THE CROWN OF LIFE

K K Sutton

Inscribe Publishing, Guildford, England

The Crown of Life

Copyright © 2016 K K Sutton.

First paperback edition printed 2016 in the United Kingdom.

A CIP catalogue record for this book is available from the British Library

ISBN 978-1-909369-08-5

Published by Inscribe Publishing, Suite 232, Chremma House, 14 London Road, Guildford, Surrey GU1 2AG, England.
Cover Design and typesetting by Inscribe Publishing.
Printed and bound in Great Britain by IJgraphics, Guildford, GU4 7WA

THE CROWN OF LIFE

BOOK III

IN

THE RESTORATION

OF

THE CROWN OF LIFE

BY

K K Sutton

Dedication

To Gill my wife, Benedict, Genevieve and Francesca, my
children, without whose love, practical help and encouragement,
this third book in the trilogy would never have been written.

BOOK III

A COLLECTION OF WRITINGS

The Story So Far

Uncle Morthrir spoke a word to release the Dé-monos into the Waking World and give him power to become King. He also spoke a word to bring confusion between Kyros and Lenyé, to destroy Kyros as his rival and force Lenyé to become his bride.

As a result, Kyros and Lenyé argue and separate. Lenyé is overwhelmed by Uncle Morthrir's charisma and falls in love with him. Kyros speaks words of reversal from the Dangst Rock to break his Uncle's power. He is sent to heal people in Terrazarema and teach them about the True King. He rescues Lenyé, but she is no longer interested in him and doesn't know whom she loves until encountering the True King for herself. She is released from her Uncle's influence and reconciled to Kyros.

Morthrir cries out to Abbérron, "...*release to me something else to confound my enemies*".

Kyros is given his seventh test by Hoffengrégor, the Ancient Prophet, to seek the sunken island and recover the Crown of Life from a strong-room at the top of the Royal Ziggurat, the great building that reached to the skies and reminded them of the True King's presence above. The Prophet tells Lenyé to find the key that will unlock the Ancient Writings to enable them to overcome Abbérron, the evil power behind their Uncle.

Rafé is sent by Morthrir to locate a new source of spiritual power at Mount Nastâri.

Beth and Quinn recover from the Grand Convocation on Mount Malkamet and journey with Ishi-mi-réjá to find something that will replace their Uncle's authority in the Waking World before trying to rescue their parents.

PART I

THE TREK

Chapter One

I, Morthrir, born as a son into the Royal Krêonor Family, Lord of Onadestra, and Crown Prince once all my rivals are dead, anticipate the Day of my Coronation and Marriage to Lenyé.

I was caught up, whether in body or out of body, I know not, but saw my physical form below standing on the plain leading to the Forest at the head of Lake Sanchéso, with a handful of sand trickling from between my fingers. I rose above the Lake, rushing towards a cave mouth on the islet, before hurtling down a passage that spun me around its spiral. At the exit I flashed past two beings, ablaze with light, who swung their swords but missed because of my speed. Then out over a plain and into another cave mouth where I thudded to the ground and rolled over and over till I ended up on my face at the bank of a river.

I heard a voice in front of me saying: 'Write what you see and hear, lest you forget what is revealed, and keep the document hidden for your own use. Do not let anyone else read it, or destruction will come upon you.'

I stood up to see who was speaking and discerned, amidst the grey light, a dark patch of mist on the other side of the river.

'Come,' the voice continued, and I set foot in the water. But instead of sinking, I walked across towards the darkness ahead.

As the mist was blown away, I saw someone in the form of a man, but of greater stature, dressed in a black robe down to his feet, his head and features partly hidden in his black hood. His feet were like the skeletal bones of a man, and his voice was the venomous hiss of death.

In his left hand he held a scythe: the blade was black, the shaft was black, and the two handles were black, as black as night; so intense, it was more as if he held a cut-out shape which opened onto a different realm that knew no other colour. In a flash of insight I realised no one from the Waking World could escape that terrible instrument. Out of his mouth came the whispered words of decay breeding despair for those who live in the Waking World. What I could see of his face was a hollow skull: white, as though bleached by a sun far stronger than the one in the Waking World; white, with the sickly pallor of death about it.

When I beheld him, I fell at his feet as one stricken and never to rise again. But he seized me by the hair and dragged me to my feet, the exposed bones of his right hand burning into my scalp like ice. I was terrified by that scythe and couldn't look at him.

'You have reason to fear me. Everyone from the Waking World has to cross my river and come down to the grave. I am Lammista-ké, King of Death, and no human can escape me.'

He forced my head up till I was staring into the sockets of his skull; for no eyes did he have, only a lurid flame that flickered with the stench of death.

'There is one who has recently passed through my river unscathed,' the venomous whisper took root in my mind, 'and returned to the Waking World clothed in great power.'

'I don't understand.'

'Your nephew, Kyros!' Lammista-ké continued.

My mind reeled, trying to fathom what this was all about.

'We stirred up strife and bloodshed at the Beginning so that humans and creatures and the very substance of the Waking World would be subject to death. Our objective was to rob the True King of populating the Waking World once more with free Peoples who no longer lived in bondage to death and a life-long fear of Me!'

He let go of my hair, gripped me by the arm and pulled me closer, the hiss of his words in my ear. 'This is how we have gained mastery over him, so that he dare not bring us down for fear of destroying his own house.'

'Surely not everyone is subject to you?'

'Only if people turn to the one who has broken free from death can they escape my clutches. But they won't do that. Humankind is too fickle concerning what lies beyond the grave, preferring the comforts of hearth and home and their deep-rooted animosity towards the rule of the True King, which we actively encourage. They grasp tightly to the things of the world they know at the expense of seeking after what is yet to come. So if we are destroyed, they are dragged down with us.'

I struggled to see where I fitted in.

'Have you not cried out to Abbérron: "*release to me something else to confound my enemies*"? He and I are united against Kyros. You have been sent to me so I can take you to the bottom of the Pit. Your task,' Lammista-ké gripped me tighter and the naked bones of his right hand froze onto my arm, 'is to break the chains that hold Nastâr imprisoned. The Hidden Power of Abbérron is with you in great measure, and only you can do this. Make him obey you in the Waking World to destroy your nephew.'

'What about Lenyé?' I whispered in response.

'Lenyé?' I heard the derision in Lammista-ké's laugh. 'Don't even try your fancy instant-travel method to seize her. As long as she is under Kyros' protection, it won't work. Once he's been dealt with, you can have her as a reward.'

I felt myself falling into a dark pit without end, and Lammista-ké fell with me. Great bulls gored me with their horns and enormous dogs tore at me with huge teeth, but Lammista-ké beat them off with his scythe. An intense heat engulfed me and I thought I would die. Who was Nastâr? Surely the Nastrim were dealt with? Yet Lammista-ké talked of a person in his own right.

Then I heard the King of Death's voice. 'Nastâr was one of the Great En-Luchés cast down to the Realm of Dominion when we attempted to place Abbérron on the Highest Throne. He tried to break out and lead an army of Dé-monos to invade the Waking World, but was apprehended and thrown down to the Pit.'

How long I fell, I could not say, but as I reached the bottom, Lammista-ké pointed to a huge door reinforced with large straps of iron, and spoke a word of command. We walked through the very fabric of the door into an enormous chamber. At the far end was the open mouth of a furnace and the heat was unbearable.

I recoiled as something lunged at me, with a clanking of chains, missing by a hair's breadth. The creature was hard to see in the flickering atmosphere, but was winged and of giant human stature. The five fingers and thumb on each hand were curled like claws. It leaped at me again, the wings fanning the searing heat around me, but was brought up short by its chains.

'Back, Nastâr,' Lammista-ké yelled. 'We are here to free you. This is Morthrir, who carries the Hidden Power of Abbérron.'

'Abbérron?' The massive creature glared at us. 'He's taken this long to release me. Why should I be interested now?'

'There is a man in the Waking World who has passed through death and returned clothed in great power. He must be stopped, otherwise our long labours will be overturned, the Realm of the Departed will be broken open, our hostages released and all of us will be consumed in that furnace. Including you.'

'What do I have to do?'

'Destroy this man. Is that clear?'

Nastâr nodded.

Lammista-ké turned to me. 'Do as I have instructed you.'

I grasped Nastâr's chains and cried, 'Be free, in the name of Abbérron!' I felt power flow through me as the chains parted, but the great being lunged at me and grabbed me by the throat.

'Make him obey you in the Waking World,' I heard Lammista-ké's voice in my ear as everything began to go hazy, 'so that you may destroy Kyros!'

4

Chapter Two

Lenyé started in her sleep and was instantly awake; someone was shaking her by the shoulder. She could make out the special beech tree at the edge of the Pool of Alesco by the faint starlight, but froze as a dark figure bent over her. 'Is that you, Kyros?'

'Don't make a sound.'

She was relieved as she recognised his urgent whisper.

'Help me wake the others. Tell them to get the horses saddled and harnessed and the hay shoes on.'

'Why? What's happened?'

'Those warriors must have carried on during the night. There's a scouting party below the Pool of Alesco coming this way. We need to hide all traces of our camp and leave quietly.'

Lenyé still wore her cut-down blue dress and cloak with the long boots. She strapped the two swords across her back and rolled up her bedding. Within minutes she led her horse out of the camp, followed by Ramâno with Kyros' horse, and the others. Chuah-te-mok flew ahead with Ra-Na-Jiri in his talons. Ariella and Mamma Uza-Mâté were at the back so as not to terrify the horses and Kyros came behind, checking for warriors. Twice they halted at his whispered command and stood in silence waiting for the all clear. Then they mounted and cantered through the forest. Ramâno sat behind her with his arms around her waist to free up Kyros' horse so he could keep watch with Harbona at the rear.

'Surely those warriors will change sides,' the boy whispered in her ear, 'when they see how different Kyros is to your Uncle?'

'They would capture us before we could convince them.'

'Harbona did. They'd take notice of a great warrior like…'

'Shh, Ramâno. There's someone ahead.'

Lenyé held up her hand to warn the others and reined in her horse but was distracted by a sound from her right.

A warrior crashed through the undergrowth and charged straight at her with lance lowered in the attacking position. She swept both swords out of their scabbards and turned her horse to face him, conscious of the boy scrambling to his feet behind her to stand on the horse's rump and hold on to her shoulders.

'What are you doing, Ramâno?'

As she parried the lance between both swords and knocked it out of the warrior's hand, the boy flung himself at the man and tumbled him off his horse.

She wheeled round in time to see more warriors break out of cover and charge at the rest of her party. Her brothers and cousins leaped off their horses, the two girls scrabbling in the loose soil for any stones and small rocks, while her brothers hurled them at the oncoming warriors. Ariella sprang into the fray, fangs bared, claws extended and roaring; terrifying the horses and making them rear up and throw their riders. Mamma Uza-Mâté waded in, frightening more horses and dealing with any warriors on the ground. Ramâno was up, raced over to the others and began throwing stones as well. She caught sight of Chuah-te-mok, with Ra-Na-Jiri still in his talons, dropping out of the sky in a steep dive directly at an oncoming warrior. He released the cobra at the man's chest and hurtled past, talons extended, straight into the face of the warrior behind, dislodging the man from his saddle.

Lenyé fought her way to the rear of the line, where Kyros was protected by Harbona holding several warriors at bay. He was the only one not fighting. She saw him raise his right hand and heard his clear voice ring out: 'Oh, my King. We do not strive only against these warriors, but the dark power behind them that drives them on to do my Uncle's will. Break that power, I ask.'

The battle was intense, but over in a few minutes. About twenty warriors lay dead on the ground. Their horses had bolted into the forest neighing in terror.

Lenyé dismounted and hugged everyone, so glad that they were all alive and unharmed. She shook her head as she approached Kyros. 'Same old problem,' she said. 'Failure to carry any weapons almost cost you your life.'

'You didn't see the Dé-monos swirling around those warriors heads, did you? They are a far worse enemy than men.'

'We may have defeated those warriors,' she replied, 'but the sound of their horses will bring others before we know it. We must get away from here.'

But even as she spoke, a figure in white appeared before them. 'Yanantha!' Lenyé was overjoyed and rushed to greet her friend.

'Mount your horses and follow me,' Yanantha seemed a little distant, and Lenyé wondered at that. 'Quick. The forest is alive with warriors hunting for you. I have spoken a word of power to blind their eyes to your whereabouts, but it won't last long.'

Lenyé led the others and kept pace with Yanantha as her friend turned and ran, twisting and turning along criss-crossing animal trails as the sound of pursuit from behind and on either side closed in on them. They raced towards a dense line of trees, but at the last minute Yanantha turned left and led them through a narrow entrance. Lenyé sighed with relief as she recognised the familiar shape of the house in the light of dawn and knew they were safe.

Ramâno slithered off first so she could dismount. Then Yanantha was tugging her by the hand.

'Leave the horses to the others. I must talk to you.'

Yanantha led her to the back of the house and drew her into the shadows on the verandah. 'You know when you fell in love with your Uncle and Kyros spoke words to reverse his power against you both?'

'Yes. I thought that had all been sorted out.'

'It has. But I was also badly affected when Kyros asked me to marry him.'

'What?' Lenyé was stunned. 'When we were reconciled he asked me to forgive him and told me, "*I too have gone away from you in my heart and desired another*". But I had no idea it was you.'

'Lenyé. I was so torn; wanting it to happen, but knowing it wasn't part of the True King's purposes for my life. In the end, Kyros was stronger than I, and obeyed the True King and released me from his offer. I'm sorry if that hurts you, but I have to be totally honest, otherwise there would forever be a barrier between us. Will you forgive me?'

'Of course.' Lenyé embraced her friend, feeling the hot tears on her cheek as Yanantha sobbed in her arms.

'I've failed you, Lenyé.'

'No you haven't. You've always been strong for me.'

'And now it's you being strong for me?' Yanantha looked up and smiled through her tears.

'Thank you for telling me. I want you to know nothing has changed between us. We both need each other.' Lenyé held her friend a while longer until the tears subsided, and Yanantha eased herself away.

'Your Uncle once spoke words of incredible power before Kyros intervened,' there was a sense of urgency in Yanantha's voice. 'My heart warns me that he is about to release something far worse against you.'

Chapter Three

Morthrir hovered above the plain near Lake Sanchéso, looking down on his body and saw the sand trickling from between his fingers. How could he return to the Waking World with Nastâr still gripping him by the throat?

'If you think I'm going to submit to you,' the great being growled in his ear, 'you're mistaken. I obey no one except Abbérron.'

Morthrir struggled against the choking grasp. He couldn't break that terrible grip.

'But if you submit to me,' Nastâr's voice was softer now, more persuasive, 'then I can give you all knowledge, all wealth, and all power. Why be content with the Krêonor Throne in the Waking World? I can set you on the Highest Throne in the Known Universe. You would be King Morthrir over all Realms, and every being, great or small, will bow down to you. Even Abbérron!'

Morthrir felt himself spinning. Lights came and went, dazzling his eyes and plunging him into blackness. He saw scrolls of writing pass before him, containing the secrets of life. Then he was in a cave filled with gold and silver and precious gems, glinting and sparkling in the light of a flare. He stretched out his hand to grab what he wanted and everyone bowed before him. He was free in an eternal existence with no sense of time and would live for ever. He could go anywhere, understand all things and have unlimited power: so much easier than the burden of his old life forcing him to strive against everything that opposed him.

This was what he craved above all things.

But then he thought of Kyros, as if another being had planted it within him, and his intense hatred for the man flared up: he had to destroy his nephew. And his burning desire for Lenyé: she'd escaped once, but not again. He must have her as his bride! A great rage arose within him. Surely Abbérron would never have agreed to release Nastâr if the being was uncontrollable?

The image of his body standing on the plain with the sand trickling out between his fingers arose in Morthrir's mind and filled all his vision. Time was running out. Kyros and Lenyé were getting further and further away from him, and all because of this delay by Nastâr. They could be anywhere by now!

Chapter Four

Kyros sat in one of the easy chairs on the verandah at the back of Yanantha's house as dawn broke. He felt awkward being here with Lenyé after what had occurred between himself and Yanantha, but let it pass as he glanced round at the expectant faces. Lenyé was in a chair on the other side of the doorway with his two sisters settled at her feet, leaning against her knees. Her two brothers sat on the lawn facing him with Marie-anna close to them and Harbona nearby. Kyros was amused to see Marie-anna haul Ramâno onto her lap, so he couldn't distract the other boys. The four animal-friends sprawled in various positions around the circle. Not many for such an important quest. Ariella yawned as Yanantha came out of the house with a tray of drinks.

'We're grateful to Yanantha for rescuing us from those warriors,' Kyros spoke up, 'but we can't stay here. Lenyé and I have to find the lost island.'

'You mean, like the game we used to play at the Pool of Alesco?' his cousin, Wilf, was quick to ask.

Kyros outlined what Wilf meant for the benefit of Marie-anna, Harbona, Ramâno and the four animal-friends, then glanced at the others. 'We need to recover a Crown and a key.'

'What key?' Wilf's brother, Festé, frowned. 'We know about the Crown. But there was never any mention of a key.'

Lenyé explained about the parchment sealed in a cylinder and needing the key to unlock critical information to help them win against Uncle Morthrir. 'But it's a bigger thing we're involved in,' and she talked about the True King and the spiritual powers they had encountered.

'Was that what we saw when you were fighting the giant?' Wilf chipped in.

'Yes.'

'Will the True King help us again?' Kyros' sister, Olathe, sounded excited.

'I'm sure he will,' Kyros broke in, 'but last time the Pilgrims of Lohr interceded until the light of the True King shone through and help was sent. We don't have them with us now so we'll have to call upon the True King ourselves.'

'Can we ask as well?' his other sister, Nasima, spoke up.

'We'll all have to,' Ramâno's high-pitched voice startled everyone. 'It wasn't until those men fell to their knees and cried out to him for more aid that the En-luchés came, especially the big one with wings. I saw it all happen from Kyros' horse.'

'You may not have seen the Dé-monos those En-luchés were fighting,' Kyros drew their attention back to himself, 'but they'll be after us again. Do you still want to be involved?'

'Yes,' the youngsters all chorused together.

Lenyé looked round at their eager faces. Olathe was already a willowy fifteen-year-old and very sure of herself. Wilf was only a year younger. Nasima was the quiet one and shy with strangers, and Festé's voice was at that croaky stage of a boy changing into a man. How fast they were all growing up. She tried hard not to think of Beth and Quinn no longer with them, and would prefer the rest of them to stay here in safety while she and Kyros went. She was about to ask Yanantha when Kyros beat her to it.

'You do realise sailing to find the Crown and key will be far more dangerous than our game at the special beech tree. Lenyé and I have to go. Are you sure you want to come with us?'

'Of course,' they all shouted.

Lenyé sighed. It was clear no one wanted to be left behind.

'Before you begin planning the next step,' Yanantha spoke up, 'you need to be able to understand one another.'

Kyros met her eyes, realised what she meant, and stood up. He went to Wilf and held his hands above the lad's head, 'I grant you the gift of understanding and speaking to all creatures.' He nodded at Lenyé and they walked amongst the rest of the group speaking over each in turn. Lenyé approached Marie-anna as he reached Harbona and then finished off with Ramâno.

'Hey, Ariella,' Ramâno shrilled. 'Can you understand me?'

'Yes,' the great cat growled slightly.

'Come and chase me, then,' and he darted away from the group across the lawn before turning to see if she was following.

Ariella grunted and sat on her haunches with the air of someone who doesn't chase seven-year-old boys, no matter how excited they are.

'I thought all cats wanted to play?'

'I can see it's going to take a while for you and me to get to know each other.'

Everyone else laughed.

Kyros raised his voice, 'That's enough, Ramâno.'

'What's the point of understanding the animal-friends if I can't have any fun with them?' But he came and sat on his mother's lap again at her urgent beckoning.

'We need to charter a sailing ship,' Kyros eyed them all. 'I suggest we head due West from Terrazarema, and aim for Pordé-Sûnca.'

'Port-of-the-Setting-Sun?' Lenyé broke in. 'I never realised till now what it means. How poetic.'

'It's also a joke amongst the locals,' Kyros glanced at her, 'making a play on words for Port-of-the-Sunken-Isle. That's where Hoffengrégor met the survivors of the Great Inundation when the island was flooded at the Beginning: right on the Westernmost bulge of the coast. If we're serious about recovering the Crown and key, it's the best place to sail from.'

They discussed what they would need. Lenyé insisted on taking a few Nastrim longbows from the gorge out on the plain

13

to arm their ship against any attacks their Uncle might make.

'How are we going carry them?' Kyros sounded dismayed. 'Plus provisions and water to get us to Pordé-Sûnca.'

'We'll have to use some wagons.'

'They were all smashed to pieces,' Kyros pointed out.

'We could salvage several to make two serviceable wagons, My Lord,' Harbona spoke up. 'That's all we'll need. You and I can try as it will require some heavy lifting.'

'Very well.'

'Can I help?' Ramâno sounded so eager.

'Let's sort out the other jobs first and then decide,' Lenyé smiled at Ramâno. 'Wilf and Festé, you search for longbows and arrows, and any provisions and water skins and horse fodder in what's left of the wagons.' She glanced at Chuah-te-mok, 'You keep a lookout for the warriors and also hunt for rabbits. Ariella, you go for something larger, like a deer. The girls can skin and roast them on campfires.'

'That's such a messy job,' Olathe glared at her. 'Can't someone else do it?'

'No. Marie-anna and I need to round up a few horses for the wagons. We'll help as soon as we can.' Lenyé paused to check she hadn't forgotten anyone. 'Ra-Na-Jiri and Mamma Uza-Mâté, you scare the horses towards us. Ramâno, you help the girls gather firewood and then work with the men.'

'This is all going to take time,' Kyros muttered. 'And I don't like the idea of lighting campfires, even if it is to give us food for the journey. Those warriors will be after us straight away.'

'If it's any help,' Yanantha interrupted. 'I can speak another word to blind those warriors' eyes to your whereabouts. But it will take me some time to prepare my thoughts.'

'How long will that last?'

'Three days, at least. Enough to give you a good start.'

'Then the sooner we set out, the better.'

Chapter Five

Lenyé sat at the table in the dining area of Yanantha's house reading the scroll she was given by Hoffengrégor, while the others finished clearing up the breakfast things and repacked the saddle bags. Inwardly she was struggling with her emotions over Yanantha's revelation about Kyros. 'My best friend,' she muttered, 'who rescued me from Uncle Morthrir's warriors and helped me believe in myself and set me on the path to find the Sword of Justice.' She returned to the beginning of the scroll, puzzling over the strange title: *A Cosmography of the Known Universe*; but wasn't taking it in. Something about the vision being shown to the Ancient Prophet to instruct the Peoples of the Waking World in wisdom.

She looked up as Kyros entered. 'I'm only going to mention this once,' her voice was cold, 'then I want to put it behind us.'

Kyros winced. He could guess what was coming.

'When I fell in love with Uncle Morthrir, you proposed to Yanantha. She told me as soon as we arrived she was so upset about it. Kyros. How could you do that to me?'

'I thought we'd cleared all this up.'

'You never told me who it was. I forgave you at the time, and I won't go back on that. And now I'd like to forget all about it. Here,' she passed him the scroll. 'You'd better read this.'

Kyros sat next to her, grateful for the way she'd handled the issue. 'Does it tell us about finding the Crown and key?'

'No. Just read it. Then we can discuss how it applies to us.'

She was relieved to have vented her feelings and softened

towards him, resting her head on his shoulder. He raised his hand to ruffle her hair and she slipped hers over the back, then lifted her head to smile as he turned towards her. She settled her head back on his shoulder, slipped her arm around him and watched him run his finger down the parchment, pausing over various paragraphs before moving on to complete it.

'Look here,' he pointed. *'And then I beheld Him: the True King, seated on his Throne in such splendour and majesty that words fail me to describe Him. And to his left, and slightly removed behind Him was another, even greater Throne, but it was as yet unoccupied and remained empty for all the time I was there.* What's this empty Throne?'

'I don't know,' Lenyé scanned down the parchment. 'What about the rebellion of Abbérron that Stellatus mentions, and the casting down of some of the Great En-luchés?' She pointed to another paragraph. 'And here, about the Waking World: *Even though the Lord Abbérron rules here...* It reminds me of something Yanantha said: *"behind your Uncle Morthrir there sits a far greater power than any mortal can ever challenge unaided. That power is what you have to bring down and vanquish. But it is beyond mere human wisdom and strength to ever master".* That's what she must have been referring to.'

'So our task is not just finding the Crown and key,' Kyros frowned.

'No. Yanantha warned me that Uncle Morthrir will release something far worse than those words he spoke against us.'

'And that means him calling on Abbérron again. When I spoke against Uncle Morthrir before, I said: *"let the power of Abbérron in the Waking World be broken".* And that has happened.'

'So what's going to be different this time?' Lenyé asked.

'I have to confront Abbérron directly, like the True King did.'

'But he used the Sword of Justice.' Lenyé reached up and touched the Sword on her back. 'You'd better take it.'

'No. You keep it. Did I not say to you at the Pool of Alesco concerning both swords, "...*the Sword of Justice, in your hands, is a powerful weapon. Bear them a little longer on behalf of us both. For you will have need of them*"; and that "*I am destined to walk armoured only with the power contained in the name of the True King*".'

'Very well,' Lenyé smiled at him.

'The Prophet talks about the Dé-monos in the Realm of Travail,' Kyros pointed to a paragraph near the end, '*These are the Dé-monos, who are like the En-luchés of my order...For at the rebellion, they were cast down here and are contained that they may not work any mischief in the Waking World.* Those were the ones released through the Breaking-in, and are still here at Uncle Morthrir's command.'

Lenyé frowned. 'A lot of En-luchés helped us in that battle. And wasn't there a greater presence you mentioned?'

'Yes. He must have come from the Realm of Eternal Flight,' Kyros skimmed through the parchment and pointed. '*I saw beings like Stellatus, filled with the same light, but of greater stature, and winged so that their movement was of swift flight...These are the Great En-Luchés,' Stellatus whispered to me. 'The highest members of my order, and have direct access to the Blessèd Throne.'* Kyros paused. 'I think he only came because of the intercession of Osâcah and the Pilgrims of Lohr.'

'After the destruction of Uncle Morthrir's remaining army,' Lenyé stared at Kyros, 'surely he will call up one of those fallen Great En-luchés to contest the power released to you?'

'You're right. And that fills my heart with foreboding.'

'Surely the True King will help us if he does?'

'Yes. Look at the last paragraph. *And herein I saw the key to all things: that the Known Universe was in balance and contained and waiting. For the final struggle, if it should ever come, would be waged in the Waking World.*' Kyros paused and looked at her. 'The True King will not leave us helpless. For we are at the centre of a war that affects the entire Known Universe.'

'What can we do?' Lenyé sounded alarmed.

'It confirms our discussion with the others earlier,' Kyros sat back and studied her face. 'We need to call upon the True King ourselves...'

He was interrupted by a yell from Olathe that had them both up from their seats and racing for the garden.

'What's the matter,' Lenyé called from the doorway onto the verandah.

'He started it,' Olathe was on her feet and pointing at Wilf where he sat on the lawn.

'All I said was, *"Pity Quinn and Beth aren't here,"'* Wilf sounded defensive, '*"wouldn't they just have loved..."'*

'Wilf, how could you?' Olathe shouted at him.

'It's all right, Olathe,' Lenyé hurried over and tried to soothe her cousin.

'You girls tended the graves with flowers,' Wilf carried on, 'but I don't feel I've said good-bye properly. Do you, Festé?'

Festé shook his head.

'I can't help it if Quinn's dead,' Wilf muttered. 'I miss him, and want him to be here and join in the fun. Is there anything wrong with that?'

Kyros walked across to his cousin, squatted down next to him and slipped an arm around the lad's shoulders. 'No. Of course not. Quinn would have jumped at the chance. You know what he was like. But we need to be kind to one another and recognise that some of us still haven't got over the shock of losing them.'

'Can't we even talk about Quinn?' Festé looked up at Kyros. 'And Beth? She was my little sister!'

'We need to give each other space to talk.' Lenyé beckoned Nasima over and put her arm around her as well. 'It helps if we can let our feelings out to each other.'

'That includes you, Festé,' Kyros slipped his other arm around the lad's shoulders.

'I know this is a difficult time for your family,' Marie-anna spoke up, 'but perhaps we need to be more practical now.' Kyros saw her glance at Lenyé and then back to him. 'Yanantha may have blinded the eyes of those warriors but they won't give up. We need to make the most of the time we have.'

'You're right,' Kyros smiled at her before turning to Lenyé. 'We need to ride out.'

Lenyé gave Hoffengrégor's Cosmography scroll to Yanantha for safekeeping while the others finished packing up. She asked Ariella and Mamma Uza-Mâté to travel behind the girl's horses and in front of the boys to keep them apart. She was concerned there was still some friction between them over Quinn and Beth. Ra-Na-Jiri travelled in her saddle bags with a loop of his body across the rump of her horse, leaving Chuah-te-mok free to hover above and keep watch with Kyros and Harbona at the rear. She felt uneasy leaving the safety of Yanantha's house, glancing around for any sign of pursuing warriors.

She led the way, reined in her horse at the top of the escarpment and sat looking down on the gorge, suddenly aware of the cobra's head at her left elbow. It wasn't quite midday for the sun was still above the Forest, and slightly behind them, leaving the face of the escarpment in shadow. Lenyé sighed in dismay as she shaded her eyes with her hand, taking in the shattered remains of wagons spilling out of the mouth of the gorge.

'What's the matter?' Ra-Na-Jiri hissed.

'It's worse than I remember. The wagons are in a terrible state. And look at all those horses scattered on the plain. This is going to take longer than I originally thought.'

'How much time do we have?'

'Until nightfall. We must ride out at dawn if we're going to have any chance of out-distancing those warriors.'

Chapter Six

Quinn led the way to Druis-cyf-rin, the Great Oak Tree, riding the horse with Beth sitting behind him. He was surprised at how fast they were able to travel. Ishi-mi-réjá was fit for her age and alternated between a fast walk and a run, despite being weighed down by her backpack with those two odd-looking spades strapped on either side. He cantered the horse at times and then reined him in as they waited for her to catch up. At this rate they should be at Druis-cyf-rin in a few days' time.

He and Beth switched between riding while the other sat behind. He felt sore from the awkward angle and nearly fell off when Beth pushed the horse into a canter without any warning.

'You did that deliberately, just because I wasn't holding on.'

Beth laughed. 'That'll teach you to show off.'

'You wait till it's your turn to sit behind me!'

But he didn't take it out on Beth. He was pleased to see the delay in getting to Fantrios hadn't dampened her sense of fun, and it was a good diversion from thinking about not rescuing their parents first.

'What do you miss about your Mother and Father?' he craned his neck round to talk to her as they waited for Ishi-mi-réjá.

'When I was locked in the cellar at Onadestra, I was so close to them. All I wanted was to feel my Mother's arms around me and hold me safe. Then my warrior-friend, Paco, couldn't get me out and I was taken off to Terrazarema and you rescued me; and we were on the run for so long that I haven't had a chance to think about it since. What about you?'

'My Father's voice, and his strength and his humour. Kyros is so like him. I miss them both. And my Mother's music. Do you remember she used to play her lute and sing to us in the orchard at harvest time, and all the pears that were still firm enough to sell to the merchants or store at home were packaged up and loaded onto carts, and we were left with the ones that had ripened too much on the trees? They were perfect for eating.'

'And we got covered in juice all the way up to the elbows. Your Mother made me wash my hands and passed me her lute so I could play while she had some pears. She was very strict about sticky fingers on her instrument.'

'I'm not surprised.'

'But she always let me play whenever our two families were together. She was so encouraging. I wish we could get to Druis-cyf-rin quicker and find this thing Ishi-mi-réjá wants. Talking about our parents makes me want to go and rescue them straight away.'

'I know,' Quinn nodded. 'Your Father is quiet and gentle, but comes alive at storytelling. He once recited part of the *Book of Beginnings* at a mid-winter party. He's the best.'

'I remember that party,' Beth chuckled. 'I was only three and we played reverse hide-and-seek. We were all trying to find Lenyé. I tiptoed into the upstairs salon and heard her giggling behind the settee against the wall. So I looked round the back and saw Kyros lying behind her with his arms around her waist and she was holding his hand. I wriggled on top and we waited for ages trying to be as silent as possible before Nasima found us. Then the rest of you came quite quickly.'

'I don't recall the game; there was so much else happening that evening.'

'Lenyé told me only recently that was when it all began.'

'All what began?'

'Her and Kyros.'

'What do you mean: her and Kyros?'

'She knew he was the one for her.'

'What? That long ago!'

Beth nodded. 'She was furious it was me who found them first, but had to stay quiet in case someone else came into the room.'

'I don't remember about them being in love then.'

'Boys never do.'

'Makes me miss Kyros and Lenyé even more, just talking about them. Why has Uncle Morthrir done this to us?'

Before Beth could answer, Ishi-mi-réjá caught up with them, leaned forwards with hands on knees and recovered her breath.

Chapter Seven

Lenyé held out her hand and clicked her tongue as she moved towards the black stallion. Mamma Uza-Mâté and Ra-Na-Jiri had separated him from a band of free-roaming horses grazing on the scrubby grass and were deliberately upwind to scare him towards her with their scent. Marie-anna was behind her to stop the horse bolting if he got past. Even from that distance Lenyé caught the sound of Marie-anna singing to herself about the True King. She focused on the task, wanting to get as close as possible and catch the horse with gentleness rather than using force.

These horses must be left over after Uncle Morthrir's final army was destroyed by the second wave of Nastrim, as they were still saddled and bridled and presumably found grazing awkward. This one had foam around his mouth from agitating the bit with his teeth to try and get rid of it.

The horse pricked up his ears at the sound of a human voice. He trotted towards her, stumbled on the dangling reins and then nuzzled her hand. She stroked the cheek and wiped away the foam with a soft cloth. 'There. That's better, isn't it?' The horse jerked his head up, but nuzzled her hand again. She held the cheek strap to stop him running off, lifted the reins over the head, caught hold of his mane and swung herself into the saddle. The horse reared slightly, but settled down as she gripped with her knees and patted his neck. 'Good boy.'

She set him off at a walk and then straight into a gentle canter as she headed down to where the men were salvaging a couple of wagons. Marie-anna hurried after her.

'Hey, Lenyé. Mamma. Look at me!' Ramâno's shout made them both glance round at the work on the wagons. He was sitting on the seat of one, pretending to hold a set of reins. 'I'm going to drive it when we're ready. Kyros said I could.'

'It's a long way,' Marie-anna called back. 'Aren't you going to take a break sometime?'

'I'm going to ride a horse on my own the rest of the way. Harbona's promised to teach me.'

Lenyé saw Marie-anna pause with something more than a Mother's love in her eyes for her son. She followed Marie-anna's gaze and realised she wasn't looking at Ramâno so much as the men at work. Lenyé felt awkward in asking the obvious question so soon; after all they were still getting to know each other. Maybe it would come out in conversation later.

'That's great, Ramâno,' Lenyé shouted back. 'You'll make a warrior yet.' She saw the flash of his smile and then looked beyond him to where Wilf and Festé were foraging in the gorge. She was impressed by the piles of longbows and arrows, the wooden boxes of provisions stacked together and a growing mound of fodder. The girls were behind Ramâno's wagon busy skinning rabbits and cooking the meat over their campfires. The smell of roast rabbit filled her nostrils: they would eat well tonight. She glanced over to the escarpment and saw Ariella making her way down, dragging an antelope between her front legs. That was going to take some preparing: she and Marie-anna would help as soon as they were through with the horses.

Chuah-te-mok distracted her as he dropped out of the sky with more rabbits.

Lenyé turned back to Marie-anna and dismounted. They removed the saddle and harness before grooming the horse.

'Crook your fingers,' Marie-anna held up her hands and nodded her head towards the eagle, 'like Chuah-te-mok's talons.'

Lenyé smiled, 'We use that trick ourselves if we're out camping and don't have any combs and brushes for grooming.

Hurts your fingers after a while.'

They looked at each other and laughed as though sharing a secret.

Between them they scrubbed down the horse, digging their fingers into his coat to act like a stiff brush, Lenyé conscious all the time of Marie-anna singing softly whenever they weren't talking. It was hard work, but the horse enjoyed it. They checked each hoof, and ran their fingers through his mane and tail. Then they tethered him with a rope halter and went back for more horses. This time they agreed to do one each.

As Lenyé cantered the last horse they needed down towards the others she tried to put into words what she'd been sensing all afternoon. Everyone had worked hard preparing for the long trek, but there was such a happy atmosphere, with the chatter and the calling across from one group to another. She finished her horse, strolled over to where Marie-anna was helping the girls with the antelope carcass, and sat next to her.

'It's like a big happy family,' Marie-anna broke off singing and waved to where Kyros and the boys were loading the wagons, and Harbona was urging a horse on a long lead to walk in a ring round him, with Ramâno riding bareback. 'Thank you for making us feel so welcome. I thought Royalty would be different.'

'We've learned enough in running from Uncle Morthrir to know that people are far more important than palaces and big rooms and servants. Haven't we, girls?' She looked across to Olathe and Nasima and they both nodded.

'Ramâno feels it as well,' Marie-anna continued. 'Kyros is like a big brother to him. Maybe a Father. I wish it was so. That's what he needs more than anything.'

'And Harbona?' Lenyé felt she had to raise the issue, but hoped she hadn't pushed Marie-anna too far too soon. She glanced across and saw the other woman blush, but there were tears in her eyes as well. 'I'm sorry,' Lenyé faltered, 'I had no right to ask.'

'I'm glad you did. He's the first man who's tried to teach my boy to ride since my husband, Ranyak, died.'

'Why's that?'

'With his Father gone, no one else would do it.'

'I don't understand.'

'The warrior clans are close-knit, but very practical. Almost cruel, even to their own. *"What's the point of teaching a crippled boy to ride?"* they would say. *"If he falls off in battle, he cannot help himself."* So they wouldn't bother to teach him. The other boys despised him for being useless, and he felt bad about himself.'

'How did it happen?'

'When Ramâno was nearly two, he was with me and the other women and children down by the river washing clothes. Our settlement was attacked while our men were away fighting. I dropped him as I ran and broke both his ankles and many bones in his feet. I've never heard anyone scream like that in my life and it has haunted me ever since.'

'I'm sorry. I shouldn't have asked.'

'No. It's all right. You're the first person I've ever told outside my family. Ranyak rescued us. But the damage was done and we had to raise a crippled boy. Ranyak tried to teach him to ride, but Ramâno had no strength in his legs to grip with and kept falling off. I carried him to the river whenever I went washing, and he learned to swim and stay down a long time. It was the only thing that gave him hope to go on living. As he grew he developed a powerful chest and became very strong in the arms for his age.'

Lenyé glanced across to Olathe and Nasima and realised they were watching Marie-anna intently. When they caught her eye she smiled and encouraged them to go on listening.

Marie-anna was oblivious to the girls glances as she carried on. 'Ranyak's hatred for that clan never died. He led many raids against them. One day he rode straight into a trap. They dumped his body outside our settlement with so many arrows sticking in

26

him I was sick with shock. Even for warriors gaining their revenge: that was far too cruel.' She paused and wiped her eyes. 'I couldn't let my son see him like that and broke off all the arrows and covered him with a cloth so only his face was showing before I let Ramâno anywhere near him. It was just before his fifth Birthday and the boy was devastated.'

Lenyé felt tears pricking in her own eyes as she listened.

'That was the last time I saw Ranyak,' Marie-anna continued, 'before we buried him and sang songs of his great valour. It was the end of my life. No one wanted to marry a woman with a crippled son: it would bring bad luck. I had no man, and a child who would never walk. So we came with our clan warriors to Onadestra looking for a new life and I took a job in the castle kitchens. Then your Uncle moved the warriors to Terrazarema and commanded the cook with the special pike recipe to be brought to the Royal kitchens. He didn't know me by name and probably didn't care. Most of our warriors were killed fighting for your Uncle. There are many women still weeping at Onadestra and in my home country, and many children who are Fatherless. I cannot go back,' Marie-anna looked up through her tears. 'I don't belong there any more. You have accepted us so naturally. You are my People now. Thank you for listening.'

Lenyé wiped her sticky fingers on the cloth she used for the horses and slipped her arms around Marie-anna, feeling the other woman's racking sobs.

'Thank you for telling me. I loved Ramâno from the very first time I met him. I love him even more now I've heard your story. And I love you as well.'

She felt Marie-anna's sobbing die down, as the woman eased herself away slightly and dried her eyes.

Lenyé nodded at the two girls and they began chattering amongst themselves, passing pieces of skewered meat to roast on the fire, and covering the sudden silence.

Marie-anna started helping and smiled at the girls. 'Thank

you for listening as well.'

Olathe reached across, wiped her sticky hands on Lenyé's cloth and hugged Marie-anna. Nasima did the same.

Then Marie-anna burst out laughing and they all looked at her in surprise. 'You know the rest of the story because you've been part of it. The True King healed Ramâno's legs through Kyros and everything's changed. Now I can't stop singing about the True King, I'm so happy.'

They joined in laughing with her and talking as they finished off cutting the meat and roasting it and clearing up.

As they sat watching Ramâno's riding lesson, Lenyé thought about Marie-anna's story, and wondered where Harbona fitted in. Why was he teaching the boy to ride? Did he see it as his duty now that Ramâno's legs were healed?

Then she began mentally checking off what they needed for the journey. As far as she knew, everything was ready. It was at least three days' journey from here. Most of them would ride on horseback. But the animal-friends would have to travel in the wagons. They couldn't possibly keep up with horses all day; not even Chuah-te-mok soaring on the air currents. Had she prepared enough horses? Eight to each wagon, eight more as spares and eight in reserve for themselves. That was a lot of horses to lead. Maybe they could sell them later to help pay for the ship and crew. She and Kyros hadn't discussed that part yet. It might be worth taking the saddles and harnesses as well and sell them with the horses for more money.

Lenyé felt a momentary stab of fear about those warriors, but knew Yanantha's words would protect them. And she was too excited to think about sleep as the dusk deepened into night and the men and boys gathered round for the evening meal. At first light tomorrow, they would be off for Pordé-Sûnca.

Chapter Eight

Rafé sat at his campsite cooking an evening meal, prodding the fire and occasionally adding more wood. He was pleased with his progress; two days of riding one horse and swapping with the other as the first tired. He reckoned on six days to reach the Plains of Lohr and then two more to Mount Nastâri. He hoped to find the golden globe quickly and start on his return journey.

He was relieved to be away from Terrazarema, and the recent pressure of events. No. That wasn't strictly true. He was relieved to be away from Morthrir. With the defeat of Vashtani, the Dé-monos leader Morthrir used to hunt his nephew, and the escape of Lenyé and Kyros, the man had become obsessive. Even when Morthrir did his instant-travel stunt and chased after Kyros and Lenyé at Rafé's urging, he still sensed the effect of Morthrir's presence as though lingering in Terrazarema to keep an eye on him. It wasn't until he was out of the city and riding through the countryside that he felt free of the man.

He was thinking of his friend, Eawen: the utter rejection of Abbérron, despite a lifetime of serving him on Mount Malkamet; his acceptance of the True King and the resulting miracle of the man's healing. That proved beyond all doubt the True King was real. Rafé felt troubled: he either had to obey Abbérron or follow the True King for himself. There was no middle ground. It was hard enough serving a human master. But an invisible being in some location he didn't know: how could you do that? Abbérron was more tangible: he saw the image on Mount Malkamet and felt the power when he conjured up that snake; and Eawen imparted strength to him to use the cobra in tracking Lenyé's movements. But he wasn't sure he wanted to do that any more since Eawen had turned his back on Abbérron.

If the Healer really was Kyros, then what a change in the man. Despite the beard and long hair masking his identity, Kyros used an altogether different kind of power from Morthrir: he gave, unreservedly, to people in need; whereas Morthrir took, greedily and possessively, for his own gain. Was that the difference between the True King and Abbérron? Maybe that repelled him from Morthrir now; the man wielded seemingly unlimited power. Could Rafé finally push him to destruction, or would the man end up as an even greater monster?

Rafé wasn't able to answer that question.

And so his thoughts turned to his own mission to find the golden globe for Morthrir and bring him an alternative source of power. He still needed the cobra, which meant connecting with Abbérron. He shuddered at the thought, but steeled himself to go to his pack and pull out the brown Priest robe and put it on. Then he sat cross-legged amongst the roots of a tree and focused on the snake.

He located it quite easily and was surprised to see Lenyé through its eyes. She was in a covered wagon judging by the rear view of four pairs of horses and the lurching motion of the cobra.

A boy sat next to her driving the team. Rafé frowned: the timing was wrong. It was dark night around him, but this appeared to be morning and they were heading West with the shadow of the wagon falling forwards onto the horses. Was it something that had happened, or was it in the future? Despite his uncertainty, he wanted to check he still had control of the cobra and forced it to look more closely at Lenyé.

Chapter Nine

The following morning Lenyé sat on the wagon seat and handed Ramâno the reins as they set out for Pordé-Sûnca. 'Keep the horses at a steady pace, steer between those two lines of grasses and aim for the smoothest sand to stop the wheels digging in too deep.' The lad was keen to get it right, and she saw the frown of concentration on his face as he whipped up the horses.

Mamma Uza-Mâté and Ra-Na-Jiri were riding in their wagon, while Ariella and Chuah-te-mok were in the other to spread the weight more evenly. She heard the gentle breathing of the she-bear dozing in the back; but the cobra was wide awake, coiled up behind the seat with his raised head close to Ramâno's shoulder, and swaying with the movement of the wagon.

'How long will it take to get to Pordé-Sûnca,' Ramâno had settled into a rhythm for his steering and felt free to talk again.

'Kyros said three days. But it might take more, even driving all day and changing the horses regularly.'

She glanced at the cobra and was startled to see him staring fixedly at her with eyes that brought back those uneasy feelings from the past. She shivered at the reminder.

'Ra-Na-Jiri, sometimes you act as if another person is staring at me through your eyes. It's happened three times: at the dinner with King Ogandés and Acwellan; then when you brought me the verse about *"Two Swords in splendid jewels bound..."*; and after the big battle when we were preparing to march to Terrazarema.'

'Snakes see and hear and sense vibrations in the ground or the air. But mainly it's from within. Like voices speaking or thought-waves coming to us, and we try to understand them.'

'You were doing it again just now. Why does it always make me feel uneasy?'

'Because snakes are snakes. If we never made anyone feel uneasy, we wouldn't catch anything to eat.'

'And we nearly left without you, when we set off for Terrazarema, because you were saying goodbye to your recess in the mountain. What's going on?'

'I feel especially warm and tranquil there and full of peace, and I'm able to dream of good things. I've never known anything like it. That's why I want to go back and live there.'

'Hmm,' Lenyé slumped back in her seat and folded her arms. She was more convinced than ever that Yanantha hadn't sent him after all. But if not Yanantha, who did? And, more importantly, why? She was so engrossed in her thoughts that she was only vaguely aware of Ramâno talking to the cobra.

'Hey, Ra-Na-Jiri. When I found out you were a friend of Lenyé's, I wanted to meet you, but there wasn't time. I told Kyros about it afterwards, and said, "*I wish I could talk to a snake. I wonder what he'd say to me*?" So what would you say to me?'

Lenyé was conscious of Ra-Na-Jiri remaining silent for a while before answering.

'My ancestor fell from the sky at the Beginning, and many people think we're divine and worship us.'

Ramâno laughed. 'Ra-Na-Jiri. Even I know that's not true.'

'I can teach all knowledge and how to obtain wisdom.'

'Really! What are you going to teach me?'

'If you want me to teach you, then I must be divine. And if I am divine, all people need to bow down and worship me. If others see you do it, they'll want to join you.'

'Ra-Na-Jiri,' Lenyé broke in. 'Don't tease the lad.'

'But the Nastrim believed it. You've no idea what wonderful feelings I had when all those giants bowed down to me.'

Lenyé snorted, 'You're not still after that, are you?' She sat wondering whether she could believe everything he said. Was he trying to hide something?

She would have left it at that, but heard the True King's voice in her heart, "*You must speak words of release over Ra-Na-Jiri. He is a continual drain on your spiritual strength by allowing access from your enemy*". 'Ra-Na-Jiri,' Lenyé turned to him. 'There's some power at work in you that's not good. I would like to break any link you may have with it. Will you let me do that for you?'

'I am still your servant to command.'

Lenyé raised her right hand, 'Be released from any evil that is using you, in the name of the True King!' She was astonished to see the cobra's head thrown back amongst his coils as if she struck him between the eyes. 'Ra-Na-Jiri. Are you all right?'

'I feel as if a cord has been cut that was making me dangle and writhe in mid-air. And I've been freed from someone.'

'Do you know who that person was?'

'A man. That's all I can tell you.'

'If he makes contact again, find out what you can. But don't let him gain control over you. Are you prepared to do that?'

'Yes. Of course.'

Chapter Ten

'How dare you touch me, Nastâr!' Morthrir roared. 'As far as you are concerned, I am Abbérron. Therefore you will obey me.'

He felt the hand release him and was back in his body, standing on the plain near Lake Sanchéso, with that handful of sand still trickling from between his fingers and intensely aware of time and the constraints of living and breathing in the Waking World. A sense of urgency gripped him: there was never enough time to accomplish all that he wanted.

But the struggle wasn't over yet. Nastâr towered over him, wings partly raised, and glared into Morthrir's eyes.

Morthrir felt his source of power strengthen, adopted his flexed-knee stance, slowed his breathing and focused on the image of Abbérron. He stared back into those treacherous eyes.

'Let me remind you of why you were released. Your task is to destroy Kyros. If you challenge me again, I will cast you down to the Pit. Do I make myself clear?'

Slowly the great being sank to its knees and slumped forwards till it was bowing down with its face to the ground.

'Yes, My Lord.'

Morthrir had no idea how long the battle raged until Nastâr was subdued, but it was now late evening, judging by the setting sun. He smiled to himself. If his struggle with Nastâr had been this closely matched, then the Great Being would be powerful enough to destroy Kyros.

He glanced up and saw Nastâr had risen and was standing in front of him, the tops of his folded wings protruding above his shoulders. 'Quick,' Morthrir pointed at him. 'Accompany me to the Vault of Malrema in the palace.' Morthrir closed his eyes and raised both hands, 'I summon all participants to meet me there, wherever they are and whatever they're doing.'

When he opened his eyes he was standing on the altar in the centre of the Vault in complete darkness. He sensed Nastâr still in front of him, and was aware of the rustling of robes. As the light in him grew and illuminated the chamber he saw the Summoners, Priests and Dé-monos leaders in their positions.

Nastâr bowed before him. 'My Lord, you brought the two of us here quicker than I can fly, and all these others by your spoken word; therefore, the Hidden Power is with you in great measure. I will do everything you command.'

Morthrir grunted his acceptance, and then studied the Dé-monos leaders, probing their minds. He glared at Vashtani. If he'd been stronger against Kyros, he wouldn't need Nastâr.

'Vashtani. For your failure in dealing with Kyros, you and your division can take over from the others appointed to carry out my specific commands. That way I can watch you closely, and you need never try your strength against Kyros again.'

Was that resentment he detected, or relief?

'The other five leaders and their divisions are assigned to Nastâr's command. Is that clear?'

'Thank you, My Lord,' Nastâr bowed.

Morthrir held and released each pair of eyes of the Summoners and Priests, despite the hoods hiding their faces in shadow, and found one Priest unable to meet his gaze. What was he hiding? He would ask Rafé later.

'Eawen the Henosite, our Chief Priest, failed to respond to my command,' Morthrir held the man's eyes a moment longer before moving on. 'When I called, there was more than just resistance. He has gone over to the other side and is now clothed in a light I cannot penetrate. He is therefore a traitor. I will have him imprisoned till I decide what to do with him. The same applies to anyone else who aids him.' His eyes flicked back to the other Priest: this time his gaze was returned without any wavering.

'Nastâr, take over the Chief Priest's position at the Eastern point of the Circle.'

'Yes, My Lord,' Nastâr moved across to the point indicated.

Before Morthrir could continue, Jumar-jé, the lead Summoner, spoke up. 'My Lord, Morthrir. May I make a suggestion?'

'Go ahead,' Morthrir was intrigued at the man's boldness.

'At the Beginning, on the island of Bara-mâla, Abbérron urged us to search for traces of a substance called *Imbrésonite*. We gathered all we could find. On the eve of the final battle, four of our Tsé-shâmé soldiers broke through Zerigor's defences and concealed it in the Royal Ziggurat. We thought the True King would stir up the sea to submerge the island and so render it impossible to use. The Inundation came, and we whispered in the ears of those who survived that this was in response to bloodshed and so hid the real reason for the flood.'

'What did Abbérron want it for?'

'He never told us, but was furious when it was lost to the sea.'

'What are you proposing?'

'Those four soldiers were disturbed and fled, but dropped it just inside the Southern door of the strong-room. It was too heavy to move easily, so I think Zerigor probably left it there. If you recover it, and present it to Abbérron, I think you will gain greater favour with him than you already have.'

'I see,' Morthrir paced up and down on the altar. 'How do you propose finding this *Imbrésonite*?'

'The Ziggurat was known as *the great building that reached to the skies and reminded them of the True King's presence above.* We have one of the Great Ones with us,' Jumar-jé bowed to Nastâr. 'He can stir up a violent storm, and maybe the calm afterwards will lower the sea level enough to expose the top, so we can dig through the stonework into the strong-room.'

'What about destroying Kyros? That's why Nastâr is here.'

'My Lord, Morthrir,' Nastâr spoke up. 'When I stood on the plain, I sensed the presence of Kyros, such is the power he carries. I know it of old, and hate it, for it comes from the True King, curse his name! Your nephew was moving West towards the coast. Maybe he knows of the *Imbrésonite* and is being used by the True King to destroy it. If so, we have to get there first.'

'How?'

'I can stir up the wind and the seas as Jumar-jé says. If your ships ride on the skirts of the storm you'll arrive before he can.'

'What if he is driven by the same storm and gets there first?'

'I will make sure the storm destroys him.'

'Lenyé escaped with him. As I intend to make her my bride, I do not want her killed as well. What do you suggest?'

'The storm can place his ship at your mercy,' Nastâr replied.

'So,' Jumar-jé intervened, 'you can recover the *Imbrésonite* to impress Abbérron; capture Kyros to destroy him; and rescue your bride at the same time.'

Morthrir paced up and down again smacking his fist into the palm of his hand. 'We'll do it. Jumar-jé, you and the Summoners charter four ships with officers and crews for the expedition.'

'Yes, Sire,' Jumar-jé replied.

'You Priests, send out your thoughts so that we may have speedy travel and success on this mission.'

'Yes, Sire,' they answered in unison.

'Vashtani, you stay here with me while the other Dé-monos leaders and their divisions accompany the ships.'

'Yes, My Lord,' Vashtani didn't sound too resentful.

'Nastâr, you stir up the storm when everything is ready.'

'Yes, My Lord.'

'What about yourself, Sire,' Jumar-jé interrupted, 'will you be directing activities from here?'

'No. Prepare yourselves as I release power for this mission.' His eyes swept around those present. 'I'm coming with you.'

Chapter Eleven

That night Lenyé sat next to Kyros at the campfire, thinking about her conversation with Ra-Na-Jiri. She watched Ramâno, silhouetted against the fading light in the Western sky, as he stood on the far side of the camp and threw a stick into the air. Chuah-te-mok did his incredible fall-out-of-the-sky-like-a-stone act and caught it before it hit the ground.

'Hey, Chuah-te-mok,' she heard the shrill of delight in the boy's voice, 'can you teach me to do that?'

'I think if you tried, we would be minus one young boy very quickly.'

She laughed with the others as Ramâno picked up the stick and threw it again. 'I don't need wings now that my legs are healed. Look at me.' He raced round the campfire and dived on the she-bear's back where she lay sprawled in front of the fire. 'Mamma Uza-Mâté, I hope you're not going to be as boring as Ariella!'

The she-bear lurched onto all fours. Ramâno sat on her with his legs dangling down either side. 'I can ride a horse bareback, and now I'm riding on a bear's back.'

Again everyone laughed.

Mamma Uza-Mâté rose up on her hind paws and Ramâno had to leap and cling onto her shoulders to save himself from falling off. She lumbered across the campsite putting her arms behind her back and hitching him higher so he could hold onto her neck. Then she grabbed his hands, swung him off and dumped him on the ground in a standing position.

Lenyé clapped her hands in delight and leaned over to Kyros. 'She did that to me once when I was recovering from the shock of my first battle.'

'Really?' Kyros frowned. 'You never told me that before.'

'I haven't been able to tell you everything that happened to me after we were separated in the hamlet.'

She glanced up and saw Ramâno and the she-bear circling around, facing each other and looking like wrestlers about to dive in under each other's guard.

'Go on, Ramâno,' Wilf yelled. 'She's much too big and clumsy to beat you.'

'Too big and clumsy am I?' Mamma Uza-Mâté roared, and took a pace forwards, but Ramâno darted in and leaped at her chest. The she-bear grabbed him.

'Help. She's squeezing all the life out of me,' and he lunged upwards to grasp her face.

Mamma Uza-Mâté sat down awkwardly and flopped onto her back. 'You're much too strong for me, Ramâno. I submit.'

Ramâno sat on her chest, an exultant grin on his face, but the she-bear grabbed his hands, lifted him into the air and caught him neatly so that his stomach was supported by her hind paws. Then she spun him round several times.

'Hey, Chuah-te-mok. Look at me. I'm flying.'

The she-bear dumped him on the ground again in a standing position.

Before he could move, Ariella nosed him in the back. 'Boring, am I?'

'What?'

She pushed him again. *"Boring, am I?"* she repeated.

The boy whirled round. 'I'm not scared of a cat like you,' and he flung himself at the lioness' neck and whipped round so he was sitting on her back. 'That's a trick I'm going to teach Harbona when I have my next riding lesson. Sneak up on a horse and slip onto his back when he least expects it.'

'And here's a trick no horse is ever going to teach you,' Ariella collapsed her front right leg, rolled her shoulder and the boy tumbled off, landing on his back. Then she was on him, pinning him to the ground by the shoulders, her bared fangs only inches from his neck.

Kyros whispered in Lenyé's ear, 'Ariella did that to me at the Pool of Alesco when she wanted to know why you and I walked away from each other after our argument. If it hadn't been for Mamma Uza-Mâté, she would have eaten me for breakfast.'

'Really?' Lenyé raised an eyebrow in mock surprise. 'You never told me that before.'

'I haven't been able to tell you everything that happened to me since I returned from the Realm of Travail.'

'Touché,' she laughed, but Ramâno's voice drew her back to the big fight.

'You don't frighten me,' the lad wrapped his arms around the lioness' neck. 'I'm going to squeeze all the air out of you.'

Ariella shook her head and stood over the boy, her tail lashing from side to side. But Ramâno scrambled away from her before she pounced on him. She rolled over onto her back with him trapped between her huge forepaws, but he sat up on her stomach and began bouncing up and down. Ariella shook him off and stood up.

'No seven-year-old boy should ever do that to a cat of any size, let alone me.'

Ramâno laughed and climbed on her back again. This time she stalked back towards the campfire before throwing him off.

Lenyé leaned closer to Kyros, 'I'm so glad we were able to impart the gift to the others. I think Ariella and Chuah-te-mok still found it awkward hunting yesterday because the girls were shy of speaking to them. And Mamma Uza-Mâté and Ra-Na-Jiri were with me most of the afternoon so I didn't notice.'

Even as she spoke, Ramâno raced across to throw the stick for Chuah-te-mok in the last few minutes of the failing light, while

Olathe and Nasima took his place, leaning against the lioness' flank and stroking her fur. Wilf and Festé were chasing Mamma Uza-Mâté, and Ra-Na-Jiri was coiled between Harbona and Marie-anna where they sat on the other side of the campfire.

'Look at them now though,' Kyros pointed at the eagle as the great bird caught the stick and dropped it at the lad's feet. 'Ramâno's so natural with them and gets the others involved.'

Lenyé felt Kyros slip his arm round her and leaned her head on his shoulder. 'Do you realise it's your Twenty-First Birthday in less than three weeks?'

'Who knows where we'll be and what we'll be doing by then?'

'But we should have the Crown, and you will have come of age. This is the True King's timing for your Coronation.'

Lenyé was distracted by a movement on the other side of the campfire, nudged Kyros and nodded towards Ra-Na-Jiri where Marie-anna had cupped her hand over the cobra's head. She was startled by Marie-anna's scream as Ra-Na-Jiri flared his hood, but was reassured by Harbona's chuckle as he too reached out to feel the cobra's head. Lenyé noticed their hands coming together.

'Do you think that was deliberate? It looked like Harbona was daring her to touch the cobra.'

'Just so he could hold her hand?' Kyros laughed. 'Why not?' He grinned, his teeth very white against his beard and tanned face in the light of the campfire. 'They're so well suited for each other...' He started at a sound from behind, 'What was that?'

'An animal smelling our food. What did you think it was?'

'I'm concerned about those warriors being so close.'

'When Yanantha did a similar thing and blinded the eyes of the Nastrim so I could recover the Sword, I didn't see any warriors for four days. We've at least two days left since she sent us off. As long as we keep moving, we'll be all right.'

Chapter Twelve

At dusk on the second day Beth, Quinn and Ishi-mi-réjá camped in a dell ringed by trees. They were making good progress but it would take another three days to reach Druis-cyf-rin. They lit a fire and sat talking round the embers well into the night.

Quinn asked Ishi-mi-réjá if she knew how his Uncle moved so quickly, and told her about seeing him appear at Onadestra.

'As I understand it, your Uncle commands spiritual beings to transport him instantaneously to wherever he wants to go.'

'And can he move things with him,' Quinn frowned. 'Like the altar stones from Mount Malkamet?'

'Most certainly. I once looked into Eawen the Henosite's mind and he knew of the practice.'

'I followed Rafé to that old man's cottage and sat in the rafters and heard him tell Rafé about the Grand Convocation.'

'Be very careful about Rafé. He thinks he's only joining in with the Grand Convocation to keep an eye on your Uncle. But he is being drawn in deeper himself. Once you get involved in these practices, the powers that govern them will not let you leave easily in case you betray them.'

Quinn sat thinking over Ishi-mi-réjá's description of how the instant-travel worked. 'That old man said my Uncle *"will stand and speak a word of power that will echo through the Waking World and call into being a new spiritual order to direct the future course of our existence"*. Is that what happened on Mount Malkamet?'

'That's why my stone disintegrated and we were overcome.'

'And is it still having effect?' Beth asked. 'We seem to be all right now.'

'Your Uncle's words opened up a way for those spiritual beings I mentioned to enter our world. They are the ones who do his bidding. But do you remember when you rescued me and I said: "*a greater power broke something over me and I began to rise up in the pit away from the heat*"?'

'Yes,' Beth nodded.

'It was Quinn's brother.'

'Kyros?' Quinn jerked his head up to look at her.

'I saw a vision where he stood on the Dangst rock, faced Mount Malkamet and reversed everything your Uncle spoke against himself and Lenyé. I particularly recall: "*Let all power that Uncle Morthrir relies on be stripped away*". So to answer your question, Beth, your Uncle's words may still be having effect, but because Kyros has spoken more powerfully, they will eventually cease. I think that's why you were able to reach down and pull me out.'

'And will Kyros' words help uncover the secret behind Uncle Morthrir's rise to power you told us about?' Beth leaned across to throw more wood on the fire.

'Yes,' Ishi-mi-réjá replied. 'Once we've recovered what I think you'll find at Druis-cyf-rin, we must give our attention to that.'

When they settled down to sleep, Beth lay turning things over in her mind. Why did Ishi-mi-réjá want to head for Druis-cyf-rin instead of going directly to Fantrios and rescue their parents? She said earlier, "*There's something you need to find first, that no Krêonor has seen for a thousand years. Something that will finally replace your Uncle's authority in the Waking World*".

What was it? And would it lead to uncovering the secret behind their Uncle's rise to power and bring him to justice as Ishi-mi-réjá had promised?

Chapter Thirteen

Kyros felt uneasy as the wagons continued across the plain the following morning. Despite Lenyé's reliance on Yanantha's words, they must be visible from the escarpment. He dropped back with Harbona and Ramâno. Chuah-te-mok hovered above.

He knew Harbona was keen to continue Ramâno's training, but was surprised to see him carrying a small lance.

'We can stay here for the boy's lesson,' Harbona watched Ramâno practise his galloping, 'then catch up with the convoy.'

Kyros left them and cantered back towards the escarpment with Chuah-te-mok ahead, but didn't find anything suspicious. He glanced behind and saw some of the lesson: Ramâno weaving his horse in and out of a line of stones; then dismounting on one side, springing back into the saddle and doing the same on the other side as the horse was moving.

He surveyed the escarpment ahead, but his eyes were drawn to the plantations of tiny saplings and swathes of young grasses growing up. He turned and looked West. Nothing except sandy plain till you reached the coast. But again, young plants were emerging. These must be the replanting undertaken by Osâcah and the Pilgrims. He recalled his friend's words, *"This is a picture of what is happening in the spirit-realm of the Waking World: bringing forth life where once there was only desert"*. He felt encouraged and took it as a sign for the fruitful outcome of his quest.

'Well done,' Kyros applauded as he cantered back. He dismounted and sat in the shadow of his horse to watch the boy.

Harbona handed the lance to Ramâno, 'Hold the butt on your

hip, balance the shaft against the horse's shoulder and make sure the tip is beyond the horse's nose. Try trotting with it.'

Kyros watched in fascination. A seven-year-old boy holding a lance quite steady, and this was the first time he'd ever done it.

'Good. Grasp the lance a bit further along, hold it up at an angle so that it's just behind the horse's head, and canter.'

The boy did as he was told, a frown of concentration etched on his face as he tried to keep the lance from wavering.

'Very good. Now drop the point of the lance and keep it a few inches above the ground. Rest the butt under the length of your forearm to give it stability. Keep your elbow bent. If it's straight, you'll break your arm when you hit the target.'

The boy cantered up and down a couple of times, the point wavering close to the ground, but he managed it.

'Excellent. Let's try for the peg.'

Harbona walked away and thrust a peg in the ground before walking back. He swung himself up behind the boy and steadied the lance with his own arm underneath. 'Feel what I do.' They cantered towards the peg and lifted it from the ground with the point of the lance. 'You could start at a trot, but it's easier at speed. Try it at a canter and feel that rhythm.'

He dismounted and re-set the peg. 'Now do it on your own. Don't let the point drop.' He watched intently before yelling, 'And back again.' But Ramâno missed. Harbona caught hold of the harness. 'Keep your eyes fixed on the peg and visualise it coming out of the ground on the point of your lance. Try again.'

Kyros watched the boy race towards the target, the lance steady in his hand. From this distance the peg looked tiny. Harbona was a brilliant teacher, but could the boy do it so soon?

Ramâno missed again. Kyros wasn't surprised. It had taken Lenyé and himself three days to learn the trick. He watched Ramâno try several times, but the boy kept missing.

'Nearly,' Harbona shouted. 'It'll come with practise.'

Kyros rode with Harbona as Ramâno led the way, galloping

to catch up with the convoy.

Lenyé sat next to Mari-anna as she steered the wagon and was glad there was no one within earshot.

'The other night when you screamed over the cobra and Harbona came to the rescue. Was there any…?' She hesitated, not knowing how to finish her question.

There was an awkward silence before Marie-anna whispered, 'Harbona's a good man.'

Lenyé caught the gleam in Marie-anna's eyes as she glanced in her direction. 'Do you know him well?'

'He's from another clan, but highly respected in my country. Feared for his prowess, and honoured. He called for a gathering of elders from both clans after Ranyak's death and gave them a month to resolve their differences, or there would be reprisals. When Harbona says something like that, everyone jumps.'

'Sounds like a formidable man,' Lenyé replied.

'Yes, but he also carries a deep sadness,' Marie-anna continued. 'His wife died in childbirth six years ago and the boy was stillborn. He's never looked at another woman since. Keeps it all locked up inside. Some men are like that. Just thrown himself completely into his work and his accomplishments. He looked at me when he rode into our settlement. I saw something in his eyes and understood we were two hearts suffering the same loss. Then he turned away to meet the elders and that was the last time I saw him, until I escaped with you.'

Lenyé smiled as Marie-anna glanced up.

'He should have been your Uncle's Commander, but somehow Youdlh got the job. When your Uncle found out what a great man Harbona was, he was furious, but it was too late, so made him his bodyguard. Youdlh was terrified of him. I heard rumours that he's recruiting warriors to rebuild your Uncle's army. But in reality he's protecting himself. He knows one day there's going to be a showdown between himself and Harbona.'

'So is Harbona teaching Ramâno to become a warrior?'

'I don't know. Now that Ramâno has been healed, my heart is full of hope for the future. I am not worthy of such a man, but for my son's sake...' her words tailed off. She drew a deep breath before continuing. 'All I can say is Harbona is one of the best. And I don't care who knows it.'

Lenyé reached over, placed her hand on the back of Marie-anna's and squeezed gently. Marie-anna looked at her and they both smiled as a deep understanding grew between them.

Lenyé heard galloping hooves from behind and peered round the edge of the wagon as the men caught up with them.

'Ramâno,' she shouted. 'I thought you were going to drive to Pordé-Sûnca. When are you going to take your turn?'

'He has me to blame,' Harbona spoke up for the lad. 'We've been learning some more horse skills.'

The wagons stopped. Everyone climbed down or dismounted to stretch their legs. Ramâno took his place in one of the wagons when they started again. They trekked till there was hardly any light in the sky, swapping the horses and driving them hard.

On the third day Kyros left Harbona to carry on with Ramâno's training, riding further back down the trail and scanning the sky for Chuah-te-mok. The eagle was away longer than usual and he couldn't even see the dark speck in the air. When the eagle returned, Kyros was stunned at the news.

'Those horsemen have left the escarpment and are riding after us, accompanied by four unarmed men hooded and cloaked in white, black, red and grey. Also, there's a dark mist shrouding the warriors, and one dark being with enormous wings that emanates an evil power I can feel.'

'Was my Uncle with them?'

'I didn't see him.'

Kyros rode to the others and found an exultant Ramâno with a peg on the point of his lance being congratulated by Harbona.

The bond between teacher and pupil was very close already.

As they galloped to rejoin the convoy, Kyros heard the warning of the eagle above him and whipped round in alarm. He could see the dark mist racing towards them.

'Ride ahead and tell the others to speed up,' he yelled at Harbona. 'I'll stay here and confront these Dé-monos.'

He cantered to one side, dismounted and used the heel of his boot to gouge a furrow in the sand at right angles to the track of the convoy. Then he stood in the middle of the line, raised his right hand and spoke, 'In the name of the True King, I forbid you to cross this line or harm my companions.'

The Dé-monos dived out of the sky, straight at him, swarming around and screaming abuse:

'One man. How can you stand against so many of us?'

'You have no power to counter us!'

'The True King cannot hear you!'

'Back, I say,' Kyros cried. 'You cannot pass me.' He was conscious of a huge, winged being behind the Dé-monos. Was it a fallen Great En-luchés? He cried out in his heart to the True King for wisdom about how to counter it and also for a releasing of the En-luchés to come to his aid.

The great creature remained well above him and took no part in the attack. Eventually the Dé-monos wheeled away, like a flock of crows and headed back towards the escarpment.

As Kyros mounted and followed the wagon tracks he realised this was only a trial of strength and the great being was testing him for any weaknesses. When he joined the others they were all shocked at the speed of pursuit, especially Lenyé. Yanantha's words had been overturned already!

Kyros kept the convoy riding well into the night and allowed no campfire. They had to reach Pordé-Sûnca by tomorrow to escape.

Chapter Fourteen

Rafé stood in the private council chamber and watched Morthrir pacing up and down.

He was still coming to terms with how he'd arrived in Terrazarema last night. He remembered making the snake show him Lenyé but was seized by a more powerful force and the link was broken. The next thing he knew, he was standing in utter darkness, but aware, by the rustling of robes and the sound of breathing, that he was not alone and realised he was in the Vault of Malrema. He knew Morthrir was able to move himself instantly, but how could he transport another person over such a distance? What if the other participants were drawn there in the same way? It made him feel helpless against Morthrir.

He was vaguely aware of Morthrir speaking about the Priests, but didn't fully catch the words.

'Are you listening to me, Rafé?'

'I'm sorry, Sire. I'm a little confused. Last night I was away on my journey; then suddenly I was in the Vault of Malrema. I thought I was dreaming.'

'Rafé, I take it you heard the discussion about recovering the *Imbrésonite*, destroying Kyros and capturing Lenyé.'

'Yes, Sire.'

'And took part in the ceremony to release the words of power to accomplish those three things?'

'Yes, Sire.'

'Then you weren't dreaming. I asked you why Eawen was not present. One of the Priests had a guilty look. Was that you?'

'No, Sire. Whoever it was may have been similarly confused about being in the Vault without any warning or preparation.'

'Hmph!' Morthrir shrugged. 'What do you know of Eawen's defection? He stuck up for you on Mount Malkamet. I assume there must be some sort of friendship between the two of you. Has he confided anything to you?'

Rafé hesitated, not knowing what to say. If he was seen to be siding with Eawen, what would Morthrir do to him? Throw him in prison? Execute him for helping a supposed traitor?

'I'm waiting.'

'Only to say he could no longer serve Abbérron.'

'In other words,' Rafé heard the chill in Morthrir's voice as the man spoke slowly and deliberately, 'he means he can no longer serve me.'

'He did say he could only be faithful to the True King, Sire.'

'He cannot leave the Priesthood by himself. Someone had to witness his renunciation; otherwise I would still have a claim over him. Was that you?'

Rafé felt trapped, wanting to be loyal to his friend, but unable to resist the probing of Morthrir's questions.

'I find you less than helpful today, Rafé. What's going on? Let me repeat the question, *"Was that you"*?'

Rafé stared at his feet, wishing the floor would open up and swallow him whole.

'Well?'

'Yes, Sire.'

'I see. You have done a grave disservice not only to the rest of the Priesthood, but to me personally. Do you understand?'

'I thought each member of the Priesthood was free to come and go depending on the promptings of his own conscience.'

'If that has been the case in the past, it is no longer so. I want undivided loyalty from all who serve me. I shall make that clear at our next gathering.'

Rafé glanced up at Morthrir's face and saw the anger still

burning in the eyes.

'As for the Henosite,' Morthrir continued, 'I will have him imprisoned until I decide what to do with him.'

'Be careful, Sire. I saw him this morning when I went outside for some fresh air. He was standing on the fountain in the Central Square talking to a great crowd about the True King.'

'He was even speaking to a crowd last night when we were in the Vault,' Morthrir slammed his open palm against the wall panelling, 'when he should have been with us as Chief Priest. The Central Square was ablaze with people's lanterns, they were so keen to hear him. I cannot let him roam the streets undermining my authority like that!'

'He appears to have taken over where Kyros left off, Sire. They were hanging on his every word. If you arrest him now there will be a riot, and we don't have enough warriors left to contain any uprising.'

'Do you think I don't know what he's up to, and the risk involved. Youdlh told me about his activities just before I came in here. I've ordered him to catch the Henosite at night when he's on his own with no crowds to protect him.'

'But if they find out he's in prison, they'll still riot.'

'Listen, Rafé. I don't believe in mob rule, and I'm not going to let it happen now. We'll think of something.' Morthrir paused and Rafé felt the man's eyes boring into his own. 'You may go.'

'What about my own mission, Sire?'

'Ah, yes. Your mission. If it was not for that and the benefit I expect to gain from its success, I would be treating you the same as the Henosite. Consider yourself lucky this time.'

'My horses are two days' journey away at my campsite, Sire. Am I to start again on foot?'

'Of course not.'

Rafé watched in horror as Morthrir raised his hands and spoke: 'Return Rafé to his campsite immediately.'

PART II

THE STORM

Chapter Fifteen

Kyros sat in a corner of *The Wreckers' Bar*, a drinking house on the harbour front at Pordé-Sûnca, talking to Hanniel, one of his former Captains from the Royal Garrison in Terrazarema. He and his men chose exile after Uncle Morthrir's coup, rather than serve in the warrior army. Kyros spotted the man soon after he entered Pordé-Sûnca late that evening, and explained who he was. Hanniel brought him here to talk.

'You sound like Prince Kyros, and have the same build, but I don't recognise you with that dark skin and long hair and beard.'

'Neither did my Uncle. I was able to walk into Terrazarema and talk to the People about the True King and the coming Restoration and heal those who were needy.'

'You mean, you're the Healer? We've heard of him out here. Wasn't there a boy whose legs were healed?'

'Yes, Ramâno. He's here with me, and Princess Lenyé, and my sisters and two cousins. My brother and youngest cousin are dead and buried at Terrazarema.'

'I'm sure I'd recognise members of the Royal Family; but you're the problem.'

Kyros pulled his signet ring out of a pocket. 'This is my seal.'

'Why aren't you wearing it?'

'I've been on the run from my Uncle long enough not to be that foolish. Hanniel, I don't have time to argue any more. My Uncle's warriors are not far behind. You have to believe me.'

'Very well,' he handed the ring back. 'Wait here.'

Kyros watched Hanniel walk to another table and talk to the

men, obviously discussing him. Now that his attention was drawn to them, he recognised a number of his former soldiers: the room was full of them. He saw some glance in his direction.

Hanniel came back with a couple of men and introduced them. 'What are you doing in Pordé-Sûnca? You can't avoid your Uncle any further unless you're planning to sail somewhere.'

'That's exactly what I am doing. I need to recover an ancient artefact to prove my Kingship beyond any shadow of doubt.'

Hanniel raised his eyebrows. 'An ancient artefact? That can only mean Bara-mâla.' He and his companions laughed. 'This Port's full of dreamers trying to find that place. What makes you think you'll be any more successful?'

'I've been sent by the True King, and I trust him to guide me. But I need a ship and a crew, and I have forty warrior horses with saddles and full harness to sell to pay for them.'

'Don't do that,' Hanniel glanced at his companions. 'It would attract too much attention selling so many in one go. Especially if Morthrir's warriors are in the area. Listen,' he lowered his voice and leaned forwards. 'Me and my men already have a ship, with a Captain and crew. We were going to raid our way down the coast in Tsé-shâmé country, flying the Krêonor flag, to provoke them into war against your Uncle. That would draw his warriors away from the capital so we can lead a surprise attack. But we can delay that and make our ship and ourselves available to you instead.'

'What ship?'

'*Brave Heart*. A warship captured from the Tsé-shâmé some years ago and renamed. Big, sleek and very fast. Captain Josiah hires his services to bounty hunters. Been out in more storms than anyone else in these parts, and even rides the worst winds to get there quicker, despite what it does to his passengers' stomachs. He goes out looking for trouble with the sea and is completely fearless. Trusts completely in his sea anchor skills.'

'Sea anchor?'

'Yes. A canvas cone towed behind the ship in rough weather. The small end is open and the whole thing's fitted with steel hoops to keep its shape with vents in the canvas to stop it being torn to shreds. Acts as a drag and slows the ship as it tries to career down a steep wave. He's perfected the size and amount of rope compared with the length of the ship needed in different conditions. Hasn't failed him yet.'

'Let's hope it won't come to that.'

'He's faced the worst weather at sea of any man I know, and always beaten the odds. I'm sure he thinks he'll never go down with his ship. Watch him like a hawk, in case he does anything foolish and endangers your company.'

'Can I trust him to keep quiet about where we're going?'

'Josiah will be very discrete. He and my Father go back a long way. Let's just say there's been a certain amount of cargo landed by *Brave Heart* and sold on by my Father. He won't fail you.'

'Good.'

'We can sail immediately and chart a course to tack against the Southwesterly wind.'

'Excellent,' Kyros was impressed.

'What are your plans once you've recovered this artifact?'

'I head for Terrazarema to deal with my Uncle.'

'In that case, corral your horses at my Father's homestead. I have plenty of men who can make good use of them on our return and ride with you as Guard of Honour. We will be proud to serve you again.'

Kyros reached across the table and they shook hands.

'Where's the rest of your group?' Hanniel asked.

'Hidden in the woods just outside the town.'

'Right,' Hanniel nodded to his two companions, and then raised his voice to the rest of the room, 'let's get going.'

Chapter Sixteen

Morthrir paced up and down in the private council chamber pausing every now and then to glare at Youdlh. 'Well?' The man could be so infuriating at times.

'My warriors tried to arrest the Henosite in the Central Square this morning, but were set upon by the crowd. They had to beat a hasty retreat.'

'You're not suggesting that Eawen and his mad ravings are having the same impact on the People as my nephew, are you?'

'The crowd think he's carrying on where the Healer left off.'

'This is getting ridiculous. Is it generally known the Healer was Kyros?'

'I don't think so, Sire.'

'Good. Let's keep it that way. If Kyros is ever allowed to return, and the People find out, he'll be welcomed back as a hero, and they'll never listen to me again.'

Morthrir carried on pacing up and down. 'What about your efforts to raise and train more warriors. How many have you managed to round up?'

'A thousand, Sire.'

'Is that all? How long will they take to train?'

'Most of them are seasoned horsemen from the buffalo plains further South. But they're not warriors. I've trained them to handle a sword and a lance. They just need to use those skills for attacking horses.'

'Why is that so difficult?'

'Plainsmen ranchers love their horses like members of their

own family. To attack a horse is like committing murder to them.'

'You know these people better than I do. Make sure they're up to strength and fully trained within the next two weeks.'

'Yes, Sire.'

Morthrir watched the man stand his ground, obviously wanting to ask a question. 'What is it, Youdlh?'

'The reserve guard of one thousand warriors that rode out the other night. I have no news back from them. What am I supposed to do?'

'They are on a special mission to locate Kyros and Lenyé. When that task is accomplished, I will return them to you.'

'Will that be all, Sire?'

'I may be away from Terrazarema on urgent business. Make sure you find a way to arrest Eawen properly and have him imprisoned before I return.'

'Yes, Sire.'

Chapter Seventeen

Lenyé stood on the main deck of Hanniel's ship, *Brave Heart*, where it lay moored to a quay in the harbour, and felt the gentle motion beneath her feet. Those warriors were bound to track them to Pordé-Sûnca and give chase at sea. She was exasperated at the slowness of Tadeas, the Crafter, and watched him trying to draw one of the Nastrim longbows. If only he would hurry up!

'See what I mean,' she said. 'It's too powerful for a human but would work as a crossbow with a winch to draw back the string.'

Tadeas talked of clipping the crossbow to a stock, bolted to the deck, on a swivel for up and down and sideways movement to act as bow- and stern-chasers and slow enemies at a distance. But to destroy a ship in battle, Lenyé would need to loose many fire arrows as quickly as possible. Tadeas suggested a barrel with six chambers to hold an arrow each, use the energy from the longbow string to spin the barrel and loose each arrow in turn.

He examined an arrow. 'But they won't go very far.'

'That's all right,' Lenyé replied. 'I can steer *Brave Heart* across the stern of an enemy, pour fire arrows into the cabins and hurl kegs of resin after them. That should set their ship ablaze.'

'I'll fit the barrel in spring-loaded clips so it can be quickly replaced. That should increase the rate of arrows you can loose.'

They talked about tying strands of hemp to the arrow tips to burn. Tadeas didn't have many kegs of resin but offered her an unclaimed consignment of molasses from one of the warehouses.

'Take a while to catch,' he said, 'but will burn for ages.'

'How do I throw the kegs onto the other ship?'

'I can rig some ropes between the masts. On the upwards roll of your ship, jerk the lanyards to release the kegs.'

Tadeas agreed to fit two crossbows on either side of the bows and stern, with a multi-barreled crossbow next to each of them.

'How soon can you get all that done?'

'Should be ready for testing by this evening.'

Lenyé breathed a sigh of relief. She thought it would take much longer and delay them leaving.

Throughout the conversation Lenyé was aware of pattering feet and yells from the youngsters as they explored the ship. She shouted down a companionway, 'Wilf, Olathe. Help the men unload the provisions and the rest of the longbows. The Nastrim ones are for Tadeas in his workshop, but the ordinary longbows and all the arrows can go to the armoury on board.'

Lenyé stood by the starboard gunwale watching the activity and was aware of a movement from behind. She felt Kyros slip his arm around her and turned towards him. 'I thought you were working with the others?'

'Hanniel insisted his men do it. Can Tadeas sort out the crossbows?'

'Yes. He'll be finished by this evening. Then we test them. Do you think those warriors have reached the city gates yet?'

'I don't know. How long do you need for the tests?'

'Tadeas said two days at sea, and then we'll have to return for adjustments. Any idea how we're going to find the island?'

'No,' Kyros glanced at her. 'But Hoffengrégor was able to see the island and the people and even Zerigor wearing the Krêon of Tulá-kâhju from the mainland. So it can't be very far from here.'

'Unless it was a vision the True King gave him, or a special gift of sight. It might be much further off than you think.'

'In that case, we'll have to trust the True King to bring us there by whatever means he chooses.'

Chapter Eighteen

Morthrir stood on the altar in the Vault of Malrema and calmed his mind. The Priests had sent out their thoughts to ensure speedy travel and success on the mission. Everything was coming together as planned. But he was still bothered by his conversation with Rafé. He dismissed the man to his campsite using Vashtani's division of Dé-monos, but Rafé was turning into a serious threat. And as for Eawen. The sooner Youdlh had the man behind bars the better. He was annoyed that his Chief Priest had defected, and now Rafé may be suspect.

He let his mind drift and sensed the light take root in him and fill the room. Although he was the only one present, he felt power in the atmosphere. He focused his mind on Pordé-Sûnca, the largest port on the coast to charter the ships, and spoke words to hasten the loading and departure. Suddenly he found himself staring at Nastâr.

'Is the mission progressing well?' Morthrir kept his voice low.

'Four ships have been commissioned by Jumar-jé, My Lord. But there's some misunderstanding with the Captains.'

'And Jumar-jé is unable to resolve it?'

'I think your presence may be necessary to make these Captains see sense, My Lord.'

'Are you sure? I planned to come once the ships had sailed.'

'Yes, My Lord.'

'Where are the Summoners staying?'

'At *The Flagship Inn*. Right in the centre of town.'

'Very well. Tell Jumar-jé to organise a meeting with the

Captains for 2.00pm today. I will order Vashtani to transport me so I can join you before then.'

That afternoon Morthrir sat with Jumar-jé glowering at the Captains across the table in the meeting room. His voice was controlled, but inside he was seething with fury.

'Let me see if I've got this right. You're questioning the need of four ships on what you call a bounty hunt?'

'Yes, Sire,' one of the Captains spoke on behalf of them all. 'We usually compete with each other, and want to know how any bounty monies will be split between us if we work together.'

'Is this why you've stopped loading your ships?' Morthrir banged his fist on the table.

'Yes, Sire.'

'Each ship will get the same,' Morthrir stared at them in turn.

'Then there's no incentive to excel over each other,' the Captain snorted. 'What about any loss or damage to our ships?'

'What makes you ask that?'

'There's another ship being chartered. Does that mean we're in competition and is there any risk of using force?'

'That depends on how matters turn out.'

'These ships are our livelihood,' the Captain replied. 'If they are damaged or destroyed we stand to lose a lot of income. So we request a deposit with the Shipwrights' Guild to cover any costs of repair or replacement for our ships.'

'How much?'

'One thousand gold krêons.'

'Very well. I'll have the money deposited by noon tomorrow.'

'That's one thousand gold krêons per ship.'

'What?' Morthrir jumped to his feet, the chair crashing to the floor behind him. 'For that kind of money, I insist on fifty of my warriors being aboard each ship.' His dark eyes swept the four men as they protested. 'To make sure you carry out my orders!'

Chapter Nineteen

Beth reined in the horse as they reached the Great Oak Tree. It was mid morning. She shuddered as she re-lived the convocation unfolding before her eyes: the time candle marking the midnight hour; the moving of the leaves in the breeze while the hoods and cloaks of the robed figures hung motionless around the wearers; the arrival of her Uncle; and the bolt of power that threw her into a trance. She was so afraid!

But by day, she couldn't help admiring how magnificent the Oak Tree looked with its wide canopy forming a huge, perfectly shaped crown. Most oak trees she'd seen were lopsided in shape as they grew amongst others, competing for the light. But this one commanded its own regal space, uncontested by any trees near it, like a great monarch of the forest.

Quinn slid off the horse first and she dismounted as Ishi-mi-réjá pushed her way through the bushes at the edge of the clearing. Beth replaced the reins with a rope halter while Quinn unbuckled the saddle and dumped it near a young tree.

'That's right,' Ishi-mi-réjá called across. 'Keep your things away from the big tree. We'll need to dig all the way round it.'

Beth led the horse over to Quinn, tethered it to the young tree and watched the old woman remove her backpack and unstrap the two spades.

'I've carried them this far. Now it's your turn. You'll have to dig between those tree roots at an angle going under the tree itself. That's why I brought the ones with long thin blades.'

'What are we looking for?' Beth saw her cousin frown.

'I think we'll recognise it when we find it.' Ishi-mi-réjá walked round the tree, feeling the hollows between the roots, then stood back and studied its position before looking into the distance. 'The question is,' she glanced at Quinn and raised an eyebrow, 'where do we start?'

Beth watched closely as Ishi-mi-réjá took the stone out of her bag and walked round the tree again, muttering to herself.

'There's a lot of confusion surrounding this tree that we need to get rid of before it will offer up its secret. I need your help. We must hold hands around the trunk and see what happens.'

Beth was startled by Quinn's laugh. 'Ishi-mi-réjá. The tree's massive. You'd need at least a dozen children to do that.'

'Maybe.' Beth saw the curious smile as the old woman turned to him. 'We need to get to know the tree.' She put her stone on the ground; Beth realised it was right on the spot where the altar had been. 'Quinn, you stand there facing the trunk, and hold your arms out as though hugging it. Beth, you come with me.'

Ishi-mi-réjá led her round the trunk till Quinn was out of sight. 'Not quite half-way round,' Ishi-mi-réjá whispered. 'But when I take up my position, we'll all be the same distance apart.'

As Ishi-mi-réjá walked on round, Beth rested her left hand against the trunk and was aware of the texture of the bark. She put her finger into one of the deep fissures and traced the curious twisting and turning pattern up the trunk. She stroked the rough bark with her other hand and was astonished at the feeling of life in the tree itself. She'd never known that before.

Then she heard Ishi-mi-réjá's voice. 'Stretch out your arms as wide as you can round the trunk and concentrate on feeling each other's hands meeting. Do not doubt, thinking it's impossible. I'll give you a few moments to concentrate on what you're doing.'

Despite the old woman's words, Beth couldn't accept what she was being asked to do. Quinn was right. It would take a dozen of them stretching their arms to meet up round this tree.

She gasped in surprise. With her right hand she felt finger tips exploring hers. That must be Ishi-mi-réjá. Then she could feel the same with her left hand. It must be Quinn.

'What's going through your minds?' Ishi-mi-réjá asked.

Beth found herself saying, 'I think we should move round the tree together.'

'Very well,' Ishi-mi-réjá replied. 'You lead us.'

Beth started them off with one sideways step to the left and a pause, then another, and another. After the fourth step she cried out, 'Stop. Go back one pace. I sense something coming to me, not quite a voice. More like words in my mind: a desire to hide; a desire to protect; and a hope for the future.'

'Good,' Ishi-mi-réjá sounded pleased. 'Mark the place in the ground with your foot, but don't break the circle of our hands. Anything else?'

'No. Shall we move on,' and she led them several more steps before wanting to stop again. 'This time I feel: a breaking open; a releasing of evil; and the coming of great fear.'

'Don't forget to mark the place with your foot.'

Beth was about to move them on when Quinn shouted: 'Wait. I feel something too. A sense of excitement and expectancy and revealing, but it's faint, as if what Beth said is masking it.'

'Mark the spot with your foot and then Beth can move us on.'

Beth talked them round to her original place which was just before the mark Quinn made. Odd that he felt it and she didn't. And strange that Ishi-mi-réjá hadn't noticed any of them.

'I think that's all we can do for the moment,' Ishi-mi-réjá spoke up. 'We need to break the connection, but don't take your hands away yet. Concentrate on letting go of each other.'

Beth felt Quinn's hand slipping out of hers first, then the old woman's.

'Don't drop your arms. Wait till I come to you.'

Beth was aware of the old woman approaching round the trunk, taking her by the hand and leading her to Quinn. Whether she still had her arms spread out or not, she couldn't tell, but suddenly the three of them were holding hands in a ring around Ishi-mi-réjá's stone and staring at each other.

'And break the circle,' Ishi-mi-réjá let go of both their hands together and she let go of Quinn's.

'Now sit down where you are.'

'I'm starving after all that hard work.' Quinn glanced up at the sky. 'It's well past lunchtime. Can we have something to eat?'

Beth laughed, 'You're always hungry.'

Ishi-mi-réjá chuckled. 'If we get the next bit right, it'll save some really hard work when we come to do the digging.'

'What do we have to do?' Beth looked at the old woman.

'My stone will help us,' she replied. 'But it may take a few days of waiting and listening till we understand what those words mean and how we are to use them.'

Chapter Twenty

Kyros paused with his hand on the rail of the gangplank leading up to the entry port on *Brave Heart*, and watched one of their wagons driving fast along the cobbled quay of the harbour towards him. It was late evening and there were no lamps on the wagon. Tadeas, the Crafter, was at the reins, cracking the whip. Kyros stepped off the gangplank and caught hold of the lead horse's harness as the team came to a stop.

'What's the hurry, Tadeas?'

But Tadeas turned away from him as his two sons jumped out of the back and began hefting bundles of arrows on their shoulders and lugging them up the gangplank.

'That's it, lads. Get them secured below. Quick as you can.'

He climbed down and walked across to Kyros. 'I'm returning the arrows Lenyé gave me to test the crossbows. I've included some heavy duty bolts. If she uses those first, they'll smash the glass on the stern cabins of her enemy's ship so her fire arrows can embed themselves straight into the wood inside and do more damage. She'll know what I mean.'

'Of course.'

'And remind her that the longbows are fitted to the stocks with quick release clips so she can remove them when not in use and store them below. Wouldn't want them out in a heavy sea; it would ruin the strings and maybe rip the longbows out. The stocks and swivels should be all right lashed to a ring bolt on the deck.'

'I'll tell her.'

Kyros saw the man glance along the quay behind the wagon before lowering his voice and drawing him away from the gangplank. 'There are four men in town with a number of warriors. They're trying to charter some ships. They've ordered enough provisions for six months at sea. I'm sure they're from your Uncle.'

'Do you know what they're after?'

'They're not giving anything away. Just say they'll be sailing South-West on an expedition as soon as the ships are ready.'

'What do you advise?'

'That's the direction every bounty hunter heads for to try and find Bara-mâla. I suggest you weigh anchor immediately and get going on your sea trials. But don't come back. From what I've seen of these men, they mean bad news for you.'

Chapter Twenty One

The following day Morthrir was with Nastâr in the meeting room at *The Flagship Inn*. He'd used Vashtani's powers of instant-travel to collect the deposit money from Terrazarema, and now the Captains were loading their ships. But it still wasn't fast enough. He paced up and down the room, smacking his palm against a beam now and then and fuming at the delay.

'I should execute those Captains for holding up our departure and hire some others.'

'There are no others prepared to act for us, My Lord.'

'Hmph!' Morthrir thumped his fist against the oak panelling of the wall. 'Do we know anything about Kyros?'

'I tracked him across the plain. And he was here in Pordé-Sûnca. I sensed his presence as soon as I arrived.'

'Where is he now?'

'Those Captains were right. Another ship set sail last night.'

'Why are you telling me this?'

'Because I'm certain Kyros was aboard.'

'This is outrageous! What about Lenyé?'

'I don't know, My Lord.'

'Those Captains are going to completely thwart our plans at this rate. How soon can they set sail?'

'Tomorrow morning, My Lord.'

'Tell Jumar-jé to use the warriors to load those ships. We need to start this afternoon. Stir up the storm as soon as we're at sea!'

Chapter Twenty Two

Two days out from Pordé-Sûnca and Lenyé was satisfied with her sea-trials. The ship's Crafter adjusted the bow- and stern-chasers and the ones with rotating barrels. She experimented with Tadeas' free-hanging ropes and tested the swing effect of the kegs and the quick-release mechanisms. Lenyé was convinced those warriors had put to sea already after Kyros' conversation with Tadeas, and half expected to see sails on the horizon behind them. She was relieved the crossbows were ready in time and there was no need to return to port.

She was pleased to see Captain Josiah ran a well ordered ship. Not only were all of Hanniel's men being trained in hoisting and lowering the sails and taking a turn on the capstan, but also their party as well: Kyros and Harbona doing the same sort of manual work and she and Marie-anna taking turns in the galley. The youngsters helped when they weren't doing basic navigation tasks like turning the hourglass, taking bearings or scrambling aloft with a telescope to keep a lookout. Also she showed them how to load the crossbow barrels, and they were eager to carry up bundles of arrows from the armoury and practise lighting and tending the braziers to ignite the fire arrows.

But she was concerned about the animal-friends. Even the slight movement of the ship in harbour was very unsteadying for them and they stayed in the cabin most of the time. She said they were free to remain ashore but they insisted on coming.

Lenyé stepped back from inspecting the rope lashing the port bow-chaser to a ringbolt on the deck to prevent it moving in high seas. With the longbow removed and stored below in the armoury it looked more like a see-saw for children to play on. She glanced at the rest of the crossbow stocks on the fo'c's'le and poop decks and smiled: they would far out-distance an attack by ordinary longbows, and be deadly against another ship.

She stood with knees slightly flexed enjoying the movement of the deck under her feet. Two days on board and she'd gained her sea legs. She listened to the thrum of wind in the rigging and the hiss of water alongside. They were close-hauled, tacking across the constant Southwesterly wind and making good speed. But for how long? This was the weak part in Kyros' plan. She relived his words: *"I suggest we ride West and head for Pordé-Sûnca…If we're serious about recovering the Crown and key, it's the best place to sail from"*.

She thought it a bit vague at the time, but didn't want to dampen his enthusiasm. When they discussed it with Captain Josiah, the man roared with laughter. She recalled his booming voice echoing in the confines of the rear cabin: 'Every bounty hunter points South-West and says, *"take me there. We're bound to find Bara-mâla"*. But we never do. It's out there somewhere. But how far?' He shrugged his shoulders and raised his hands in a gesture of despair. 'Nobody knows. I've sailed there so many times in fair weather or foul, and never spotted a thing. If it's under the sea, then it's so far down you can't see it, even in bright sunlight. So why should your quest be any different?'

'Because the True King has sent me,' Kyros replied.

'The True King, you say?' Lenyé heard a mixture of incredulity and suppressed laughter in the Captain's voice. 'That was a thousand years ago with all those stories about Zerigor.' He paused to get the better of his mirth. 'I've seen many bounty hunters in my time and can read them like an hourglass. But now you mention it, there's something different about you.'

'I have a specific artefact to recover.'

'No one finds anything. It's just a myth; but it's a good living.'

'It's no myth. I've seen the True King myself, and he doesn't make mistakes. I'm not coming back without it.'

Lenyé heard Kyros' tone of voice and knew he meant every word. She recognised that look of determination and a thrill of anticipation arose in her heart. If the True King had sent him, even if it was through Hoffengrégor, he wasn't going to fail.

She saw Captain Josiah step back, a look of awe on his face. He obviously felt it as well. 'I don't know about all this Zerigor business.' He sighed, 'I'm a practical man with a living to make. I'll take you as far as you want to go. But don't be shy about asking me to turn back. Even the bravest bounty hunters give up eventually. I hope that doesn't disappoint you.'

And so she was back to that nagging question no one could answer. She wondered if Kyros had any more thoughts since their conversation and glanced across to the quarter deck where he stood on his own against the starboard gunwale and gazed out to sea, the wind streaming through his long hair and blowing it out sideways. She walked across to the port companionway to join him, but was distracted by Ramâno. The lad's face was frozen in concentration, waiting with one hand on the ship's glass for the last grains of sand to trickle through the neck before turning it round and reaching up to ring two bells for the afternoon watch. 1.00pm. Marie-anna and the others would still be in the galley clearing up from the midday meal. Then he was busy marking the time and their position on the helmsman's slate. She smiled at the lad as he looked up and caught her eye. He'd taken to his new tasks with such an eagerness to learn that he was even getting comments of praise from Captain Josiah.

Lenyé ran lightly down the companionway, facing forwards, one hand on the rail; a far cry from the first day when every step on deck was followed by a lurch of the other foot to steady herself, and she had to turn round and climb backwards going down a companionway clutching on to the side of the steps as if she was using a steeply-angled ladder. She hurried across the sloping deck and joined Kyros, feeling his arm slip around her as she settled her head on his shoulder.

'What's the matter, Kyros? Is it the problem of finding the sunken island?'

'No. I trust the True King completely to guide us there.'

'What, then? Something's been troubling you ever since we read Hoffengrégor's parchment.'

'The True King said: "*I set before you seven tests that you may prove yourself worthy of being a King. You are free to face them, or walk away. Whichever you choose, you must stand before me when I sit on my Throne and give an account of how you have used this freedom*". If he dwells in the Realm of the Blessèd Throne, that's where I'll have to go.'

'How do you feel about that?'

'When he said that to me I had no idea who he was or where he dwelt. Now I've read the parchment I will be entering the actual centre of the Known Universe. It fills me with fear, not for my life, but what I will become.'

'It's very simple. You will be King.'

'I know. But I'm not sure I can carry that responsibility.'

'Surely that's what all the tests have been about? The True King would never let you become King if you weren't ready.'

'You're right. You're so wise, and so gentle with it. I don't know what I'd do without you.' He glanced up, 'Look at that.' He pointed back towards Pordé-Sûnca.

She followed his finger expecting to see the sail she feared, and took in the hazy look of the sky far astern. 'What is it?'

'I don't know. Change in the weather of some sort.'

As she watched, the clouds came pouring down to meet the sea, darkening all the time, with the sea mirroring their colour so that it became impossible to tell them apart, and she could only guess at a line on the horizon separating them.

'Whatever it is, it's coming up fast.'

A cold blast hit her in the face, and they both clutched at the gunwale as the wind veered round, spilling out of the sails and leaving the canvas flapping and the yards banging.

'All hands,' the Captain bellowed from the poop deck.

Everyone came pouring out of the hatches.

'Leave me the fore and main courses and the two jibs,' the Captain yelled above the sound of tramping feet.'

Lenyé felt the gust catch the sails directly from behind and the ship staggered sideways, but already the helmsman was bringing her head round to run before this new wind.

'Get those topgallants down,' the Captain roared, 'or we'll lose a mast. Lively now, or this one'll blow the sticks out of her.'

Lenyé raced after Kyros, up the stern companionway onto the poop deck and began hauling the spanker into a manageable roll as the sail came slithering onto the deck. She glanced over the stern. The deep blue of the sea from only a few moments ago was now being overtaken by a dull lead grey, coming up fast from behind; the waves rising and lengthening as if growing in power and deadly intent, mixing with the blue and changing its colour in seconds. The wind was already howling in the rigging and shrouds, and the remaining sails were hard-bellied, threatening to tear. A sudden bang made her whip round in alarm to see the main topsail rip straight down the middle, the men on the yard arms fighting to control the shreds.

'Get the main course off her,' the Captain bellowed only a few feet from Lenyé, 'and reef the fore course.'

She felt the ship bucking and swaying as high cresting green seas surged past, streaked with foam. A freak wave slammed into their port quarter thrusting them round and causing the ship to heel dangerously far over to starboard. Someone gripped her wrist. She looked up to see Kyros mouthing words at her and cupped a hand to her ear as he yelled again.

'Get below and check the others are all right. I'll finish off up here and help Josiah as much as I can.'

Chapter Twenty Three

Rafé glanced round his campsite and took in the two horses tethered on long leads in a patch of woodland grass where he'd left them. They were grazing unconcernedly, as if he hadn't been snatched away and returned in like manner. Morthrir's treatment of him, summoning him to the Vault of Malrema like that and sending him back again, was intolerable. What struck him most was the burned-out campfire, long since gone cold, as though something in his life had been snuffed out and he couldn't go back to it. That was when he decided he was no longer going to find the Golden Globe for Morthrir but for Lenyé. Maybe it would make himself appear more favourable in her eyes after their argument in the armoury over her swords.

He recalled afresh the startling view he had of Eawen speaking to a great crowd in the Central Square at Terrazarema, taking over from where the Healer had left off. He didn't appear to be healing anyone, but nevertheless argued most vigorously with the crowd concerning the True King.

'You know who I am and how I once was,' Eawen's voice rang out so clearly, 'with physical eyes that couldn't see. And you said to the Healer you would accept the words of the True King if he healed me. And here I am. I can see.'

'But it didn't happen in front of us,' a man called out. 'So how do we know it was the Healer who did it?'

'That's right,' someone else responded. 'He spoke over you, but nothing happened.'

'He even took some dust from the paving stones, spat on it

and rubbed it into a paste before smearing it on your eyelids,' another spoke up, 'but still it didn't work.'

'Do you not remember,' Eawen continued, 'he said to me: *"Your eyes will not be healed immediately, but only after your inner eyes have been opened to see the truth in what I say"*?'

'What inner eyes? That doesn't make sense.'

'We all have inner eyes that potentially can see into the spirit realm. But they became darkened in the days of Zerigor, and we have inherited the same disability. Only as we acknowledge the True King and turn to him with our hearts and trust in him are they opened so that we can see again.'

'What is it that you see and we can't?'

'The True King himself. He fills my inner vision, and, as a result, my heart is at peace.'

'How can we know this for ourselves?'

'I was blind from birth. And you have to acknowledge that because you saw me and knew me, and were perhaps a little afraid of me because I was the Henosite and had strange powers. But I have renounced all that and turned away from Abbérron to serve the True King. I did that before my physical eyes were healed. So this is confirmation of what has taken place within me. Never in the history of the Waking World has a man born blind had his sight healed. You cannot deny the testimony of someone who has experienced the True King like I have. My healing is a sign to you that the Restoration is upon us.'

There were some mutterings in the crowd but no one spoke up to challenge Eawen any further.

'What about you, my friends?' Eawen continued. 'My urgent plea is that you become like me. Abbérron may not control your life in such an obvious way as I experienced, but his influence is there. You have to choose for yourselves to reject Abbérron and turn to the True King. For a Day of Reckoning is coming when all who call on the Name of the True King now will be delivered from the grave and brought through to the life beyond. But if you reject him, he will honour that choice. Do not think you can keep putting this off, for that Day will come upon you suddenly, and it will be too late to change your mind.'

Instead of muttering, Rafé could see tears in their eyes. As he watched, people knelt and he heard a rising tide of voices calling on the Name of the True King. The crowd was largely Krêonor, but there were also many Tsé-shâmé and Harmoth. Race and background didn't matter as each one cried aloud. He sensed a great weight lifting from them to be replaced by a deep peace.

Eawen stepped down off the side of the fountain and walked amongst them, pulling people to their feet and embracing them. Rafé heard Eawen's voice lifted up for all to hear. 'At the end of my life, the True King has raised me up to prepare the way for the one who will rule amongst us. Now that you have turned to the True King yourselves, I urge you to walk with him and know his ways and serve him in love.'

Rafé saw his friend turn in his direction and scan the edge of the crowd before waving him over. Rafé pushed his way through as Eawen resumed his place and sat on the edge of the fountain.

'Come and join me, my friend. I am still learning.'

Rafé sat next to him. 'How do you mean?'

'When I ask about the sky, men say those soft white fluffy things are called clouds. And they pour rain down upon us. How does water float in the sky? And why is it white when the water we see is clear? If I climbed the stairs to the sky, I would leap off the top rung and fling myself, arms outstretched, into those beautiful clouds and feel myself falling through and pouring out of the sky with the rain.'

'Eawen. That's impossible. No one can do that. You have to understand what is real and what is imaginary.'

'I went to the river and sat beside it; for surely that is where the rain goes to after it has fed the ground. All my life I have listened to the mountain streams and heard their sounds and felt their icy waters. But now I can watch as well, and see where a submerged branch breaks the surface and changes the voice of the water; or a fish as it leaps for insects and flops back again; even feel the shock of a moorhen pulled under by some great fish, like a pike; and people hasten past and do not pause to wonder where the water goes and how it returns to the sky.'

'I don't know what you're talking about, Eawen.'

'No. Because you have ceased to wonder.'

'I don't think so. It's because there is too much else to do in life to bother with questions like that.'

'I asked someone the colour of a poppy, and he said, "*red*". And I see other things that are red, but are not poppies. That is not what poppies are all about. The red of a poppy is the shout of life, so vibrant and striking, you cannot miss it. I see in it the very handiwork of the True King. And he has made all things well. But people walk past and don't even notice.'

'That's because we're so used to poppies.'

'Ah. My friend. That is the point. When you first saw a poppy, did you not marvel?'

'I was but a child and learning so many new things.'

'Then I am also a child, and my cry to the True King is that I will never grow up or lose my sense of wonder.'

'Eawen, if that is the case, there are too many things to wonder at in the Waking World. We would never live out our lives if we stopped to do what you're saying.'

'Do you remember the gift box I told you about and how I tied it up and returned it to the True King?'

'I certainly do.'

'And you asked me whether he'd given it back?'

'Yes,' Rafé frowned.

'It is still in his safekeeping. But every day I write a little note in my heart, telling him of some new wonder I've encountered and place it in the box in my mind. I want that box to be so full and the ribbon forced so tight that he cannot undo the bow, and has to cut it and the lid of the box will be thrust off. Then all my sense of wonder at so many things he has made will flood out and pour over him and be his reward at what I have experienced in this life. I love this world in which he has placed me. And I cannot think of anywhere else I'd rather be.'

'But Eawen. Are you saying that the True King made all these things?'

'The shout of the poppy is unmistakable. How else can it be so red, and the marigold so orange and the daffodil so yellow? It's the same bee that pollinates each of them. Is it for their benefit alone? Who can behold the wonders of what is around us or search out their mystery without acknowledging the hand of the True King in all things?'

'I cannot answer you.'

'No. Few people can. And most don't want to because of the implications. If the True King is in all this, then they have to accept him for themselves. I was given a box to fill. That is the most important occupation of my life. I would hate to stand before him and confess I was too busy with my own concerns to even bother with putting just one thing in his box to show my appreciation of the life he has given me. Everyone has a gift from the True King. It is up to them to find it and fulfil it.'

Rafé didn't know what to say in response, but glanced up and saw some warriors pushing through the crowd towards them. 'I think it's time I was moving on. I need to meet with Morthrir as I am on a special mission for him.'

'Listen, my friend,' Eawen lowered his voice to a whisper. 'I have a gift for you.'

As Eawen thrust something into the palm of his hand, Rafé closed his fingers around a short, uneven cylinder that felt like something made of wood.

'What is it?'

'When I took my tools from the room where I was working on that bust of the Healer, I also took my old walking cane. Now that I could see, I no longer needed it to feel my way and cut it into ten equal parts. I kept one for myself as a reminder of what the True King did for me, and gave the rest to the other Priests. I implored them to reconsider their involvement with Morthrir and the Summoners and the convocations and, especially, Abbérron. For what they do is altogether evil, and a snare and entanglement that will take a man down to destruction. This is the last piece which I kept for you, so that I could give you the same warning. Think carefully about my words, my friend.'

Rafé hesitated. There was something so convincing in what Eawen said that he wanted to make some kind of response there and then, like the people earlier, kneeling down and calling on the name of the True King. He glanced across to the warriors, realised they were much closer and the moment was gone. 'What about you? If Morthrir decides you have spoken against him and praised the True King too much, those warriors will arrest you.'

'I do not fear men in this world, but I fear to deny the True King and the consequences that would count against me. If I lose my life in the Waking World declaring the greatness of the True King, I have lived well.'

Rafé stood looking down at the charred patch of ground in his campsite, fingering the piece of cane in his pocket and thinking about Eawen. He couldn't deny the man's testimony, but was worried about the implications for himself. He had to find that golden globe and the cobra was the only means of doing so. How could he switch allegiance away from Abbérron at such a critical point despite Eawen's warning? He would use the cobra one last time, and then decide.

Chapter Twenty Four

Kyros felt the impact of the sea anchor on *Brave Heart's* motion as the rope was paid out fully. Instead of staggering at the top of a wave and corkscrewing down the other side, the ship hung suspended on the crest, before easing down as the helmsman brought her under control with only the reefed fore course and two jibs. He glanced up at the poop deck and saw the Captain pacing up and down, grinning and smacking his fist into the palm of his hand. Hanniel was right. Josiah was utterly fearless, confident in his ability to tame the power of the sea with his skills and obviously enjoying himself. He saw the man cup his hands round his mouth, 'We're going to run before this one, Kyros, and use it to our advantage. Maybe it'll get us far enough out for you to find something after all!'

But the storm was building fast: the wind screaming in the rigging and huge green seas cresting behind them, lifting the ship's stern and plunging her down into the trough in front, the bows ploughing into the wave ahead as she fought to come up and ride the next one. Kyros saw the Captain's frown of alarm as he ordered another man on the helm to steady her, and Kyros rushed to take the place. He felt the power of the sea through the wheel and steering linkage to the rudder as the next wave crashed into the stern and hurled them down the slope in the trough to the next teeth-jarring impact of the bows and the stagger of the deck as the ship plunged through the head spray.

He was vaguely aware of Ramâno, still at his post, turning the hour glass, and reaching for the lanyard. He watched the boy's hand ring out four bells as if defying the might of the ocean with the simplicity of routine to keep the ship on course. One hour. That's all it had taken to change from calm blue to raging green; and there was more to come.

The wind veered slightly and the ship yawed as the next wave smashed into them at an angle, a huge crest rising up close to the stern and crashing on board in a maelstrom of heavy green water and white foam. Kyros gripped the wheel tighter as the waist-high water surged past him, and fought with the helmsman to bring *Brave Heart* back on course; but the boy was washed away. Kyros released the wheel to race after him, but the spokes spun and the ship lurched further over: the helmsman couldn't hold her steady on his own. Kyros grabbed the wheel and looked up as Ramâno was swept aside into the scuppers, the power of the water slamming into the starboard gunwale and pouring back again over the deck. He heaved on the wheel and felt the ship straighten herself for the next onslaught. Ramâno picked himself up and crawled back to his post.

'Get below, Ramâno. It's not safe for you up here.'

'I'd rather do a job that frees a man for more important work, than be stuck down below.'

'Then find a safety line and tie yourself on.'

He saw the flash of the lad's smile as he darted away to the rope locker.

Kyros found steering the ship in those conditions exhausting. The Captain only allowed half an hour on the wheel before replacing him. He was distracted as Ramâno rang five bells, and gratefully relinquished his post to another man. But he stayed on deck. Hanniel's warning about Josiah was still fresh in his mind: *"I'm sure he thinks he'll never go down with his ship. Watch him like a hawk, in case he does anything foolish and endangers your company"*. It was impossible to go below when conditions were like this. They had to bring the ship through and survive. He must give Josiah his support, and be on hand if anything did happen.

Kyros took comfort in the fact that if they were experiencing such a tough time, then any pursuing ships would be the same.

It became an intense round of on-and-off duty, not only with the helm, but manning the pumps and checking nothing was carrying away. He was soaked to the skin, intensely cold, tired beyond belief and the rims of his eyes stung where they were caked with salt. But still he fought on as the light began to fade and the sea changed to a dense black, the crests marked out by an occasional glint of foam as a patch in the clouds revealed the starlight. They were sailing by feel more than anything else. And so they continued for two nights and the day in between.

As dawn broke on the third day and the raging seas became green and white again, the Captain ordered four men to the wheel. At one point Kyros found himself shoulder-to-shoulder with him as Josiah took his turn.

'Storm's holding steady,' he heard Josiah yell in his ear.

Kyros nodded.

'That's good news for us. It must slacken off soon.'

There was a pause and Kyros didn't even try to say anything.

'I was out with a consort once, not as big as *Brave Heart*, in conditions like these. The wind veered and caught her as she headed down a huge wave. Very nearly broached and turned over, but managed to go on round till she was sliding stern first into the trough, but didn't come up the other side. Her stern kept going right under and the wave pitch poled her.'

Kyros stared at him, not fully grasping what he meant.

'Flipped her end-over-end. Heard the smack of her masts on the water above the sound of the wind. Just lay there hull up, with wave after wave lifting her and smashing into her before she went down. We would have joined her if it wasn't for my sea anchor. It has never failed me yet.'

Even as he spoke, the wind changed from an intermittent shrieking to a moan and back again, with large patches of foam all over the rising and falling waters. Then the shriek was a moan and staying constant, the seas rising and rolling higher about them. Kyros glanced at Josiah and saw the shock in his face. There was a sudden pause in the sound, like a welcome silence, but the power of the sea was still rising. Suddenly Kyros caught it in his belly, more a vibration than an actual sound, as though someone had connected a huge pair of bellows to an enormous hollow pipe and pumped as hard as possible, filling him with a deep tonal resonance that threatened to shake the ship apart. But the bellows went on pumping and the diameter of the pipe kept changing, making the resonance move up and down the scale without any recognisable melody: just a maddening effect that threatened to tear the very life out of him, as though some giant sea sprite was playing a mischievous tune to torment him.

Kyros was aware of eight bells striking, and someone forcibly pulling him from the wheel so another could take his place. He glanced over the side: the seas were white from a continuous layer of spume stirred up by the pounding waves, and the air was thick with spray. He was hardly able to breathe from the pressure of the wind and the spray in his mouth and up his nose.

Then he heard the True King's voice in his heart, as though recalling something from so long ago he was scarcely able to remember it: *"Because you have surrendered your dream unreservedly to me, we will prevail together to fulfil it. Any dream that becomes my dream must come to pass in the Waking World"*. Dream? His numbed mind couldn't make the connection. What dream? Suddenly it came to him: recovering the Krêon of Tulá-kâhju, the Crown of Life, from the ancient site of Bara-mâla itself. And his conversation with Hoffengrégor: *"I feel it deep in here…Sometimes I'm doubled over with pain just thinking about it"*.

He collapsed to his knees, writhing in agony, trying to hang on to his dream while the tonal voice reverberated within him, grinding down his resistance and demanding he give up on his quest. Something was trying to rip that dream out of him.

Chapter Twenty Five

Morthrir paced up and down on the quarter deck of his ship, fuming to himself, the strong wind whipping around him and singing in the rigging. Those Captains were still complaining amongst themselves, sending urgent signal flags running up the masts and trying to form some kind of conspiracy against him. Stupid fools! He had fifty warriors in each ship to enforce his orders, but was far from happy.

The wind veered suddenly from the seasonal Southwesterly till it was raging from the North-East, bringing with it the deadly cold of the mountain regions. His Captain kept muttering about how this uncanny storm had sprung up almost as soon as they put to sea and saw it as an omen against them that would bring nothing but trouble, and destroy their ships before they even reached their goal. The others signalled that one thousand gold krêons per ship was not enough, and asked Morthrir to lodge more money with the Shipwrights' Guild. As if he could do that while at sea. What did they think he was? A conjuror? He yelled at his Captain, 'Signal back that the storm is retribution for their delay, and making up for lost time. Tell them to trim their ships accordingly and get on with what I've commissioned them for.'

But secretly he was ecstatic about the storm. It was exactly what he had commanded Nastâr to stir up so they could ride fast on its tails and catch up with Kyros before the storm hit his ship. He was determined to have Kyros at his mercy, and then rescue Lenyé for himself. He looked up from his musings and saw the great being flying towards him out of the storm. Morthrir pointed at the cabin to talk with Nastâr in private.

'Well?' He paced up and down, glanced across to Jumar-jé and the other Summoners and back to Nastâr.

'I saw the white sails of a lone ship on the horizon. Kyros is definitely on board. I could feel him. The storm is upon them and they were hauling in their sails.'

'And Lenyé? Was she there?'

'I can't be sure. Something is blocking any knowledge of her.'

'We'll have to assume she is. I want you to watch the storm carefully. Destroy Kyros and rescue Lenyé. Is that clear?'

'Yes, My Lord. But there is something else.'

'What?'

'I felt it coming from Kyros. Not only does he carry great power, but also a dream from the True King.'

'Dream,' Morthrir frowned. 'What dream?'

'I don't know. I sense it is to restore all that Zerigor once had.'

'And what will that do?'

'Bring you down and utterly wreck all that we are labouring to accomplish.'

'In that case,' Morthrir began pacing up and down and smacked his fist into the palm of his hand, 'you must act quickly. I want that dream torn out of him before it destroys us.'

'I've already tried, my Lord, but he's resisting me.'

'Use the power of the storm if necessary.'

'His ship is successfully weathering it.'

'Then increase the ferocity!'

Chapter Twenty Six

Lenyé hurried to the cabin to find Mamma Uza-Mâté staggering on her hind legs and occasionally dropping to all fours. Ariella paced up and down in the narrow confines lurching from side to side. She strapped them both into their leather harnesses, recalling, as she did so, Captain Josiah's words when they first came aboard. "*Get the Crafters to make up some restraining harnesses for the lioness and she-bear. They won't last five minutes in a heavy sea. And get them to bolt a couple of large wooden boxes to the decking for the cobra and eagle. Wedge them both in with spare canvas, if you need to*". She helped coil Ra-Na-Jiri in his box and secured him with some canvas, but Chuah-te-mok was more difficult to settle. He kept moving up and down on the decking and hopping every now and then with wings slightly lifted to balance himself against a sudden lurch of the ship.

She made her way across the main deck to the galley and helped Marie-anna and the others finish clearing up. The two of them sat down and worked out menus for however long the storm would last, while the others drifted off to their various tasks: Wilf to relieve Ramâno at the hourglass, and the others down to the bilge to take turns on the pumps.

'We must keep them occupied, Marie-anna,' Lenyé whispered once they'd all gone. 'Otherwise they'll give in to sea sickness too quickly and everyone'll be miserable. Ariella's already looking quite bad,' and she recounted how the animal-friends were coping.

She knew it was too dangerous to light any fires in the galley with the ship lurching about as wildly as this, so it would have to be cold fare: dried fish, sun-dried tomatoes, biscuit, cheese and fresh fruit. And there was some bread left. It would be stale by tomorrow, but was better than nothing. The salted meats would be too hard to chew without cooking.

She smiled to herself. One good thing about the storm: any enemy ships would be scattered in this wind and unlikely to catch them unawares.

The rest of the day revolved around preparing and distributing meals, helping out on the pumps, checking her crossbow stocks which gave a welcome breath of fresh air after being below decks for so long and retiring to the cabin to check on the animal-friends. Mamma Uza-Mâté was sound asleep, as though she had determined to go into temporary hibernation and remain oblivious to the pitch and roll of the ship. Ra-Na-Jiri was coiled up fast asleep. Chuah-te-mok couldn't settle in his box and was doing his hop-and-flutter and getting very tired. Ariella was the worst. The great cat was unable to sleep. She felt dizzy and her face looked so forlorn that Lenyé was quite worried about her.

The cabin became a hub for people drifting in as their respective duties came to an end. Harbona visited regularly to check on them. Only Kyros stayed on deck all the time and she wondered at that. Surely he needed a break from that incessant wind and the sheer exhaustion of being out in it and keeping his footing?

Ramâno was the chirpiest, finishing his turn on the hourglass and immediately hurrying down to help on the pumps. 'It stinks down there,' Ramâno burst into the cabin. 'I'm glad we're up here as far away as possible.' He sat cross-legged with his face pressed against the panes of glass on the stern window and gazed at the waves rolling up behind and sliding under the ship. 'How long's this going to last?'

'Hush, Ramâno,' Marie-anna's calm voice made Lenyé smile

to herself. It must be hard work for any Mother with such an energetic young boy to look after.

He jumped up. 'I'm going to help Kyros and Harbona.'

'Don't get in anybody's way.'

'I won't. I had a safety line last time. Kyros made me because a great wave crashed over the side and washed me up against the gunwale. It was great fun.'

'Be careful. The sea's much rougher than when you were last out there.' But it was too late: the boy was already gone.

Lenyé lost track of time. She was vaguely aware of the bell striking, but forgot to count. Only the changing colours through the stern window told her when it was night and dawn and then night again. She knew Marie-anna was struggling, by the look in her eyes, but they both held to an unspoken agreement between the two of them: they had to stay strong for the others and not give in to this. She fought her own battle, willing herself not to let the giddiness take over, forcing herself out on deck for some fresh air to clear her head; but always against the uncertain lurch and heave of the ship and the numbing sensation of rise and fall and side to side roll, on and on without any let up. And then back to the cabin to care for the others.

The girls were overcome with sea sickness quite quickly and she comforted them in her arms as much as possible or helped them into their boxlike cots that hung from the deckhead above and gave some relief from the rolling of the ship. Wilf and Festé weren't much better off and lay moaning to themselves or staring at nothing in particular as if focusing on something made the giddiness worse. Even Ramâno succumbed eventually by the following evening and spent most of the night face down in his cot or crawling to his Mother and lying in her arms.

Chapter Twenty Seven

Beth felt frustrated with the delay at the Great Oak Tree instead of rescuing their parents. For several days she and Quinn sat in a circle with Ishi-mi-réjá, taking turns to stroke the old woman's stone. Gradually her resentment changed to a feeling of peace. What they were seeking here would have a profound impact not just on her Family, but the whole Krêonor Kingdom.

On the fourth day she looked up expectantly.

The old woman smiled, 'I think we're ready. What are your impressions of coming here? Quinn, let's start with you.'

'I wanted to know why Rafé slowed us down in getting to Onadestra. He must have known the date of the convocation and was delaying us to be here at the right time.'

'What about on the night itself. Were you afraid?'

'Only when I couldn't find Beth. But mostly, I was curious.'

'And you, Beth?'

'I was scared from the outset. We were in that clump of trees over there. As Quinn said at the time, we couldn't leave without being seen and caught. Especially after my Uncle arrived.'

'Curiosity and fear. Do you still feel that, either of you?'

Beth wasn't surprised when Quinn said he was curious as to why they here again. Her cousin was curious about everything. But for herself, she knew Ishi-mi-réjá's stone had cured her of any fear of this place. Then she related her impression of the tree when they arrived, as a great monarch ruling over the forest.

'So you think it grew up here before there were any other

trees to compete with it. Anything else?'

Beth told of her wonder at exploring the bark and feeling the life of the tree itself.

'A sovereign with the power of life? Interesting. Let's talk about those words now, and particularly where you heard them. Beth, you spoke first, and the mark you made points directly towards the Dangst Rock.'

'Really? What does that mean?'

'Something came to this tree from the Dangst Rock with "*a desire to hide; a desire to protect; and a hope for the future*". This tree grew over it, so the first two words have been fulfilled. The third is outstanding, and relates to the tree itself: "*a sovereign with the power of life*", representing a hope for the future.'

'What about the second mark?' Beth was intrigued.

'That points towards Mount Malkamet. You heard: "*a breaking open; a releasing of evil; and the coming of great fear*". It came to this tree for a reason. Do you know what Druis-cyf-rin means?'

'No.'

'Mystic Doorway. Whatever came from the Dangst Rock originated in another Realm. So this location has become a thin place allowing a cross-over between the Waking World and that Realm. It's not the tree itself that's important, but what's under it. Mount Malkamet is where evil was released into this world. We know Abbérron and the Summoners used it. I think they were drawn here by the power to cross-over into another Realm. That's the "*coming of a great fear*".'

'What about Quinn's words; where do they point to?'

'Terrazarema.'

'How does that fit in with the other two?' Quinn asked.

'The "*sense of excitement and expectancy and revealing*" you felt?'

'Yes. Why was it so faint?' Quinn persisted.

'Firstly, you said, "*it's…as if what Beth said is masking it*". I think that was the fear from Mount Malkamet trying to use this place for Abbérron's purposes. And secondly, in the first two instances, something was coming to this location: the thing we're looking for and the fear. What you sensed was something going away from the Great Oak Tree to Terrazarema. And that is tied to the sovereign with the power of life.'

'You mean, my Father?'

'No. I think it has more to do with your brother, Kyros.'

'But once we've rescued our parents, my Father will resume his reign. He's still King, isn't he?'

'A lot has changed since your Uncle seized the Throne.'

'I don't understand. If Father is alive, how can Kyros…?'

'We'll have to wait and see when we get to Terrazarema.'

Ishi-mi-réjá stood up and held out her hands to them both. 'Come. We need to break the power of Mount Malkamet over this tree before we can do anything else.'

They stood in front of the tree with Ishi-mi-réjá's stone on the ground between them and held hands. Beth was stunned at the potency she felt in the old woman words: 'By the power released when Kyros spoke against his Uncle on the Dangst Rock, I command a reversing of all evil forces that have ever gathered here, and break whatever intent and action they have sought!'

They let go their hands and Ishi-mi-réjá smiled. 'Now we can start digging. Beth, I suggest you choose the hollow in the roots closest to your Dangst Rock mark; and Quinn, you start at the Terrazarema mark.'

Beth and Quinn carried on digging and scooping the soil out with their hands till dusk when it became too dark to see what they were doing.

They camped again for the night under the canopy of the great tree.

Chapter Twenty Eight

Lenyé lay in the cabin with Olathe and Nasima in her arms trying to recall something Kyros said. *"Osâcah and the Pilgrims interceded until…help was sent. We don't have the benefit of them with us now. So we'll have to call upon the True King ourselves…"*. Already she felt the sea surging with greater strength as dawn began to break and the wind was more of a shriek than she remembered. If ever they needed the True King's intervention, it was now. But the shriek of the wind was changing again, this time to a moan and she could feel the seas rising and the ship plunging up and down through greater waves.

She didn't know what to do or say, but quietly, to herself, she began speaking his name. As she did so, her voice grew in power as though thinking about him and that wonderful smile she'd experienced at the Pool of Alesco came rushing back to her: nothing could take away the awareness of his presence for long, not even this storm. She felt a great sense of hope welling up within her till she was about to burst.

'What are you talking about?' Olathe's feeble voice made her look up.

'Remember when we said back at Yanantha's house that we would have to call on the name of the True King?'

'Yes.'

'That's what I'm doing.'

'Can I do it with you?'

'Of course.'

'And me,' she felt Nasima stir beside her. 'What do we have

to do?'

'Speak his name, like this,' and they joined in with her.

'Can we say it too?' Wilf was astir and she saw Festé and Ramâno lift their heads and stare at her.

She glanced around at the animal-friends but they were asleep. 'We're all going to.'

Before she could say anything more, the moan of the wind changed yet again, not to a sound so much as a deep vibration that shook the whole ship.

'Repeat after me, "*O True King, you see how bad this storm is. Please come to our aid*".'

In the midst of his struggle, Kyros realised what was going on. This was no ordinary storm; some greater power was behind it. As he wrestled and cried out to the True King, he felt a jarring sensation from the stern of the ship as though they'd been kicked by an enormous boot, followed by that corkscrew motion, and knew instinctively that the sea anchor had torn away. He felt *Brave Heart* gather speed as she lurched down towards the trough. As Kyros turned to stumble up the ever-tilting deck towards the cabin, he saw behind the ship, much higher than the rising poop deck, a huge rogue wave bearing down on them.

He grabbed the Captain by the front of his waterlogged jacket. 'Have you got another sea anchor like that one?'

The man shook his head. 'That was the biggest I had; and it wouldn't hold. The men are paying out two smaller ones, but they won't be in time.'

'Is that the same kind of wave that up-ended your friends?' Kyros stared into the Captain's eyes and gripped the jacket tighter. 'Is it?' The man didn't answer. Josiah had given everything to get the ship this far: now he was fearful for his life. No. It was more than that. Kyros saw stark terror in the man's eyes. Josiah knew the wave was going to pitch pole them and there was nothing the man could do about it.

Kyros thrust him aside and staggered towards the stern cabin, falling to his hands and knees and clawing his way up the steeply sloping deck. He reached up and turned the handle on the door.

Lenyé and the others were still calling out to the True King and saying his name together over and over again when the door burst open and Kyros collapsed into the cabin.

Kyros raised his head and surveyed the scene, everything etched on his mind in startling clarity, despite the urgency of the moment: Lenyé cradling Olathe and Nasima in her lap; Marie-anna with Ramâno in her arms; his two cousins lying on their cots with canvas stuffed around them to stop them falling out; the lioness and she-bear strapped to the sides of the cabin; he couldn't see the cobra but knew he was somewhere, and the eagle taking little hops and steadying himself with his wings; Harbona hunched in one corner, taking a respite between watches, and utterly exhausted. Everyone he loved and cared for: all those who were left to him. And through the great stern window that enormous rogue wave, grown in size and potency since he saw it from outside, still bearing down on them.

He heard them muttering to themselves or speaking quietly, almost in unison, and his confused mind tried to piece together their words. But there was no time.

Lenyé saw him pause for a split second that seemed to last for an age; then heard the note of desperation in his voice.

'Quick. All of you. We must call upon the name of the True King to deliver us.'

There was a sudden silence.

'That's what we're doing,' Ramâno's voice was harsh and croaky. Everyone laughed.

Lenyé saw the look on Kyros' face, wrenched herself away from the girls and sat up. He wasn't laughing at all.

'What is it?'

She followed his pointing finger and stared out of the stern window at the most immense wave she had ever seen, rolling in from behind and lifting the stern of the ship higher and higher. She felt the ship rushing down the steep slope of the wave as though it would plunge bows-first into the trough of sea that must be opening before them, and go on ploughing down and never come up again. She gripped his arm, fearful of what would happen if they could not avert the deadly power of this wave.

Suddenly a figure was flung through the glass, but nothing broke, her long hair lashing about her face in a wild frenzy, her arms pinned out straight behind her back and her legs caught up behind her as well, so that she was bucking and thrashing like a demented being. Her eyes were starting from their sockets such a terror was upon her, and her mouth open fit to split her face in a silent scream, every sinew in her neck standing out knotted and taut as whipcord.

'Save me, save me!' her voice was the same tonal discord throbbing in the heart of the ship.

Lenyé shrank back in horror, and would have screamed herself but for the quiet voice that arose in her heart as it had done once before when they were in the forest at the Pool of Alesco, gently prompting her. 'Kyros,' she gripped his arm tighter. 'This is no ordinary storm. It's like Uncle Morthrir releasing the Breaking-in. You have to speak against it. Only you can do this.'

Whether the True King was still speaking to her or not, she couldn't tell, but in a flash of insight she knew who this was: Asa-Dura, the Sea herself. A name she'd never really considered before, merely seen carelessly scrawled on a map when you reach the coast and everything ahead is blue; a name sailors banded about concerning something they had to navigate through to get somewhere else; a name embedded in an old song that had come down to them from time out of mind and they carelessly sang at play as children; and here she was, right in front of her. Not just a name, but a real person, with the full weight of the sea and the power of the wind at her command.

Lenyé saw the hair as a shifting hue of blue and grey and green, shot through with brown and swelled along the length of the strands with little air blisters like sea wrack. Her clothing was greeny-brown, of a seaweed-like texture, but torn to shreds as though she'd been hauled across a reef of razor sharp coral. Her shoulders were wrenched so far back and her legs drawn up so tight that it looked as if she was being dismembered. 'I am being torn asunder by the Merciless One,' the terrible voice came again. 'Have pity on me in my distress.'

Lenyé couldn't tear her eyes away from Asa-Dura, but she had to, and glanced across at Kyros.

What did he say to counter Uncle Morthrir and reverse the words spoken? Did he say it in a loud voice? Did he command? What would he say now? She knew he was about to speak; saw him lurch to his feet, raise his right hand and open his mouth in anticipation. Would it be enough? Lenyé tensed herself, waiting for the blow to fall. Surely it would have to match the volume and power of the raging seas to have any effect. Would this be the end of Asa-Dura and all that she suffered?

'Hush. Be still.'

Lenyé was astonished. She caught the words, despite them being spoken so quietly and with such compassion.

Immediately the gigantic wave collapsed under them and the

ship settled down with it into a calm sea, and no accompanying sound of wind to trouble their minds. And Asa-Dura collapsed with it as though her tormentor was hurled away, releasing her limbs, and she fell forwards onto the decking at Kyros' feet. She raised herself up on her hands and knees and bowed her face before him, 'Thank you, My Lord and King.'

Lenyé stared at Kyros in awe. Who was this man she'd grown up with and known all her life and come to love, that even the wind and waves obeyed him?

She watched him stoop, take hold of Asa-Dura's hand and lift her to her feet. 'Peace, Dear One. Be at rest.'

Asa-Dura let out a long sigh of appreciation, 'How can I ever repay you?'

Kyros paused in silence before responding.

'There is one thing.' Lenyé heard above the gentleness of Kyros' voice the tremor of his urgent plea. 'In the Beginning you rose up in wrath, flooding Bara-mâla and covering the island so that the Peoples of the Waking World would not go down to the grave with blood-guilt on their hands. Alas, that has not stopped the shedding of blood on the mainland. But now is the time of unveiling. Only if you release to me the seal of Kingship that Zerigor once bore, can the Peoples be turned back to walk in the ways of the True King and be at peace amongst themselves.'

'How can I know this is the time?'

'Because the Restoration is upon us and all things will be made new.'

Asa-Dura leaned forwards, slipped her arms about his neck and embraced him. 'Now I know the True King has sent you. I will not fail you in this. Farewell.'

With that, she was gone through the glass of the stern window, and Lenyé was left with the memory of Asa-Dura diving into a quiet blue sea with all her hair swirling about her head and floating around her on the surface before she disappeared into the depths.

Chapter Twenty Nine

Morthrir lay face down in his cot moaning and fighting against the dizziness he felt at every lurch of the ship. What was Nastâr playing at? The storm should be against Kyros' ship only, not theirs as well! Jumar-jé kept bringing him news, and was little affected by the motion of the ship. 'Curse the man,' he muttered. 'Why him and not me? Why do I have to suffer like this?' The news was not good: all the warriors were in their hammocks completely given over to seasickness. Most of the sailors were no better off, utterly exhausted by the constant retching of their empty stomachs and slumped where they had fallen while trying to do their tasks. They were complaining amongst themselves they'd never known anything so bad. Then the Captain came in. The ship was carrying minimum sails to maintain steerage, but he didn't have enough fit sailors to work her any more. The other ships were in the same state and likely to be scattered. They must turn back and get out of the storm before it was too late.

'No,' Morthrir tried to raise his head and shout at the man, but his body wouldn't obey him any more and it came out as a feeble croak. 'We have to keep going.'

'But spars have carried away. The main topmast broke before we could get all the sails down. We cannot go on like this, Sire.'

Morthrir's head flopped back onto the cot and he tried to wave the man away, not even sure if his hand moved or not. He didn't care any more. He just wanted to die.

Suddenly the terrible motioned stopped and he felt the ship settle into a calm sea. What was going on? Had Nastâr destroyed

Kyros and that foul dream of his already? He heard the Captain clatter out of the door, shouting orders.

Morthrir swung his legs over the side of his cot and dragged himself onto the deck outside. He lurched to his feet, staggering wildly like a drunken man, despite the gentle motion of the deck under him, felt the dizziness ebb away, and was able to stand, holding onto the door frame of the cabin.

He looked up and saw Nastâr speeding towards the ship and land on the deck in front of him.

'Is Kyros dead?' Morthrir stared at the great being.

'No, My Lord. This calm is not of my doing. The final wave, that was about to destroy his ship, collapsed under them like a pack of cards.'

Morthrir shook his head to clear his mind. 'Then recreate the storm immediately.'

'I cannot, My Lord. A greater power has overruled in what I can do to the seas.'

Chapter Thirty

That afternoon Kyros sat on deck with his back propped against the main mast. Although the storm had gone, they were still sailing fast with a North-East wind behind them, with virtually no side to side roll of the ship in the gentle swell. But even more strange was the layer of sea mist on the water, practically up to the top of the gunwale, as the cold wind from behind met the warmer water. The ship appeared to be floating in a soft white feathery blanket, and he wondered if this was Asa-Dura's answer to his request: a smooth sea to uncover the island, and a brisk wind to get them there. He was half watching the younger ones as they heaved at the capstan and heard his cousin Wilf call: *'On the Isle of Bara-mâla...'* He couldn't believe the difference in their happy smiles after the green faces and heaving stomachs during the storm.

He grinned to himself at the reminder of the game they used to play at the Pool of Alesco. This was the first line of a song from the Lay of Hoffengrégor they always sang.

'Lived the Bara-mâla-ké,' the others chanted back in time to the tramp of their bare feet on the deck planking as the capstan began to turn. He was amused at Mamma Uza-Mâté as the she-bear leaned her great bulk against one of the capstan bars, while Ariella, on her hind legs, kept pace as she pushed against another with her fore paws.

They were helping some of the soldiers let down the anchor on its huge hawser so the crew were able to haul it up on a temporary tackle to inspect it. After the storm everything was

102

being checked for any damage: the anchor was the last item.

'*Ancient People, ancient Nation…*' Wilf called the next line.

'*Blessèd Kingdom, blessèd Day,*' the others responded.

The song told of the divisions that arose amongst the first Peoples and the Inundation that swept them away and the bedraggled survivors who escaped to the mainland. Maybe the storm prompted Wilf to choose this song, but it was certainly very appropriate for where they were heading. Kyros knew the words so well that he kept forming the lines in his mind as the others sang.

But in reality he was lost in that game at the Pool of Alesco. They would swarm over those two branches that swept out over the water and the platform they'd lashed between for the deck of their ship, and set the whole thing swaying as violently as possible. Now he came to think of it, in the light of what they'd just been through, there was something uncanny in the way they always pretended to be caught in a terrible storm at sea before finding the island and launching their canoes in the water. It was like a ritual before anything else could happen.

And Quinn, younger brother though he was, would always make up for his age and size by his enthusiasm to shake the branches and encourage the others.

Quinn!

This was the personal cost to him of Uncle Morthrir's actions. He felt devastated that his brother was gone. He hadn't realised how much he loved him till now, till it was too late: that eager inquisitiveness, always wanting to know and explore and examine; the boy knew no fear in his desire to find out. He'd been idly comparing Quinn with Ramâno: one lost brother and another found, almost as a replacement. But that wouldn't do. Quinn was a person in his own right and demanded his own place and appreciation and mourning. Kyros couldn't bring himself to admit that was what he was going through, but he knew it was true, deep down inside. He missed his brother, and nothing would ever bring him back.

He was vaguely aware of the others chanting three more verses till one of the crew called out: 'Belay capstan!' He watched the man set the securing pin and the youngsters were free to chase each other around the deck till they were needed on the capstan again to haul up the anchor.

'Teach me the rest of that song,' Ramâno yelled as he flashed past Kyros, trying to catch Wilf and Festé. 'I never heard it before.'

'Kyros knows it best,' Wilf called back. 'I always get stuck after verse five.'

Ramâno raced over to Kyros and squatted down in front of him. 'Teach me the song.' There was such an expression of impassioned pleading on Ramâno's face, and especially in his eyes, that Kyros couldn't help laughing: so alike in that desire to know; but so different. Ramâno's infectious smile, and if Kyros didn't jump in quickly there would be that unstoppable chatter; compared to Quinn's more serious expression, and deeper thought behind his questions. The others came crowding over and sat around him on the deck. 'Oh please, Kyros,' Ramâno was already plucking at his sleeve.

'Not now. Find something else to do. You'll be needed back on the capstan in a few minutes.'

'But we'd like to sing the other verses,' Ramâno was insistent. 'What's the good of singing the same ones over again? I want to know as much as I can about Bara-mâla. That's where we're going, isn't it?'

Kyros stood up, walked away from the group, leaned against the gunwale facing out to sea and trailed his hand in the sea mist. It felt so cold. 'Not now,' he called back over his shoulder. 'I need to be alone for a while.'

'Oh, Kyros,' the tone in Olathe's voice made him kick against the gunwale in frustration. 'You can be so boring at times.'

Everyone else laughed.

Kyros was aware of a movement next to him and turned his head slightly as Lenyé slipped her arm around the back of his waist.

'What is it, Kyros?'

'That song,' Kyros was aware of the irritability in his voice, and tried to soften his tone for her. 'The last two lines have haunted me all my life: "*Parted now, the grieving Peoples; Sundered from each others' side*".' He spat the words out as if in disgust.

'That was a thousand years ago. Things are different now.'

'I feel this in the pit of my stomach. Hoffengrégor told me it was like a woman about to give birth.'

'He also said finding the Crown was your seventh and final test.'

'What use is a Crown without the Peoples? I cannot rest until the Sundering is finally healed.'

Surely once you've recovered the Crown, everything else will fall into place?'

'It cannot be as simple as that.'

'Kyros. It's important to be honest about your doubts. If you don't face up to them, you're always going to be tossed about like a ship in a storm. But when you challenge them, you emerge much stronger and focused on what you have to accomplish.'

'I know.' Kyros sighed.

'If all the other tests have been fulfilled, Hoffengrégor must think you're ready. He wouldn't have sent you if you weren't.'

'Maybe you're right. But it's too much for me to face.'

'No one likes preparing for any sort of test, but they come in our lives to prove us. Once we've passed through them we are released into greater things. The True King is preparing you for Kingship. That is no small task and takes a very special man…'

He felt her hand on his shoulder as she gently turned him towards her from his stance against the gunwale, and saw the depth of her feelings for him in her eyes as she searched his face.

'…my man,' she whispered. 'I will always love you, whatever the outcome.'

Kyros slipped his arms around her waist and felt hers entwining about his neck, before burying his face in her shoulder. 'I don't deserve anyone half as good as you.'

She shook her head and whispered again, 'Neither do I. But we have each other to hold onto.'

He sensed Lenyé ease herself away from him and felt the tip of her finger on his cheek as she smoothed away a tear before it trickled into his beard.

'If you want to hug me like that again,' he saw the frown of concentration on her face, 'get rid of that beard; it tickles too much. And cut your hair so that you look like a Krêonor man!'

He stared at her in astonishment; then they both burst out laughing together.

She hesitated, suddenly serious, 'Something else's bothering you, isn't it?'

When he remained silent, she prompted him.

'You're right,' Kyros felt his emotions tugging at him for a very different reason. 'It's Quinn.'

'I wondered what you were feeling. You've hardly mentioned him, and then, only really, to help the others.'

'It's been too soon. I didn't realise how much I miss him until I heard that song again.'

'I know. It's hard. I feel the same way about Beth. But at least I've had longer to come to terms with it than you. I miss Quinn as well. There are no words to describe him, but…well…Quinn.'

'By rights, Quinn should be here, with us. He would have loved this. No more pretending like at the Pool of Alesco, but the real thing. And Beth, as well.'

Kyros saw Lenyé hesitate and look him in the eyes before continuing. 'I may as well tell you, now that he's gone.'

'What?'

He heard her draw a deep breath before continuing. 'You

know that day we were walking in the mountains and you fell into the crevasse?'

Kyros nodded.

'Quinn was the first one there he was so concerned about you. Both our Fathers had to drag him away from the danger before they pulled you to safety. He clung to me sobbing as they hauled you out. Then he whispered, "*Don't let Kyros know, but I was terrified I was going to lose my brother*".'

'Why didn't he tell me?'

'Because you were his hero, and he couldn't handle the strength of his feelings for you.'

'I keep thinking it's all a terrible mistake, and one day he'll walk back into my life.'

'Do you think I don't feel the same about Beth? I've gone through that conversation with Doctor Nostrea over and over again in my head, trying to find some flaw in his story. He was very defensive about you till I got the truth out of him, but was totally convinced it was Beth and Quinn they buried.'

'But wild animals,' Kyros smacked his hand on the top of the gunwale. 'I can't believe it. Even if it was lions, Quinn would never have let themselves get into such a dangerous situation. His woodcraft was too good.'

'He learned most of his skills from me,' Lenyé's voice sounded thick with emotion.

'Exactly. That's what makes it so unlikely.'

'He pushed me to my limits in his eagerness,' she continued, 'and helped me think things through afresh for myself. I wouldn't have done that without him.'

Kyros saw the beginnings of tears in Lenyé's eyes and glanced away at the sea, suddenly distracted by the thinning mist, before replying. 'Even if they did get into trouble, he would have tried to fight off any lions and give Beth a chance to escape and run for help!'

'I know. It doesn't seem fair. All we can do now is mourn

their loss and hold onto our good memories of them.'

'He was such fun,' Kyros felt his lip tremble as he looked up into her eyes. 'I'll never get that back, however hard I try just by remembering. I caught him stealing a pie from the kitchen, once, and chased him up the corridor. That's how he and I discovered the secret passageway we all escaped through. When he realised I wasn't after a piece of his pie but merely angry with him, he thought it was hilarious and rolled around in the corridor laughing his head off. I couldn't be angry with him after that.'

They embraced again, the silent tears and their racking sobs uniting them in their shared grief over something less lofty than the Restoration, but far closer to home in their loss of loved ones.

Kyros heard the cry from a crew member and the scamper of bare feet as the others raced to the capstan.

'Hey, Kyros,' Ramâno's shout made him look up. 'Give us a hand. It's much harder hauling the anchor up than lowering it.'

He wiped his sleeve across his eyes, and saw Lenyé do the same. 'Come,' he held out his hand to her. 'It's about time we joined in,' and he led her across the deck to the capstan, taking his place on a wooden bar opposite Lenyé, but positioned so he could see Ramâno's grinning face.

Kyros glanced across at Lenyé and knew she was urging him on to break through his doubts by leading the chant. He took a deep breath and called the first line, *'But the waves of Asa-Dura...'* and Lenyé led the others in response: *'Round the fated Mâla-ké'*; he called again, *'Could not bear to see the life blood...'* and nodded in time to the response: *'Of the Peoples ebb away.'*

He called the first line of the next verse, *'So in anger, Asa-Dura...'* and again she led the response: *'Raised a mighty Invadrook.'* He was distracted by Ramâno's sudden frown during the response as the boy stumbled over the words, and thought again of Quinn: so alike, yet so different. This lad had entered deep into his affections in a way he thought would be impossible outside of his immediate family. Maybe he was a replacement for his brother after all. '*Rushing inwards, cleansing ocean…*' he called again, and felt the tightening of the hawser through the resistance on the bar of the capstan: '*Sank the island: all forsook,*' came the chant of response.

'Belay!' a shout from the port bow made them halt.

'If the island was sunk by all that water,' Ramâno's high pitched voice made him turn to the lad, 'how are we going to find it?'

'I've no idea,' Kyros started chuckling to himself and then burst into laughter.

'What's so funny?' Ramâno sounded indignant.

'At least, I've no idea until I've had a haircut and shaved this beard off.' He caught Lenyé's eye and started laughing again as she laughed with him. 'It's going to take a good many hugs to help me work it out.'

'Oh, really?' Ramâno shoved his face forwards and stood with hands on hips. 'Well ask my Mamma to help you. She's very good with a pair of scissors and a razor!'

Chapter Thirty One

Rafé descended to the Plains of Lohr in the early evening. The setting sun hung over the flat horizon and he had enough light to go on riding for several hours before he camped for the night.

He huddled close to the campfire and thought about how to move the cobra to Mount Nastâri when he needed it. The last time he'd only managed to raise the snake off a rock and hold it in mid air for a few minutes before letting it fall back. But to move it several miles to Mount Nastâri was another thing.

Then he remembered the convocation at the Great Oak Tree when he called the cobra from its nest and dumped it on a rock, miles away. So he could do it.

He pulled the brown robe out of his pack, put it on and sat staring at the flames of his campfire, but for some reason had difficulty locating the cobra this time. He sat gazing down a long, hazy tunnel before he saw the snake. But it wouldn't respond or let him into its mind. What was going on? He willed the cobra to move, but instead of being easy to manipulate, the cobra turned on him, head raised, hood flared, tongue flicking in and out as though it was going to strike at him, even from that distance. He felt his own mind probed from within: *"Who are you?"*.

He saw the cobra moving slowly towards him, the mouth opened wide and those deadly fangs set to attack. He was fascinated, but leaped to his feet as the snake struck at his throat.

His sudden movement broke the connection and he was left puzzling over why he couldn't control the snake any more?

Chapter Thirty Two

Kyros sat on a chair on the quarter deck and felt Marie-anna's soft fingers on his skin as she finished shaving his chin and wiped away the last traces of lather with a cloth. She held up a hand mirror for him to see.

'I had no idea you were so handsome.' Kyros heard the mischievous giggle as Marie-anna glanced at Lenyé where she played cards with Olathe and Nasima. 'She's a lucky woman.'

Kyros examined his skin in the mirror. 'It'll take a while for my chin and cheeks to tan as dark as the rest of my face.'

Marie-anna giggled again. 'I'm sure the salt air will help.'

'What do you think?' Kyros sat more upright in the chair and called across to Lenyé. 'Fancy one of those hugs now?'

Lenyé looked up from her game and poked her tongue out. 'Not till you've got rid of all that long hair as well.'

Kyros sighed, 'You're so hard to please!'

Lenyé laughed and turned back to her game.

Marie-anna draped a cloth over him and began cutting. He was aware of great locks dropping from his head and felt the keenness of the breeze on the back of his neck. She moved round cutting closer to the sides and finally stood in front of him to complete the top before holding up the mirror again.

He nodded his approval as the boys came running by, with Wilf and Festé slightly ahead of Ramâno.

'Hey, Kyros,' Ramâno shrilled in passing and skimmed the top of Kyros' head with the palm of his hand. 'Nice haircut.' The lad partly turned and continued jogging backwards, a broad grin on his face. 'Bet that's a weight off your mind!'

Everyone within earshot roared with laughter.

'You cheeky little monkey,' Kyros snatched the cloth from Marie-anna's hand and lurched to his feet. He wiped his face, flung the cloth away and gave chase.

'Kyros is on the loose,' Ramâno shouted. 'Everyone get him.'

Kyros pushed the others aside and trapped Ramâno between the port gunwale and the fo'c's'le. As the boy scampered up the companionway, Kyros seized Ramâno by the foot, but Wilf and Festé sprang on him and brought him down. He staggered to his feet as Ramâno swivelled round on the companionway and leaped straight at him. He flung Wilf and Festé off, caught Ramâno in mid air and slung the lad over one shoulder with the boy hanging half way down his back. He swung round a couple of times, the lad gripping his jacket to steady himself. 'Right, young man. You're going overboard.'

'Help!' Ramâno thrashed his arms and legs, trying to free himself. 'Get Kyros, everyone, or I'm done for.'

Kyros felt the lad pummel his back, and swung him round, but was distracted by Wilf and Festé jumping into the fray, followed by Olathe and Nasima. Even Lenyé was running towards him. He went down in a mêlée of arms and legs with everyone on top, but heaved them sideways and crawled out from underneath. Ramâno scrambled up the companionway, but Kyros grabbed the boy by the ankle, pulled him down the steps and caught him. He stood in the corner where the port gunwale met the fo'c's'le, with his back to the sea, and Ramâno wriggling in his arms. He began the movements to throw the lad overboard. 'One,' he counted, 'Two,' and was about to yell, 'Three,' when Ramâno shrieked, 'Look out. You'll kill me if you throw me onto that!'

Kyros spun round to look where Ramâno was pointing. The sea mist had practically disappeared.

'What is it?' The lad's voice was suddenly loud in Kyros' ear, as he dumped the boy in a standing position on the deck.

'Captain,' Kyros was running aft to the wheel and shouting. 'Hard a-starboard. We're almost aground.'

'What's going on?' Lenyé was the first to recover and ran to the port gunwale, with the others racing after her.

Kyros joined them as soon as he felt the ship change course.

'What do you think, Kyros?' Ramâno looked up at him.

'I'm not sure.' Kyros traced the strange rock with his eyes, trying to measure the odd flat shape that stood only a few inches above the calm surface of the sea. It was at least eight ships' lengths by five, and regular, with sharp corners and a bulge of rock in the dead centre. There were long strands of still wet seaweed stretched out from their anchor points as though the sea had only recently subsided enough to leave it exposed, and it was totally covered in barnacles and therefore impossible to see the underlying rock itself and make a guess as to what it was.

The Captain called down from his position on the poop deck, 'I've sailed in these waters several times and never seen anything like that before. But the sea is extraordinarily calm this far from land, and after that storm, appears to be uncommonly low.'

'Look,' Wilf pointed into the water. 'It goes straight down to a shelf sticking out, then carries on going straight down again.'

'It's not a rock,' Olathe exclaimed, 'it's far too symmetrical.'

'You mean, it's a building?' Ramâno looked up at her, his eyes shinning with excitement. 'Is this what we've come to find?'

Kyros glanced over to Lenyé and caught her eye. 'If I'm not mistaken, this is the Royal Ziggurat.' He looked up at the poop deck. 'Captain, put the helm further over to starboard and anchor as soon as you can.'

'But it's deep ocean here,' the Captain replied. 'The anchor won't even touch bottom.'

'If this is what I think it is,' Kyros eyed the man, 'you'll find a good anchor point not too far down.'

Kyros was impatient for the soldiers to complete their task and open up the Ziggurat. The ship was moored some way off in calm water, and the longboat was hauled up on the Ziggurat itself and they'd carried their equipment to the rock in the centre. Except it wasn't a rock. He was confident it was a seal that Zerigor had put in place to allow access from the top. The men chipped at the encrustations with hammers and chisels and levered with their wrecking bars. They needed to be quick about it. Already the sun was beginning to set and he felt a chill wind pick up from the North-East and blow the clouds towards them. If the weather turned bad, they wouldn't have much time.

A cheer went up from the working party as, with a scrunching of steel against stone, the seal opened, and the huge piece of masonry lifted up and toppled over, leaving a symmetrical hole into darkness.

The air smelled musty, and Kyros realised with a shock that it had been trapped in this chamber for a thousand years. He tied a flare to a rope and lit it before lowering it into the hole. As he paid out the rope he saw that the chamber was completely dry and about fifty feet deep. He shouted at the men to prepare another rope to lower him down.

'Can I come too?' Ramâno's voice broke his concentration on surveying the inside of the chamber.

It should have been Quinn. After all those years of make-believe at the Pool of Alesco anticipating this moment, Quinn should have been the one here with him. But he wanted someone light in weight for the men to haul up if he needed to send any messages from the bottom, and he'd chosen Ramâno over Wilf or Festé. Why? He couldn't say, except for his thoughts earlier when he was comparing the two boys. Besides, he had a lot of respect for the lad's quick thinking and resourcefulness.

'Let me get down and check it first,' he replied. 'If I give two tugs on my rope, it's safe for you to come. Bring that net of flares with you; we're going to need as much light as possible.'

Kyros sat on the edge of the hole with his legs dangling, took his weight on his hands, swivelled round and dropped into the hole. There was a sickening moment before the rope tightened and the men above took the strain, then he was free to look about him as he steadily descended.

He realised straight away that it was safe for Ramâno and gave two tugs on his rope as soon as he reached the bottom. He untied the rope and checked the things closest to hand while Ramâno was lowered.

There was an oblong shape directly below the hole. Once he'd wiped the dust away he found an intricately painted casket, with no sign of hinges or lock or even a straight line within any of the surfaces to indicate where it opened. It was too heavy for him to move. Next to it stood a clay pot. Again he wiped away the dust to reveal its cork top sealed with wax. He shook the pot and heard a metallic rattling sound from within. Then he helped Ramâno and untied the lad's rope.

'Light some more flares from this one, Ramâno.'

The lad did as he was asked and they went exploring holding two flares each. The strong-room was as long and wide as it was deep. Ramâno gave a hoot like an owl, and the sound echoed back at them.

'Shh!' Kyros glared at the boy, as Ramâno hooted again. 'The men at the top will think we're in some kind of trouble.'

They stopped and listened, but there was no sound of anyone calling through the hole.

They continued exploring in silence. Thick dust was everywhere, but they could make out wooden chests packed against the walls, with clay pots, presumably full of parchments, stacked in front of them. Close to the Southern door was a large item wrapped in a cloth. They wiped the dust away and Kyros tried tugging at it but it was too heavy to move. He peeled back a loose corner of the cloth to reveal a golden coloured substance with gemstones embedded in the surface that flashed and glinted in the light from the flares.

'What's that?' Ramâno asked.

'I've no idea. But it doesn't concern us. I'm pretty sure it's that casket and clay pot we're after.'

They retraced their steps and Kyros shoved at the casket with his foot. 'Not even Mamma Uza-Mâté could shift that. We'll have to break it open while we're down here.' He tried shouting up, but the men at the top appeared to be confused over his request.

'Ramâno, you're going to have to go up and tell them. I want four men with hammers and chisels and wrecking bars and plenty of rope. Got that?'

'Yes.'

'Shake those flares out and give me the net.'

Kyros opened the net, placed the clay pot in it, drew the free ends up and attached them to one of the ropes. 'Make sure that's sent to Lenyé immediately. And tell the men to bring the boat straight back. She can send us any messages by one of the other boats if necessary.' He tied the second rope around Ramâno's waist and gave a single tug on each. The boy and the clay pot began rising swiftly to the hole.

The hammers and chisels and wrecking bars made no impression on the casket, so Kyros decided to take it back to the ship. He and the soldiers wove a web out of rope and levered up the casket to slip it underneath. They attached four separate ropes for hauling up; but the men at the top couldn't move it.

'We'll need some lifting tackle from the ship,' Kyros smacked his hand on the top of the casket in frustration. 'That means waiting till tomorrow and the light of day to see what we're doing. It must be dark up there by now. It's going to be hard enough re-sealing the hole and rowing back to the ship.'

PART III

THE SCROLL

Chapter Thirty Three

Lenyé sat at the desk in the main cabin of *Brave Heart*. She was ecstatic over the clay pot the soldiers brought her and examined it in the light of the lantern hanging from the deckhead above. She shook it and heard a metallic clink, but muffled, as though something else was inside.

She broke away the wax, removed the cork, held the pot upside down and a key fell out on the desk. This must be the one Hoffengrégor sent her to find. She put her hand into the pot and felt a roll of parchment. Immediately she was reminded of when she used to play adventurers with Kyros and the others at the Pool of Alesco, when they were younger, diving for the treasures of the sunken island. She always wanted to find something like this with the writings about the Ancient Wisdom of the Peoples, and work out how to use it in their game. But Kyros wasn't interested, and told her not to be so stupid: "*If that wisdom caused the break up of the civilisation in the first place, it wasn't worth having*". She remembered arguing with him and didn't speak to him for the rest of the day. Lenyé withdrew her hand and stared in wonder at the only parchment ever recovered from the real island. Her fingers trembled in anticipation at what it might contain. As she unrolled it, a secondary and smaller parchment fell out which she set aside as she started to read the main scroll:

I, Zerigor, head of the Krêonor and King over the island of Bara-mâla, ruling by decree of the True King in close friendship amongst the three Peoples: the Krêonor, Tsé-shâmé, and

Harmoth, who are marked out by the Light of Life around our brows as a sign of the favour we enjoy from the True King; do hereby set forth an account concerning the events of the last few months.

For some time a shadow lay over the Tsé-shâmé, and they spurned our company. Even a number of my own People were drawn away and looked upon us with darkness in their eyes.

Then one day I was disturbed by much shouting and raced to the main gates of the city, and was shocked to see many Krêonor and Harmoth streaming through the arches from their work in the fields and vineyards and heaving the gates closed. There was a crashing sound against the gates and much jeering from outside.

I climbed to the gallery above the gates and looked down at a crowd of Tsé-shâmé led by a few dark-haired Krêonor. Some brandished long poles with pointed tips that glittered in the sunshine as though fashioned of steel, and others waved what looked like long straight ploughshares ending in a sharp point. Another group bore great sticks pulled into a curve with cord. Onto that cord was fitted a slender stake, glinting at its tip as though also forged of steel, and clothed with feathers at the end nearest the cord. I had never seen such implements before and knew not their purpose.

'What is the meaning of this, my People,' I cried, 'that you come to us in such anger and the city has closed its gates against you? Never before have they been shut, for everyone is free to come and go without hindrance and enjoy great friendship.'

'We consider ourselves no longer your People,' one of the dark-haired Krêonor replied. 'The Tsé-shâmé do all the work. The Harmoth paint pictures and play their instruments and dance all day. Your race lord it over us as if we were but dung from the plough horses that is left to rot in the ground. And you, as King, don't even notice. You are not fit to rule over us!'

I recognised the man as Jumar-jé and was saddened by his

present actions, for many times he had gone up in my company to the Royal Ziggurat to acknowledge the True King together. I raised my voice to address him, 'So why, my friend, do you speak against your own race? For you are Krêonor rather than Tsé-shâmé.'

'I will not stand aside and let this go on. If I have to renounce the People of my birth in order to uphold others so wrongfully treated, I will do so.'

He gestured with his right hand and the men with curved sticks let go of their tightened cords. I heard a strange singing in the air as their shafts raced towards me. Some stuck quivering in the gates, others whistled past my face and still more soared overhead and fell behind. Those with the long poles and straight ploughshares surged forwards and beat against the gates, setting up a hollow sound that echoed in my ears.

And I thought to myself that something was wrong with their appearance, as though it had changed in accordance with their rejection of my Kingship. Then I saw the Light of Life about their heads as it flickered and disappeared altogether.

I turned away in grief. For up till now, each person put their hand to the activity that delighted them most and so their individual giftings served the whole community. The Tsé-shâmé were the best cooks and the Harmoth were especially skilled in creativity. How had the Tsé-shâmé come to resent the giftings of others rather than rejoicing in the work of their own hands? And were they now cut off from us with the extinguishing of the Light of Life in them?

As I walked in the city gardens at the cool of the day, the True King came to me and I bowed low in greeting. But he raised me by the hand and looked me in the eyes and said, 'Something disturbs you, my good friend.' And I recounted my disquiet at the events of the day.

'A great evil has come to trouble this world,' he replied. 'The

Tsé-shâmé have given their minds over to it, and, as a result, have died on the inside. Their inner peace with me has been destroyed, the Light of Life has deserted them and darkness now fills their hearts. They have opened a door to let this into the Waking World so that all humankind is tainted by it. In their enmity, they will wage war against you to destroy you. Therefore I urge you to beat your ploughshares into swords and your pruning hooks into spears, and cut the yew tree to fashion longbows. You must fight them to preserve all that is good.'

Swiftly I made the connection in my mind of swords, spears and longbows with the strange implements I observed in the hands of the Tsé-shâmé, and realised they were for deliberately inflicting harm. 'But why?' I frowned in puzzlement as I glanced afresh at the True King. 'I have only known the harmony of close family and all my Peoples I consider as friends.'

'So far you have dwelt in the experience of good,' the True King continued, 'but now the knowledge of evil has come amongst you. The Light of Life will be stripped away; your open relationship with me will be broken; and you will know separation from me.'

'What will be the outcome of all this?' I queried.

'Death and sorrow and despair.'

'What are these words, for I know not what they mean?'

'Alas, my good friend. You will come to know them only too well. These words are as a curse coming upon you; but I will ensure the worst part of this burden falls on me. From now on, as each person hears me calling their name and chooses to come to me, the relationship can be restored. You must teach your People to hide themselves in the strength of my name. Only then can I protect them and bring them through death to what lies beyond.'

With that, he was gone and I was left turning those three words over in my mind, trying to discern what they meant. For my days so far had been filled with the Light of Life, joy in the presence of the True King and a great hope and expectation of what was yet to come of his purposes for us. I knew nothing else.

I shuddered, for even the sound of the words filled me with dread: everything that we enjoyed and received with gratitude from the True King was about to be snatched away from us.

And so, reluctantly, we forged these weapons. As I held a sword for the very first time, I realised that the cross at the top of the Royal Orb of Dominion was actually a tiny sword, far more elaborate and bejewelled than the one in my hand, with over half its blade buried in the Orb itself. Was this a sign from the True King predicting at my Coronation that dominion could only come through conflict?

For some months we trained and thought we were well prepared. About three weeks later we confronted a major attack from our enemies out in the fields. So great were their numbers that we were forced back in disarray and hastened towards the safety of the city. As we ran, our enemies harried us from behind and sought to overtake us. Then the True King appeared and stood between the two companies with arms outstretched as if to shield as many of my People as possible. Yet it seemed that he would also gather the Tsé-shâmé to himself and hold them as a Mother gathers her children and comforts them in her arms.

But even he was forced back towards the city.

My company scrambled past the gates and closed them, but the True King was not with us. I heard a great shout and running feet, accompanied by a dull thud against one gate as though a spear was thrust into the wood, followed in swift succession by lesser thuds as of arrows. There was a cry of agony as the gates rocked to and fro and banged against each other, and were still.

A collective gasp arose from outside, the shouting ceased and everything was quiet, save for the sound of many feet retreating from the entrance of the city and the intermittent dripping, as of water, onto wood.

At last I could bear it no more, and thrust at one gate to see what had transpired. It moved a little and then stuck fast. I glanced down, and, in the centre of where the closed gate had been there was a dull red patch in the dust, and a curved trail of brighter red leading from it to the partially opened gate. That, too, was rapidly soaking into the dust and turning a dull colour.

I put my shoulder to the gate and heaved. It jerked open grinding over a broken sandal and swung free. I looked out, but there was no sign of our enemies. My eyes traced the red arc that continued on the ground as the gate swung open and puzzled over it as it soaked into the dust and darkened as before. I was about to investigate, when a quick movement distracted me. I hastened beyond the gate a little way, but it was only a bird which flew off as I approached. And still no one in sight.

A gust of wind sprang up and I spun round at the bang of the gate closing behind me. There, impaled on the wood, with a spear thrust through his chest, was the True King. Amidst the scattering of arrows embedded in the gate, his outflung arms were held in place by a few through his wrists and the palms of his hands, as though he was still trying to gather his attackers to himself. His feet hung limp, one sandal missing, the other dangling from his foot with the strap half torn away. Blood was coursing down his chest and onto the gate where it continued to drip on the original puddle of dark red in the dust. His head drooped sideways, and the Light of Life around his brow was no more.

I stood, rooted to the spot, unable to move or cry out. Then I was running and shouting for help and others came tentatively out of the gates as I reached the True King. We lifted him gently down and laid him on the ground. We'd seen blood before from accidents in the field with working implements, but never in this quantity, and it was beyond our skill to revive him. There was no life in him and we were appalled, for we had never encountered this before, and knew not what to do for him.

We bore him to the Sanctuary in the Royal Ziggurat, where

we gathered once a week to remind ourselves of the teachings of the True King and lift up his name in honour by word of declaration and song to refresh the knowledge of him amongst us. There we laid him on a stone dais and covered him with a linen cloth, and left him in the cool quietness of that place.

Daily we came to mourn and cry out for the returning of his life, but to no avail, and we wept bitterly. I spoke over him the words of his origin and of his ending, 'He was before us in time, and appeared to live for ever, but now we behold the end of his being.' And I invited the People to a memorial meal. At the end we broke bread and dipped it in the stew as a reminder of his broken body and the Light of Life that had departed; and passed around cups of shared wine to remember his blood poured out to save us from our enemies and the evil power that drove them to this terrible deed. For never before had we seen death in the Waking World. He was the first person alive to walk in the place, and he was the first to go down into death at the Beginning and the very founding of the Peoples.

Often I would linger after the others had gone, for I, perhaps more than any other, was distressed at the passing of my closest friend. More dear to me was he than the breath I breathed, and I was uncertain how my life could continue without him.

So horrified was Lenyé at what she read that she bowed her head in grief and wept. For the knowledge of evil coming into the Waking World had led directly to the True King's death. How could this have happened to Him?

Chapter Thirty Four

Morthrir yelled at the Captain, 'Get your sailors working the ship and searching the sea ahead. There's something I need to find. Signal the other ships to do the same.'

A chill wind was still blowing from the North-East, and raising a thick sea fog where it met the warm seas around them.

'I protest, Sire. I must repair my ship and replace the sails that were torn. Everything has to be checked to make sure she's fully seaworthy again. And the others need to do the same. You can see how knocked about they are.'

Morthrir followed his pointing finger, taking in the spars dangling from the masts and shreds of sails flapping in the breeze and seasick sailors still sprawling on deck. 'They can do that later once we've found what I'm looking for. Make sure you post some good lookouts in all the ships.' He stumped off to the rear cabin as he saw Nastâr flying towards them.

He slammed the cabin door and turned to face the great being. 'Well?'

'Kyros' ship is hidden by this sea fog, My Lord. And some power is preventing me from locating him. I can't feel his presence anywhere. It's as though he's completely disappeared.'

'Then we'll have to find the ship by physical means. I've ordered the Captain to search the area with all our ships, and he's posted his best lookouts.'

'They'll have to be quick, My Lord. It's dusk already.'

Chapter Thirty Five

With a shock, Lenyé realised that if the evil had tainted the whole human race in Zerigor's day, it must have passed on down to her generation and she was affected by it. Only the True King's intervention had rescued her from its power. For she had seen him and met with him and been changed by him. How did that happen if he was dead? She dried her eyes and glanced at the stern windows: it was pitch black outside. She continued reading Zerigor's parchment by the light of the lantern:

Many times I saw some Tsé-shâmé from the top of the gate, and was distressed at the absence of the Light of Life, and thought: "*Even if they still lived in physical form, they were now full of darkness*" as the True King had said. But the Light of Life about my own People's heads flickered, and the blaze of the Krêon of Tulá-kâhju, the Crown of Life, about my own head diminished and went out. And I knew confusion in my mind about the True King and how I remembered him, and whether his power was still available to me; for I assumed that with the passing of the True King, the Light of Life was extinguished in us as well. And therefore, would the People still accept my Kingship over them? But then I also knew, as if for the very first time, that I could rule over them myself, without any intervention from the True King at all; and was, at long last, my own master!

On the morning of the third day I hastened to the Sanctuary for my thoughts were driving me mad. Maybe I would find comfort from seeing him afresh. I stopped aghast as I beheld the dais, empty of his body, with the linen coverlet neatly folded and laid to one side. I was in great distress of mind, for who had done this, and where had they taken him?

Sorentina, my eldest daughter, came running to me, her face flushed with exertion and her rapid breathing prevented her from getting her words out. It was some time before I understood the import of what she was saying.

'His body is no longer here,' she finally gasped, 'for he has returned to us from the place of death. I've seen him! He met with me in the public gardens where I was bowed in grief and spoke to me. He said: *"Go to your Father and tell him the good news. Death cannot contain me and I have burst his gates asunder"*.'

She flung herself into my arms and her tears of joy were hot on my face.

'What are you saying, my daughter? This cannot be.'

'He's alive. He's come back from the place of death.'

'But we left him in this chamber,' I countered, 'with no Light of Life about his brow. Surely that Light can never be re-kindled? I cannot accept this, unless I see him with my own eyes.'

As I reasoned with her, I heard my name spoken by a voice I recognised instantly. I looked up and there was a figure, ablaze with light, in our midst. I fell at his feet, as though all life had gone from me and I was unable to move.

'Do not be afraid,' he said. 'Behold, I am alive and have come back amongst you. See the wounds of spear and arrows to prove to you who I am.'

'Whether I remain as King, I care not,' I whispered, remembering his words from a few days ago. 'I choose, this day, to forsake all my vain thoughts of ruling in my own strength and return to you, that I may walk with you once more.'

'Well done, good and faithful friend,' his voice was so vibrant with life, like the sea washing over me. 'You heard me call and made the choice despite the sore trials of your mind. You are the first to do so, and are therefore worthy to still lead your People.'

He raised me by the hand and lifted me up. Either the brilliance of the light had diminished, or my eyes were strengthened to see him afresh, and I was able to look upon him whom they had pierced and recognised the face of my friend. But he radiated so much more light than before that I was filled with consternation as to what this might mean.

'Be assured,' he said, 'for now you see me as I really am. The Light of Life in me can never be extinguished again.'

'Does that mean it will be restored to us, your People?'

'Alas, no. For the evil that has been set in motion must be worked out to its fullest extent and utterly destroyed. You already know its effect as you struggled with your thoughts concerning your response to me. Everyone who chooses to return to me will suffer that and must be constantly on guard if they wish to remain faithful to me. It will be many generations before the Light of Life is re-kindled for all People, and only by the hand of one of your heirs. You need to prepare for that day with the wisdom you already have.'

Then he appeared to many Krêonor and Harmoth in the city and showed them his scars, and there was great joy in their hearts, for the True King had come back amongst us. But never again did he appear to me in the cool of the day as I walked in the public gardens. Occasionally I saw him, and was comforted by his presence. And I wondered at what this might mean, and why things had changed. Was it because he had passed through death, and we had yet to follow him on that path?

I knew not what the Tsé-shâmé now intended, for that collective gasp I heard and the sound of their feet running away must indicate their shock at what they had done. Surely they would come back and acknowledge the grief they had caused? But not so. For the birds of Sorentina flew from my daughter's hand and brought us news. Far from being filled with sorrow, we learned that already they were preparing a mighty attack to sweep us away. For they said amongst themselves: *"The True King is dead, therefore we can inherit the whole of the Waking World if we first destroy the Krêonor and the Harmoth who stand in our way"*.

Daily I stood above the gates and pleaded with them that the True King had returned from the place of death. But they refused to accept it. I said, 'If you lay down your weapons, I will take you to the Royal Ziggurat and show you the empty Sanctuary where we laid him.' They refused again, saying, *"We never saw where you laid him, so how do we know it is the right chamber, and therefore, if he has returned. You have no proof"*.

It puzzled me greatly why the True King did not appear amongst them to convince them himself. Then I realised it was because he had chosen those of us who had seen him to convince others that he really was alive by the strength of the new relationship we now had with him. But without the Light of Life about our heads as before, what evidence could we present to convince them? So caught up was I in wrestling with this issue that I failed to take note of the Tsé-shâmé preparations.

One morning we awoke to find the whole city surrounded, their war boats surging up river towards us and great wooden towers on wheels, filled with their fighting men. All they had to do was push these towers against our walls, for scores of warriors to pour over the top. Alas, the walls were made to stop any building works from spilling beyond our city and occupying too much farmland, not for keeping enemies out.

We sent our own fishing boats down river towing others packed with brushwood and kegs of pine resin to set on fire to attack theirs; and lined the river banks and landing stages with archers equipped with fire arrows. We set cauldrons to contain boiling oil on the walls and appointed archers with fire arrows to destroy the moveable towers. The children formed human chains to pass buckets of water from the river to prevent the spread of any fires within the city. And we awaited their onslaught.

By evening, the war boats were less than a mile from the landing stages and we sent our fire boats amongst them. The Tsé-shâmé began rolling their towers forwards under cover of darkness, to attack, and we harassed them with fire arrows and poured down boiling oil if they came close enough to our walls.

I left my post briefly, placing my senior Captain in command, gathered my wife and sons and daughters and hid them in the hold of a large fishing boat drawn up out of the water for the cleaning of its hull, and some way from the landing stages. For I had a sudden premonition that the very seas themselves would rise up in anger at what was happening this day and sweep all away, rather than let us go down to the grave with the bloodguilt of many deaths on our hands. I was determined to preserve the Royal line and establish my heir who would one day put all things right. So a boat was the safest place for them, and I ordered several fishermen to stand by to steer it.

I gave my wife the Royal Orb, wrought in the Realm of the Blessèd Throne and still glowing with golden light as it had done ever since the True King presented it to me. "*Let this be a sign to all the Peoples*", he said, on the day of my Coronation, "*that you have received authority from me to have dominion over the entire Waking World*". Similarly, the Sceptre of Authority, carved from a living tree of the Realm of the Blessèd Throne, I thrust into Sorentina's hands. If they escaped from the destruction of the city, they would bear the emblems of Kingship to safety, apart from my Crown, and so establish the future of our race.

I lit a flare and hastened to a strong-room in the topmost chamber of the Royal Ziggurat, the door of which was impregnable to any flooding from below.

There I removed the Crown and contemplated it afresh one last time. Made in the Realm of the Blessèd Throne, it was a frame of gold that sat on my head and reached down the back of my neck, round past the hinge of my jaw and up over my ears to rejoin the top and covered my hair, leaving only my face and chin showing. From this frame hung strands of gold filament laced through flat disks of sliced rubies. Each strand overlapped another like the scales on a pine cone, so that there were no gaps. When first set on my head, it blazed with a deep red from the Light of Life about my brow. Only now did I understand the significance of that rich colour from the recent death of the True King and the shedding of his blood to deliver us. For suddenly I realised that Kingship in this world could only have effect by acknowledging his sacrifice for us all.

I placed it in a canvas bag, covered in pitch, and reverently laid it in a casket, lest the Light of Life break out amongst us again and my heir should have need of it to re-establish his Kingship. And this parchment, whose contents may yet instruct him to make known afresh the knowledge of the True King's sacrifice, I will place into a clay pot to be sealed with wax, once I have finished the last few sentences of writing. Also in the same pot I placed a key to unlock a document cylinder that I will take with me. For surely there is more knowledge I yet must write when I have more leisure than this present emergency allows, in order to help my heir win through and restore all things. Only when he finds this key can he open the cylinder. My last cry to the True King, before I return to lead my People in battle against our enemies, is that my heir will be the first to enter this strong-room and recover the three things I have hidden here: Crown, key and parchment.

Signed and sealed in haste this day by my hand, in the year the True King was slain and returned to us from the dead,

Zerigor,
King of Bara-mâla.

Postscript: To open the casket, look for the concealed sword within the decoration on the front, which was facing East when I left the casket. The sword can only be seen when a light is falling on it from above. Hidden in the pommel at the end of the handle, the tip, and both ends of the hilt guard are four buttons. Press them in this order: top; bottom; right, when facing the casket; and finally, left.

On a spare parchment Lenyé drew a diagram of the position of the buttons and ordered a soldier to take it to Kyros.

Then she sat back, relieved over the contents of the rest of the parchment. The True King was greater than death, had defeated its power and returned to them. But how could his sacrifice and triumph no longer be remembered and honoured in the Waking World? And how was this to be made known again now that it had been revealed through Zerigor's writings?

Lenyé re-read the last part of the parchment that had held her attention. Zerigor was right. A Great Inundation of the sea had swept them all away. And the True King did answer Zerigor's request: for Kyros was the first to enter that sealed chamber. She had the parchment and the key in her hands, and Kyros had the instructions to open the casket and recover the Crown.

She rolled up the parchment, tied it with cord and picked up the key. What was the knowledge locked in the cylinder that was so important in defeating their enemies? And from what Hoffengrégor said, it wasn't penned by Zerigor as he'd obviously intended, but by the Ancient Prophet instead. Why did Kyros insist they leave it with Yanantha? She needed to know what it contained now!

Lenyé started reading the secondary parchment but was distracted by Kyros bursting into the cabin, holding her diagram.

'Pity I didn't get this before my boat returned. We could have the Crown safely on board by now.'

Chapter Thirty Six

Morthrir was furious. The four ships had searched a large area of sea; but in the dark and the heavy sea fog that had descended on them, a lone ship might have slipped through unnoticed. The Captain was complaining again that they weren't hired to risk their ships at night, especially as they couldn't even see any stars to navigate by because of the sea fog, and Morthrir had ordered no lights to be lit. They could blunder into each other if they weren't careful.

Where was Kyros' ship?

He returned to the rear cabin, flopped down in a chair, and sat drumming his fingers on the arm. Why was Nastâr unable to sense Kyros' presence any more? He thought back to the convocation at the Great Oak Tree. The Priests had experienced the same thing. One of them said: "*This man is covered by a greater power than ours. One which we dare not challenge. He has the greatest level of protection we have ever encountered*". They also said it was beyond their arts to locate Lenyé. He recalled Eawen, when the Henosite was still Chief Priest, saying that it "*…will take the direct intervention of the Lord Abbérron himself to resolve*".

So why shouldn't he try? After all, he had grown enormously in power since Druis-cyf-rin. As far as others were concerned, he was Abbérron. All he had to do was reconnect with that power he encountered on Mount Malkamet.

He stood in the centre of the cabin, knees slightly flexed and moving intuitively to the gentle roll of the ship. Morthrir began to slow his breathing and focus his mind. But all he sensed was a hindering of his spiritual vision, as if the sea fog had seeped into another realm and was blocking his power. In desperation he resorted to the usual instant-travel method and commanded Vashtani to lift him up and move him to Kyros' ship, but there was no response. He couldn't even connect with the Dé-monos leader. It had to be Kyros, and he was directly in front of them. Wait a minute. If that was the case, all they had to do was continue sailing as they were and eventually they would come upon Kyros' ship.

He broke his stance and was about to open the door and yell for the Captain when he sensed Nastâr was suddenly with him in the darkened cabin.

'Well,' he demanded. 'Have you found them?'

'No, My Lord. But I've found something else. We may have to suspend searching for Kyros and Lenyé for a while to focus on recovering the *Imbrésonite*. I've discovered the top of the Royal Ziggurat.'

'Where?'

'Straight ahead of us. Tell your Captain to reduce sail and all four ships can anchor in about an hour.'

Chapter Thirty Seven

Kyros paced up and down on deck willing the early morning sun to break through while the ship's boat was being made ready. Everything was hidden in a sea fog: that chill wind from the North-East meeting the warm sea over night had done its worst. He couldn't even make out the top of the Ziggurat, or tell whether the sea level had risen and covered it.

He went over the things in his mind from the Parchments and Postscript that would help him recover the Crown. According to the secondary parchment, that item near the Southern doorway was called *Imbrésonite*. Zerigor didn't know what it was for, or why it was so important. Maybe he should recover it. But the sea fog would make it difficult to mount any lifting tackle. And he would have to drag it sideways for about twenty feet to get it directly under the hole before hauling it up. No. He would do a quick in-and-out recovery exercise for the Crown. Now he knew how to open the casket, he wouldn't need any lifting tackle: only a rope over the edge of the hole for the Crown in a net.

The expedition consisted of himself, Harbona, four soldiers and Ramâno; hence the smaller boat from yesterday. The men could easily remove the seal now that it had been loosened, and he and Ramâno would go down on ropes, open the casket and recover the Crown. He was startled as Harbona called up to him out of the sea fog, 'Everything's ready, My Lord.'

They rowed to the Ziggurat and found the sea had risen and covered the top by about four inches of water; just enough to lift the seaweed and make it difficult to walk across without getting it wrapped around their ankles.

'This is going to be tricky,' he muttered, as they hauled the boat onto the Ziggurat. 'I hope none of this has seeped through the seal in the night and flooded the chamber.'

They carried the ropes and wrecking bars over to the seal.

'Ramâno, tie a rope round your waist.' He made sure the knots were secure before he did his own. 'As soon as that stone is out of the way, water is going to pour in, so we'll have to be quick. Harbona, tie a flare to a rope, light it and put your arm right round one edge of the hole and lower it carefully so it doesn't get put out by any falling water. You other men get ready to lower us down as quickly as possible, with a separate rope and net. Keep hold of all the ropes, and, as soon as I give a single tug, haul us and the Crown back out again.'

The men levered the stone away and everyone went into action. As he was lowered next to Ramâno, Kyros saw that water was already in the chamber, and practically up to the top of the casket. The chests and clay pots must have been weighted as none of them were floating on the surface.

Kyros was drenched when he landed on the casket and leaned over to run his hand down one side. 'I can't see the sword and I'm reluctant to find the buttons by feel.'

'Do you want me to jump in,' Ramâno's normally shrill voice sounded dead with all that water in the chamber and pouring down on top of them. 'If you hold that flare over the edge, I can open my eyes and see under water.'

'Let's give it a try.'

'Is this the correct side?' Ramâno glanced up at him.

'That bundle we saw yesterday is over there by the Southern doorway, and also by a compass bearing, this is the East side.'

Kyros held the flare overhead beyond the curtain of water pouring down while Ramâno eased himself into the water, took a deep breath and dived under the surface. Kyros watched him moving his arms and legs as he held himself steady in front of the casket, before jerking his head out of the water.

'I can see it!'

'Good. Remember the sequence to press the buttons in: top, bottom, right and then left.'

Ramâno ducked down again, steadied himself with his arms and reached out his hand to press each button in turn. As the boy touched the fourth one, Kyros felt through the casket, rather than heard, a sliding of the locking mechanism.

Kyros leaped off the casket into the water and raised the heavy lid. He held it up with his shoulder and grabbed the only thing he could see inside: a canvas bag coated in pitch to keep it waterproof. The contents of the bag clinked as he moved it. 'This is it,' he yelled and dropped the lid before too much water poured in.

Ramâno's head broke the surface and he stood up, gasping for breath.

'Well done, Ramâno,' Kyros hugged him in delight. 'You did it!'

He placed the bag carefully in the net, tugged once and felt himself being hauled up as Ramâno and the Crown were pulled up with him.

'Quick,' Kyros shouted as soon as they were clear of the hole. 'Start levering the seal back into place.'

Chapter Thirty Eight

Lenyé sat at the desk and read the secondary parchment again to see if she'd missed anything the night before. It was clearly an urgent addendum that had been rolled up and shoved through one end of the original scroll, as the writing was badly scrawled, but clearly still in Zerigor's hand:

I am in haste and do not have time to open and re-seal the main parchment, but those coming after me must know of this. As I prepared to leave the strong-room, I heard others approach and hid in a corner covering my flare with an empty clay pot. Presently I saw a light and a man entered holding a flare and three others followed bearing a heavy bundle wrapped in a cloth and hoisted on their shoulders. All four were Tsé-shâmé, and I marvelled that they had broken through our defences so quickly and had the courage to enter this Ziggurat when the city had not yet fallen. I shouted and flung myself at the leader and the other three yelled in fright, dropped their bundle and fled. I wrestled my captive to the ground and threatened to throttle the life out of him if he didn't tell me what they were doing. So terrified was he that he blurted out the most astonishing tale:

"The Tsé-shâmé had been instructed for many months to recover a certain substance from the ground and smelt it into one piece for ease of transport. Four dark-haired Krêonor took the lead in this and commanded us and were very sensitive to this substance through the use of divining rods, and so every instance of the substance throughout the whole island had been located and excavated to recover all that the

island contained".

I asked why they were bringing it here.

"To preserve it for a later time, once we have won the battle".

I demanded to know what the substance was to be used for, but he didn't know. When I asked what it was called, he said the Krêonor leaders whispered, *"Imbrésonite"*, amongst themselves.

I let him go. When I peeled back the cloth, I saw in the light of the flare that the substance shone like gold and sparkled with many gems of blue, red, yellow and white impregnated within its surface. And I wondered again as to why this substance was so important to preserve beyond the current battle, and possibly, the inrush of the sea, and what it was to be used for.

I was puzzled over the name *Imbrésonite*, for it meant nothing to me. But I record these details for my heir to read and understand the significance of what else lies hidden in this strong-room. For the bundle was too heavy for me to lift and there was no time to summon guards and have it removed, and remains close to the Southern doorway where they dropped it.

Kyros was startled by the splash of running feet across the top of the Ziggurat and the shim of swords being drawn. He whipped round at a voice from behind: 'Stop! What do you think you're doing?' In the swirling sea fog he could just make out a semi-circle of about twenty men; some holding tools, others with drawn swords in their hands, but most had longbows, fitted with arrows and pointing directly at them.

One tall, dark-haired Krêonor, dressed in a white robe, spoke up. 'What have you got there?' he indicated the canvas bag. When no one answered, he strode forwards and grabbed Ramâno by the hair. 'Tell me, or it will go badly for the boy.' He held a dagger against Ramâno's throat. 'What's in that bag?'

Ramâno struggled to break free, but the man held him tighter.

'We know this is the Royal Ziggurat and contains many treasures from the Beginning. Tell me, or I'll cut the boys throat.'

Kyros sighed. 'The Crown of Life that Zerigor once wore.'

'Interesting.' The man indicated to one of his comrades who took it from Kyros. 'Morthrir will want to see that. But we are here to recover a heavy bundle wrapped in a cloth. We thought it was what you came for. Did you notice anything like that?'

Kyros shook his head.

'It wasn't far from the Southern doorway. I'm going to count to ten; then I'll slit the boy's throat. One…two…three…'

'Wait.' Kyros held up his hand. He paced away from the hole in a Southerly direction counting his steps. 'It would be about here. But by now, it's under several feet of water.'

Lenyé rolled up the secondary parchment, shoved it back into the end of the original scroll and sat tapping her fingers on the desk while she decided what to do.

She recalled Kyros' words from last night as they discussed the bundle of *Imbrésonite*: 'I'm not sure we should leave it there.'

'But you said yourself that you would need some lifting tackle, and it would take time.'

'Lenyé, everything in that strong-room is neatly packed: wooden chests; clay pots; even the casket is precisely in the middle directly under the hole. The bundle is inside one of the doors, at an angle. It has nothing to do with Zerigor. This is our only opportunity to find out what it is.'

'We mustn't delay trying to take it with us. Just go back and get the Crown. That's what we came for. Then we can set sail. If those pursuing ships are anywhere near us, I don't like being here at anchor for longer than we have to.'

'When I touched it, I knew immediately there was something about the substance that would affect our lives. I even heard the

True King's voice in my heart: "*Be careful what you do with it*".'

'That still doesn't mean we should take it with us.'

'What about those clay pots? Presumably they're full of parchments. You can use the time going through them.'

'Kyros. Hoffengrégor sent us for the Crown and the key. We've even got the last parchment Zerigor wrote. We cannot stay and search everything, however valuable. We'll have to seal it up and go. Maybe someone else will uncover what we leave.'

'I want you two men,' the dark-haired Krêonor indicated Kyros and Harbona, 'down in that chamber and wrap some spare ropes around the bundle.' He pointed to his men carrying tools. 'Get back to your boat and bring the lifting tackle.'

'I'm not going down there,' Kyros walked towards the hole, 'without the boy. He's my best swimmer. It'll take the two of us to lift each end, and he can slip the ropes underneath.'

'Very well. But no tricks.'

'On one condition. We keep our ropes tied around us all the time and no one cuts them!'

'You can trust me on that score. Morthrir will want to question you and find out exactly why you are here and what you are doing recovering the Crown of Life. Now, get on with it.'

There was no point using flares as the flow of water through the hole was too intense to keep them dry. When they reached the bottom the water was about ten feet deep. They swam in single file using the light from the hole above to direct them, Ramâno leading with Kyros right behind holding the lad's rope to guide him and Harbona doing the same with his.

They found the bundle. He and Harbona dived down, stood on the floor of the chamber, and heaved one end up so that Ramâno could drag a length of rope under it. They broke the surface and gulped great lungfuls of air before doing the same with the other end, and knotted the ropes around it to form a web. They tied more ropes to this and paid them out under water as they swam back, and tied them in turn to four ropes hanging down from the hole. Kyros tugged a rope and felt them all tighten as the lifting tackle took the strain. With a surge of water from the far end, the bundle began edging towards them till it was right under the hole. The men above hauled it straight up and guided it out of the strong-room.

Lenyé was still undecided about the *Imbrésonite*. The most important thing was to recover the Crown. That's what they'd come for. But like Kyros, she was intrigued about this new discovery. Maybe they should take it with them and try to find out its purpose. He was right; this was the only opportunity they would have. She pushed the chair away from the desk, stood up and walked towards the cabin door. She would send another boat across to Kyros' with the lifting tackle, see how they were getting on with recovering the Crown and tell them to haul up this bundle as well while they were down there.

Kyros heard a shout and their own ropes tightened as they were lifted out of the water and hauled up through the hole.

They were about to be led away when Kyros spoke to the leader, 'What about resealing the chamber? There are a lot of valuable items down there.'

The leader shrugged before signalling to the men with tools to heave the stone back into place.

Kyros, Harbona and Ramâno were escorted under armed guard to one of the longboats. Six men were sent to recover their own ship's boat and the rest of the party, with Kyros' four soldiers, dispersed to the other longboats.

Lenyé thrust open the door leading to the deck. The wind had swung round to a Southwesterly and was stirring the sea fog, but she still couldn't see across to the top of the Ziggurat. She stopped dead in her tracks and yelled, 'All hands on deck.'

Everyone came scrambling up the companionways.

'Man the crossbows and light the braziers for the fire arrows!'

Captain Josiah emerged from his cabin.

'Captain.' Lenyé pointed over the stern. 'How come no one spotted those?' Rocking slightly at anchor she saw the mast tops of a ship where the sea fog was beginning to shred in the upper air currents. No. More than one ship.

'Hoist the inner jib and fore and main courses,' the Captain shouted, 'and shorten the anchor cable!'

Lenyé stared the Captain in the eyes. 'How did they know we were here?'

'I've no idea. But whoever they are, they mean trouble.'

❖

Kyros sat in the longboat with his hands tied behind his back and felt a shift in the wind as the sea fog lifted. He saw four ships moored a little North of the Ziggurat, with the longboats heading for them. He noticed *Brave Heart* had weighed anchor and was under steerage with its jib, fore and mainsails set. He also saw the telltale haze of hot charcoal drifting up from behind the nearer gunwale, presumably from the braziers. They were obviously preparing to use fire arrows if necessary.

He nudged Harbona, touched Ramâno's foot with his boot and jerked his head in the direction of their ship. 'Stay alert while I work out what Lenyé's doing, and be prepared for action.'

Chapter Thirty Nine

The following morning Quinn carried on with the digging while Beth stowed their breakfast things in the saddle bags.

'I've uncovered a lot of big roots,' Quinn shouted across to Ishi-mi-réjá, 'but can't see far enough down the hole any more.'

'Can you feel anything?' Ishi-mi-réjá came over and squatted down beside him.

'There's something not attached to the tree,' Quinn wriggled onto his side. 'But my arm's not long enough to grip it properly.'

They changed places and Ishi-mi-réjá slipped her arm down the hole. 'Can you reach it from where Beth was digging?'

Quinn raced round and tried. 'There's too much soil blocking it.' He scooped more out and Beth knelt beside him to push it out of his way. Beth took over and he went back to Ishi-mi-réjá.

'It's a bit looser now,' Ishi-mi-réjá gasped from exertion.

'I can't reach any further,' Beth called out.

Ishi-mi-réjá took her arm out of the hole and went to help Beth. Between them they scooped more soil out. 'I've got my hand on it now,' Ishi-mi-réjá called to Quinn.

'Do that again,' Quinn shouted back. 'It's coming. Keep twisting and pushing up... It's stuck on a root. Ease it down and clear more soil away so I can tilt it... That's better, it's moving and I can angle it past the root... It's coming... It's coming.' Quinn had a good grip on it and kept pulling upwards. 'I can see it at the top of the hole. It's coming... Keep pushing. It's out.'

Quinn stared at the object as he cradled it across his knees. It was a rod, slightly longer than a man's arm, and fashioned from a light coloured wood, with a carved acorn surrounded by a garland of oak leaves at one end, and shaved down to a rounded knob at the other. The shaft was decorated with parallel lines carved into the wood itself, and the acorn at the end appeared to be bursting into life. 'Come and look at this,' he shouted.

The others raced round and he passed it to Ishi-mi-réjá. 'What is it?'

'And why is it so clean?' Beth took it from the old woman.

'That's what I thought,' Quinn stretched out his hand and ran his fingers down the length, feeling the smoothness of the polished wood and the little troughs of the parallel lines. 'If it's been under this tree for a thousand years, why hasn't any soil stuck to it, or discoloured it?'

Ishi-mi-réjá took it from Beth and held it up. 'I think it's the Sceptre of Authority which Zerigor brought with him from the sunken island.'

'I thought you said it was from another Realm?'

'It's from the Realm of the Blessèd Throne. That's why it came to Zerigor at the Beginning.'

'And is that why it's remained so clean all these years?'

'Probably.'

'What are we supposed to do with it?'

'It marks the re-instatement of the reign of a King in the Waking World who restores all that Zerigor once represented.'

'Is that why Abbérron and the Summoners were so interested in using the tree as a cross-over from this world to the Realm of the Blessèd Throne?'

'Possibly,' Quinn felt Ishi-mi-réjá's eyes boring into him as she replied. 'But what they were seeking, I cannot say.'

After their midday meal they headed North. Quinn smiled at Beth. She was obviously feeling the same as he was: after the last few days, they were both reluctant to leave Druis-cyf-rin because of the wholesome atmosphere that had been released here.

Chapter Forty

As they weighed anchor, Lenyé felt the new wind freshen. She watched the mast tops of the nearest ship, as *Brave Heart* turned to head before the Southwesterly. The sea fog was still thick about their own mastheads. She heard shouts and saw the vague outline of a boat being raised from the water. Maybe they were unaware of *Brave Heart*'s approach. She crouched behind the port gunwale, both swords strapped across her back and ready to swarm over with the soldiers as soon as the grappling hooks were embedded in the other ship's gunwale.

She registered the name, *Flying Cloud*, as they surged past her starboard bow, and was nearly knocked sideways when the hulls jolted together. She cupped her hands to her mouth, 'Grappling hooks!' and heard the grunts of sailors hauling on the ropes to bring the two ships grinding together. 'Lower fore and main courses,' and she felt *Brave Heart* held against their opponent with the force of the wind on the jib and spanker.

She signalled with her hand and they swarmed over the sides, swords drawn and hunted down the opposing crew. Even the animal-friends joined in: the lioness and she-bear snarling and growling; the eagle flying into the sailors' faces with talons extended and the cobra rearing up, hood inflated. The battle was fierce, but one-sided. The crew of *Flying Cloud* were caught completely by surprise and surrendered quickly. Lenyé ordered them to be escorted below, only to find about fifty warriors in their hammocks still suffering from the ravages of seasickness. She sealed the hatches, set a guard in place and questioned the

Captain in his cabin.

'How many ships are there?'

'Four, including ourselves.'

'And who's in command?'

'Morthrir.'

'Morthrir! What ship is he in?'

'*Monarch of the Seas.*'

Lenyé snorted with amusement. 'Still thinks he's King does he? What are the other two ships called?'

'*Tempest* and *Sea Sprite*. *Tempest* is closest to us with the old *Monarch* between her and *Sea Sprite*.'

'And why are you in these waters?'

'I was requested to make my ship ready for a bounty hunting voyage and accompany Morthrir.'

Lenyé was startled as the door burst open. Two of her soldiers entered, marching four other men between them.

'What's the meaning of this interruption?'

'My Lady,' one of the soldiers replied. 'These men rowed Kyros to the Ziggurat this morning.'

'What happened?'

'We were overpowered by a much larger force from these ships,' one of them answered, 'and Kyros, Harbona and the boy were forced to go back into the Ziggurat and recover the bundle of *Imbrésonite* for them. They've also got the Crown.'

'I see. And where are they now?'

'In a longboat being rowed to *Monarch of the Seas*. They should be on board by now.'

'Very well. Captain, I am commandeering your ship as spoils of war. Morthrir is my enemy and has captured three people who are dear to me. One of whom is Prince Kyros. By so doing, he has committed a treasonable offence. If you, or any of your crew, escape and seek to aid my Uncle, you will also be guilty and liable to execution. Do you understand?'

'Yes, my Lady.'

'I will leave a guard here and some sailors to man the ship. You and your officers will be confined to this cabin.'

Once back on *Brave Heart*, Lenyé felt the wind strengthen, thinning the sea fog, as they cast off the grappling hooks and regained steerage under courses and topsails. She saw *Tempest*, beyond *Flying Cloud*, hauling up a longboat on its davits and preparing to get under way.

A plan was forming in Lenyé's mind to capture *Tempest* and use her against the other two ships. She had a stab of conscience about being the first to attack, but those warriors on *Flying Cloud* bothered her. What if the other ships had that many as well? Besides, Uncle Morthrir had seized Kyros, Harbona and Ramâno, and taken the Crown and *Imbrésonite*. She had to rescue them and recover what had been stolen.

'Set the topsails and topgallants,' she yelled, so she could reach *Tempest* as the ship turned.

'Crossbowmen, to your places!'

She watched as eight ropes were rigged to swing freely between the masts for the incendiary devices. Kegs of resin and molasses were hauled up and attached to the ropes.

As *Brave Heart* approached, *Tempest* swung round on an Easterly tack and *Brave Heart* cut across her stern. Lenyé dropped her hand and shouted, 'Bow chasers!' The heavy duty bolts smashed through the upper and lower stern windows. As the many-barrelled crossbows began to bear, she dropped her hand again, 'Loose fire arrows!' A dozen arrows raked the stern and embedded themselves in the wood of the cabins.

'Incendiaries,' she yelled, and the kegs swung on their long ropes in perfect time with each other. On the upwards roll they were released into the cabins and erupted in a firestorm.

Lenyé saw flames licking through the poop deck skylights. Sailors rushed down the ship towards the bows and jumped into the sea as the fire spread. A group of warriors, obviously still suffering from seasickness, stumbled after them. The ship was left unmanned and continued turning, the pressure of the wind on the jib and spanker forcing her round. Lenyé ran *Brave Heart* alongside. *Brave Heart's* crew hurled grappling hooks across to hold the ships together, while soldiers and a few sailors surged over the gunwales and took charge of the ship. More kegs were lobbed across to *Tempest* and dropped down the hatches: the quick burning resin igniting the slower burning molasses. Once the ship was ablaze, the skeleton crew knew their orders: sail between the other two ships, engage *Monarch of the Seas*, and set her on fire.

Her own sailors hacked away the grappling lines, and *Brave Heart* sailed before the wind to cut off the other two ships as they turned to head North-East. Clearly *Sea Sprite* was the faster of the two, a much sleeker hull compared with her heavier consort, and already hoisting extra yard arms for stunsails to run faster before the wind. Lenyé would have to let her go. It was Uncle Morthrir she wanted, and presumably he had Kyros and the others on board as prisoners with the Crown and *Imbrésonite*.

'Captain,' she shouted, 'hard-a-port and slacken sail so that *Monarch* will run alongside us as she turns.'

There was a crash as the hulls banged against each other.

'Crossbowmen, loose fire arrows when you bear.'

As *Monarch of the Seas'* momentum brought her alongside *Brave Heart* and pushed forwards, the rear crossbowmen loosed their fire arrows, followed in quick succession by those in the bows.

'Incendiaries,' Lenyé yelled. Kegs of resin were swung across and released. One burst over the poop deck and a blazing trail poured down through the open skylights into the cabins below.

She glanced across *Monarch's* deck and saw *Tempest* thrust between *Monarch* and *Sea Sprite* on the other side. Sailors threw grappling hooks and opened the hatches of *Tempest*. A roar of flames shot up the masts, caught the sails and leaped across the yard arms into the sails and rigging of the old *Monarch*.

By now, her rear crossbowmen were loosing again and another wave of fire arrows poured into the doomed ship.

Lenyé mustered a squad of soldiers, laid gang planks to the other ship's gunwale and clambered across the gap. She had to find Kyros in the rapidly growing inferno.

She glanced behind and saw the lioness and she-bear following her. 'Get back,' she yelled. 'This ship's about to go up in flames.'

'We promised Yanantha to guard you at all times,' Lenyé caught Ariella's growl above the din of battle.

'And we're not going to stop now,' Mamma Uza-Mâté roared. 'Flames or no flames.'

Chapter Forty One

Quinn walked the horse along a narrow trail in the woods and felt Beth stretch her arms as she sat behind him. Ishi-mi-réjá strode ahead with the Sceptre wrapped in a cloth in her backpack. He gripped the horse tighter with his knees and turned his head slightly to talk to Beth, 'Now we've found it, we can head straight for Fantrios and rescue our parents.'

'Do you think Paco's still there?' Beth asked.

'Don't know. It's some time since that escort left Onadestra. He's probably gone back by now.'

'Why change the guards so soon?'

'Security.' Quinn kicked the horse into a trot to catch up with Ishi-mi-réjá. 'They wouldn't want anyone talking to our parents and getting too familiar with them.'

'But Paco told me Lenyé destroyed one of Uncle Morthrir's armies and is marching on Terrazarema,' Beth persisted.

'What's that got to do with it?'

'He also said, "...*there are many families back home grieving already, waiting for an official announcement*". The remaining warriors must be worried about what Uncle Morthrir's doing, and don't like the risks any more. Maybe Paco would help us.'

'Doubt it,' Quinn turned to face forwards and concentrated on riding. 'Even if Lenyé is winning, any warriors up here will be more concerned about their commander's discipline. If Paco is caught helping our parents escape, he would be executed.'

'I was only thinking about how to get them out. If the Hunting Lodge is heavily guarded, it's going to be difficult.'

'They'll be in the bedrooms,' Quinn turned his head round slightly to talk more easily. 'But we won't know which ones.'

'And another thing,' Beth frowned. 'Lenyé once said to me that she thought Uncle Morthrir wasn't even part of our family.'

'Kyros said the same thing to me, but told me to keep quiet because Lenyé got into trouble when she asked the question.'

'If it's true, we need to do something about it.'

'Like what?' Quinn frowned.

'If we proved it, Uncle Morthrir couldn't be crowned King.'

'He'll have himself crowned whether we can prove it or not. That's why we have to rescue our parents and prevent him!'

Quinn saw Ishi-mi-réjá stop and wait for them to catch up.

The old woman cupped her hands around her mouth and called, 'Don't forget Beth was asking about "*uncovering the secret behind your Uncle's rise to power*".' She glanced from one to the other as the horse halted in front of her. 'We still need to do something about that before we head for Fantrios.'

'I thought we were going to rescue our parents next,' Beth sounded distressed. 'Will it delay us for long?'

'No. It's on the way,' Ishi-mi-réjá replied. 'I'm not exactly sure what we're looking for. But I know roughly where to go.'

Chapter Forty Two

Kyros sat on a chair in the main cabin of *Monarch of the Seas*, with his wrists still tied behind him and facing his Uncle. Harbona and Ramâno stood to one side, also with their hands tied.

'At last I have you,' Morthrir paced up and down. 'Not only with the *Imbrésonite* I was after, but also a Crown: the Krêon of Tulá-kâhju that belonged to Zerigor, to be precise. Any King with that Crown would be immediately accepted by the People.'

Kyros protested. 'Only the one chosen and appointed by the True King can wear it.'

'Oh, really? I suppose you think that's you,' he sneered at Kyros. 'Why don't we put it to the test? Bring in the Crown,' he yelled, turning to the cabin door.

A tall, dark-haired Krêonor entered carrying the black canvas bag containing the Crown, and presented it to Morthrir. He was accompanied by three others.

'This is Jumar-jé. You've already met him,' Morthrir chuckled. 'And his associates. Old friends of mine. Try it on him first,' he pointed at Kyros. 'I want to see what it looks like on my rival.'

Jumar-jé walked across and tried to set the Crown on his head, but Kyros jerked away.

'I will not have such an act of violation performed against me. Only by proper Coronation can this Crown be set upon the head of anyone.'

'Nonsense. I only want to see what it looks like.' Morthrir indicated for the other three to help. Between them they succeeded in placing the Crown on Kyros, ensuring the dangling layers of rubies settled around the back and sides of his head.

'One day you will regret this,' Kyros glared at his Uncle, but whipped his head round at a gasp from Ramâno, hearing the layers of rubies tinkling together as he did so.

'What is it, boy?' Morthrir stared hard at the lad.

'I…' Ramâno hesitated, glanced at Morthrir and back to Kyros. 'I had no idea the Crown would look so beautiful when someone was wearing it.'

'Try it on me, then,' Morthrir indicated to Jumar-jé to remove the Crown and set it on his own head.

'What do you think?' Morthrir turned round so they could see the back. 'Well, boy. Do we look the same, or is there any difference?'

'I, er,' again the boy stumbled over his words and blushed noticeably, despite his brown skin. 'It looks beautiful on you as well.'

'Good. That's settled. We'll use this for the Coronation.'

Jumar-jé removed the Crown, returned it to the waterproof bag and re-sealed it. He was about to open the door when there was a bang against the hull and the ship lurched sideways.

'What was that?' Morthrir shouted.

Kyros heard approaching footsteps and a hurried knock.

'Come.'

The door burst open and the Captain entered, saluted smartly and asked for permission to speak.

Morthrir nodded.

'*Tempest* is on fire against our starboard gunwale and a strange ship is grappling us on the port side. She emerged out of the sea fog, Sire.'

'Is that your ship, Kyros?' Morthrir glared at him.

'Probably.'

'And is Lenyé on board?'

'Naturally. She wasn't going to let you get away with the Crown,' Kyros stared back at his Uncle. 'Or the *Imbrésonite.*

Incidentally. What do you want it for?'

'Never you mind!'

'The fire's spreading to *Monarch*, Sire,' the Captain interrupted. 'I ordered hoses to be connected, but the fire in *Tempest* is too intense to douse properly.'

'Where are the other ships?' Morthrir gripped the man by the arm and prevented him running for the door.

'*Flying Cloud* has tacked down the West side of the Ziggurat to turn and sail up the East side to join us. She's a long way off and no help at present. *Sea Sprite* is hoisting stunsails. If we have to abandon ship, she's our only hope of escape.'

'Jumar-jé,' Morthrir turned to him. 'Tie Kyros to the chair and leave him. He can either burn to death or go down with the ship. I don't care which, but I need to get rid of him once and for all.'

'Yes, Sire.'

'Take Harbona and the boy.'

'Yes, Sire.'

'Get a boat into the water, have the *Imbrésonite* lowered in and make sure you've got the Crown with you. I'll join you and we'll head for *Sea Sprite*.'

'Yes, Sire.'

'If Lenyé is on board that other ship, I'll entice her to chase us. *Flying Cloud* can come up behind and catch her in a trap!'

Chapter Forty Three

Rafé puzzled over his experience with the snake as he travelled North under the blazing sun. The mountains loomed nearer and he decided the one thrust out onto the Plain was Mount Nastâri.

He couldn't get that image of the cobra out of his mind. It was as though the snake was there in front of him. He even felt a movement of air against his skin before he leaped back. How could that be?

As he rode his horse and held the bridle of the spare to canter beside him, he heard the snake's voice inside his head again, 'Who are you?'

'No. This is not possible.'

'Who are you,' the voice was more insistent now.

He quickened the canter of both horses, as if by speed he could leave the voice behind.

'Why do you always seek to know about Lenyé?'

He tried to shut his mind to the questions.

'You will never escape me till I know.'

Rafé slowed his horses and brought them to a halt. He dismounted, tethered them to a couple of pegs in the ground, and began pacing up and down, but was still troubled. He settled down in the shadow of the horses, ate some food and drank from his wineskin, hoping the wine would block the voice from his mind.

But the voice was still inside his head.

Chapter Forty Four

Lenyé dodged the knots of warriors caught up in the chaos of the blazing *Monarch*. Like their comrades in the other two ships, they were still too badly affected by sea sickness to fight her soldiers. She thrust open the door to the upper stern cabin and recoiled at the flames within. She was startled by howls of fear from Ariella and Mamma Uza-Mâté behind her, but braced herself to enter. She swept both swords out of their scabbards, not knowing what she would encounter.

Lenyé entered the cabin, saw there was no one about and sheathed the swords. If Morthrir had been interrogating Kyros this would be the most likely place and she had to get Kyros out. She dropped to all fours, crawled towards the stern, coughing and choking and saw a dark object on the planking against the port side. She lay on her belly to get below the smoke, and hauled herself across. Kyros was unconscious and bound to a chair, on its back. He'd obviously tried to shuffle to the windows, but the chair must have tipped over.

She cut the ropes with her dagger and slapped his face, but no response. She dragged him out, still coughing and choking, slammed the door shut, and slapped him again. She was relieved to hear him moan and start to move and finally sit up.

'What...?' he groaned. 'Lenyé. How did you get here?'

'Never mind. The ship's on fire. Can you walk?'

Kyros struggled to his hands and knees and stood up, clutching at the cabin door to steady himself. 'I'm all right.'

'Where's Uncle Morthrir?'

'Gone. We need to catch him. You'd better lead the way.'

As they reached the starboard bow, Lenyé could see past *Tempest* and down onto the water where a longboat was pulling for *Sea Sprite*. 'There he is, and four men I don't recognise.'

'They were with Uncle Morthrir in the cabin.' Lenyé saw him shield his eyes against the crackling flames in *Tempest*. 'Apart from those five, there are only sailors at the oars. Where are Harbona and Ramâno?'

'I don't know. They'll have to fend for themselves.'

'They must have escaped. I'm not leaving without them.'

'But we have to stop Uncle Morthrir. Look,' Lenyé pointed at the longboat, 'that bundle must be the *Imbrésonite*.'

'Yes. And one of them has the Crown. You go back to *Brave Heart* and chase Uncle Morthrir. I'll find Harbona and Ramâno. Be careful. He thinks he can lure you into a trap with *Flying Cloud* coming up behind you.'

Lenyé laughed. '*Flying Cloud* is South-West of us and manned by some of our crew. So he's in for a nasty shock. If you find the others, get into a boat and *Flying Cloud* can pick you up.'

They hugged each other.

'Take care, my Sweet,' Lenyé whispered; then raced for the port gunwale and the safety of her own ship. The last she saw of Kyros, he was heading for the companionway to take him down a deck and deeper into the raging flames.

Chapter Forty Five

Morthrir strode up and down on the quarter deck of *Sea Sprite*, shouting at some sailors as they rigged a temporary tackle to hoist the *Imbrésonite* on board. He ordered it to be taken to the rear cabin and it needed four of them carrying it slowly on their shoulders. He yelled at the Captain to get the ship under way with all sails set for Pordé-Sûnca and glanced up at Nastâr, towering over him. Morthrir smiled to himself knowing that the rest of the ship's company couldn't see the great being, except the Summoners, wherever they were.

'What would you have me do, My Lord?' Nastâr asked.

'Release Vashtani to me in case I need him to move me out of here if we're overtaken. If Kyros is dead, it should be easy. Then head for that ship and check if Lenyé's on board. Finally, find *Flying Cloud* and bring her up behind to form a trap.'

Morthrir eased open the cabin door to find the Summoners with their backs to him, gloating over the *Imbrésonite* and too absorbed in their conversation to notice him. Jumar-jé still had a hand on a loose corner of the cloth where he'd obviously peeled it back to reveal its golden colour and gemstones. 'Look at that,' he exclaimed. 'Abbérron commanded us to recover it all those years ago. Why should Morthrir benefit from it?'

'Let's offer a child sacrifice.' Morthrir watched the Summoner in red glance at his companions. 'Like we used to.'

They all jumped as Morthrir slammed the door behind him.

'That's a very interesting remark,' he stared at the man and let his eyes search out the others. 'You may all have lived a thousand years and seen Abbérron on many occasions, but you are now obedient to me.'

He was amused at their guilty expressions.

'Do you not recall me saying on Mount Malkamet: "*Abbérron will no longer appear to you at any Convocation, for his power has been transferred to me. As far as you are concerned, I am Abbérron*"? If there's going to be a child sacrifice, I intend to be present. Do you understand?' He glared at all the Summoners. 'What exactly will it do?

'Release Abbérron to us in a new way.'

'I see. Where can we find a suitable child?'

'Not any child, My Lord,' Jumar-jé spoke up. 'A very specific child. I suggest the boy who helped Kyros when he was trying to be a Healer. His death would be in revenge against all those who speak about the True King.'

'You mean, Ramâno?' Morthrir was surprised at the suggestion. 'He's locked in one of the cabins.'

'Then all we have to do is perform the ceremony and Abbérron will come.'

'Hmph!' Morthrir began pacing up and down in the cabin. 'I was planning to use him to draw Lenyé into a trap to catch her. If the boy is dead, he's no further use to me.'

'That would delay Abbérron's appearing and the reward you will receive from him for recovering the *Imbrésonite*.'

'I need to think about this further. In the meantime, let me have another look at that Crown.' He held out his hand as one of the Summoners opened the bag and handed it to him. 'Why was the boy so excited when you put it on Kyros' head, but tried to hide his feelings when I asked him what it looked like on me? Tell me the truth: was there any difference?'

'No, Sire,' Jumar-jé was quick to jump in; too quick. What was the man hiding?

Morthrir put the Crown on his head. 'From your recollection of when Zerigor wore it, what did it look like?'

'It blazed a deep red.'

'And is that the case with me?'

'No, Sire.'

'What about when Kyros wore it?'

'There was no difference, Sire.'

'So it didn't blaze red on his head?'

'Not that I could see.'

'What about the rest of you?'

'No, Sire,' the other three Summoners spoke together.

'Then, at my Coronation, how are we to make it look like it blazes on my head as it did for Zerigor to prove my Kingship?'

'I suggest you hold the Coronation in the Amphitheatre, on a sunny day,' Jumar-jé replied, 'and it will be bound to blaze with light.'

'And on other days, or indoors?'

'We will have to arrange the lights carefully to achieve the same effect.'

'I see. So if there was any occasion when it didn't blaze red, my authority as King may be called into question.'

'All of us will work hard on your behalf to maintain the deception, Sire. No one else will ever know.'

'But I still need to marry Lenyé on the Coronation Day. I will use the child sacrifice to capture her and present the *Imbrésonite* to Abbérron at the same time to incur his favour.'

PART IV

THE LURE

Chapter Forty Six

'Man the crossbows,' Lenyé shouted as her feet touched the deck of *Brave Heart*. She sent Wilf and the others scurrying to the armoury for more arrows and hemp. She paced up and down on the quarter deck in frustration as the sailors hacked the ship free from the blazing *Monarch* and unfurled the sails. But *Sea Sprite* was already well in the lead.

Lenyé ordered maximum elevation of the two bow-chasers. One fire arrow passed through the mizzen topgallant sail, but the other embedded itself in a yard arm. The flames caught in the rigging and blazed through the canvas. Men swarmed up the ratlines on *Sea Sprite* with leather buckets and formed a human chain to douse the flames. But the damage was done. She ordered the other two crossbows to join in and loose arrows as the front bow-chasers reloaded. The barrage kept the firefighters ducking and dodging. An arrow embedded itself in the woodwork and set another sail on fire. *Sea Sprite* was noticeably slower in the water as sailors hoisted a spare topgallant, and *Brave Heart* was beginning to gain on her.

Every time a burning sail was cut away and replaced, *Sea Sprite* surged forwards again, and the gap lengthened. At this rate Lenyé was never going to slow her quarry enough to board her and recover the Crown and *Imbrésonite*. As the sun began to set, Wilf called up to her that they only had half their stock of Nastrim arrows left. She couldn't go on loosing fire arrows indefinitely. Also, what should she do when night set in? Stay on their current course and expect *Sea Sprite* to do the same?

❖

Kyros struggled down the companionway of the old *Monarch* to her main deck, the intense heat forcing him to take shallow breaths. He must find Harbona and Ramâno before it was too late. He collapsed to his knees at the bottom and realised he was below the worst of the smoke and able to breathe more freely.

He glanced up at a boat, already aflame, hanging by its lashings from the beams in the open space above. The second must have been the one his Uncle used. The third he'd seen in its davits, waiting to be dropped into the sea while he was on the quarter deck, but abandoned by terrified sailors as they jumped overboard rather than delaying to lower it. Once he found Harbona and the boy; that would be their means of escape.

He crawled past several bodies, and stumbled on Harbona lying face down, blood oozing from a wound to his head. The man's hands were still tied behind his back, but Kyros felt a faint pulse. He slung the man across his shoulders, crawled to the companionway and climbed the steps. He laid Harbona on the quarter deck in the open air, cut the rope around the wrists, then slapped the man's face a couple of times and saw Harbona coming to.

Kyros felt the man grip his wrist. 'Is that you, My Lord?'

'Yes. Have you seen Ramâno?'

'They've taken him. I tried to break free but they separated me from the boy. The last I saw they were tying his ankles and bundling him into a sack. They must have dumped him in the bottom of the longboat before they lowered it into the water.'

Kyros banged his fist on the deck. 'No wonder I didn't see him with Uncle Morthrir. Let me help you into a boat, and we can lower ourselves down.'

❖

Lenyé was distracted by a flash of light from the stern of *Sea Sprite* and raised her telescope: it was the reflection of the sun on glass. Men were holding a struggling figure out of the window and lashing its wrists and ankles to the frame. She focused on the features and recognised Ramâno. 'It can't be,' she muttered to herself in an agony of conflicting choices. 'I thought Kyros had rescued him from the fire on *Monarch*.'

'Cease crossbows,' she yelled. 'Chuah-te-mok,' she called to the eagle as he perched in the crosstrees above her head. 'Fly over and see what they're doing. It looks like Ramâno to me.'

She watched the eagle fly between the two ships and trained her telescope on him as he hovered at the stern. He tore at the ropes holding the boy to the window frame, but men appeared at the windows with lances and thrust him away. Others loosed arrows. Chuah-te-mok scrambled into the sky and sped back, swooping under the sails to land beside her.

'What's going on?' she snapped her telescope shut.

'It is Ramâno. According to the boy, your Uncle had him tied in a sack and dumped at the bottom of the longboat. But there's more. He overheard a conversation threatening to use him as a child sacrifice and release more spiritual power for your Uncle to make you return to him and be his bride.'

'What?' Lenyé was dumbfounded.

'I tried undoing his bonds,' the eagle continued, 'so he could drop into the water and swim towards you, but they fought me off with lances and arrows. I can't get near him now.'

Lenyé smacked the palm of her hand against the mainmast in fury. How did she miss seeing Ramâno in the longboat? Secondly, she daren't loose any fire arrows while he was tied there in case one injured him. And thirdly, what must the lad be suffering? This was much closer to her heart: not only the physical pain of hanging over the water like that, but also the mental strain of knowing about her Uncle's threat.

Kyros' boat was filling with warriors and sailors: as many as he could rescue without sinking. More were in the water clinging to the gunwales. Far better to save his enemies than leave them to drown. He rested on his oars and watched the death agony of the *Monarch*. The firestorm shot up through the main deck and consumed the masts. A hole appeared in the starboard quarter and the sea swept in. The stern opened out and the ship listed as the fire raged through her, ripping into the decks above. She settled further backwards until the bows were out of the water and still the ship was tipping. There was a roar of flame and inrush of sea as she slid below the surface and disappeared.

Tempest was no better off. All that remained was a burning hulk, settling deeper into the sea as the masts sagged and collapsed, dragging the hull over so she was lying on her side.

He resumed rowing towards *Flying Cloud*, just visible in the gathering dusk and sailing towards him.

Lenyé watched *Sea Sprite* as they tailed her well into the night, feeling totally impotent to do anything with Ramâno hanging there. She saw his mouth opening wide, shouting for help, and her heart went out to him. As the light faded from the sky, the lad was untied and dragged aboard.

It was a moonless night, and the cloud layer hid any stars, so nothing could be seen in the blackness ahead. Lenyé loosed an occasional fire arrow to check that *Sea Sprite* was still ahead of them. She didn't care about the Crown and *Imbrésonite* any more, she had to rescue Ramâno. The big question in her mind was when would her Uncle carry out this terrible deed?

Chapter Forty Seven

Beth reined in the horse, pulled his head round so she could see back down the trail, and waited for Ishi-mi-réjá. The old woman was going slowly, stopping every now and then, peering into the foliage and sniffing as if for some elusive scent. But she was only looking on the right hand side of the path.

'Is anything wrong?' Beth called.

'No. It's here, somewhere. Give me a few minutes.'

'There's a little track off to the right, further up,' Beth called again. 'I saw a rabbit darting into it.'

'Really?' Ishi-mi-réjá came striding up the trail towards them. 'Let's try.' She squeezed past the horse and led the way. 'You're right. This is going in the direction we want,' and she plunged off down the track.

Beth pulled the horse's head into the gap, but he seemed reluctant to follow. 'What is it, boy?'

The horse snorted and tossed his head.

'I think we need to get off and lead him,' Quinn whispered in her ear. 'Can't you see? He's afraid of something.'

'Wait,' Beth shouted after Ishi-mi-réjá.

'Shh,' the old woman spun round and put her finger to her lips. 'I don't want to scare whoever it is.'

Quinn dismounted first and helped Beth down, but still the horse refused to go along the track.

'I'll stay here with him,' Quinn held the bridle as the horse tried to buck and rear and get out of the entrance to the track. 'You go after Ishi-mi-réjá.'

Beth sighed, 'All right. But if the horse is scared already, I hate to think what's down there.'

She ran after Ishi-mi-réjá, rounded a bend in the track and gasped in surprise at a tiny cottage hidden by a curtain of creepers. Already Ishi-mi-réjá was forcing her way through a small gap leading to the front door. Beth crawled after her. 'It looks so run-down. Does anyone live here?'

'I think so,' the old woman pointed to the hard-packed ground in front of the doorstep. 'And I smelled smoke as I thrust through the creepers. So there's been a fire recently.' Ishi-mi-réjá rapped on the door and waited in the silence. She rapped again, but no one came. She moved to the window, looked through a crack in the shutters and tapped on the wood. Still no answer.

Beth followed her round to the back of the cottage and clutched at Ishi-mi-réjá's sleeve. 'Can you feel it?'

'Feel what?'

Beth moved back and forth along the little path round the side of the cottage they'd walked along. 'There. It feels like fear. No wonder the horse wouldn't come down the track. It's so strong. And it's been here a long time.'

Ishi-mi-réjá stood closer to Beth. 'You're right. You must be very sensitive. I was concentrating so much on finding the occupier that I missed it.'

A shutter of one of the rear windows was open, and they were able to peer in.

'Is anybody home?' Ishi-mi-réjá called, and Beth distinctly caught a movement on the other side of the room and heard the scuff of a chair as it scraped on the wooden floor.

'May we come in?' Ishi-mi-réjá called again.

'Who's there?' a woman's voice croaked. 'I don't have many visitors. Only the birds when they're hungry.'

'We're looking for someone who can help us.'

'Help you? Your voice sounds too strong for anyone who needs my help. Who are you?'

'My name is Ishi-mi-réjá.'

'What do want? And who's the little girl hiding behind you?'

'Her name's Beth.'

'Beth who? She's not a common girl by the feel of her on the air. I want to know before I let you in.'

'You guessed right. She's the daughter of Lord Alkram.'

Beth leaped back from the window at the sudden scream.

'No,' the woman's voice croaked again. 'I've been dreading this moment for years. Send her away. I can't bear to see her.'

'We're not here to hurt you,' Beth heard the gentle tone in Ishi-mi-réjá's voice. 'We're here to help you.'

'No one can help me. I'm lost. I've done such a terrible deed. I must go down to the grave and take my secret with me.'

'There is no secret in this world that is too terrible to share.'

'You don't know,' wailed the voice again. 'No one knows. Except them!'

Beth felt Ishi-mi-réjá's hand in hers as she led the way to the back door, tried the handle, opened it and stepped into the cottage. On impulse, Beth darted across to a chair and slipped her hand over the back of the woman's. 'Come out with me into the fresh air and sunlight and we can talk more easily.'

'Thank you, my dear.' The woman allowed herself to be helped up and led out through the back door.

Beth guided her to a slatted wooden bench in a burst of sunlight and sat next to her. 'Why don't you want to see me?' She held the woman's hands in hers and felt the brittle skin, so thin and dry and wrinkled that she wondered why it didn't all flake off at her touch.

The woman didn't answer.

'What is your name?'

'I have no name. I am no one. I am lost.'

Beth glanced up at Ishi-mi-réjá for help, but realised she was signalling to go and get Quinn. Beth felt a twinge of fear at being left on her own with this strange woman, but realised

Ishi-mi-réjá was going deliberately to give her more time.

How long they sat holding hands in the warm sunlight with a soft breeze stirring the shock of wild flowers about the bench, Beth couldn't say; but something was going on between them, as though all the years of the woman's terrible secret were melting away and a trust and a bond was growing between them. If only she would say what it was that troubled her so much.

When Beth opened her eyes, Ishi-mi-réjá and Quinn and the horse were standing in front of her.

The woman looked up. 'A horse.' She let go of Beth's hands and struggled to her feet. 'I haven't seen a horse or felt a horse or smelled a horse in years.' She stretched out her hand to him. 'Don't they have such lovely soft noses? I used to ride a horse. Let me ride him, one last time, and I'll die a happy woman.'

Beth glanced at Quinn and saw him shake his head and mouth silently at her, 'She's too old.'

Beth nodded, but the woman saw the movement and pointed. 'Who's that?'

'My cousin, Quinn.'

'Quinn. Quinn who?'

'He's the youngest son of King Dareth,' Ishi-mi-réjá cut in.

'No. No. Not him. The girl I can bear. Alkram was always the quiet one. But not him. Not Dareth's boy. So Dareth's King now, is he? Send his boy away or I die.'

Beth saw Ishi-mi-réjá glance at Quinn and heard her whisper: 'Take some provisions from the saddle bags and go and find your parents. We'll catch up with you when we can. Leave us the horse. It's the only thing that's getting through to this woman.'

Dusk was falling as Beth watched Quinn set off. The old woman sat on the bench for some time stroking the horse's muzzle and holding tufts of grass on the flat of her hand for him.

'Isn't he wonderful,' she kept saying. 'I'd like to ride him.'

'It's too dark now,' Beth whispered. 'Maybe in the morning.'

Chapter Forty Eight

Kyros encountered two problems once on board *Flying Cloud*. Firstly, the rudder was damaged during the storm. The pintles on which it turned had sheered off and would take some time to replace. That meant lying at anchor for the rest of the night. *Brave Heart* was well ahead already in pursuit of *Sea Sprite* and they had little chance of catching up.

The second problem was what to do with the sailors and warriors from *Flying Cloud* and those he'd rescued from *Monarch* and *Tempest*. There were too many for his crew from *Brave Heart* to keep under guard and sail the ship. Most were still suffering from the ravages of seasickness, so he spent the evening moving amongst them, speaking over them in the name of the True King and seeing the look of surprise on their faces as they began to feel better. The rescued sailors grumbled about the loss of their ships, but were prepared to help sail for Pordé-Sûnca. It was the warriors that caused Kyros concern.

He gathered them on the main deck in the light of the lanterns to address them, but let Harbona speak first. The warriors all thought Harbona had died on active service for his Uncle and were demanding an explanation.

'My friends,' Kyros watched Harbona address them. 'You are warriors who serve Morthrir. I was his personal bodyguard under orders to arrest Prince Kyros for treason against him.'

A murmur of agreement arose from the assembled men.

'I chased him down a spiral on the Eye of Hoffengrégor into another Realm and was captured by some very evil beings called

Dé-monos. Prince Kyros rescued me and brought me back to the Waking World at no small cost to himself.'

The men sat in silence, listening to the unfolding story.

'I have therefore renounced my oath to Morthrir and given my allegiance to Prince Kyros.'

There were shouts of, 'Traitor, traitor,' and waving of fists.

'In Prince Kyros I have found only virtues of self-sacrifice and the desire to give unreservedly to others: friend or foe. Did he not rescue you from the sea, even though you were his enemies? In Morthrir I see only traits of grasping things for himself.'

Still the shouts of, 'Traitor, traitor,' echoed around the deck.

Kyros watched Harbona stand firm, like a rock with raging seas crashing about it, and raise his hands for silence.

'One thing I have learned, warrior though I am: we do not fight only against humans but also a spiritual army from another Realm we do not see, but is nevertheless real. I swore to serve Prince Kyros and all those he loves, and, in so doing, I am now committed to waging war with him against those unseen forces.'

'How can we accept what you're saying?' someone shouted.

'You are warriors of the land and understand the ground beneath your horses' hooves. But at sea, you're in a strange environment. You do not know its ways, and suffer as a result.'

'Like sea sickness?' someone shouted.

There was a roar of laughter.

'Exactly,' Harbona continued. 'Yet Prince Kyros comes amongst you and heals you.'

Dead silence.

'He was the Healer in Terrazarema with power from the True King to open people's eyes to what I'm talking about. This other Realm is as different to humans as being at sea is for a warrior.'

'Harbona,' someone called out. 'What shall we do about this?'

'You have two options. Either to treat me as a traitor. You know the law of the warrior clans.'

'Death!' someone shouted.

'Death, certainly, if I am guilty of the charge. But I will fight each one of you personally if you go down that road.'

Kyros watched Harbona survey the men. Not one could meet his eye. He smiled to himself, recalling that terrifying wrestling bout he had with Harbona in the forest, and felt the life being squeezed out of him. Not for nothing was Harbona's reputation established. And these men must hold him in awe because of it.

'Or you can renounce Morthrir, swear allegiance to Prince Kyros and serve me as your Captain.'

Utter silence.

'Well. I'm waiting.'

One man stood to his feet. 'Harbona, you have a reputation amongst the warrior clans that no one can match. Not even Youdlh. And you are also known for your integrity and fairness. I'm glad now that Youdlh was appointed as Morthrir's Commander rather than yourself, because now I can do as you suggest. I renounce my allegiance to Morthrir and ask Prince Kyros to take me into his service.'

'And me,' another was on his feet.

'And me; and me; and me;' till all the warriors were standing, heads bowed, awaiting Kyros' response.

Kyros stepped forwards. 'Everything Harbona said is true, and carries more weight coming from him rather than me. I know a warrior's oath is unbreakable, but I warn you this is not for the faint hearted. You will see strange things and encounter beings with great power and be tempted to run from a fear you have never experienced before. Allegiance to me is not enough. You must learn to call upon the name of the True King. Only he can stand by you in the hour of need and deliver you. That is the greatest lesson a human being can ever learn and it becomes the greatest joy to serve him too. Are you still with me?'

There was silence. Kyros stood staring at each bowed head in turn. Was it too great a challenge for them? Had he gone too far that backing out would make them appear cowards in their own and each other's eyes?

When the silence became unbearable, one man spoke up. 'If Harbona has switched allegiance and sworn on oath to you, My Lord, that's good enough for me. I do not understand these other realms and beings, but I trust you, and I trust in this True King you talk about. I will swear allegiance if you will have me.'

As if a sluice gate had been opened in a dam, all the others spoke with one voice, 'And I will, too.'

'Well said, my friends.' Kyros raised his right hand and indicated for them all to do the same. 'Repeat after me: "By the authority vested in Prince Kyros to act for the Crown",' he paused to let them speak the line, and the sound of their many voices sent a thrill down his spine at the solemnity of the occasion and the significance of what was happening and the bond that was growing between himself and these men. He raised his voice to continue. '"I hereby receive my freedom from servitude to Morthrir. I swear on oath to serve Prince Kyros, being faithful in all things, even to the laying down of my life in the Waking World. So let it be!".'

After they finished, a great cheer erupted from the men.

'I take you into my service,' Kyros continued, 'as free men. Not to serve out of duty, but with love and respect as well. For service freely offered is more precious than anything I could force from you. Do you agree?'

'We do,' all the warriors responded.

'As you are the first company of warriors to do this, I appoint you to ride in the van of my army against my Uncle. For most certainly we are returning to the mainland to challenge him and the dark forces he calls upon.'

Another cheer erupted from the men which carried on for some time as he and Harbona stepped down from the quarter deck and embraced them. They were definitely his men now.

Chapter Forty Nine

Morthrir didn't sleep well during the night and was still awake at dawn, pacing up and down in the confines of the rear cabin, ducking his head now and then to avoid the lanterns hanging from the deckhead above and frustrated with the turn of events. He was startled by a shout and glanced out of the stern window to see a fire arrow arcing its way from the pursuing ship.

He strode across the cabin, flung open the door and yelled for his lieutenant. 'Get that boy strung out on the window frame. Leave him for an hour after they cease the fire arrows. If they do it again, make it two hours. Keep doubling the time till they give up. And make sure you stop his yelling. How do you expect me to think in my cabin when he's making that din directly below me? Report to me in here when that's been done.'

He slammed the door and carried on pacing, then shoved his head out and bellowed for the Captain. He continued his pacing while he waited for the man, smacking his hand on the sides of the cabin in annoyance. The man was incompetent. When he demanded the Captain send for the master Crafter yesterday to rig up an enlarged longbow to counter their pursuer's fire arrows, he was met by some nonsense about this being a bounty hunter not a warship. 'Don't be ridiculous,' Morthrir fumed at him. 'You must come to blows with other bounty hunters when you're after the same artefacts.' But the man stared at him. The Crafter was little better, saying they had no wood on board with the required flexibility. Fancy putting to sea so ill equipped. Their pursuers must have had the right sort.

Wait a minute. Morthrir slumped into a chair, drumming his fingers on the arm and thinking back to when his first army was destroyed at Mount Nastâri. Some warriors escaped and brought news that the Nastrim had developed a longbow with an incredible range and used fire arrows. If Kyros was right and Lenyé was on board that ship, she must have some of those longbows and arrows with her...

He was interrupted by the Captain bursting into the cabin.

'How dare you,' Morthrir scowled at the man. 'Knock first before...'

'But, Sire,' the man was clearly agitated. 'My men have mutinied against my command. They've surrounded the door to this cabin and told me to air their grievances with you.'

'Grievances. What grievances?'

'They know you have artefacts in here from Bara-mâla. This is the first expedition to have ever found anything. According to their contract they're entitled to a bounty payment, and nothing has been forthcoming. Also, they're worried about being pursued and having to deal with fire arrows. They never signed up for any fighting. And if that ship overpowers us and seizes the artefacts, their payout won't happen at all. They've got a living to make, and they want to be treated fairly.'

'I see. And what if I ignore their demand for money?'

'They will lower all the sails and surrender to the ship behind us. They know it's *Brave Heart* and Captain Josiah is respected everywhere as a fair man. He'll see they get something, even if it's shared between the crews of both ships.'

'Get out.'

'But Sire...'

'I said, "*Get out*".'

As the man stumbled through the doorway, he caught a glimpse of the massed sailors outside. He also heard his lieutenant whisper through the skylight.

'Sire. I have my warriors with longbows in a ring around

those sailors so they can't escape. What would you have me do?'

'Demand that they retreat from my cabin door so I can come out and talk to them unhindered.'

He heard the man walk across the poop deck above his head and yell a command. A few minutes later the door opened and the lieutenant stepped into the cabin.

'The sailors are ready for you to address them from the poop deck, Sire.'

'When I've finished talking to the crew, rouse the four Summoners and join me in here. We need to decide what to do.'

'Yes, Sire.'

Morthrir climbed the companionway and stood looking down on the men below him. 'My friends,' he began. 'Your Captain has come to me as though there was no concern in my heart to be generous towards you for the outstanding way in which you have handled this ship and are thereby hastening our return with two artefacts from Bara-mâla. I am sorry that there is a predator behind seeking by whatever means they can to slow us down and steal these precious items. You may know the ship. And you may know the Captain. But you do not know those who have commandeered it and are forcing the Captain, no doubt against his will, to chase us like pirates closing in on a helpless prey. You saw how they destroyed *Tempest* and *Monarch of the Seas*. They are utterly ruthless. If you will continue to handle the ship and help me deter our enemy and get us safely back to Pordé-Sûnca, I promise you there will be a generous payout in excess of any contract you have signed.'

Morthrir watched the men glance at each other, obviously waiting for someone to take the lead.

'How do we know you will honour this?' a sailor called out.

'I have lodged one thousand gold krêons for *Sea Sprite* with the Shipwrights' Guild in Pordé-Sûnca.'

'That money is to cover any excessive damage to this ship,' another spoke up. 'If we are attacked, and *Sea Sprite* is set on fire, we'll need all of it to repair her.'

'And we never signed up to fight against any ships,' someone else shouted.

'If you're worried about being attacked by our pursuers, let me put your fears to rest. I will post my warriors amongst you, to ensure that no harm comes to you and to protect these artefacts from piracy on the High Seas. They will do all the fighting.'

There was some half-hearted clapping and one or two cheers but no one was particularly enthusiastic.

'I assume you are agreeing to my terms,' Morthrir continued. 'Your Captain also told me what would happen if we do not reach an agreement today. Any man who attempts to slow this ship down and betray us to our enemies will be strung up from the nearest yard arm as an example to everyone else. My warriors will enforce it. Is that clear? I suggest you go away and think carefully about my offer. You are dismissed.'

The men broke into small groups, muttering amongst themselves and occasionally glancing up at Morthrir and then at the warriors still encircling them with longbows poised.

He returned to the cabin to find the Summoners waiting for him, and heard sharp words of command and the tread of many feet as the sailors returned to their posts. The lieutenant joined them and closed the door.

Morthrir sat in his chair, drumming his fingers on the arm. 'Lieutenant, I do not trust this crew. Post your warriors so that they're guarding the sailors and forcing them to perform their duties whether they like it or not.'

'Yes, Sire.'

He was about to open the meeting for discussion when Nastâr appeared through the stern window. Morthrir swung round in his chair to face the great being. 'Well?'

'The pursuing ship is called *Brave Heart*.'

'I know that.'

'And Lenyé is definitely on board.'

'I know that as well.'

'But I saw no sign of Kyros.'

'So he must have perished in *Monarch of the Seas* after all.'

'I don't think so, My Lord. I flew on to find the other ship, *Flying Cloud,* was delayed at the Ziggurat with rudder problems. And I sensed Kyros' presence very strongly.'

'You mean, he's on board *Flying Cloud*?'

'That's the only conclusion I can come to.'

'They must've taken him prisoner. But if he's still alive, what about releasing Vashtani to me?'

'Kyros is too far away, My Lord, to have any effect on your instant-travel method now. Vashtani will come when you call.'

'Hmph!' Morthrir drummed his fingers on the arm of the chair again thinking about using Vashtani to seize Lenyé straight away, but decided on trying another approach first. She was close enough for others to do it instead. A plan was forming in his mind…

'*Flying Cloud* cannot help in capturing Lenyé,' he continued, 'but we could do it with just this ship, if we surprised them.'

'How?' Jumar-jé intervened.

Morthrir scowled at the Summoner before turning to his lieutenant. 'No doubt *Brave Heart* was lulled into a false sense of security by our actions last night.'

'Yes, Sire.'

'They will assume we'll continue on our present course tonight. Do you have any material to make fire arrows?'

'There must be something on board we can use, Sire.'

'Good. I will order the Captain to sail without lights again tonight. I want your warriors to be prepared for a night attack at close range with ordinary longbows.'

'Yes, Sire.'

Chapter Fifty

In the morning Beth was astonished at how easily the woman swung herself up into the saddle, despite her age. It was so natural; she appeared to be bred to it. Who was this person who had hidden herself away in such a remote cottage and cut herself off from the rest of the world? And, more importantly, why didn't she want anyone to know where she was?

'I used to live in a palace,' the woman leaned down slightly to talk to Beth while she adjusted the reins. 'Called the boys by their first names. I was the only one allowed to do that.'

Then the woman was off, straight into a fast trot down the track at the back of the cottage, leading away from the main path that Beth and Ishi-mi-réjá had used, but still heading North.

'Slow down,' Beth yelled, and started chasing after her, aware that Ishi-mi-réjá was following.

'Come back, boys,' she heard the woman shout. 'Dareth, you're such a bad example to your brother. You know he can't ride as well as you. Alkram. Look out! You'll be off and flat on your back before you know it.'

The woman alternated between a slow canter and a fast trot. Beth struggled to keep up with her as the horse disappeared round a bend, but could still hear the shouts to the woman's imaginary companions. No doubt she was reliving an actual scene out of her past. But why use names from the Royal Family? The horse carried on, out of sight as the path looped its way past clumps of trees, but still within earshot.

The chase went on for miles. Beth heard a scream, pelted

round a sharp twist in the track into a clearing and nearly collided with the horse. She stopped, leaned against a tree and gasped for breath till Ishi-mi-réjá caught up with her. The horse had its head down, reins trailing on the ground and was cropping some woodland grass. The woman was on her knees, bending forwards with her face to the ground.

'Oh no. It's here. Right here. Where is my little boy? My poor baby boy.'

Beth knelt down and slid her arm about the woman's shoulders. 'Are you saying your baby is here?'

'Yes. Yes. It's my secret. But no one must know.'

'So why did you bring us here?'

'I didn't bring you here. The horse did. And you followed. I must see him. One last time, before I go down to the grave as a ruined woman.'

Beth watched as she lurched to her feet and stumbled around the clearing.

'He's here somewhere. Oh, help me find him. Where have they hidden him?'

Beth ran over to her. 'How can I help?'

'There.' The woman sank to her knees and started scrabbling amongst the dry leaves with her bare hands. 'Where the ground sinks away. Can't you see? Even after all this time, it dips down in a depression. He must be here. Oh, help me.'

Beth glanced across to Ishi-mi-réjá, but already she was taking off her backpack and undoing the straps on the spades before she joined them.

'Spades. Yes, yes. We'll find him quickly now. Oh, help me.'

Beth and Ishi-mi-réjá were quickly through the layer of leaves and loosening up the fine dark humus of countless years of decay before digging down into the harder soil. There was a clink against one of the blades and the woman was scrabbling away with her hands to reveal something solid and darkly yellow. They both dropped their spades and helped her, only to uncover a skull.

'He's dead. He's dead. I knew he was dead. Oh, why did he have to die? Such a beautiful baby boy.'

They carried on digging with the spades and scooping away with their hands till they'd revealed the intact skeleton of a baby.

'He's mine, he's mine,' the woman began clawing at the bones to loosen them completely from the last of the clinging soil and gather them into her lap.

'Wait,' Ishi-mi-réjá raced to her backpack and returned with a shawl. 'Gather the bones up into this.' She laid the shawl on the woman's lap and helped Beth place the bones on top, roughly in the shape of the skeleton. Beth watched in amazement as the woman drew the edges of the shawl together and tied them up so tenderly and sat rocking backwards and forwards on her haunches moaning to herself.

'He's mine. He's mine. Oh, why did I ever part with him?'

Beth slipped her arms about the woman's neck and let her sob against her shoulder. Then she heard the clink of a spade and glanced up to see Ishi-mi-réjá begin to fill in the hole but stop at the sound.

'There's more here.'

Beth left the woman sobbing and helped Ishi-mi-réjá uncover another skeleton.

'Looks like the remains of a young woman. What do you think, Beth?'

'You're right. There's some damage to the ribs over her heart. She must have been injured somehow.'

'Or murdered.'

Beth shuddered at Ishi-mi-réjá's words. She went over and slipped her arms around the woman's neck again. 'Tell me what happened here.'

'Nothing.'

'Who is this other woman?'

'There was no other woman. Just me and my baby boy.'

'Was she your daughter?'

'I never had a daughter. I am no one. Nobody would marry me and have children by me after what happened.'

'So why was she killed?' Beth persisted.

'There never was another woman. Just me and my… Another woman? Killed? Oh, no. He said she was only a girl. Is that what they did to her? To silence her. How could they be so cruel?'

'Was the baby her son?'

'He was my boy. My baby boy.'

'Who are they, and what did they do?'

'No. No. I cannot say. He made me promise. If he ever found out I've told anyone, he would come for me. Even after all these years. He will find me.'

Beth heard Ishi-mi-réjá's quiet voice. 'You have to trust us. Whatever happened here cannot be kept secret any more.'

Beth watched Ishi-mi-réjá use the sharp edge of a spade blade to hack down a small sapling and shove it into the ground at the head of the grave, then begin to scoop the soil back over the remaining skeleton. 'At least we can find this again.' She leaned forwards and offered her hand to pull the woman up. 'You must trust us to help you.'

'No. I will not speak of this to anyone.'

'There has to be someone,' Beth whispered into the woman's ear. 'You cannot remain silent any longer.'

'Very well. I will give an account to the King when he sits on his Throne. But only if you promise not to tell anyone else what you've seen here. Especially that cousin of yours. Promise me?'

'I promise,' Beth spoke softly, and felt the woman slump in her arms.

'Then bring me to the King.'

Chapter Fifty One

Lenyé was up with the dawn. *Sea Sprite* hadn't increased her lead during the night. But as soon as she ordered fire arrows the boy was lashed to the stern window. This time he was gagged. Once her crossbowmen ceased, he was left there for an hour before they brought him in. She tried later, but the boy was out again within minutes and left for two hours into the blaze of the noonday sun. She couldn't keep doing this or he would be exposed to the glare of the sun until late afternoon. But if they used him for a human shield against fire arrow attacks, at least she knew he was still alive.

The day dragged on into another black night with her quarry infuriatingly close. She ordered no lights and refrained from the occasional fire arrow to check *Sea Sprite* was holding her course, hoping to fool them there would be no more activity at night. Instead, she had her crossbowmen draw back their bowstrings and ready for action. Wilf and the others lit arrows but kept them hidden behind the gunwale. Lenyé wanted enough for several rounds to surprise her enemy with a sudden barrage, and in the ensuing confusion try to shorten the gap and board her.

Morthrir paced up and down on *Sea Sprite's* quarter deck in the pitch black of night. There were no lights, except a shaded lantern for the helmsman. But nothing from *Brave Heart*, not even a glimmer. Was *Brave Heart* holding on her expected course?

He trusted his lieutenant to lead the warriors in the dark. But as for that fool of a Captain. How did Morthrir know the man was steering in the right direction? Those sailors would probably carry out their threat and bring down the sails at the first volley of fire arrows. Did the lieutenant have enough men to guard the sailors and attack *Brave Heart*? Morthrir expected the surprise to carry them through and allow their boarding party to swarm onto *Brave Heart's* decks. If there were no mishaps, his warriors would seize Lenyé, bring her aboard *Sea Sprite*, and they could sail for Pordé-Sûnca in the confusion.

He ran through his own plans for escape in case things went badly wrong and *Brave Heart* overpowered them. The four Summoners had the boy bound hand and foot and tied onto the bundle of *Imbrésonite* in the main cabin. One of them also had the bag with the Crown. Nastâr was posted at the cabin door. Morthrir could race across the deck, fling open the door and command Vashtani to whisk them all away to the Vault of Malrema in Terrazarema. That was the safest place to keep such a precious cargo. Nastâr would stay here and fight; no one could withstand the great being. Whatever happened, Nastâr's orders were to capture Lenyé and bring her to Terrazarema. As far as Morthrir was concerned, she was the most important prize at the moment. He would attend to Kyros another time.

Lenyé tried to spot any giveaway signs, or even a hint of *Sea Sprite's* wake. She stole between the crossbowmen, whispering instructions. 'Now,' her voice was just loud enough for the men to hear, and she saw the tips of the fire arrows move as Wilf and the others set them in place. The men loosed off five arrows from each crossbow in rapid succession and the blaze lit up quite an area; but *Sea Sprite* wasn't there.

Chapter Fifty Two

That night Rafé tried calming his mind by watching the flames of his campfire, but before he was ready to probe for the snake he felt the cobra's mind looking into his. How could this be? Did the cobra have power over him? He tried to break the connection, but couldn't. It was as if he was a tiny bird being mesmerised by this deadly killer.

'Who are you?' the voice was clearer now. 'And why do you seek to control me?'

Rafé tried shutting his mind to the questioning, but the voice in his head was becoming more insistent.

'Why are you spying on Lenyé? Every time you control my eyes, you look at her and ask questions about what she is doing.'

'But, I...'

'What is your name?'

The thoughts in Rafé's head were overwhelming. It kept repeating, 'Your name... your name... your name?'

'No. No.'

'Once I know your name, I will let you go.'

He felt like a rabbit caught in a beam of light from a lantern in a night-time hunt. The gaze of the cobra was dazzling. He covered his eyes, but couldn't help forming his name in his mind. Suddenly the blaze vanished.

Chapter Fifty Three

Lenyé was distraught as the last fire arrow disappeared into the waves and darkness closed in around *Brave Heart*. Where was her Uncle's ship? She raced to the main deck companionway and roused more lookouts to climb aloft. 'Chuah-te-mok, get up in the sky and try to find *Sea Sprite*.'

As the eagle took off, she was startled by a sudden volley of ordinary-sized fire arrows embedding in their own yard arms and setting the main course alight; followed by a shout from one of the lookouts, 'There she is!'

Lenyé whipped round. 'Captain, put your helm over hard a-starboard.' She could just see a glimmer from *Sea Sprite's* bow wave. In a flash she realised they must have tacked in a circle under cover of darkness and were now racing towards *Brave Heart's* starboard quarter.

The flames ripped through the huge sail above her, and Lenyé felt a loss of power as the ship slowed and turned.

'Cut that sail free,' she shouted. 'Fire fighters, get aloft. You sailors,' she pointed at a group that came running at her urgent command, 'hoist a replacement sail. I must have that power available when I need more speed.'

At least the blazing canvas gave her enough light to see by.

As *Brave Heart* prepared to manoeuvre, the crew furled the main sails so they were going about under fore course and topgallants alone.

'Stern crossbows,' she yelled, 'loose your fire arrows as you bear. Aim for the jib and foremast sails.' She turned and shouted to the other crossbowmen, 'Bow-chasers, load with the heavy duty bolts and wait for my signal. You others, get your barrels fitted with arrows and loose them immediately afterwards.'

She grabbed at Wilf as he raced past and caught him by the shoulder. 'Get as many barrels loaded fore and aft and light the hemp. We're going to let her pass on the starboard side and tack across her stern. I've only got this one chance to hit her where they least expect and hit her hard. We're going to rake their stern like we did to *Tempest*. You understand?'

Wilf nodded and ran on.

She ordered up the kegs of resin and molasses and had the swinging ropes rigged in place.

Lenyé felt the check in pace as *Brave Heart* turned into the wind, maintaining headway as her quarry raced past. The stern crossbowmen poured fire arrows in quick succession into *Sea Sprite's* exposed starboard side, while her soldiers in the crosstrees rained down fire arrows from their ordinary longbows. She held her breath as *Brave Heart* tacked across *Sea Sprite's* stern. She pointed to her crossbowmen, 'Bow-chasers, now,' and she brought her hand down. The heavy duty bolts crashed through the upper and lower windows in a shower of flying glass, followed by a volley of fire arrows from the other two crossbows. They replaced the barrels and loosed again as the kegs of resin and molasses were released from the swinging ropes and hurled in. The upper and lower cabins erupted in an inferno as flames came pouring out of the stern windows and licking up through the skylights.

As *Brave Heart* turned again and picked up the wind from directly behind, she surged alongside the stricken ship, her sailors hurling grappling hooks to close the gap and haul the two hulls together. Lenyé shouted to the soldiers aloft, 'Switch to ordinary arrows. Leave the sailors and bring down their warriors.' Then she was across with the rest of the boarding party and fighting her way towards the stern. She had to find

Ramâno and rescue him at all costs.

Lenyé saw Chuah-te-mok up amongst *Sea Sprite's* crosstrees dislodging longbowmen. Ariella and Mamma Uza-Mâté followed her while Ra-Na-Jiri slithered ahead.

'There she is,' a warrior yelled. 'The one Morthrir wants!'

She found herself hemmed in by a ring of warriors no longer suffering from seasickness, but armed and ready for battle. A man rushed at her, but she parried his blade and thrust him into the path of two more attacking from behind. Then she blocked and deflected and sidestepped a myriad of blades as she hurled herself at the warriors to break through their line, conscious of the lioness and she-bear flinging themselves into the fray using teeth and claws and roaring and snarling. Even Chuah-te-mok was on them, talons extended, and Ra-Na-Jiri was striking at any attacking from behind.

Most fell to her sword or the animal-friends and she hacked her way up to the main cabin, flung open the door and was met by a blast of intense heat. But the cobra was in before she could stop him.

'Nobody there,' he hissed as he slid out a few minutes later.

She was about to try the cabin beneath, but was confronted by a great shadow, black against the raging flames, bigger than a man, even bigger than Vashtani, with huge wings that fanned the crackling flames behind it. Ariella and Mamma Uza-Mâté roared and sprang past Lenyé, but she grabbed them and pulled them back. 'You cannot prevail against this enemy.' She thrust them aside and drew both her swords.

'I am Nastâr. Morthrir told me you are the one who despatched those who bore my name in the Waking World to Elasis and thereby rendered them useless in the ongoing struggle to rid us of the True King. You are therefore doubly my enemy.'

Lenyé edged sideways with both swords raised. She adopted an attacking stance, and raced at her adversary. 'You must be a fallen Great En-luchés, and are subject to the swords I bear.'

'No sword from the Waking World has power over me.'

'Really? Vashtani was. This one is the Sword of Justice,' and she lunged at Nastâr with her left arm extended.

The great being leaped back but she kept advancing till he was pinned against the outer bulkhead of the rear cabin.

'This won't be the last you see of me,' Nastâr snarled at her. 'I haven't been released from the bottom of the Pit to be held at bay by a mere girl!'

Lenyé stared down his glare and smiled to herself in grim satisfaction as Nastâr disappeared.

Ra-Na-Jiri slithered up to her, 'No sign of anyone in the lower cabin either.'

She shook her head, 'What? Where's Ramâno, then?'

'I don't know.'

Lenyé spotted the Captain surrounded by some of his sailors and cut her way through the press of fighting. She grabbed him by the collar and thrust him up against the poop deck companionway. 'My Uncle and that boy. Where are they?'

'I don't know.'

'You must have seen them.'

The Captain shook his head. 'Morthrir ordered me out of the main cabin to begin the attack, and I haven't seen them since.'

'Could they have climbed out of the stern windows and used a boat?'

'No. All the boats are still lashed in place.'

'Someone must have helped them.'

'Your Uncle had the boy and four men with him in the main cabin. And some artefacts from Bara-mâla. The crew expected a handsome payout, but nothing was forthcoming, so they mutinied. Your Uncle sent in his warriors with drawn swords and longbows and it's been a slave-ship ever since. None of my men would have helped him.'

'What about the warriors?'

'Doubt it. They've been too focused on attacking your ship.'

The man was obviously telling the truth. She relaxed her grip on his jacket. 'I can offer you and your crew safe passage to Pordé-Sûnca. But no trying to take over *Brave Heart*.'

'My thanks for your kindness. But we'll stay here and salvage *Sea Sprite*. She's all we've got to make our living.'

Lenyé rounded up *Sea Sprite's* sailors and warriors and kept them in two separate groups while her soldiers searched the ship. There was no sign of her Uncle, or Ramâno. None of the crew or warriors had seen them either.

She gave the order to return to *Brave Heart* and left the Captain to his salvage work.

Lenyé was baffled. Her Uncle had either taken a longboat, but the Captain disproved that; or jumped overboard rather than be captured, but that was highly unlikely; or he had some power that enabled him to move between locations without anyone else seeing. If that was the case, he would most likely attempt to get back to Terrazarema. Was that where he intended to carry out the child sacrifice? She ordered *Brave Heart* to replace any damaged sails and set a course heading North-East to run before the following wind as fast as possible.

The burning ship dwindled into the distance as the night wore on.

'Captain,' she called to the figure at the starboard railing of the quarter deck. 'How long till we get to Pordé-Sûnca?'

She heard him sniff the air. 'Nightfall tomorrow.'

Lenyé called up to the eagle. She'd been wondering for some time where *Flying Cloud* was. Kyros couldn't be far behind. Surely they would steer for that burning wreck? 'Chuah-te-mok, try and find *Flying Cloud*. They need to rescue some sailors.' She watched him disappear into the ink-black sky.

Whatever the outcome of the stricken ship, Lenyé had to return to Pordé-Sûnca as quickly as possible and find Ramâno before her Uncle carried out his threat.

Chapter Fifty Four

Kyros leaned against the gunwale of the quarter deck on *Flying Cloud* and watched the waves race past. *Flying Cloud* was making good speed running before a Southwesterly breeze, but with no chance of overhauling *Brave Heart* and *Sea Sprite*. Not even the lookout clinging to the foremast crosstrees could see so much as a hint of sail on the horizon ahead.

Harbona talked to the warriors earlier and discovered there were nearly one hundred and fifty on board: three platoons out of four; the other was aboard *Sea Sprite*. The original regiment of warriors that chased them numbered one thousand. That meant eight hundred were camped outside Pordé-Sûnca, with orders to detain Lenyé and himself. If Lenyé had destroyed *Sea Sprite* while rescuing Ramâno and recovering the Crown, she would be caught if she landed at the port.

He looked round as Harbona joined him.

'I've set the warriors to follow their fitness drill, My Lord. Can't have them going soft because we're at sea.'

Kyros smiled. 'Will they remain loyal to us when we reach Pordé-Sûnca and are stopped by their comrades?'

'I can persuade those warriors to join us as well. They don't know ours have switched allegiance, and won't hinder us.'

'That's true. What if they've captured Lenyé and the others?'

'We'll cross that bridge when we get there.'

Kyros thought back to his conversation with Lenyé at one of their campsites when they were trekking to Pordé-Sûnca.

'And Marie-anna?' he glanced away thinking how best to put

this. 'You're closeness with her the other night when she screamed as Ra-Na-Jiri flared his hood; was that deliberate?'

'I put my hand on hers because she was scared by the cobra.'

'So you have no further interest in her?'

'Why do you ask?' Harbona seemed surprised at the question.

'Lenyé told me Marie-anna is very attracted to you.'

'I cannot go down that path, My Lord. I tried marriage once and it ended in sorrow. I have devoted myself to my work ever since.'

'That was a long a time ago. Surely you need the gentleness of another woman to make you feel whole again?'

'I cannot mislead her as to my intentions. It was wrong of me to sit so close that night.'

Kyros decided to push Harbona further with one last plea.

'And Ramâno? He needs a Father.'

'I cannot do that either. I can teach him warrior skills, but a Father's role is too hard for me.'

'Harbona, at the moment, he's like *Flying Cloud* without a rudder. The Captain told me the ship could sail at reduced speed in a calm sea with a following wind. But if the wind changed or the seas became rough, *Flying Cloud* wouldn't stand a chance.'

'So another Father's influence is like repairing the rudder?'

'Exactly. Ramâno is responding to your strength as a man and a warrior, but he needs your affection and love as well.'

'He's told me a lot about you, My Lord. And how he wants to be a Healer and take after you. Surely…'

'He's torn between the two of us; but only needs one Father.'

Kyros was roused in the dead of night by a tapping on the window of his cabin and realised it was Chuah-te-mok. He pointed to his cabin door and emerged onto the quarter deck to find the eagle waiting for him.

Chuah-te-mok bobbed his head. 'Kyros, I bring terrible news. I was able to speak to Ramâno aboard *Sea Sprite* as he was tied to the stern windows. He overheard words in the cabin above that Morthrir needs more power from Abbérron to force Lenyé to come back to him and be his bride. They think offering a child sacrifice will release this power. When they mentioned his name the poor boy was nearly sick he was so shocked. I tried to undo his bonds so he could jump into the sea and let *Brave Heart* pick him up, but they saw me and fought me off with lances and bows.'

'Where is he now?'

'No one knows for certain. *Brave Heart* caught up with them last night and set fire to the ship. But when Lenyé boarded her there was no sign of him. Your Uncle and the *Imbrésonite* and the Crown and the boy have all disappeared. None of the crew saw him go. Lenyé thinks your Uncle has power to travel swiftly wherever he wants to and has taken the boy straight to Terrazarema. That's where she plans to go herself as quickly as possible. She's left the burning hulk for you to rescue the crew and warriors and is sailing for Pordé-Sûnca.'

'How far ahead is the hulk?'

'A day and a half, maybe two at your present speed.'

'And how far away is she from Pordé-Sûnca?'

'*Brave Heart* should be there by nightfall tomorrow.'

'Fly to her as fast as you can.' Briefly he explained about the rest of the warriors surrounding the port. 'She's sailing straight into a trap.'

Chapter Fifty Five

Morthrir stood on the altar in the Vault of Malrema and studied the four Summoners. One of them had the bag with the Crown in his hand, and the boy was still strapped to the bundle of *Imbrésonite* where it lay on the floor next to the altar. He was startled by the sudden appearance of Nastâr.

'You were right, My Lord, to make provision for a quick escape. That girl wields the Sword of Justice. I have no power to capture her while it's in her possession.'

'If you can't do it, how am I supposed to regain her?'

'I don't know, My Lord. I was not released to seize wayward brides, but to destroy Kyros. Now that I have sensed his presence, I'm not surprised Lammista-ké is worried.'

'Very well. Go back to *Flying Cloud* and deal with him.'

As soon as the great being had disappeared, Morthrir glared at the four Summoners. 'Cut that boy free and have him imprisoned in one of the upstairs rooms. See that he gets food and water; but make sure there's no chance for him to escape.'

'Yes, Sire,' Jumar-jé spoke for all of them.

'I need him to increase my power with Abbérron. We will hold the sacrifice once Nastâr has dealt with Kyros.'

Chapter Fifty Six

Lenyé gripped the rail to mount the companionway leading to the quarter deck on *Brave Heart* and head for the cabin to catch up on some sleep, but felt a hand clutching her wrist. She stopped and turned to find it was Marie-anna; her friend's face very dark in the glimmer from the helmsman's lantern, with only the whites of her eyes and the occasional flash of teeth showing.

'Ramâno,' Maria-anna whispered. 'Where is he?'

'I didn't find him on board *Sea Sprite*.'

'Then what have they done with him? We need to go back and search the sea around the burning ship.'

'Marie-anna,' she knew she would have to break the eagle's news to her at some stage, but was dreading how to begin. 'Come and sit with me and talk.'

'I must know!'

Lenyé caught her by the hand, led her up the companionway and sat with her back against the port gunwale. She drew Marie-anna down with her, but the woman was restless, trying to break away from her grasp.

'Marie-anna, listen to me. He's with my Uncle.'

'How can you be so sure? Did you see a longboat pulling away? And why aren't we chasing it?'

'No. All the longboats were still lashed in place.'

'They must have thrown him overboard.'

'Ramâno is too important for my Uncle to get rid of like that.'

'What are you talking about?'

'You saw the way they used him as a human shield to stop us

loosing fire arrows at them?'

'That was terrible. Your Uncle must think my boy's life is cheap and it doesn't matter what they do to him.'

'He's using him as a hostage to try and capture me.'

'Why?'

'He wanted me to be his bride, but I refused. I don't think he's given up, though.'

'How do you know all this?'

'Chuah-te-mok brought me news when he tried to rescue your son.'

'What news?'

Lenyé took a deep breath and spoke as calmly as she knew how. 'Ramâno overheard a conversation about releasing more spiritual power to capture me...'

'How does my boy fit into that? Tell me.'

'My Uncle is going to use him as a child sacrifice.'

Lenyé saw the shock in Marie-anna's face before she drew her legs up under her and rocked backwards and forwards on her heels, moaning. 'Not my son. Not Ramâno. Please. Why him? What has he done to deserve this? I can't believe anyone can be so cruel. What does the death of an innocent boy achieve? I don't understand. Why him? And why me? He's all I've got...'

Lenyé drew Marie-anna to her and cradled the woman in her arms.

'I cannot believe the True King would allow this to happen. He's only just healed my son's legs. But to let him be healed for such a short time before he is killed by some monster like your Uncle...' she broke off, sobbing. 'How can the True King treat me like this? I would rather the True King had never healed my son. Or that I was dead. Why do I have to go through this?'

'Marie-anna...'

'It's all the True King's fault. Your Uncle must know that Ramâno was the boy who was healed, and helped Kyros as the Healer. If he arrested me for just singing about what the True

King had done for my son, he must be taking revenge on Ramâno by killing him!'

Lenyé was fighting back the tears herself. Ramâno's life was on a knife-edge. She didn't know when her Uncle would carry out his threat. It could happen at any time. And she was also fearful for Marie-anna's state of mind.

'Marie-anna. You have to let go of your son and trust him into the keeping of the True King. We both do. I cannot answer your questions. Or remove your doubts and fears. But the True King is good. None of us know when we will face death, or in what circumstances. But the True King will guard us and bring us into his presence. He will do this for Ramâno. I promise you.'

'I cannot accept this. I can't. If Ramâno dies, I die. For I will have nothing. I wish I was back in the Central Square, doing my shopping, living an ordinary life working in your Uncle's kitchens, and none of this had ever happened.'

'Marie-anna, you cannot change the past. Your son is a walking miracle and a sign to everyone of the good things that come from the True King. I will not let you deny what has happened.' She held Marie-anna a little longer till the racking sobs subsided and the woman was quiet in her arms. 'If you can't let go of your son, are you at least prepared to trust me?'

There was no answer.

'Well?'

'Even if I do, I need to know where my son is.'

'Because of this power my Uncle has, I think they're in Terrazarema now.'

'So how are we going to get Ramâno back?'

'I cannot answer that question. But if I have your trust, then at least I can start making some plans and work out a course of action. Are you prepared to do that for me?'

She felt Marie-anna nod against her shoulder and heard the faint, 'Yes,' in her ear.

Chapter Fifty Seven

It took Quinn the rest of the day until well after nightfall, when he camped, and most of the following day to get to the Hunting Lodge at Fantrios. He kept within the shelter of the woods, watching and listening and sniffing the air and studying the frontage. The building was only one storey high with a pitched roof, the red tiles weathered to a dull tone against the white of the walls. Not many rooms, he recalled: a lounge and dining room either side of the main door at the front; an entrance hall between them leading to a reception area where people removed their boots and jackets; two sets of bedrooms either side and kitchens at the back. There was a stable in a separate building beyond for twenty horses. The whole place looked deserted.

He was so excited at the prospect of finding his parents at long last that it was a bitter disappointment. Supposing they weren't here after all. Maybe it was better that he came on his own: Beth would be devastated.

He was about to creep to his right and make his way down that side of the Lodge, when a movement distracted him. His eyes were well adjusted to the dim light in the woods and he saw a warrior by one of the trees close at hand.

Quinn shrank back at the sound of a bugle and a squad of warriors marched from behind the back of the building and stepped into the woods. He watched as the warrior close to him was replaced, and was able to work out the other points where more warriors stood. The relieved warriors formed into a squad and marched back behind the Lodge. Quinn checked the sun and waited. These warriors were changed two hours latter. So his parents must be here. They wouldn't guard it so well otherwise.

Apart from the doors at the front and back there was no other way in, except through the roof if he removed some of the tiles. As dusk fell he crept round to the back avoiding the warriors at their hidden posts and emerged to see a cluster of warriors coming out of the open back door and crossing the well-worn path to disappear into the stable block. Two others walked across from the stables, laughing and chatting. That must be where most of them were housed in the grooms' lodgings above the stables.

He skirted round beyond the stable block and came up the other side of the Lodge. It was too dark for anyone to see him now, so he used the opportunity to scramble up the drainpipe at the corner and climb onto the roof. He felt around and found a loose tile and eased it to and fro till it came out in his hand. He laid it on the roof and let it slide down gently into the gutter to stop it falling, then eased out the next tile. He had to remove the two above in order to make a hole big enough to crawl through.

He gripped the edges of the tiles on either side of the hole, slid his feet in first and felt for the rafters before letting go of the tiles with one hand and swinging himself in. It was pitch-black, except for a faint grey smudge showing the hole in the tiles. He crawled across the rafters on hands and knees till he was over the rear bedroom on his side of the building. This was going to be trial and error, but he couldn't think of any other way.

Quinn knocked gently on the lath and plaster between the rafters. Nothing happened. He tried a little louder. Still nothing. At the third attempt, a voice called out, 'What's that noise?'

'Who's there?' Quinn whispered.

'King Dareth.'

'Father!' He couldn't believe he'd found them first time.

'Is that you, Quinn?'

'Yes.'

'Your Mother's here with me.'

'We've come to rescue you.'

'We?'

'Just me at the moment. Beth's on her way.'

'What about the others?'

'As far as I know, Lenyé's raising an army to challenge Uncle Morthrir. There's no news about Kyros, and the rest are all imprisoned at the palace by Uncle Morthrir. We've got to get you out and decide what to do.'

'You'll have to be quick, then. One of the more friendly warriors, called Paco, let on that they were moving us again soon. Wouldn't say exactly when or where to, and was very evasive after that, so it must mean bad news.'

'Did you say, Paco?'

'Yes.'

'He's a friend of Beth's.' Quinn was about to continue when he heard the turning of a lock.

'Shh,' his Father whispered. 'Someone's coming.'

Quinn crept back to the hole, eased himself out onto the roof, replaced the tiles and began to climb down the drain pipe. He'd found out which room his parents were in and he'd also learned that Paco was still around. If only he could get that warrior to meet up with Beth, they must be able to work out a plan.

He slid to the ground, but was so excited that he failed to pay close attention and landed awkwardly, scrunching some gravel under his heel.

'Who goes there?'

He heard the sliding of a shutter on a lantern and was caught in a sudden beam of light. As he dived to his left to escape, he felt a hand grip his collar from behind and was held fast.

Chapter Fifty Eight

Lenyé lay on her cot in the cabin of *Brave Heart* but was too worried about Ramâno to sleep. She kept seeing him strapped to that window frame with his arms and legs spread out and the sun blazing down on him. But *Sea Sprite* was reduced to a burning wreck and Ramâno had disappeared. Where was he?

Suddenly she was flying over the sea, crossing the coast, soaring over the Plains of Lohr and the Forest at the head of Lake Sanchéso and dipping towards Terrazarema. She floated above the palace before plunging down to the largest cellar and hovering in a corner just below the vaulted ceiling.

The room was black, except for a light emanating from her Uncle in the middle of the floor by a pile of stones. There were strange white markings on the floor. Figures in brown robes and four in white, black, red and grey stood in a circle with hoods hiding their faces in shadow. Six Dé-monos, including Vashtani, were with them. Nastâr stood at the Eastern point of the circle. She saw Ramâno bound hand and foot, lying on his back on the pile of stones, and shivered with fear. The whole spectacle felt evil: the stones were an altar and this was the child sacrifice.

The figure in white robes stepped forwards, unbuttoned Ramâno's shirt and pulled it open so that his chest was revealed.

Her Uncle held a long dagger. She watched in horror as he raised his hand, and heard him speak: 'My Lord, Abbérron. I adjure you, by the shed blood of this child sacrifice, to break the protection surrounding Lenyé and bring her to me once again, so that she may be my bride.' He plunged the dagger straight into Ramâno's heart.

Lenyé felt an ice-cold stab of pain shoot through her as the boy jack-knifed into a sitting position, his bonds melting away as he raised his hands in supplication, his eyes pleading with her: 'Help me!' She felt the blow again and again, and saw the boy jerk up twice more before collapsing back and lying limp on the stones: all life gone from him.

She was shocked to see the great being unfold its wings and lunge forwards, grabbing her by the throat and pulling her down to the altar. The boy had disappeared and the being held her in his place and she felt the stones digging into her back. Her Uncle ran the middle finger of his left hand along the blade of the dagger in the blood of his victim.

'With this blood,' she felt his finger trace a circle on her forehead and draw the six-pointed shape of a hexacle inside it, 'I seal you as mine. Come to me, for this time, you shall surely be my bride!'

Lenyé awoke and found herself drenched in sweat. She sat up and wiped her face with her hands, expecting to see blood, but there was nothing. Where was she? It was dark, but not as dark as the cellar: the pale light of dawn was creeping through the stern windows of a ship. She slumped back in relief: she was in her cot onboard *Brave Heart* and it was only a dream. She shivered and drew the bedclothes close about her.

Then she caught a glimpse of the True King's face, but he wasn't smiling. 'What you have witnessed is an abomination to me and shows the depths of evil to which these men will stoop. You have to destroy them. But remember Yanantha's words: *"Not by might or human strength shall the final victory be won…"*. These powers are too great for humankind to challenge. Only through me and upholding my Name can you prevail. Lenyé, this is your calling, and the honour granted to you. Do not fail me in this.'

Chapter Fifty Nine

The following day Kyros paced up and down on the quarter deck of *Flying Cloud* as they sailed North-East. What was trying to tear his dream out of him during that storm, and had it gone with the collapsing of the great wave?

He looked up and saw a black cloud approach, surrounding a dark speck of such malevolence that Kyros felt he would be sucked up from the deck to be consumed by it in mid air.

He heard the whisper of the True King in his heart: "*This is Nastâr, released by your Uncle to destroy you. He is the fallen Great En-luchés from whom the Nastrim took their name. As the Nastrim struggled with their two conflicting inner natures, he represents the struggle of the human heart: to be your own master or follow me. Destroy him and you will release my people*".

The cloud of darkness swarmed about the ship. 'Oh, my King. Guard the hearts and minds of these men. For they do not know how to defend themselves against the Dé-monos yet.'

He was distracted by Nastâr dropping from the sky, settling on the deck in front of him and folding his wings.

'What do we have here? A ship filled with men newly converted to your cause? They will not last long against me.'

'Be gone, in the Name of the True King.'

Nastâr threw back his head and laughed. 'I have heard those words before. Only when someone greater than me appears can my activities be stopped. But there is no one strong enough. We will meet again.' With that, he spread his wings and flew off.

Chapter Sixty

It was still daylight when Beth slipped round to the rear of the stables at Fantrios and peered through the gateway that riders used. She left Ishi-mi-réjá with the horse to take the old woman to Terrazarema at their own pace. But the image of that woman's face lingered in her mind and she could still feel the texture of that flaky skin. She thrust her thoughts aside to concentrate on how to get into the Lodge and rescue her parents.

Beth stiffened as she saw a warrior polishing a pair of boots and recognised Paco. She whistled softly. Paco raised his head, beckoned her over and ushered her into the empty stable behind him, partly closing the bottom of the door to keep her hidden yet still able to talk.

'I've been waiting for you. Thought you'd be along soon. Ever since your cousin was caught snooping around the Lodge last night, I knew you wouldn't be far away.'

'Where is he? Is he all right?'

'He's locked in one of the bedrooms,' Paco gestured with his arm, 'on that side of the Lodge. Your parents are in the one next to him, right on the corner. King Dareth and his wife are in the corner on this side. Morthrir's wife is in the one next to them.'

'Aunt Faria? What's she doing here?'

'The Captain at Onadestra was told to include her for her own protection. Your Uncle didn't say what from. It was whispered that your parents were going to disappear and never be seen again.'

'We knew something was going to happen to our parents, but

not Aunt Faria.'

'Maybe his wife was making things difficult for him and he wanted to dispose of her at the same time.'

'That's terrible. How can I rescue them all?'

'Since I failed to get you out at Onadestra, I owe you a favour. I'm on late guard duty the night after tomorrow. I'll hide the keys amongst the jackets hanging on the wooden pegs by the back door. Make sure you replace them or I'm in trouble.'

'Why are you doing this for me?'

'You once said,' Paco smiled, 'memories link people together.'

'How can I ever thank you enough?'

'You'd better take this for your cousin,' Paco held out Quinn's leather food satchel. 'Filled it up myself from the kitchen.'

'Thank you,' Beth slung it over her shoulder with her own. 'Won't there be any warriors around?'

'I suggest you create a diversion. You know the log store round the side?'

Beth nodded.

'Next door is the lumber room. Inside are kegs of pine resin. Douse the log stack and set fire to it. Leave a trail of pine resin to the kegs, and it'll go up in no time.'

'And the guards will rush round to deal with the fire?'

'That's the idea. Get your parents and your Aunt out, and take some horses from the stables. Can you all ride bare back?'

Beth nodded again.

'Good. Use the rope harnesses as they're quicker to put on. Any questions?'

'I don't think so. When should I start?'

'When it's completely dark. I'll have hidden the keys by then. I won't fail you, this time. Don't forget. Night after tomorrow. Keep yourself well hidden in the woods till then.'

Part V

The Challenge

Chapter Sixty One

The following morning Lenyé paced the quarter deck of *Brave Heart*. It was one thing to pacify Marie-anna with trusting in the True King to rescue Ramâno, it was quite another to plan how to do it. Hoffengrégor had sent her to Bara-mâla for a very specific purpose. Lenyé recalled his words: *"the key for Lenyé to unlock the knowledge you will need to overcome your enemies"*. Now that she had it, her course of action should be to ride to Yanantha's house and read the scroll. Perhaps it would help her rescue Ramâno. It was on the way to Terrazarema so wouldn't be much of a detour. But every minute brought them closer to her Uncle's threat against the boy. Where was Chuah-te-mok? Had he found *Flying Cloud*? She needed to know how far behind her Kyros was, and whether she should wait for him. How was she to decide?

It wasn't until well into the afternoon that the eagle returned. Kyros was at least a day and half from the wreck of *Sea Sprite*, because of problems with the rudder. She couldn't afford to wait for him at all. But his warning about the warriors at Pordé-Sûnca filled her with alarm. How was she going to get to Yanantha's?

Captain Josiah had the answer. 'We can heave to for a while till dusk so we won't be seen from the land, and then head further West. There's a small deep-water harbour in the rocks not far from the homestead of Hanniel's Father. I've used it many times when I haven't wanted the authorities at Pordé-Sûnca to know what cargo I've been carrying. It's tricky in the dark, but I can set you down there. Hanniel and his men can guard you as you travel overland.'

They landed safely under cover of dark and Lenyé noticed immediately how unsteady she was back on dry land after the constant movement of *Brave Heart's* deck beneath her feet. They walked for the rest of the night and arrived at the homestead as dawn was breaking and were greeted by a warm welcome and a cooked breakfast.

Lenyé sent Chuah-te-mok, with Ra-Na-Jiri in his talons, to head for Terrazarema and leave the cobra in the palace gardens to try and make contact with Ramâno. As the eagle flew away, she whispered in her heart to the True King on the boy's behalf, 'Grant Ramâno your strength to come through this ordeal, and give him words of wisdom and power to confound his enemies.'

They saddled the horses and set off for Yanantha's house, escorted by Hanniel and his men, until the soldiers broke away and aimed for Terrazarema to scout out the area and await her arrival. Their progress was swift, travelling light with only a blanket and enough food and water to last two days. As usual, Ariella and Mamma Uza-Mâté kept well behind the horses so as not to terrify them.

On the morning of the second day they arrived at Yanantha's house. Lenyé flung her arms around her friend in greeting as they were all welcomed.

'Lenyé, it's so good to see you after all this time. Come in. I've been expecting you these last few days and have food prepared.'

'Before I do anything else,' Lenyé looked into her friend's eyes, 'I must read the scroll from that cylinder. Where is it?'

'Here,' Yanantha fetched it from her parchment store.

Lenyé felt her fingers trembling with excitement as she fitted the key. It turned easily in the lock and the end of the cylinder came away in her hand. She shook the cylinder and eased the parchment out. Yanantha passed her a pair of linen gloves and put on a pair herself. Lenyé broke the seal and unrolled the parchment onto the table before leaning over to begin reading.

Chapter Sixty Two

Morthrir drummed his fingers on the desk in the private council chamber in the palace at Terrazarema and glared at Eawen. The man stood in front of him with his wrists bound and a guard either side. What annoyed Morthrir most was the serene expression on the man's face and that incredible sparkle in those bright eyes. What was he playing at? The man was on trial. He should be cowering down and begging for mercy by now!

'Listen, Eawen,' Morthrir reined in his anger. 'You are a prisoner because of your stance concerning the True King.'

He stood up and paced across the room, conscious that the man didn't even turn to watch his movements. 'You weren't healed at all, were you? I think you've been play-acting at being blind and could see all the time and had some kind of fake sunken eyelids over your eyes for effect. Am I right?'

'No, Sire. I was blind from birth. I learned everything by feel. My Father taught me the ways of the mountains till I was able to run as nimbly as a goat without stumbling. But I couldn't see till the Healer intervened and the True King gave me my sight.'

'Gave you your sight. How?'

'The Healer made a paste from the dust of the ground and smeared it on my eyes and said to me: "*This is not a question of healing your sight, but rebuilding your eyeballs*". The True King had to make new eyeballs for me before I could see.'

'That's rubbish, and you know it.'

'You witnessed my eyes being healed yourself, Sire. You cannot deny that.'

'I'm not denying what I saw. But to expect this True King of yours to do it; that is what I'm questioning. You had time to rub something on your eyes before I came to your workroom. That's why I say it was fake sunken eyelids that were dissolving and revealing your real eyes underneath.'

'When you had Doctor Nostrea examine my eyes earlier this morning, Sire, he was astounded. He said I had the eyes of a thirteen-year old boy in clarity of vision.'

Morthrir rounded on the man. 'Doctor Nostrea was lying. He's always trying to undermine my authority.'

'But the crowds acknowledge a great miracle has taken place.'

'Those crowds always want a miracle, and will strain the credulity of any sane person to get one. They've also been taken in by your fake blindness.'

'What about the boy, Sire? No one who saw him before can deny a great miracle of healing took place on his legs.'

'You mean, Ramâno? He was faking his crippled legs.'

'Why don't you ask those who saw it happen?'

'I haven't got time to find those who saw it. And even if they did, they were taken in by a clever conjuring trick.'

'Ask his Mother. She'd know whether he was crippled or not.'

'That woman tried to poison me. Why should I believe her?'

'What about your own warriors? Many of them were healed of old battle wounds, and the scars disappeared.'

'They said they had wounds that still hurt, and this so-called healer waves his hands over them; and, suddenly, no scars. But you can't prove it. They never had any wounds in the first place. The Healer was only doing it to draw away the loyalty of my warriors and undermine my position.'

'No, Sire. If you'd been there, and felt the compassion the Healer had for everyone, you'd know it wasn't faked.'

'Hmph! If it wasn't for Youdlh, those warriors would defect to anyone. If he was ever killed, I'd have a major rebellion on my hands. As for that boy,' Morthrir smacked his hand on the wood panelling of a wall, 'he was only play-acting to support the claims of that vagabond to be a healer. Once the crowd accepted him, anyone with a vague ache or pain would come to him, and agree they'd been healed. It was mass mind control. That's all he was doing. Then he could peddle his drivel about the True King. You can't prove his existence with a few fake healings. But people will accept anything if you dress it up in the right way. One day those people are going to wake up and their aches and pains will have returned and they'll accuse the Healer of tricking them. Only a fool would accept his ranting in the first place.'

'The greater fool, Sire, is the man who does not acknowledge the existence of the True King.'

'If I was the True King and someone came along with a few cheap conjuring tricks to try and prove I existed, I would take that as a personal insult.'

'Healings do not prove the existence of the True King. They merely display his compassion for those who are suffering.'

'What would prove his existence, then? Convince me.'

'You have only to look at the flowers in your garden, Sire, to see the hand of the True King in everything.'

'Those flowers are there because my gardeners planted them.'

'If you cannot accept this, you are to be pitied above all men.'

'Rubbish! At least with Abbérron you get what he says he will deliver and that is giving me power to rule the Waking World for the benefit of everyone.' Morthrir paused and decided to try a different approach. 'Listen, Eawen. You rescued me from the River Rubichinó. We're still friends, aren't we?'

'I would do the same for anyone struggling in that flood.'

'You even gave me my name. Surely that indicates you are personally involved with my cause?'

'By renouncing Abbérron, I have come to regret anything I have ever done in furthering his purposes.'

Morthrir strode across the room, grabbed Eawen by the front of his jacket and thrust his face close. 'What kind of a monster is this True King of yours who turns friends into enemies?'

'If you carry on as you are, you won't have any friends left.'

'Hmph!' Morthrir pushed the man away.

'I think you're secretly jealous of your nephew, Sire.'

'Jealous of Kyros? How dare you!'

'The True King has given him a compassion that touches all the People and draws them to him. He is Dareth's heir, and one day will become such a great King that he will outshine Zerigor.'

'What you're saying is treason.'

'No, Sire. It's the truth.'

'And treason is punishable by death.'

'You have no power over me except what has been granted to you by the True King.'

'That's nonsense. Besides, no one knows the Healer is Kyros.'

'Then I see it as my duty to inform everyone, Sire.'

'Listen, Eawen. I'm a fair man. I have a document on my desk confirming that the healing of your eyes was a fake and the True King does not exist. It also re-instates you as my Chief Priest. Sign it and I will forget about the past and you are free to go.'

'I cannot do that, Sire.'

'If you are set on undermining me, I could have your eyes put out and we start from scratch and see if this True King of yours will heal them again. Maybe then I might begin to accept some of the things you say.'

'I would rather carry on living in this world maimed, than do as you ask.'

'I could have you executed.'

'I would rather lose my life in this world than face the consequences of denying the True King.'

'Enough,' Morthrir snapped. 'Guards. Take this man away and lock him up. See that he gets sufficient food and water, but do not let anyone near him. I don't want the whole city hearing what he has to say. I need time to decide what to do with him.'

Chapter Sixty Three

Lenyé sat at the table in Yanantha's house and skimmed through the parchment and then read it more thoroughly. The Ancient Prophet talked about evil originating from a spiritual being rather than as a vague influence that suddenly came over people.

She passed it to Yanantha and sat contemplating what the parchment contained. It all focused around Abbérron. *For this surely is the entering in of evil: the malicious will of Abbérron actively turning others from following the True King.* But Abbérron wasn't always like that. For Hoffengrégor said of him: *There is no one more beautiful to behold.* And the True King said: *I established you in the fire of my Mountain and you were perfected in your ways from the day you were fully formed...* In looks and behaviour, he was faultless. According to the True King, he was to: *carry the Light of Life throughout the Known Universe, but especially to lead my work in the Waking World.* He even had a different name: *Rabborné, Teacher of Light.* And his beautiful coat was called *Imbrésonite* and *converted intense heat to the opposite degree of cold.* But it was stripped from him when he was cast down. So why was her Uncle seeking it in Bara-mâla, and what possible use could he have for it?

She was startled as Yanantha gave the parchment back.

'What do you make of it?' Yanantha gazed into her eyes.

'It's hard to piece together. It all revolves around Abbérron's attitude. Listen to this, and she read Hoffengrégor's words from the parchment: *I felt his mind probing who he was and the pride in self-knowledge that took root within him and the disdain he felt for others...* and his rejection of the True King.' She pointed about two thirds of the way down the parchment: *'until this iniquity of rebellion was found in you.'*

'You're right,' Yanantha ran her finger up the parchment till she found the section she wanted. 'Look at this: *as I listened, I realised he was sowing seeds of doubt in the minds of his hearers concerning their relationship with the True King.* And down here as well: *Again the words were soft and persuasive and crept into the inner heart like molten honey, and spoke of throwing off the yoke of servanthood and becoming your own master, and thereby being free.'*

'And it's not just for those in higher Realms,' Lenyé was keen to press her point. 'What about this bit: *I knew he would attempt to raise the same rebellion in the Realm of the Waking World... by enticing them to be their own master.'*

'I know.' Yanantha referred back to an earlier section and read aloud, *'I knew of a certainty that whoever heard those words had to respond: either to obey them and follow Rabborné, or remain faithful to the True King...* As I understand it, all are affected and cannot escape the testing of their loyalty.'

Lenyé looked up. 'The defence against these words that the Ancient Prophet resorted to was: *Only by meditating on the words of the True King did I have any chance of resisting them.'*

'That's right,' Yanantha said. 'It's all relative to the Presence of the True King, and Hoffengrégor sensed the importance of it: *I beheld afresh the True King, seated on his Throne...* and from that position came the pronouncement of judgement: *Therefore you will be brought down to the lowest Pit.'*

'What I don't understand,' Lenyé frowned, 'is why didn't the True King cast him down there straight away, rather than let him come to the Waking World and sow doubts in humans as well?'

'Even though the rebellion was set in motion in the Realm of the Blessèd Throne,' Yanantha replied, 'it was bound to affect every other part of the Known Universe eventually. It's a bit like a farmer sowing his field with wheat, and a rival comes along and sows weeds amongst them to ruin his crop.'

'Especially if that weed is darnel,' Lenyé grinned at her. 'We used to get it on my Father's farms back home. Looked like wheat until the ears on the wheat stalks appeared. Then you could tell them apart. My Father wouldn't let his farmers pull up the darnel because it would root out the wheat as well. So they left it till harvest time and everything was cut together. Then we had to sort the darnel into piles and burn it. The darnel-fires reeked for days. We had to wash our hands afterwards because sometimes it was infected with a fungus that made you feel sick.'

'I think that's you're answer. The True King wants to preserve his good crop of wheat at the expense of allowing those weeds to grow alongside them.'

'So those who side with Abbérron in the Waking World, are they cast down to the Pit with him?'

'Why do you ask?'

'It's implied in the Cosmography parchment I left with you.'

'In that case, I'll have to re-read it.'

Lenyé rolled up the parchment and locked it in its cylinder. 'I'll take this with me in case Kyros needs to read it. I've another one here from the island of Bara-mâla and written by Zerigor himself. You'd better keep it here with the Cosmography one.'

Yanantha was clearly astonished. 'That's three fresh parchments. Now the Ancient Wisdom is coming together to speed the Restoration. I will certainly keep these two safe.'

'The Empty Throne, the Prophet also mentions in his Cosmography parchment,' Lenyé continued, 'do you know anything about it?'

'No. I will have to seek for wisdom to understand this.'

Lenyé smiled, 'Kyros thought it was important.'

Chapter Sixty Four

After his ordeal with the cobra, Rafé wasn't troubled by the snake for some days, but still felt vulnerable in case it returned and began probing his mind again. He reined in his horses and sat in the saddle musing on what to do about it and was caught up, as if in a dream, to find himself in the basement of the palace, gazing through the bars on the door of a small cellar.

He saw a man standing against the further wall with his back towards him and talking to people through the air vents above, urging his visitors to accept the words of the True King and walk in his ways.

Only Eawen would do that. So he was arrested after all.

There was a shout from outside and the sound of running feet and Rafé realised the visitors had been chased away.

Eawen turned round and began pacing up and down in the cellar. Suddenly he pointed at the door. 'Rafé, my friend. Welcome. You look troubled. Tell me what's on your mind.'

'I want to end my involvement with that cobra. It has learned my name and gained control over me.'

'Very well,' Eawen approached the door, raised his right hand and spoke in a commanding voice, 'I release you.'

Rafé sighed with relief. His connection with the cobra was instantly broken.

'Now that's done,' Eawen continued, 'what about my advice to leave the Priesthood, and renounce Morthrir and accept the True King's guidance over your life.'

Rafé was about to ask his friend for help in this when there was a clash of keys behind him and the door at the top of the steps was thrown open. 'What's going on down there?' a harsh voice questioned.

'Quick,' Eawen whispered and drew closer to the bars on the door. 'It was important that we met today, for the True King speaks these words over you:

> I alone foil the designs of the Summoners
> And thwart the desires of Morthrir.
> For I have raised you up as part of the Restoration
> To place a King of my choosing upon the Throne.
> Therefore I will lead you and guide you in finding
> What rightly belongs to my King.'

There was a clatter of heavy boots down the stone steps. 'If I catch you talking to anyone else through those air vents,' the harsh voice was much louder now, 'there's going to be serious trouble.'

Rafé had one last quick glimpse of those incredible grey eyes of his friend through the bars on the door and saw in them such a deep compassion that he felt tears starting in his own eyes.

But the noise of the guard had disturbed the dream and Rafé was back sitting on his horse.

Chapter Sixty Five

Later that morning Lenyé gathered everyone in the room where she read the parchment. They sat round the table: herself and Nasima at one end; Yanantha, Marie-anna and Olathe down one side; Mamma Uza-Mâté and Ariella on their haunches at the far end; and Wilf and Festé to her right. She could tell they expected an action plan, but she didn't have one.

'I sent Chuah-te-mok to Terrazarema with Ra-Na-Jiri to confirm if Ramâno is there,' she began. 'Kyros is on his way to Pordé-Sûnca and needs to evade those warriors he warned us about. I have nothing else to offer except suggest we spend time thanking the True King for what has happened so far.'

'You mean, like calming that storm,' Olathe spoke up.

'And allowing us to find the island,' Wilf broke in.

'And recovering the key and the parchment,' Nasima was quick to point out.

'And the Crown,' Festé chipped in. 'But our Uncle's stolen it!'

'That's right. My natural inclination,' Lenyé wanted to keep them focused, 'is to ride out and see what we can do. But I sense we are being asked to wait and hear from the True King. Something is going on that I don't understand. Wilf, would you like to lead us in offering our thanks?'

And he did. The others spoke in turn. Marie-anna started singing of her gratitude to the True King for healing Ramâno's legs, and protecting him at this time of uncertainty; her sweet voice filling the room. Lenyé was amazed at the change in her. Then they were all singing: Wilf's tenor, Festé's rasping as his voice hadn't fully broken yet, and the rest of them a mixture of sopranos and altos. Even the she-bear and lioness joined in with soft growls that fitted the harmonies. But it wasn't just them. Lenyé was conscious of other voices, some much higher in range and others incredibly low, their vibrations shaking the room, as though a host from another realm had joined in with them.

Without any spoken agreement they all pushed back their chairs and knelt on the floor, despite the table hiding most from each other's view. But that didn't matter; they were so caught up in their singing. Lenyé began to feel a darkness squeezing her, till she slumped forwards with her face grinding into the floor. Their singing intensified as the darkness tried to crush the life out of her. Suddenly she felt something snap, like Captain Josiah's sea anchor and that lurch of *Brave Heart*, and sensed the True King had come amongst them. She was being gently pressed down by the sheer weight of the light that shone about him; and lay there peacefully, enjoying his presence. Lenyé caught a glimpse of his face and that wonderful smile and heard his voice in her heart: *'You were right to wait, for you have allowed me to break the evil power that was set against you. Be free.'* Then he was gone.

Lenyé realised one of the things she was freed from was the link through Ra-Na-Jiri. Whether the cobra found out who the man was didn't matter any more. She sat up on the floor and began laughing. Nasima sat up and laughed as well. The two of them scrambled to their feet, still laughing, and hugged each other. She went round the rest of them, hauling some to their feet and laughing and embracing them in turn. Everyone was hugging each other and laughing. She'd never seen or heard anything like it before. These were her family and friends and she loved them more now than she'd ever done. Then she was hugging them all again. She was delirious with joy. It was as though the coming of the True King amongst them had filled her up with light that gushed out of her and she couldn't stop it.

She staggered towards the door, not because her sea-legs

were returning, but because she was unable to control her legs and feet properly. It was as if she had drunk several glasses of the most intoxicating wine she had ever known, but there was no aftermath of a sore head: only the ecstatic feeling that she was going to burst she was so happy.

Lenyé heard the others as they pushed past her into the garden: Wilf and Festé were in hysterics, drowning the higher voices of the girls; Yanantha was laughing in bursts and then going quiet before laughing out loud again; the animal-friends were grunting and snorting and Marie-anna was half-singing, half-laughing, which made Lenyé want to laugh all the more.

She collapsed to her knees on the verandah still laughing uncontrollably and pointed to a black dot in the sky. 'Look everybody; it's Nomat-te-wok,' and she giggled at the unusual sound of the eagle's name. 'He's missing all the fun.'

The eagle dropped out of the sky and landed next to her.

'Tell me you bring wonderful news,' Lenyé laughed. 'You've managed to free Ramâno and he's riding here on Ra-Na-Jiri.'

'Nothing of the sort. I took the cobra to the palace gardens as you asked and left him there. When I returned he still hadn't seen anything of the boy.'

'Not surprising,' she laughed. 'Ramâno's a prisoner. They're hardly likely to let him go out and play. You'll have to get Ra-Na-Jiri into the palace somehow.'

'You can't expect an eight-foot cobra to slither up to the front door and be welcomed with open arms. They'll kill him.'

'Well, shove him up a drainpipe, or something. There must be other ways to get him in. Can you think of anything so funny as Ra-Na-Jiri crawling up a drainpipe and getting stuck,' Lenyé broke off because she was laughing too much. 'And you having to grab him by the tail and pull him out as though you were after a worm in the lawn,' and she started laughing again.

'Eagles do not eat worms.'

'Oh, don't be so stuffy, Chuah-te-mok. You can laugh for

once.'

'Lenyé,' she heard the shocked tone in the eagle's voice, and laughed even more. 'Are you drunk, or something?'

'No. Of course not. I'm having fun, that's all.'

'I don't know what's come over you.'

'The True King has been amongst us.' She waved vaguely in the direction of the garden. 'We're all like this. Even Ariella and Mamma Uza-Mâté. Why don't you join us?'

'I think I'd better get back to Ra-Na-Jiri. At least he's trying to help the boy.'

'I'd rather laugh for five minutes in the presence of the True King, than be all serious and worry about problems that are never likely to happen. When the True King steps into a situation everything falls into place.'

The eagle looked at her and cocked his head on one side. 'Did you really mean for me to pull the cobra out of a drainpipe?'

'Of course.'

The eagle threw back his head and uttered a chuckling sound. 'That's quite funny, you know.'

'Told you.'

'And Ra-Na-Jiri wriggling up a drainpipe and getting stuck in the first place. That's even funnier. Do you want me to fly back to him and try?'

'No.' Lenyé slumped over backwards and felt the bare boards of the verandah against her shoulder blades. 'Fly over and find out what Kyros is up to. Make sure he's all right. Tell him I love him madly and miss him and can't wait to see him. Apart from that, I don't care what happens next.'

She started laughing again, feeling her ribs and face ache from so much laughter, and was aware of a sudden silence.

'Are you still there, Chuah-te-mok?' She lifted her head to check, but the eagle had gone. Lenyé didn't mind in the least; she just flopped back and carried on laughing.

Chapter Sixty Six

The following day Morthrir sat at his desk in the private council chamber, rubbing his eyes. He'd hardly slept a wink last night thinking over his interview with Eawen.

That man had an answer to everything. But it was still a fake. He was convinced of it. He had seen those clear grey eyes emerge almost in an instant. It had to be some sort of disguise dissolving to reveal what was underneath. There was no other explanation. Why was the man so obstinate in refusing to agree? And his comments about Kyros...

Morthrir leapt to his feet and paced up and down. How dare he! Kyros was not going to be King. Nastâr would take care of that. How could gifts of compassion touch the People and draw them to him? They needed someone strong to make difficult choices and lead from the front. Not a weakling who was so concerned about people's ailments that he didn't have time for anything else. At least Abbérron didn't demand that of him.

There was a knock at the door.

'Go away.'

'But Sire,' he heard Youdlh's voice. 'You asked to see me.'

'Come.'

Youdlh entered the room.

'How's the training for your new warriors going?'

'Finished, Sire.'

'Then set up a ceremony for them to swear allegiance to me.'

'Yes, Sire.'

Chapter Sixty Seven

Kyros stood on the poop deck of *Flying Cloud* and addressed the warriors as they sat on the decks below him. 'My friends,' he began, 'by swearing allegiance to me and accepting Harbona as your Captain, you have now signed up to membership of an army. But not of this world. We battle against spiritual beings from another realm, and use very different tactics. I will take the weapons of this world to illustrate what happens. I'd like you to stand.'

There were some laughs and calls as they helped each other up, and he wondered how he was going to get them to take this seriously.

'I want you to stand, feet slightly apart and arms relaxed. Now go through the motions of putting on a chain mail corselet.' He saw a few nudge each other and smirk, but was aware of Harbona on the quarter deck turning to glare at the men. He was pleased to see they did it without any more fooling around.

'This represents the way we live in the world and protects us from giving in to our enemies. Now put on a belt which reminds us of the truth concerning the True King and all he stands for. From this everything else in our weaponry hangs.' He also talked them through putting on boots so that wherever they went they would speak the Name of the True King; a helmet to protect their minds and guard their thoughts; a shield to soak up the taunts of their enemies; and a sword acting as the words in their mouths to speak against their enemies in the Name of the True King.

They practised shouting out, 'In the Name of the True King,

we come against you.' Kyros felt a thrill run through him at the sheer volume of men speaking as one voice.

'Above all we must maintain our unity. You already know how to rely on each other in battle. If some of you faltered, a warrior-charge would be easily brought down by your enemies.'

He glanced at the men. They were watching him closely. 'I'd like you to get into groups of three and stand in a triangle with your backs to each other and shoulders touching and looking outwards. These are the most important men in your lives. You can watch over each other and guard each other's backs and look out for each other. It's one thing to win a battle in a large group, but quite another to be alone and tripped up by any weakness. We are never off duty in that respect, and must always remain watchful for ourselves and for each other. Any questions?'

One of the warriors spoke up. 'What happens when we're asleep? Surely we can't cover that?'

'Good point. I'll have Harbona divide you into watches. Each of these groups will be stationed in a ring of men around the main deck and up on the poop and fo'c's'le decks. During each watch, you are responsible for us all as you call upon the Name of the True King to release more power to us and continually sing and speak out his praises. Our enemies are the Dé-monos, but the True King will release the En-luchés to us to fight against them. The more we call upon the True King, the more he will release to us. Is that clear?'

'Yes, My Lord,' the warrior replied.

That afternoon Kyros watched Harbona drill the men and was astonished at the result: he sensed the power released when the men sang and spoke aloud and called upon the True King. As he paced back and forth along the quarter deck, he heard a shout above and looked up to see Stellatus standing in mid air.

'Well done, Kyros. For you have turned a company of untried men into a well organised fighting force. The True King has heard their cry and will release more En-luchés to come to your aid. I am commanded to open Harbona's eyes to look more fully into the spirit realm and so stand shoulder-to-shoulder with you.' Then he was gone and Kyros caught the faint melody of his presence lingering above him.

There was a cry from the masthead and Kyros raised a telescope to his eye. He could see the burned out hulk of *Sea Sprite* getting larger as they approached. What concerned him were the boats full of survivors and many more men in the water clinging to the gunwales or swimming between the boats. *Flying Cloud* was already full with her own crew and the survivors from two other ships. Where was he going to put them all?

When *Flying Cloud* was close enough they heaved to.

Kyros spoke to Harbona, 'This is when we're most vulnerable to attack as we concentrate on a specific activity. Gather as many men as you can to call on the Name of the True King so they can protect ourselves and those survivors.'

Harbona pointed to the sky. 'Look, My Lord. There are the enemies you told us about.'

'Get your men to their posts.'

As Harbona hurried away, Kyros saw a cloud of Dé-monos storming out of the sky and diving down onto the boats and survivors in the water.

He ordered their own boats to be lowered and as many strong swimmers as possible to bring the survivors aboard. But the disruption from the Dé-monos was horrific: the water was stirred up so much that *Sea Sprite's* boats were overturned and the survivors thrown into the water. Even their own boats and swimmers were harassed. The Dé-monos were concentrating on the helpless survivors first before they focused on *Flying Cloud*.

'Call on the Name of the True King,' Kyros yelled, and heard the cries from the main deck increase in fervour. He looked up and watched Nastâr hovering in mid air and directing the attack.

Kyros saw the great being fly towards him and a massive

onslaught of words filled his mind, grinding down his resistance and attempting to rip that dream out of him again. This was far worse than the Voices when he destroyed Malvi-Quîdda, the Dé-monos stronghold in the Realm of Travail. He slumped to his knees, holding his head and thrashing from side to side. Then he caught the whispered words of the True King, reminding him once again, *"You have to resist these thoughts, for you are beset by the same attack, but each time it grows stronger. Evil crouches at the door of your heart. But you are able to master it"*.

'Oh, my King,' he cried out. 'Grant me strength to overcome these enemies.' Even as he scrambled to his feet and stood gazing up he saw a great burst of light, and there was Stellatus leading a company of En-luchés, blazing brighter than the sun. The main force swooped down on the Dé-monos, while Stellatus and a number of others attacked Nastâr, diving down on him at a steep angle from above and behind, like blackbirds mobbing a hawk, and declaring the praises of the True King. He saw Nastâr try and shake them off, but Stellatus was relentless, distracting the great being from what was going on with the Dé-monos and driving him further away. The rest of the En-luchés forced the Dé-monos to flee, and disappeared with them.

At last the sea was calm again and the boats righted and the rescue operation was under way and the survivors were rowed in boats or towed by swimmers to the side of *Flying Cloud*. And they came aboard, clinging to the backs of the swimmers, or hauled up from the boats in nets, too weak to even climb up the dangling ropes, and were laid gently on the deck. Three nights and the days in between in the sea or the boats without food or fresh water had taken its toll: sun scorched, salt caked, with blistered faces and lips. They looked terrible.

The remains of *Sea Sprite* settled deeper in the water and sank as Kyros ordered *Flying Cloud* to set sail for Pordé-Sûnca. The survivors were washed and fed and given fresh water to drink and lashed in hammocks to sleep and recover. He and Harbona spent some time mingling with the warriors and encouraging them in their recent efforts and celebrating their first victory over the Dé-monos. But as Kyros retired to his cabin thinking over how long it would take to get to land and how he was to challenge the warriors that held the Port, he was confronted again by Nastâr, standing in the middle of the cabin with a number of Dé-monos around him. Before he could react, he was set upon and bundled to the floor face down.

'You thought you were very clever, training up your precious warriors to call on the True King and send in the En-luchés. But it didn't work. And now I'm here with you at my mercy.'

Kyros felt the sharp blade of an axe touch the back of his neck, and tensed himself in response, thinking it was the actual blow. He felt a movement of air as the axe swept upwards for the stroke and struggled to break the grip of his captors, before slumping face down again on the decking, knowing he was powerless to defend himself.

He cried out in his heart to the True King but heard Nastâr's voice exultant with victory: 'This is the end for you, Kyros!'

Chapter Sixty Eight

Quinn was startled in the darkness of his room at the Hunting Lodge as he heard a key turn in the lock and was instantly on the alert. The maid had been for his dinner dishes earlier and he wasn't expecting anyone else to come in before morning.

In the faint starlight filtering through the bars on his window, he was astonished to see Beth poke her head round the door.

'Quick,' she waved at him frantically. 'We don't have much time.'

Quinn grabbed his jacket and raced to the door. She shut and locked it behind him.

'Now for the others,' she whispered, and unlocked the door next to his. 'Here. Take the keys and use these two. Let your parents and Aunt Faria out and come back so we can lock this door as well.'

'Aunt Faria?'

'Never mind for now. Just do it.'

Quinn snatched the keys out of her hand, darted across the passageway and unlocked his parent's room.

They were even more surprised than he was, but his Father recovered the quickest and hugged him before his Mother grabbed him and flung her arms about his neck.

'Hurry. There isn't a moment to lose,' and he was tugging at them. They only had time to grab a jacket and cloak each before they were out of the room and Quinn was locking the door before opening the next one for his Aunt, and dragging them over to where Beth was. He wrenched open the door and saw his cousin sobbing in her Mother's arms.

'Beth. We must get them out.'

He saw his cousin wipe her eyes with the back of her hand, grab the keys from him, bundle her parents out and lock the door before hiding the keys on a peg amongst some jackets.

'Where now?' he whispered.

'The stables,' and Beth pushed him ahead of her.

As soon as they were outside, Quinn was aware of flames at the side of the Lodge and shouts and running feet, but the path to the stables was oddly quiet. He slipped across and opened the doors for seven horses, before grabbing a rope harness and leading one out into the cobbled courtyard. The others did the same. His horse was restless and jumpy at the smell of smoke. He stroked the neck and patted the cheek until the horse was calm enough for Quinn to lead the way out of the stable block and off into the woods in single file along an animal track. When they were far enough from the commotion, he mounted, turned to see the others do the same and led them at a brisk canter to skirt the Lodge and head South. He was startled by a cry from in front as a warrior leaped into the path, and had no option but to ride the man down. He was relieved when the warrior jumped out of the way in time.

The shout brought other warriors running. Quinn heard the issuing of commands and the clamour of men chasing them.

He recalled a section further along this path from his journey three days ago where the mud was soft as it ran alongside a shallow stream. It wasn't far off. He listened carefully to the following thud of hooves above the sound of their own and realised their pursuers were far enough behind for him to pull off this trick.

When he reached the muddy patch, Quinn gathered his horse for a leap where the water overflowed onto the path, landed in the stream and kept on cantering, the hooves splashing in the shallows and grinding on the gravel bed of the water course. He glanced over his shoulder and saw Beth and the others following him. He cantered some way before reining to a halt and let his horse scramble up the bank where it was covered in undergrowth and trailing creepers so as not to leave any hoof prints. He rode deeper into the woods away from the stream and stopped before dismounting and leading his horse under the cover of some large holly trees. The others joined him and they crouched low holding the rope tethers and waited.

'Shh,' Quinn whispered as he caught the sound of hooves. The warriors galloped past. He waited several minutes before mounting and leading them by paths that brought them to the old woman's cottage in the early hours of the morning.

'There's no one here,' he muttered to Beth.

'No. Ishi-mi-réjá has gone on to Terrazarema.'

They dismounted, tethered the horses and entered the cottage. Beth produced the two food satchels, and they made a sparse meal with some of the vegetables they found in the kitchen.

'Whose home is this?' Beth's Father asked.

Between them Beth and Quinn filled their parents in on how they met Ishi-mi-réjá, who led them here to meet an old woman. Beth was under an oath of secrecy and couldn't say any more.

'Ishi-mi-réjá told me to head for Terrazarema as quickly as possible,' she concluded. 'I suggest we get some rest here before we set off.'

Chapter Sixty Nine

Lenyé felt a chill breeze as she lay on Yanantha's verandah, and shivered. She sat up and watched the others in the garden still laughing and hugging each other, then playing tag, and laughing and hugging when someone was caught. But she sensed something significant was about to happen, raced inside to check on the Sword of Justice, and bumped into Yanantha.

'You know you asked me if those who side with Abbérron in the Waking World are cast down to the Pit with him?'

'Yes,' Lenyé was interested, but desperate to get to her room.

'I received insight as we were before the True King earlier.'

'Oh. What do you think now?'

'It's not about siding with Abbérron, but more a question of cutting yourself off from the True King and his power to bring you through death to what lies beyond.'

'And is that open to everybody?'

'If we drift away from the True King and live according to our own wisdom, the closer we draw to Abbérron. Our whole lives are caught up in this struggle. The True King can never love us more or watch over us more closely than he does now. But it's up to us to want that above anything else in the Waking World and set our hearts to follow him. If we reject him he will honour that choice. He cannot force us against our wills.'

'A sober warning, but you confirm my own thinking. Did you have any more insight about the Empty Throne?'

'I'm afraid I can't answer that one.'

Lenyé watched as Yanantha turned on her heel and walked

out to join the others, then rushed to her bedroom.

As she drew the Sword, she felt that chill again, despite being inside, and saw a waking vision, so clear that it was as if she was there in person. Kyros was still on board *Flying Cloud*, alone and face down on the decking in the stern cabin. Swirling about him was a mass of Dé-monos. But to her horror she saw a greater figure with the arch of closed wings on his back and protruding above his shoulders, standing on the decking with an enormous double-bladed axe poised to strike off Kyros' head. She recognised Nastâr from her encounter with him on *Sea Sprite*.

With a cry of, 'In the Name of the True King,' she leaped into the fray, grasping the Sword of Justice with both hands, and parried the blow as it fell. She saw the stunned look on Nastâr's face, and flicked her wrists so that the Sword swept the axe out of her enemy's hands and it clattered to the deck. Then she was in an attacking stance, the tip of her Sword poised to strike at the exposed throat. The great being retreated, but she kept on advancing and pushing her opponent clear of Kyros. 'In the Name of the True King, be gone!' The great being was sucked away and the rest of the Dé-monos disappeared with him, and she was back in her room with the Sword in her hands and still standing in the attacking stance.

Lenyé was shaking like a leaf at the encounter, but felt her heart beat slow to its normal pace and breathed a sigh of relief. Whatever Kyros had been struggling with, it was gone. With a flash of insight, she realised the True King had come amongst them earlier, and given them such a sense of security in his presence and released them in the gift of laughter so that she was ready to deliver Kyros from his enemies at a time of great need.

'How astonishing are the ways of the True King,' she murmured to herself, 'that in our emergencies he can send another from a distance to bring help and strength.'

Chapter Seventy

Morthrir strode up and down in the private council chamber smacking his fist into the palm of his hand as he listened to Nastâr's account.

'Twice now I have attacked Kyros, My Lord. The first time he had no En-luchés with him. I ground him down using persuasive words till he was on his knees, and was beginning to penetrate the layer of protection that surrounds him. But he rallied as though waking from a dream and used the name of the True King against me. I have never experienced such retaliation.'

'Did any En-luchés come to his aid?'

'Not at first, My Lord. Then they arrived and harried us, so we feigned a retreat and led them away from his ship.'

'And the second time?'

'*Flying Cloud* had rescued the survivors from the burned out hulk of *Sea Sprite* and they were sailing for Pordé-Sûnca. I think he was so focused on getting there and deciding what to do that I caught him completely off guard. He was flat on his face on the deck at my mercy with an axe in my hands. I was lining it up to cut off his head when I heard singing and laughter. Suddenly Lenyé was standing in front of me.'

'Lenyé. How did she get there?'

'I don't know, My Lord. She must have similar powers of travel that are available to you.'

'This is terrible. She could come here without me knowing and grab the boy. What happened next?'

'She leaped at me with the Sword of Justice in her hands,

parried my blow, and flicked the axe out of my grasp. Then she forced me back with the tip of her Sword against my throat and spoke the Name of the True King against me. I was sucked away with the rest of the Dé-monos.'

'I see. In that case we must act swiftly.'

'Surely now is the time, My Lord, to perform the child sacrifice?'

'No. I'm keeping him to generate greater favour with Abbérron to trap Lenyé. I have brought you up from the Pit to deal with Kyros.' He paused and looked Nastâr straight in the eyes, till the great being turned away. 'In the name of Abbérron,' Morthrir raised his voice and spoke words of power, 'let all the participants of the Hexacle be gathered together in the Vault of Malrema at midnight tonight.'

Chapter Seventy One

Kyros stood on the quarter deck of *Flying Cloud* as the warriors disembarked at Pordé-Sûnca. The ones rescued from *Sea Sprite* had also joined with himself and Harbona, and were lining up with the others. Two days with all sails set and running before the Southwesterly wind had brought them in sight of land. He was eager to find Lenyé and sent a small troop to the homestead of Hanniel's Father, but Hanniel and his men had left with Lenyé several days ago to head for Terrazarema.

Kyros shouted to his warriors and saw them line up in ranks behind Harbona. He strode down the gangplank to join them and set off to meet the warriors on the outskirts of the town. They weren't challenged till they reached the garrison; then there was a huge commotion. Harbona was welcomed as a returning hero: everyone had given him up for lost. Kyros was aware of the warriors giving him curious glances, clearly recognising him but not sure what was going on.

An officer approached and addressed Harbona. 'Sir, as my senior officer, I must relinquish my command to you.'

'You may do so after I have spoken to your men. Call them together, please.'

'Yes, Sir.'

'My company will stay separated from yours. Understood?'

'Yes, Sir.'

Kyros watched as Harbona climbed onto a rock. 'Fellow warriors. You know who I am, but not why I am here. And you may also recognise Prince Kyros with me.'

As Harbona described what had happened to him and his change of allegiance, there were the same howls of protest and cries of, 'Traitor, traitor,' that they'd encountered on *Flying Cloud*.

'Your comrades,' Harbona shouted through the din, 'who were assigned to the ships, have also switched allegiance and now serve Prince Kyros.'

There was a sudden silence.

'I am asking you to consider carefully all that I have said and report to your commanding officer with an answer in one hour's time. If you choose to join us, I will sign you up under my command. If not, my two hundred will fight you as your company stands between us and a straight road to Terrazarema.'

Kyros was impressed. Sure enough, Harbona had his answer within the hour: every warrior had chosen to renounce his Uncle and swear allegiance to himself with Harbona as their Captain.

As the two companies joined ranks together and prepared to strike camp, Kyros took Harbona aside. 'Your talk with the warriors when we were on *Flying Cloud*. Where did you get all that understanding from?'

'Being around you. Watching the change in Princess Lenyé. Talking to Ramâno about seeing you in action as the Healer when you spoke to the People concerning the True King. And hearing Marie-anna's songs about how happy she is.'

'And yourself?'

'I'm not sure. I'm worried about you not bearing any weapons, My Lord. You cannot ride amongst warriors unless you are armed. What if Youdlh has raised another army by now and attacks us? How am I supposed to protect you?'

'I've already argued with Lenyé over this.'

'At least carry a sword, My Lord.'

'*I am destined to walk armoured only with the power contained in the name of the True King.* I will not go back on that.'

The whole company set off for Terrazarema by late morning.

Chapter Seventy Two

Lenyé lay on the bed in her room at Yanantha's house, with her hands behind her head, and felt such peace. She sang a melody to touch the True King's heart out of her deep love for him, and words flowed in her song. Somehow, in the presence of the True King, she was on the offensive against her enemies from a position of complete rest:

When the dark spiritual powers of the Waking World unite
And take their stand against the True King
You laugh at them in derision
And treat them with contempt.
They are but a drop in the ocean to you
And their combined power like a boy against a warrior.

I have entered into the wild laughter of the True King
And been shaken apart by the depths of his mirth.
You, My King, have called me as your handmaiden
And placed your Sword in my hands,
To inflict your vengeance upon these rulers
And carry out the sentence written against them.
Not only to me have you given this honour
But to all those who call upon your Name.

You have hidden me in the secret place
And your strength upholds me in the time of valour.
When I am distressed in battle and greatly disturbed

You open the door to enter into your rest.
For I am like a weaned child at her Mother's breast
And you alone lay me down to sleep in peace.

Suddenly the ceiling and roof above her disappeared and the sky opened into another Realm and she was astonished to see battlements, and armies, and Kings seated upon Thrones, and ministers hastening to do their bidding. But they were not human, and she discerned a great company of Dé-monos, and their leaders, exposed to her gaze. Lenyé knew that her singing was releasing power from the True King to defeat these forces and cast down their Kings. For these were the real rulers of the Waking World, seated in high places and beyond the normal sight of humans, and only revealed by the True King himself in order to accomplish his purposes, not only in the Waking World but throughout the Known Universe.

Now Lenyé knew why she and the others had laughed so much: firstly, because of the joy of the True King amongst his People who wait upon him and hear his voice; and secondly, the Dé-monos hate the sound of human laughter directed against them because it completely undermines their work of deceiving humans about the True King.

And so she carried on singing.

PART VI

THE CONFRONTATION

Chapter Seventy Three

Kyros halted the regiment of warriors. Two days fast riding from Pordé-Sûnca and they were through the gap between the bottom of the Forest and the cliffs around the Dangst Rock at the head of Lake Sanchéso. He saw a dust cloud approaching in the distance.

'It looks like a company of horsemen, My Lord,' Harbona surveyed the plain ahead, shielding his eyes with his hand. 'I suggest we wait here and retain the height advantage.'

Kyros raised a telescope to his eye. 'Looks like Youdlh at the front. These must be recent recruits to my Uncle's army and are probably all that stand between us and Terrazarema.'

When the other company was only a few hundred yards away, Kyros and Harbona rode out to meet them with a handful of warriors and a flag of truce fluttering from a lance. A similar party approached with Youdlh at the centre. When they were within calling distance they all dismounted and paced closer together to sit in a circle, each man holding the reins of his horse.

They sat looking at each other till Youdlh broke the silence and addressed Harbona.

'As your Commanding Officer I will open these proceedings. I thought you died on active service pursuing Prince Kyros.'

'You must be pleased to see me alive, then.'

'I would if you returned with Prince Kyros as a prisoner. But I see him unbound. What is the meaning of this?'

'That you are no longer my Commanding Officer, for I have renounced Morthrir and sworn to serve Prince Kyros instead.'

A howl of disapproval arose from Youdlh's party.

'So have all the warriors who accompany me.'

The protest died down.

'As your men are between me and Terrazarema,' Harbona continued, 'you can either side with me or surrender to me.'

'Never!' Youdlh jumped to his feet. 'You've always tried to undermine me. I'm the better warrior and you know it.'

'Remember,' Harbona's tone was cold, 'if you choose to fight, I have seasoned men with me. Yours are plainsmen ranchers. Good horsemen, no doubt, but only recently trained for war. They will be decimated in the first few charges.'

'Don't count on it.' Youdlh thrust his foot in a stirrup, swung himself into the saddle and turned to ride back to his company as his warriors did the same. 'I've trained these men myself!'

'My Lord,' Harbona was in the saddle and giving orders to prepare for the first charge, but turned to Kyros. 'Stay here, with a few men to guard you, while we deal with Youdlh.'

'Don't trust in the skill of your warriors,' Kyros replied, 'for behind Youdlh's company I see a cloud of Dé-monos. I will ride with you and guard the men's hearts.'

'Very well, My Lord. Ride in the centre company. There's bad blood between Youdlh and me over his appointment as Morthrir's Commander. I have to kill him myself or he'll kill me. The men know that.'

'I understand. And I appreciate your concern for my safety.' Kyros saw Harbona turn away, and suddenly laughed. 'Lenyé reminded me a couple of weeks ago that today is my Twenty-First Birthday.'

'Then we'll celebrate your coming of age with a great victory, My Lord.'

Kyros rode at the head of one of the formations with only a few warriors in front of him. He raised his right hand, cried aloud and directed his words against a dark cloud hovering above the heads of Youdlh's oncoming men.

He saw the flash of his warriors' axe blades spinning in the sunshine, heard the *tok, tok, tok,* as they split the enemy shields, accompanied by screams as they followed through with their lances. All the formations crashed through the enemy line and swept round in a tight curve to attack from behind.

'To the right,' he yelled as he saw a group of enemy warriors gathering under the shadow of a cluster of Dé-monos. He cried out in the name of the True King, and his formation smashed through, dislodging the riders from their horses.

He was surprised Nastâr wasn't there, or even Vashtani. The Dé-monos appeared to be leaderless and engaging with Youdlh's warriors in random groups. And that was reflected in the battle as he was caught up in a myriad of individual skirmishes and the formations broke apart as his warriors harried the enemy lines. Suddenly he found his warriors had swept past him, and a lone rider charged towards him, lance lowered with a dark knot of Dé-monos swirling around his head. He recognised Youdlh and raised his right hand to speak against the Dé-monos.

Youdlh was only a few yards from him, lance poised for the attack, when another horseman raced out of the warrior ranks, galloped straight at Youdlh's exposed flank, and hurled himself from the saddle. It was Harbona with a dagger in his hand.

They both fell over the rump of the horse, Harbona twisting in mid air and landing on top. Youdlh thrust upwards with his arm and the dagger went spinning away. He was on his feet, lunging with his sword. Instantly, Harbona's sword was in his hand and they parried each other's blows.

Kyros watched the unfolding drama from horseback, aware that a running ring of his warriors encircled them and kept Youdlh's warriors out as they tried to rescue their Commander. Kyros knew by his own experience how formidable Harbona was, and seen him almost kill a man at wrestling. But he was also aware of Youdlh's prowess: a fine horseman, tall and strong, and deadly with any weapon; able to twist and turn and strike with the speed of a snake. Harbona was shorter and broader in the shoulders, but Youdlh had the longer reach.

Harbona trapped a blow on the hilt of his sword and heaved upwards, sending Youdlh's blade spinning out of his hand. Then Harbona was at him, hacking at the raised shield, but Youdlh drew his dagger, darted under Harbona's guard, thrust the man backwards with his shield and leaped on him, toppling him to the ground with Harbona underneath. There was a gasp from all the warriors, and the cries for Harbona began to drown the shouts of 'Youdlh! Youdlh!' Harbona dropped his sword and wrapped his arms around Youdlh's chest.

Kyros saw Harbona's grip tighten as Youdlh breathed out and knew what was coming next. As Youdlh struck again and again with his dagger, Harbona ducked his head and twisted further under Youdlh, away from the dagger hand, and carried on squeezing. Youdlh's attempts to stab his opponent became more erratic, his right arm weakening at each successive blow. Finally he collapsed on to his opponent and his arm hung limp, his shield arm drooped and his head slumped to one side. And still Harbona kept squeezing.

Kyros turned his head away, feeling sick. No one was going to rescue Youdlh and break Harbona's grip. It was a fight to the death and he'd seen it happen before his own eyes.

Eventually the ring of warriors opened up and two men from each side dismounted, knelt down, prised Harbona's arms apart and rolled Youdlh's body off him.

Harbona struggled to his feet and pointed straight at Kyros, his arm shaking. 'You see what happens when you refuse to bear any arms. You nearly got yourself killed!'

Kyros dismounted, removed his jacket and shirt and dropped them on the ground. 'Harbona, you challenged me to a wrestling match over my love for Lenyé. Because you rely too much on your prowess as a warrior, it's my turn to challenge you.'

Chapter Seventy Four

Rafé reached Mount Nastâri and tethered his horses between two rocks at the foot of the mountain. He took his pack, climbed up to the main entrance, and found the gates wide open. As he crossed the threshold he was startled by a movement in the darkness ahead. He shrank back thinking there were some Nastrim here after all, despite Vashtani's assurance that the place was empty. A lone fox shot past him and ran off amongst the rocks outside.

He lit a flare from his pack and walked into the mountain, marvelling at the size of the passageway before reminding himself that the place was hollowed out by giants. He came to a fork, hesitated and caught himself thinking, 'If only I had the cobra, the golden globe would be easy to find.' He shook his head. He must not go back to that. He raised his right hand and spoke into the darkness, 'If the True King really is with me, then let him guide me to find the golden globe.'

Rafé pulled a spool of twine from his pack, tied one end to a spur of rock and decided to fork left and downhill following his instinct that the golden globe would be well below ground level. He paid out the twine turning right and then left several times.

The twine jerked in his hand and he stopped, pulled another spool from his pack and tied it on. As he picked up the flare, it slipped from his hand, fell on the rock floor, sputtered and went out. He was about to re-light it when he saw a glimmer ahead and to his left. He carried the unlit flare, paid out the twine and moved forwards in the dark, using his feet to guide himself along the rocky passageway. The light grew stronger till he turned a corner and saw a gleam at ground level not far ahead. When he reached the rock wall he knelt down and tried to peer along a tiny tunnel, but the light was too bright for him to focus. He lay down, slipped in his hand and felt the smooth curve of a metal ball. He moved his fingers round it and found an odd projection that felt like the tiny sword he noticed in his vision at the armoury when he was in Terrazarema.

He'd found what he was looking for!

But when he tried to draw it out, the tunnel was too cramped for the golden globe with his hand round it. Rafé took a piece of cord out of his pack, made two small loops at one end, fitted the front loop behind the second, reached down the tunnel, slipped the loops over the tiny sword and pulled the knot tight. He eased the cord towards him, heard the golden globe move on the rocky floor and drew it out of the tunnel till it blazed in the passageway.

He sat and cradled the golden globe in his lap, feeling a sense of peace engulf him much as it had when Eawen spoke those strange words over him. No wonder the cobra wanted to come back here. Was this made by the Nastrim, or did it come from another source? And why did that tiny sword match Lenyé's? He stood up, held the golden globe in the crook of his arm and used its light to retrace his steps as he followed the twine. When he reached the entrance he concealed the golden globe in his pack.

Dusk was already falling as he climbed down to his horses and rode back into the forest. Suddenly he felt the same force trying to drag him away as happened when he arrived unexpectedly at the Vault of Malrema. Was that Morthrir attempting to control him again? This time he was able to resist it and carried on riding till he found a place to camp for the night.

Chapter Seventy Five

Kyros was aware of a rush of men to picket horses. The shadows lengthened and dusk drew in as warriors from both sides jostled for position and sat in a great circle around Harbona and himself, several ranks deep, to watch the contest.

Harbona was the first one in, ducking under his guard and gripping him around the chest, those powerful arms beginning that terrible constricting action as he breathed out. Then he felt the muscles soften to a gentle embrace, and there were tears from the man's face, streaming down his bare skin. He felt racking sobs take hold of Harbona as if the man's world had suddenly collapsed and he was completely broken.

'I cannot do this to you again, My Lord. You are far stronger than any warrior, with something greater than this world can give.'

'And what does that mean?'

'I want the same strength for myself.'

'Do you know why?'

'You come from the True King and speak words of life and give hope for the future, and have been sent to bring about the Restoration. All things will become new, and peace and harmony will fill the Waking World and we will all walk with the True King for ourselves. But I'm reluctant to lay down my weapons as how else can I protect you?'

'It's not about physical strength.'

'You mean, armies and weapons don't count?'

'They have their place in the bigger battle. But weapons of

this world are not enough.'

Suddenly Harbona started laughing, 'Thank you, My Lord. I now know that I cannot rely on my own strength any more. Therefore, I lay down my weapons before you.'

'Harbona,' Kyros whispered so that no one else could hear. 'You have learned a great deal by observation and talking to others. But what you have said can come from no human source, but only by direct revelation to your heart from the True King. Not all those who follow him are called to lay down their weapons. I need every man of pure heart who will rise up and join me. This is not about one battle, but the final overthrow of evil in the Waking World. Will you help me lead these men?'

Harbona didn't say anything, just nodded his head once.

Kyros felt a bond flow between them that would hold them together in the face of death, like a kinship stronger than brothers. This was the beginning of a comradeship that would last for ever, not only with Harbona, but for all men who love and serve the True King.

'You have changed my heart,' Harbona continued, 'so that I no longer seek to kill just as an honour in battle but to protect the weak and vulnerable from evil. I vowed to serve you before out of gratitude for being freed from the Dé-monos. Now it comes from the depths of my heart as I've grown to know you better, and I choose to serve you not as a warrior but as a friend. And you have softened my heart in other ways. I have taken heed of your words earlier and am ready to offer myself to Marie-anna, if she will have me; and to her son.'

They stepped apart to gather up their garments and Kyros saw all the warriors kneeling in a circle around them.

'What is the meaning of this?'

A warrior from Harbona's regiment looked up. 'We've sworn allegiance to you, Prince Kyros, and obedience to Harbona as our Captain. But we also want to be a part of what we've seen take place between the two of you.'

'So do we,' a leader from Youdlh's company spoke up.

Kyros talked with Youdlh's warriors and they chose to renounce Morthrir and swear allegiance to him. Then Harbona organised all the men to stand in ranks with a hand on their neighbour's shoulder while Kyros spoke over them to welcome them into this new comradeship.

They buried the dead from both sides and laid Youdlh's body in a separate grave with his shield and weapons, raised a mound over it and honoured his passing as they stood in silence. Youdlh had been a great warrior and everyone's Commander at some point in their lives; and they all had a high regard for him.

Kyros took Harbona aside afterwards. 'Spend the rest of the day training them in how to stand in this new form of warfare. We'll camp for the night and set out for Terrazarema at dawn.'

That evening they celebrated Kyros' coming of age by running him round the great ring of warriors on their shoulders, and passing him forwards to the next men, shouting, 'Long live Prince Kyros! Long live Prince Kyros!' They bundled him into a plaited rope seat slung between the shoulders of two horsemen, from each of the former companies, riding abreast. He had to remain seated with his arms in the air and trust to the skill of the horsemen not to drop him as they galloped round the outer perimeter of the circle several times. Finally a gap opened and the horsemen swept inside the ring, leaped over the flames of the campfire and hurtled towards the other side. They swerved apart at the last moment and flung Kyros head first into the eager arms of the warriors in front of him, to a great cheer of, 'Long live Prince Kyros!'

Kyros set a guard for the night and counseled the sentries to walk around the entire campsite speaking the power of the name of the True King over them against any potential attack by the Dé-monos.

Chapter Seventy Six

Morthrir stood on the altar in the Vault of Malrema as the light in him intensified and illuminated the Summoners, Priests and Dé-monos leaders in their various positions. He was pleased to see Nastâr taking Eawen's place, but was one Priest short: Rafé hadn't appeared. He felt strong resistance when he called the man: had Rafé gone over to the other side as well?

He glanced at the bag containing the Crown where it had been left on the bundle of *Imbrésonite*. 'We need to review the successes and failures since we last met,' Morthrir let his voice carry around the darkened chamber. 'I have interviewed Eawen the Henosite and he refused to renounce his allegiance to the True King or admit the healing of his eyes was a clever fake. I am still thinking of how best to dispose of him, for I cannot have him executed, even in secret, as that will cause a riot against me.'

Nobody said anything.

'Now for other matters,' he continued. 'We pursued Kyros' ship as planned, and Nastâr raised a terrible storm to destroy him, but at the last minute the storm suddenly died away and Kyros was able to escape unharmed. And Lenyé evaded our net.'

'There was something resisting me when I tried to raise that storm again,' Nastâr cut in.

'I know, and we had to abandon using the power of the wind and sea. But we did recover the *Imbrésonite*. And we also found the Krêon of Tulá-kâhju, the Crown of Life that Zerigor once wore. This was a complete surprise, as everyone thought the Great Flood at the Beginning washed it from his head and it was lost. Now I can be crowned King and the People will have no grounds to challenge me if I'm wearing it. We also captured the boy who pretended his legs were healed and helped Kyros win the hearts and minds of the People as the Healer. I will force him to sign a public confession that it was all a fake.'

'We thought you were going to use him as a child sacrifice,' Jumar-jé interrupted.

Morthrir glared at the Chief Summoner. 'I am, but not at this meeting. I will use the recovery of the *Imbrésonite* to incur Abbérron's good pleasure to release more power to destroy Kyros. I am keeping the child sacrifice for the recapture of Lenyé. Any questions?' Again he held each pair of eyes, probing into their minds.

'If not, let the ceremony begin.'

Morthrir faced East, adopted his flexed-knee stance and raised his arms. 'My Lord, Abbérron,' his voice was deep and carried an enormous sense of power. 'You released Nastâr to me from the bottom of the Pit. Grant him power to defeat my enemy, Kyros!'

Chapter Seventy Seven

Kyros wiped the dust from his face and dismounted. They were only one day's ride from Terrazarema and were preparing to camp for the night when he sensed a dark presence near him. He looked around but couldn't see anything in the fading light.

'Harbona,' he shouted. 'Set a perimeter guard and have everyone in their groups of three.'

The majority responded immediately while others tethered the horses. In a matter of minutes the men were calling upon the True King. Kyros felt a great release of power and discerned Nastâr, and a cloud of Dé-monos, circling their camp.

As they continued to cry out, Kyros glanced up and saw the familiar form of Stellatus, with a company of En-luchés, swoop down from the darkening sky and walk amongst the warriors.

'Well met, Kyros,' he called. 'Tonight we will watch with your men and keep guard. Nastâr is testing your weaknesses before his final onslaught.'

'Thank you, my friend.'

'Remember this,' Stellatus continued. 'The True King would not have you ignorant of the enemy's tactics, but will continue to speak to your heart and guide you as you grow in leadership.'

As he slept that night, Kyros found himself falling into a dark dream where the guards' ring of protection was broken down and hands were wrapped around his throat, squeezing the life out of him till he was choking and crying out in despair. He awoke with a start to find someone shaking him by the arm.

Chapter Seventy Eight

Quinn searched the old woman's cottage and outhouse for anything that might help them as they travelled, and found two hunting bows and quivers of arrows along with some small animal traps. He stood in the outhouse debating whether to take them and counting off on his fingers at least seven days to get to Terrazarema. Their own food stocks wouldn't last that long. He grabbed everything and headed back to the cottage: they would have to return these or repay the old woman somehow.

He was troubled about the journey: should he keep to the woods for as long possible and remain concealed; or try to outpace any warrior pursuit by using the road? He might reduce the number of days by travelling on the road, but the risk of being seen and caught was too great. They would have to remain undercover and head South for Ishi-mi-réjá's cottage. He could remember the forest paths and stretches of heathland between there and the Great Oak Tree and on towards Terrazarema. As long as they weren't spotted he was confident he could lead the others. The problem would come when they left the cover of the woods for the last dash across open country to the road and the ride to the city itself.

For the next few days he led the way, doubling back and covering their trail whenever he sensed pursuit and taking any opportunity to live off the land and augment their food stocks till they arrived at the Great Oak Tree and camped. They made good time, and saved a whole day on his estimate. Only one day of hard riding lay between them and Terrazarema.

Quinn left his horse at camp and ran through the woods towards the road while the others prepared the evening meal. He kept stopping and listening and checking for any sign of pursuit, but there was nothing in the woods to alarm him. He came to the final fringe of trees on the open scrubland leading to the road and stiffened. He saw the twinkle of campfires and smelled wood smoke on the night breeze as it wafted towards him. The warriors had caught up with them and were camped close to the bend in the road before it straightened out to approach the Northern Gates of the city.

Beth glanced up as he returned to their own campfire. 'Is everything all right?'

'No.' He saw the others look up at him. 'There's a troop of warriors camped close to the road above the Northern Gates. We can't reach the city without being seen. We'll have to continue South through the woods tomorrow and try the Eastern Gate, or even further round for the Main Gates. That'll take an extra day.'

Later that night, Quinn was disturbed by Beth calling out in her sleep. He was over to her immediately and kneeling beside her as she lay wrapped in a blanket. Her eyes were closed and she appeared to be deeply asleep but kept calling out, 'Lenyé...' much as she'd done when she went into that trance.

He shook her by the shoulder and saw her eyelids flicker open.

Beth sat up and grabbed his arm. 'Quinn. Lenyé needs us.'

'It's all right, Beth. You were only dreaming.'

'It was more than a dream, Quinn. Something momentous is about to happen to her.'

'Is she in danger?'

'No. It didn't feel like that. We have to get to Terrazarema in three days' time to help her. That's all I know.'

Chapter Seventy Ninety

Lenyé and the others set off from Yanantha's house, alternately cantering and walking their horses through the Forest with Ariella and Mamma Uza-Mâté behind. A day of riding and brief halts brought them out onto the plain well above Lake Sanchéso. Lenyé kept agonising over Ramâno at her Uncle's mercy, and called out in her heart to the True King about how to rescue him.

As the others settled down that night, Lenyé was aware of a dark mass on the plain further South, shown up by the faint starlight. Should she risk a night ride to avoid it and head for Terrazarema? She was distracted as Marie-anna joined her.

'What do you think that is?' she point to the area of darkness.

'I don't know. It can't be a shadow.'

'Come with me to investigate,' and she set off, riding bareback with Marie-anna following. They dismounted close to the dark area, picketed their horses and walked forwards only to find a company of warriors, all fast asleep. Most had settled down in their blankets, but others were clearly on guard duty and had collapsed to the ground in odd positions.

'What's happened?' Lenyé glanced at Marie-anna.

'It's as though something came over them to make them fall asleep.' Marie-anna knelt down and shook a warrior but he only grunted. Lenyé saw her friend glance up, the whites of her eyes showing clearly against her darkened features. 'Should we leave them and head back to our camp?'

'No,' Lenyé walked in amongst the warriors and Marie-anna followed her. 'Something strange is going on.' She picked her way carefully so as not to tread on any of them. It was a large company and it took a while to reach the middle. Suddenly she knelt down by a sleeping figure. 'Kyros,' she gasped and shook him by the arm. There was no response. She ran her hand over his brow and found he was drenched in sweat. 'Wake up.'

'Hmm,' he murmured.

She shook him again. 'Kyros, wake up.'

He opened his eyes, stared at her, then sat up. 'Lenyé. What are you doing here?'

'O, Kyros,' Lenyé flung her arms around him. 'You're safe! But who are these warriors, and why are they fast asleep?'

She whipped round at a cry from her friend. 'It's Harbona.'

Lenyé watched Marie-anna kneel down and cradle Harbona's head in her lap, but the man didn't stir.

She turned back to Kyros. 'What's going on?'

'These are my men,' Kyros reached out and stroked her cheek. 'They've renounced our Uncle and sworn allegiance to me and are serving Harbona as their Captain. We're riding to Terrazarema to capture Uncle Morthrir and rescue Ramâno.'

'Kyros, we need to talk first. I've unlocked the cylinder and read the parchment.' Briefly she recounted how evil entered the Waking World, pulled the cylinder from her pocket and kicked the embers of a campfire into flame so he could read it. 'You will need to understand these words to prevail against Abbérron.'

'How do you mean?'

'Yanantha sang the words of a refrain when she was nursing me: *"Not by might or human strength shall the final victory be won"*. The True King recently reminded me of those words and I must see them fulfilled. Now that we have this scroll to link the source of evil to Abbérron, destroying him is the last great act before you can be crowned King.'

'Lenyé. I'm not ready for that yet. Something else is going on. Three times I've been attacked by a fallen Great En-luchés, who was called up by my Uncle to destroy me. I have to deal with him first to enable the people to accept the True King.'

'That sounds like Nastâr. I met him on board *Sea Sprite* and challenged him with the Sword of Justice.'

'He was leading a vast company of Dé-monos,' Kyros continued. 'The first time he was driven away by Stellatus and his En-luchés. The second time was in the cabin. He was about to behead me with a great axe, when suddenly he vanished.'

'I saw you, in a waking vision, and parried Nastâr's blow.'

'What? I felt his axe blade on the back of my neck, and was powerless to defend myself. How is that possible?'

She described her joy in the True King's presence, her sense of urgency to check on her Sword, '…and suddenly I was there, with you.'

'Really? How amazing are the ways of the True King! I'm so grateful to him. And to you for your courage and faithfulness.'

'And the third time?' Lenyé queried.

'Just now, in a dream. All my warriors fell asleep. The En-luchés were swept away and Nastâr started throttling me. Then you appeared and must have driven him away again.'

'I didn't encounter him this time.'

'But it was so real. He had five fingers and a thumb on each hand. I felt them around my throat. I'm not making this up.'

'You certainly aren't; for all your men are asleep and there are no En-luchés. Something else must have drawn him away.'

'I've never known such evil before; far worse than Vashtani. He tried to rob me of my dream during the storm. I have to destroy him before I can challenge Abbérron.'

'Very well,' she stood to her feet and drew him up with her. 'I'll head to Terrazarema and meet Hanniel to see if he's found out how we can enter the city and rescue Ramâno. But my love goes with you; and the cry of my heart to the True King on your behalf is that you will prevail.'

Kyros wrapped his arms around her, 'Take care, my Sweet.'

Chapter Eighty

As soon as Lenyé and Marie-anna had gone, Kyros roused Harbona. 'Wake the guards, but do not reprimand them; for something more than human drowsiness has enveloped us.'

He picked his way through the sleeping warriors to the edge of the camp, crying out in his heart to the True King for wisdom to counter Nastâr and defeat him.

The warrior camp behind him was astir at the coming of the dawn. He turned to address them.

'My friends,' he cried. 'I want you to gather together to call on the True King to come to our aid and release greater power in our cause. There's a spiritual being on the loose, called Nastâr, who has attacked me three times. I need to deal with him. Yesterday, you saw a fight to the death between two men. This is different: a man against a fallen Great En-luchés, which I now understand to be a Great Dé-monos. Use your groups of three to guard one another. Whatever you see, or hear or are terrified by, do not leave your posts or cease your actions. Your continual cries to the True King are crucial to winning this battle.'

Harbona assembled them into groups. He had them rig horse blankets on javelins to shelter against the heat of the sun, and organised teams to prepare food and tend the horses.

Kyros felt detached from what was going on as though something was trying to attract his attention. He sat under one of the shelters and thought about the parchment in the cylinder that Lenyé had shown him, and was reminded about ridiculing her when they played adventurers at the Pool of Alesco. All she wanted to do was recover the clay pots containing the ancient parchments. He recalled his words: "*If that wisdom caused the break up of the civilisation in the first place, it wasn't worth having*".

But he was wrong, terribly wrong. For the parchment in the clay pot told of the sacrifice and death of the True King to rescue the people of the Waking World from the power of Abbérron. And that knowledge had been lost. Who was he to dismiss the testimony of Zerigor like that, even in ignorance?

He'd apologised to Lenyé for the damage it had done to their relationship. Now he was in tears before the True King as he heard the familiar voice in his heart: "*You cannot move any further forwards in your walk with me, or triumph in your struggle against evil, unless you let go of everything from your former life*". Suddenly he was flat on his face on the sand heartbroken over his arrogant attitude. Once the racking sobs died down, he felt a peace come over him, like tears cleansing his heart; but it was deeper than that, as though the True King was purging him of all the individual thoughts that made up his former attitude and he knew a oneness with the True King in heart and mind and spirit.

Then he laughed. That parchment in the cylinder also came from the ancient store of wisdom by virtue of the key hidden in the clay pot. Zerigor obviously intended to place his own writings in it, but decided the insights of Hoffengrégor to be more important. What was so significant about its contents? As Kyros thought about it, the thing that disturbed him most was Abbérron's name change. He sat up and wrote the letters in the coarse sand with his finger:

R a b b o r n é

"*Teacher of Light*", Kyros mused to himself. What would the Known Universe, and especially the Waking World, be like now if that office had been fulfilled?

Then he wrote the changed name:

Abbérron

He drew lines in the sand between the two, linking the same letters. Every letter was used in the second name, but in a different order. The second had been hidden and contained within the first, so the seeds of rebellion must have been there from the outset. *"Teacher of Light"* had become… What?

Kyros thought of the True King's words in Hoffengrégor's parchment, *"…**his Light source was broken beyond repair and his name became fallen and twisted and unmade from what I originally intended for him**".* Surely this new name must have a meaning as well; or why bother to re-group the letters like that?

He drew a dash between the second "b" and the "é".

Abb-érron

"A, b, b," were the first three letters of a child's endearment for its Father; and "érron" was "to deceive by false words".

Therefore Abb-érron meant *"Father of Lies"*.

So those who yielded to Abbérron and forsook the True King to become their own master were so familiar with the lie sown in their hearts that they could no longer distinguish the truth. Only by direct intervention from the True King could they be rescued from this state, and freed to decide for themselves who to follow.

Kyros realised this was the True King's answer concerning his cry for wisdom in how to defeat Nastâr. He had to challenge the Great Dé-monos with the meaning behind Abbérron's name and the effect this had on those he deceived. He also knew it was important to await the True King's timing for this confrontation, and led the warriors in their vigil for the rest of the day and well into the night.

Chapter Eighty One

Lenyé and Marie-anna cantered back to their camp in the faint light before dawn. She roused the others and they had a quick breakfast before setting off for Terrazarema. They rode all day, reached the outskirts after nightfall and were met by Hanniel.

'We saw a company of warriors ride out two days ago led by Youdlh,' Hanniel reported. 'Since then some of my men have slipped into the city disguised as ordinary people and there are hardly any guards left. If you approach the palace with my men, I don't think anyone will challenge such a powerful force.'

Lenyé was about to reply when she was startled by the eagle dropping out of the sky and settling on the ground.

'Chuah-te-mok. What news?'

'Ra-Na-Jiri was in the palace gardens yesterday afternoon and spoke to Ramâno. The child sacrifice is set for midnight tonight.'

'Then we'll have to rescue him as soon as possible. Hanniel suggests boldly riding in with his soldiers and fooling everyone.'

'He's right. There are hardly any guards left in the city.'

They parted company, Chuah-te-mok to check if the cobra had any more news, while Lenyé and Hanniel's horsemen galloped to the West of the city.

'O, Ramâno,' Lenyé cried out to him in her heart. 'Be strong for a little longer till I can get to you. Hold on to the name of the True King for he will give you the words to say. Have courage!'

Chapter Eighty Two

Morthrir stood on the floor of the Vault of Malrema as the places around the Hexacle were filled: except for Eawen and Rafé.

'My Lord, I must protest,' Nastâr spoke up. 'You dragged the Dé-monos leaders and myself back here when we were about to destroy Kyros. We spoke drowsiness over his men and he only had a few En-luchés to guard him. The Dé-monos were dealing with them. I had my hands around Kyros' throat to throttle him in his sleep. We will never have an opportunity like that again.'

'I have brought you back here to release even more power through the child sacrifice.'

'I dispute that, My Lord. You have to decide which is more important: destroying Kyros, or capturing Lenyé.'

'This sacrifice will release power to achieve both objectives.'

He turned away and studied the boy lying on his back on the altar, tied hand and foot and gagged and blindfolded.

Morthrir glanced at the time candle in its holder at the North end of the Altar. 'We have a little while till midnight before the ceremony can begin. So we'll use the time to stir up the power of Abbérron and instil fear in the mind of the boy.'

'The only reason I am here,' Nastâr continued, 'is because Abbérron and Lammista-ké want Kyros destroyed. You are acting in defiance of that by diverting power to Lenyé.'

'Morthrir glared at Nastâr then dismissed the matter from his mind. He fitted the Krêon of Tulá-kâhju on his head, climbed onto the *Imbrésonite* and felt a greater connection to Abbérron than he'd ever done standing on the altar. What was so special about this substance? He faced East, flexed his knees, placed his fingertips and thumbs together, intoned the name of Abbérron and nodded to the others to join in. Their voices became a chant in unison, dying away till they were humming on the same note: the walls and floor of the chamber resonating to the sound and setting up a vibration. They all ceased together and the ensuing silence was immense. Morthrir sensed himself falling into nothingness, but the vibrations continued. When he opened his eyes, the time candle had burned down almost to the midnight mark. There were only a few minutes to go.

Morthrir stepped off the bundle of *Imbrésonite* and indicated to Jumar-jé to remove the gag and blindfold from the boy.

'You're Ramâno, aren't you?' Morthrir's tone was harsh.

'Yes.'

'And you've fooled everyone into thinking your legs were healed, but it was a trick. You weren't crippled in the first place.'

'My legs have been useless all my life until I met the Healer.'

'Oh, yes. The Healer. What exactly did he say to you?'

'"*In the name of Luchianó-bé, Lord of Light, stand up and walk*".'

A howl of rage arose from Nastâr and the Dé-monos leaders.

'Why bother with a child sacrifice?' Nastâr broke in. 'That claim deserves death. If we let him live, others will rally to him.'

Morthrir frowned. 'Admit this has all been a trick to support a wandering conjurer.'

'Never. Mamma kept my crutches to prove I was crippled.'

'It's not that hard to make a pair of crutches to support a lie.'

'I'm not lying. My legs were healed.'

'Your Mother poisoned me,' Morthrir banged his fist on the altar in fury, 'so why should I accept anything she says or does?'

'She didn't poison you. The stallholder dropped a piece of...'

'Enough!' Morthrir sat on the altar and stared into Ramâno's eyes. 'I have a parchment confirming this was a boyish trick and you were working with a conjurer to fool people and make them think he was a healer. Sign it and I will forget about the past.'

'Why should I sign a lie?'

'It is not a lie. I'm trying to establish the truth.'

'You're asking me to denounce the Healer and deny he used the power of the True King to heal me? Never! I have a warrior's heart and remain loyal to those I love. You can't accept it because you're full of darkness. And eventually it will destroy you. The True King is the Lord of Light. Those in darkness have no idea what he's like. Those who serve the True King, like the Healer, are full of light. That's what drew me to him in the first place.'

'You've seen this light in my nephew, Kyros?'

'Like a big dinner plate around his head.'

'Is that what you saw in the ship when we put the crown on Kyros' head?'

Ramâno jerked his face away.

'Well,' Morthrir persisted. He wrenched the boy's head round so he could look him in the eyes again. 'Answer me.'

'Yes. It blazed a deep red.'

'And was it like that on my head?'

'No.'

'Is it blazing with light now?'

'How can it when you have no light in you?'

Morthrir stood up, walked over to Jumar-jé and grabbed the man by the throat. 'I thought you said there was no difference.'

'I did, Sire, because there is no difference. The boy's deluded.'

'Hmph!' Morthrir paced to the other side of the altar so that he was facing East and glanced at Jumar-jé. 'Prepare the victim.'

He was distracted by the boy shouting, 'I saw the Great En-luchés flying towards me and the rest of the En-luchés pouring out of the sky and sweeping the Dé-monos away. The same will happen again and destroy all these Dé-monos leaders you trust in for victory. Even that big one.'

Nastâr uttered a cry. 'He must die for that!'

Chapter Eighty Three

Lenyé and her soldiers swept through the gates unchallenged, and rode towards the palace. She dismounted and raced up the front steps. Hanniel's men hacked through the few guards that barred their way while she and the others hurried towards the Throne Room. She recognised the Master of Keys in the flickering light from the flares on the walls.

'Where's Ramâno?' there was an urgency in her voice.

'I don't know. I've not seen him.'

'What about my Uncle?'

'He's down in the big cellar. But you'll need the key.'

Lenyé saw him wrench one off the ring at his waist.

'Take it. Since your Uncle painted the cellar, evil things have been happening. I daren't go down there at this time of night.'

'Wait,' Morthrir whispered. 'We're going to do this properly.'

At his nod, the Chief Summoner strode to the altar, unbuttoned Ramâno's shirt to reveal the boy's chest and returned to his place. Morthrir pulled a long dagger from its sheath on his belt and heard the sound of the time candle marker tinkling against the glass as it fell away: midnight.

He glanced at everyone. 'With you stirred up like this, and demanding the boy's death, we will release power to destroy all opposition. Extinguish the time candle.' The Vault was plunged into darkness, except for the light growing in Morthrir.

'I don't care what you do to me,' Ramâno cried out. 'I commit myself into the keeping of the True King who will rescue me. But you will forever have this night on your conscience.'

Morthrir felt the boy's words hit him like a physical blow and staggered backwards. He raised both arms, his right hand gripping the hilt of his dagger. 'My Lord, Abbérron,' he cried. 'I adjure you, by the shed blood of this child sacrifice, to break the protection surrounding Lenyé and bring her to me once again, so that she may be my bride.'

❖

Lenyé grabbed the key, raced down the stone steps, crept up to the double doors of the largest cellar and heard her Uncle's cry. She drew the Sword of Justice, slid the key into the lock and quietly turned it. Several voices shouted, 'The boy must die!'

She thrust open the doors and was shocked by what she encountered. A blackened room. The only light emanated from her Uncle and lit up a white circle on the floor with the six points of a hexacle contained within in it. Exactly the same as the mark Uncle Morthrir daubed on her forehead with blood in her dream. At various points on the circle stood eight figures hooded and cloaked in brown robes, and four others dressed in white, black, red and grey. In the centre was an altar of stones with Ramâno lying on his back and bound hand and foot. Nastâr, Vashtani and five other Dé-monos leaders were rushing straight at him, and her Uncle stood poised to strike the death blow.

The whole scenario was etched on Lenyé's mind in an instant, and she felt it in the pit of her stomach. It was so evil, as if some malevolent presence was hovering in the very atmosphere of the cellar. At last she was confronting the "...*greater power that sits behind Morthrir*" that Yanantha warned her about. This is "...*what you have to bring down and vanquish... Without the lost Blade, even Kyros' return will avail little*".

Lenyé lunged forwards, the Sword of Justice in both hands, and parried her Uncle's dagger stroke.

'Hanniel,' she yelled. 'Arrest those men. Seize my Uncle and release the boy. I'll deal with the others.'

As the soldiers surged into the room, with Marie-anna close behind, Uncle Morthrir leaped at Lenyé, spun her round, held his dagger to her throat, and dragged her away from the altar.

'Stop!' he roared. 'Leave the Priests and Summoners alone. If anyone moves, I'll slit Lenyé's throat.'

Hanniel and his men backed off. One of them grabbed Marie-anna and prevented her rushing to help Ramâno.

'Nastâr,' Morthrir continued, 'grab Lenyé's Sword.'

But as Nastâr reached forwards, Lenyé raised her Sword. 'Get back,' she shouted. 'You know this Sword has power over you.' She felt the dagger press harder against her neck. 'If you try to carry out your threat, Uncle, I will …'

Instinctively Kyros knew the threshold-hour of midnight was past and called for quiet. The cries of his warriors died away. He sensed from the True King that the time was right and raised his voice. 'Nastâr. I command you to appear before me.'

Even as Lenyé spoke against her Uncle in the cellar, she was astonished to see Nastâr and five Dé-monos leaders gathered up in a dark cloud and wrenched away. She realised this was Kyros calling Nastâr to account and the others were taken with him.

'Vashtani,' Uncle Morthrir yelled. 'I need you here with me!'

Lenyé felt the Sword of Justice twisting and turning in her hands as though the evil power was trying to wrench it from her grasp and knew intuitively she had to uphold Kyros in this great struggle, despite their Uncle threatening her with his dagger.

The great being appeared in front of Kyros, folded its wings and gestured as a cloud of darkness appeared behind him. 'My Dé-monos and their leaders are also with me.'

Kyros was dismayed at their numbers, but remained resolute, crying out, 'I challenge you to single combat.'

'What?' Nastâr roared with laughter. 'So if you defeat me, all my forces in the Waking World will be subject to you?'

'Correct.'

'Abbérron, Lammista-ké and Morthrir are excluded from this agreement. If I lose, you will have to face them separately.'

'Very well,' Kyros replied.

'But if I defeat you,' Nastâr's mocking voice continued, 'then everyone in the Waking World is subject to me. Am I right?'

'Yes,' Kyros tried to keep the tremor out of his voice.

'Including Lenyé?'

Kyros didn't answer.

'Agreed?'

Finally Kyros nodded, 'Agreed.'

Lenyé thrust against her Uncle, wrapped a leg around one of his and tried to throw him off balance. He edged away and pulled so that she was thrown back into his arms. She felt the dagger slip against her skin.

'Drop that Sword!' her Uncle's voice rasped in her ear.

❖

'No man has ever challenged me like this,' Nastâr continued. 'Not even Zerigor, and he was twice the man you are.'

'That's because you were cast down before you could trouble

humankind at the Beginning. The Ancient Prophet...'

'Hoffengrégor? Drivel. That's all it was. Utter drivel. He made it up so he could appear important and impress Zerigor.'

'He was appointed by the True King,' Kyros countered.

'He took the title of Prophet to himself.'

'No man can do that. Only if the True King...'

'Zerigor failed because he relied on those writings.'

Kyros felt Nastâr's words lodge in his inner being, breaking down his resistance and destroying the trust he had in the Prophet's writings, and undermining his knowledge of the True King. He cried out to his warriors. 'Stand firm, my friends. The name of the True King in your mouths is a powerful weapon against our foes. Do not give in to them.' But even as his eyes swept the massed ranks of his warriors, he could see the dark cloud of Dé-monos pressing down on them.

'Do not trust in your warriors, Kyros,' Nastâr's words jerked him back to his own battle. 'The En-luchés won't rescue you this time. We made sure of that. Now I have been released into the Waking World,' the evil voice continued, 'your Uncle is invincible; for I was sent by Abbérron to destroy you.'

'No!' Kyros cried.

'You don't even have the Sword of Justice. So how will you defend yourself against me?'

'I rely on the name of the True King...'

'You gave it to that girl of yours, didn't you? Because you don't know how to use it. And she doesn't, either. Just waves it about and hopes it will do something.'

Kyros had a picture in his mind of Lenyé grasping the Sword in her hands and challenging Nastâr and the other Dé-monos leaders. But suddenly Nastâr turned on her, wrenched the Sword from her grasp, and seized her. 'I've just destroyed Kyros. Now you're free to be Morthrir's bride, and this time, no one will rescue you!'

Kyros shook his head to clear his mind. 'The Sword of Justice in her hands is a powerful weapon against you, Nastâr.'

'Vashtani,' Uncle Morthrir yelled. 'Lift me and Lenyé and the altar and the boy and take us to Mount Malkamet. There I will complete the child sacrifice and Lenyé will become my bride.'

'Never,' Lenyé struggled in her Uncle's grip and tried to pull away from his dagger. She watched Vashtani stoop in front of the altar and begin to raise it from the ground. 'Hanniel,' she yelled. 'Get Ramâno off there.'

Her cry came too late. Vashtani hoisted the altar onto his shoulders and Lenyé and her Uncle were raised off the floor. She sensed that evil presence pressing down on her, raised the Sword of Justice and sliced through the air above her head. 'Uncle Morthrir. You will not touch the boy!'

'That boy died painfully,' Nastâr's sneering voice penetrated Kyros' mind again. 'I saw it happen before you invited me here. Lenyé, with her fancy Sword, was unable to save him.'

'I don't believe you,' Kyros shouted. 'The boy is not dead.'

'Through his death, Abbérron has been released into the Waking World and will take up his rightful rule.'

'Not while I stand against him! The True King will…'

'The True King uses people when it suits him, and then discards them. He has rejected you, Kyros, and will cast you down to the Pit to be rid of you. Can't you feel the bulls goring your flesh already and the dogs tearing at your throat, and the heat rising to engulf you and the stench to overpower you? He won't rescue you. You are of no more importance to him.'

Kyros heard the cries of his men falter and looked up to see them collapse to the ground: the Dé-monos had overpowered them. He slumped to his knees, covered his ears and tried to shut out the incessant words that were tearing away at his own firmly held convictions. 'I call upon the True King who has lifted me...'

'You had some ridiculous dream,' Nastâr continued, 'of finding the Krêon of Tulá-kâhju and setting yourself up as King, thinking your precious True King was guiding you every step of the way. But your Uncle beat you to it. He seized the Crown and is preparing for the Coronation Day. Let the spoils go to the strong, for you will never make a King.'

Kyros fell face down on the sand unable to resist those words.

'As for that girl of yours. She's not cut out to be a Queen either. You let her ride away with that Sword in her hands when you need it here. There's no other way you can bring me down and you know it. Your words cannot prevail against me.'

Lenyé and her Uncle landed on their feet and she realised from the violent movements of the Sword in her hands that she was not only upholding Kyros in his battle with Nastâr, but also forcing the altar back down onto the floor.

Kyros sensed the great being stoop over him, and felt those five-fingered hands around his throat again, choking the life out of him. It wasn't just dark from Nastâr's shadow; his head swam and everything was going black before his eyes.

'I only let Morthrir gain mastery over me,' Nastâr's words seared into Kyros' mind like burning oil, 'because I anticipated this moment. Once you are destroyed, I can lead the Waking World in our objective to place Abbérron on the Highest Throne!'

'Oh, my King,' Kyros cried out. 'Come to my aid once more.'

Chapter Eighty Four

Beth sat with her Mother's arm around her at their campsite and snuggled into her comforting warmth. She thought she would never see her again, but now that fear was over and she felt so happy. She watched Quinn slump down next to his Father and start eating his supper. He was obviously concerned about the warriors he'd seen and kept glancing in the direction where he'd re-entered the camp.

She looked up into her Mother's face, 'Why has Uncle Morthrir done this to us?'

'Done what?' her Mother replied.

'Imprisoned you,' Quinn spoke with his mouth full of food, 'and chased us.'

'We even overheard him talking to Rafé and Youdlh,' Beth continued, 'about having you executed.'

'It was because of Rafé,' Quinn cut in before anyone else could respond, 'that Uncle Morthrir decided to wait.'

'That's interesting,' his Father spoke up. 'Rafé never let on to me about any of this before it happened, and he was my counsellor. Even at Onadestra he was very distant whenever he came to visit us, and wouldn't look me in the eyes, or give any indication about what was going on.'

Beth glanced at her own Father as he took up the story. 'Paco warned us that we were to be moved, and it sounded like bad news. So maybe Morthrir changed his mind at the last minute.'

Beth saw Quinn wipe his mouth on his sleeve before speaking. 'Why are you here, Aunt Faria? It doesn't make sense.'

His Aunt smiled at him. 'Morthrir told me the Tsé-shâmé tried to seize the Throne and take over the Krêonor Kingdom. I knew nothing about any executions. He kept your parents hidden and locked away for their own safety. He included me in the group to go to Fantrios in case the Tsé-shâmé broke into Onadestra and mistook me for one of your Mothers.'

'That's not what I heard from Paco.' Beth sighed, and mentioned the gossip at the castle.

Aunt Faria looked shocked, 'I can't believe Morthrir would do this to me.'

'What's it all about?' Quinn's Mother spoke up.

Quinn's Father put his arm around her shoulders before replying, 'This has been brewing all his life. He's always wanted to get his own back on Alkram and myself. Seizing the Throne and getting rid of us would be his obvious move. It looks as though we all owe our lives to Rafé.'

'So how are we going to sort this out?' her own Mother queried.

'I think we have to trust Ishi-mi-réjá in this,' Beth glanced round at them all. 'We must get to Terrazarema and see what happens.'

The next morning Quinn raced to the edge of the woods to assess the warriors. His party would have to strike camp and move on as soon as possible so as not to be seen.

Quinn was aware of Beth's impatience: there were only two days left to get to Terrazarema. He set a fast pace till well after dusk. When he and his Father cantered to the edge of the woods to check the Eastern gate of the city, he saw a detachment of warriors already at the gate. Some rode under the arch, but the rest carried on round the city walls before halting for the night.

They rejoined the others and continued South to shorten the journey in the morning, and set up camp.

Chapter Eighty Five

Kyros was still flat on his face on the sand with Nastâr's hands gripping him around his throat and squeezing hard. He heard the faint whisper of the True King in his heart: *"You brought nothing into this world when you were born and you will take nothing out of it when you pass on. Except my words that have grown within you. For these have become a sharp double-edged sword in your mouth. Turn and speak to your adversary"*.

Kyros eased himself backwards till his head was directly under Nastâr's chest, the powerful hands resisting him all the way. He spun himself round until he was lying on his back; the great hands slipping on his throat as he did so. Then he spoke directly at the great chest above him. 'In the name of Luchianó-bé, Lord of Light, I pass judgement over you and cast you down to the Realm of Consumption and return you to the Pit my Uncle freed you from.' He felt an enormous surge of power go out of him and pierce the Great Dé-monos.

Nastâr gave an ear-splitting screech as he was flung sideways and writhed on the sand, crying out in agony.

Kyros rolled away, gasping for breath, but knew he only had this one opportunity to counter the doubt that had been sown in his mind and nearly broken his trust in the True King and the writings of the Prophet. He lurched up on his knees and shouted at his opponent. 'Abbérron was established by the True King as *Teacher of Light* and appointed to bring the knowledge of the True King to the Waking World. His name was once *Rabborné*.'

Lenyé ducked as a stone popped out of the altar and hurtled past her head. More stones broke away from the side and front.

❖

Kyros saw doubt in the Great Dé-monos' eyes.

'How do you know this?' Nastâr demanded.

'The writings of the Ancient Prophet have been opened,' Kyros stared into Nastâr's eyes, 'and everything concerning Abbérron has been laid bare. He rebelled against the True King and drew many away before he was cast down. Including you. And he has drawn humankind away as well, tempting everyone to be their own master rather than hold fast to the True King.'

'You cannot rely on that so-called Prophet. He speaks lies.'

'Those who represent the True King speak his truth. But Abbérron was a liar from the beginning and drew the entire Known Universe into rebellion. His name means: "*Father of Lies*".'

'You're making it up. No one has ever called him that before.'

'Then it's time the truth about him is known. You were once full of light, and so was Abbérron, but his Light source was broken beyond repair.'

'That's nonsense…'

'If so, then you and Abbérron started out twisted and broken and full of hate. Who would bring such creatures into being in the first place?'

❖

Lenyé saw the altar wrenched from Vashtani's grasp and career around the cellar, skimming the tops of their heads. Everyone ducked. Ramâno was thrown from side to side and almost fell off. She gripped the Sword tighter and focused on keeping the boy pressed down on the stones.

'What's happening?' Uncle Morthrir's cry was loud in her ear.

Vashtani attempted to grab the altar but missed. It hit the floor and slithered to a stop right in front of Lenyé.

The Sword shook in her hands and the altar began to disintegrate as individual stones broke free and ricocheted around the cellar, crashing off the walls and floor in a maelstrom of hurling debris.

Kyros saw the Great Dé-monos falter as though the truth of what he was saying had pierced Nastâr's defences and his enemy could not counter it.

'Humankind was appointed to suffer with the True King,' Kyros continued, 'in order to bring you and Abbérron down to the Pit. That time is fast approaching. Formerly Abbérron was subject to the True King who cast him down to the Waking World. Now Abbérron will be subject to me.'

Kyros saw Nastâr recoil in shock. He sprang to his feet, and shouted to his warriors, 'Up, my friends. I call you to stand with me. The Dé-monos can only be defeated by those of faithful heart who cling to the True King for deliverance.' The men struggled up, stood in their groups of three, and shouted with him: 'In the name of the True King, we come against you!'

Lenyé was distracted by a cry from Marie-anna. 'I cannot let my son endure this any longer!' She saw her friend thrust through the line of soldiers, seize a dagger from one of them, grab Ramâno, pull him off what was left of the altar and cut through his bonds. Marie-anna wrapped her arms around the boy and cradled him in her lap. But her sob of relief was cut short by the lad's high pitched voice echoing in the chamber: 'Let me go, Mamma. Kyros is the only one who can sort this out, and he won't know where to come.'

❖

Kyros caught sight of a glitter out of the corner of his eye and looked round to see not one, but two Great En-luchés flying towards him, the white feathers on their wings even more apparent in the first rays of the rising sun. His heartbeat slowed to mirror the steady beat of those wings and he felt a great peace settle on him despite his eyes being dazzled by their radiant light, outshining the sun at its noonday brightness. Behind them, with a thunder of hooves and the grinding of many wheels, came horses and chariots of fire and thousands of En-luchés holding drawn swords and lances, with pennants fluttering from the tips, swooping down towards him: a far greater army than he'd seen before.

Nastâr scrambled up and spread his wings before flying off towards Terrazarema, the rest of the Dé-monos and their leaders following in quick succession.

'To your horses,' Kyros yelled at the warriors. 'Harbona bring mine. Follow me, all of you.'

Even as he spoke the two Great En-luchés swept overhead with the rest of the En-luchés surging behind, and he and the warriors were caught up with them on the song of their battle cry. But to his surprise, Kyros was in the lead, right hand raised, closely followed by his warriors with lances in one hand and drawn swords in the other. The En-luchés held back, as though allowing the honour of victory to be won by humans. They poured after the Dé-monos, hounding them all the way to Terrazarema.

Kyros saw Nastâr and the five Dé-monos leaders disappear through the roof of the palace, while the rest of the Dé-monos formed up in a dark cloud in front. He left Harbona with the warriors and rushed up the steps into the great hallway, but halted as a boy darted out of one of the corridors.

'Ramâno,' he stooped down and opened his arms to greet the lad. 'You're safe. Where's Lenyé?'

'This way, this way,' the boy dragged him along the corridor. 'She's down in the big cellar. Hurry. She needs your help.'

Kyros raced after him, plunged down the stone steps and flung the doors wide. The cellar was in chaos with a mass of stones bouncing off the walls and floor. Lenyé held Nastâr and the Dé-monos leaders at bay with the Sword of Justice, but their Uncle had an arm around her with a dagger to her throat.

He raised his right hand as the two Great En-luchés appeared through the ceiling and took up their positions either side of Lenyé. Kyros spoke in the name of the True King, 'Enough!'

The swirl of stones crashed to the floor.

'Uncle Morthrir, for attacking the future Queen, you are stripped of any authority you may have as a Krêonor Prince. Down on your knees.'

As if he'd received a blow to the side of his head, their Uncle collapsed to the ground.

'Hanniel. Arrest my Uncle and those other men.'

'Yes, Sire.'

Lenyé adopted an attacking stance and raised her Sword. The Great En-luchés drew theirs and stood with her. Lenyé advanced and Nastâr and the Dé-monos leaders backed away till they were trapped in the corner of the cellar.

Kyros spoke again, 'Let the En-luchés come to my aid so that the judgement I have already declared may be exercised today. Nastâr, I cast you down to the Pit. Vashtani, you and your division will be chained again and taken to the Realm of Consumption. The rest of you, and the remaining Dé-monos outside the palace, I summon to the Dangst Rock, the Place of Chaining.'

Chapter Eighty Six

That night Rafé felt elated at finding the golden globe, but had the True King really guided him? Surely it was his own intuitive feeling that made him turn left and head downwards?

Eawen's whispered words at their parting troubled him: "*I alone...thwart the desires of Morthrir*". Had his actions been directed by the True King all the time? And again: "*I have raised you up...To place a King...upon the Throne*". And finally: "*Therefore I will lead you and guide you in finding what rightly belongs to him*". Maybe the True King helped him find the golden globe after all.

Was the True King using him to place Dareth back on the Throne? And was that part of the Restoration Eawen mentioned?

He could ride to the Hunting Lodge at Fantrios, free Dareth and Alkram and their wives, return to Terrazarema and oust Morthrir. But there was something more important he wanted to do first. He took Eawen's example and stood up, raised his right hand and spoke into the chill night air, 'I renounce my involvement with the Priesthood, and any ties to Abbérron through Morthrir, and accept the True King into my life.' Rafé opened his pack pulled out the brown Priest robe and flung it on the fire. It smouldered and burst into flame, destroying his final link to Abbérron. He felt such peace and settled down to sleep with the soft words of: '*Trust me*', sounding in his ears.

The following day Rafé knew it wasn't his responsibility to release Dareth and Alkram after all. Instead, he had to take the golden globe to Terrazarema and present it to Lenyé.

Chapter Eighty Seven

Kyros led the way out of the cellar, to the stables. 'Lenyé, come with us. We will need the Sword of Justice to enforce this. Ramâno, ride with me on my horse.'

'I can ride myself now. Why can't I have one of my own?'

'There is only room for two horses where I plan to go, and I need you and Lenyé with me.'

They mounted and rode out of the stables. Kyros watched the Great En-luchés haul Nastâr away. Stellatus bound Vashtani and his division in chains of light. The rest of the Dé-monos fled with the En-luchés chasing them like dogs rounding up a flock of unruly goats. Kyros and Lenyé on their horses were caught up with them, rushing over the plain towards the cliffs at the head of Lake Sanchéso. The Dé-monos gathered between the Eye of Hoffengrégor and the Dangst Rock, hovering over the water.

'*Remember the Rancher's foreman who drove the stray buffalo out of his neighbour's farm and repaired the hole in the fence?*' Kyros heard the voice of the True King in his heart. '*That is what you have to do. You now stand in the gap between the Realm of the Blessèd Throne and the Waking World as my representative.*'

Kyros leaned across, caught hold of Lenyé's hand and let his horse walk gingerly onto the top of the cliff. Then they both urged their horses to leap the gap to the Dangst Rock, the hooves slithering on the smooth surface.

'Draw your Sword, Lenyé,' and he heard the shim against the scabbard as she did so.

Kyros stood up in his stirrups feeling Ramâno scramble to his feet behind him, the boy's arms resting on his shoulders. 'This is the judgement I pronounce over the remainder of the Dé-monos. By the authority of the True King vested in me, and the proof of that authority through the Sword of Justice in Lenyé's hands, I banish you from the Waking World, to enter the Spiral and return to the Realm of Travail, never to trouble this world again.'

With the sounding of many trumpets, and the raising of their battle cry, the En-luchés rushed forwards, driving the dark cloud of their enemies into the Spiral on the islet and pouring into the cave mouth after them.

Kyros twisted his head slightly. 'Now comes your part, Ramâno. If I say the words to you, can you remember them well enough to speak them out?'

'I think so.'

'Good. For out of the mouths of young children the words of the True King are powerful to accomplish his purposes.' Kyros twisted his head further round and whispered in the boy's ear.

Then he faced forwards and heard Ramâno's high pitched voice: 'In the name of the True King, let the entrance to the Spiral in the Waking World be sealed by the En-luchés so that nothing from the Realm of Travail can enter this world again.'

'Abbérron,' Kyros raised his right hand as he spoke, and his voice carried the full power and authority of the True King. 'All the Dé-monos you rely on to accomplish your will have been expelled from the Waking World. My Uncle failed to enact the child sacrifice to unleash you back into this world because of Lenyé's intervention with the Sword of Justice. And I have the boy here with me to prove it. The True King once banished you from the Waking World, and decreed that if you ever re-entered, the final judgement would befall you. I command you to appear before me when I sit on my Throne in Terrazarema. Therefore, that judgement will be released over you.'

PART VII

THE RESTORATION

Chapter Eighty Eight

The following morning Lenyé stood in the Royal Cemetery with Kyros watching the men dig up the bodies Ramâno witnessed being buried. She recalled Kyros' words in that forester's cottage when they were about to flee for their lives: "*One of us has to escape and bring Uncle Morthrir to justice, whatever that takes*". They were both still alive and back at the palace in Terrazarema, with her two brothers and Kyros' two sisters and Uncle Morthrir as their prisoner. But they were struggling to bring a case against him that could be confirmed by an independent source. They had to check this grave to verify Ramâno's testimony.

It was a bright day with clear blue skies, the casual beauty of the summer wild flowers rampant amongst the seeding grass heads of the cemetery. But it was overcast with gloom by what they had to do. She laid a hand on Kyros' arm, not knowing what to expect as the men dug into the soil.

She stifled a gasp as a shovel clinked on something metallic. The men scooped away the debris with their hands exposing the tarnished buttons of a military uniform as the first body was uncovered. Lenyé clapped a hand over her mouth as the wispy strands of hair were revealed. She choked as the face emerged, mainly the skull with traces of stained parchment clinging to it.

Lenyé was horrified. 'Is that the skin?'

Doctor Nostrea nodded. He knelt down and examined the remains of the clothing. 'See here,' he glanced up and met her eyes before turning to Kyros. 'A knife slit through the fabric to penetrate the ribs and angled to pierce the heart. These stains are dried blood. Whoever did this knew what he was about.'

'So he was murdered after all. Check the next one please, Doctor.' Kyros slipped his hand over the back of Lenyé's. 'It doesn't prove Uncle Morthrir gave the order. Youdlh could have been settling a private score.'

'Pity Youdlh isn't still alive,' she glanced at Kyros as the men carried on digging. 'He would have to tell the court under oath.'

'I doubt it. He would claim allegiance to Uncle Morthrir and remain silent.'

'Exactly the same wound.' Doctor Nostrea's shout startled Lenyé and she turned back to the grave as the men lifted the second set of remains out of the deepening hole.

She watched in fascination as the men continued digging.

'So even this doesn't produce any evidence against our Uncle!' Lenyé heard the frustration in Kyros' voice.

'Surely he's committed High Treason against your Father?'

'There's no evidence of our parents' bodies,' Kyros fumed. 'Even if we found the graves, we can't prove he did it.'

'What about Aunt Faria's death. He said she died in a hunting accident. But he might have arranged that to clear the way for him to marry me.'

'We can't prove that either. And even if he did marry you, he wasn't interfering with any direct lines of succession.'

'You'd proposed to me by then. That must make a difference.'

'But your Father hadn't given his consent. So technically, you were unattached at the time and a target for any other suitor.'

'We all know what he was after, Kyros. The Throne, me as his wife and undying loyalty from his subjects.'

'We can't convict him of any of that.'

'What about his attempt on your life? That's High Treason as well.' Lenyé was distracted again by the men scooping soil out of the hole to reveal the lid of a coffin.

'He didn't carry it out, so there's no case to answer.' Kyros' words jerked her back to their conversation.

'But he intended to do it!' Lenyé saw the lid prised open and the remains of an even more decayed body in the coffin.

'This may have been a warrior,' Doctor Nostrea called over to them. 'But it's impossible to identify.'

'He'll wriggle and squirm and bring up all sorts of counter arguments,' Kyros continued. 'It's much harder to prove intent to commit a crime like High Treason.'

Lenyé watched Doctor Nostrea gather up his instruments and give instructions to move the bodies and the coffin. She turned to Kyros. 'What about his treatment of Ramâno? He was tied to the stern window of *Sea Sprite* for hours in the blazing sun. And the child sacrifice. Surely that must count for something?'

'But you stopped him.'

'I know. I took the full force of his dagger thrust on the hilt of the Sword of Justice. If I hadn't, Ramâno would be dead.'

'He still didn't do it.'

'What about that awful chamber where he was hatching so much evil?'

'That won't help us either.'

'This is ridiculous,' Lenyé gesticulated with both hands. 'There must be something. What about his word of power you told me about? Surely that demonstrates his intentions? Can't we accuse him of conspiring by use of spiritual means to seize the Throne, put down all contenders and establish himself as King?'

'That wouldn't stand up in court. He could either deny it, and claim his word against mine; or plead insanity.'

'What about getting him to admit something in public that he can't retract?'

'Maybe. But it will require skilful handling.' Kyros paused as if thinking. 'The only other thing is the contents of the Royal safe. He may have left something in there that might incriminate him. Both sets of keys are missing, so I've authorised the Crafters to cut away the hinges and prise the front off. But it will take time.'

Chapter Eighty Nine

That afternoon Lenyé was caught up in the warrior-wedding around the fountain in the middle of the Central Square in Terrazarema. The open-air ceremony passed in a blur: the great crowd of clans-people; the double ring of horsemen encircling them, the clatter of hooves on the paving stones loud in her ears; the two aisles through the crowd, one for the bride, the other for the groom; the Headman of Marie-anna's clan awaiting them at the front; of Kyros escorting Marie-anna in one aisle and herself walking with Harbona and keeping pace with them in the other, Kyros as the chosen protector and herself as Marie-anna's friend to present the bride and groom to each other; her two brothers scattering flowers ahead of each party, her cousins holding Marie-anna's train and Ramâno behind Harbona with the rings.

Harbona chose him because today he was going to sign a document adopting Ramâno as his son. When the boy heard the news last night, Lenyé would never forget that look of shock and astonishment and joy as the flash of his smile confirmed Ramâno's feelings. And the way the lad flung his arms around Harbona's neck, and the response from the man himself, hugging the boy as if he would crush the very life out of him. Something was knit between the two, greater than a man's natural affection for his own son, as the last defences in that hardened warrior broke and Harbona shook as he sobbed. She was so pleased for Ramâno, and proud of him.

Then came the pledging of oaths, and the signing of documents. The Headman sprinkled water on the ground three times in front of the married couple to cleanse the past, seal the present and open the way for the future. Harbona and Marie-anna led the wedding party as they processed between two columns of mounted warriors, swords drawn and sloped forwards to form a protective roof over their heads, accompanied by shouts of: 'Long live Harbona. Long live Marie-anna. May their lives be blessed with many offspring and many friends coming to their home.' Children raced to the Guard of Honour, slipped between the horses and tossed flowers over the couple as they passed.

The bride was radiant and Lenyé was so happy for her friend.

She and Kyros walked arm in arm behind the couple until the procession was through the Guard of Honour and free to move amongst the crowds in the Square that had gathered to watch.

Ramâno went prancing and skipping in front, shouting, 'Look at my Mamma, she's so happy. She's just married a great warrior. And I'm so happy because I'm proud to call him my Father.' The lad was ecstatic.

Someone called out, 'Isn't that the boy who was healed?'

'Yes,' Ramâno replied. 'That's the man who healed me,' and he pointed at Kyros.

'It's Prince Kyros.' People stopped to stare and look more closely. 'We thought he was dead. He can't be the Healer.'

'He is, I tell you,' Ramâno shouted in response. 'He's had a shave and a haircut, but he's the same man.'

'The Healer's come back to us,' several people cried out.

Others came flocking to see. 'And he's Prince Kyros.'

Many more raced into the Square and stood staring.

'Eawen was right,' a woman cried out. 'He kept saying the Healer was Prince Kyros, but none of us believed him.'

The cry of the Healer returning as Prince Kyros was taken up and a great wave of joy erupted in the city.

'Why don't you free Eawen from wrongful imprisonment by your Uncle,' someone called out. 'After all, he continued speaking to us about the True King after you left.'

'I have done so already,' Kyros shouted back. 'And I am delighted he has encountered the True King for himself.'

They were swept along touching hands with well-wishers in the crowd until the whole wedding procession began to break up into separate groupings. Lenyé turned to Kyros and wrapped her arms around his neck. 'I don't think you need worry about reconciling the People to each other. The True King has gone before you and prepared the way. Look. There are the leaders of the Tsé-shâmé and Harmoth delegations joining in the fun. Let's go over and talk to them.'

She led him by the hand as they pushed their way through the crowd.

'Prince Kyros,' the leader of the Tsé-shâmé stepped forwards to greet him. 'I am bemused at the turn of events. My party was invited here by your Uncle.'

'That goes for me, too,' the leader of the Harmoth delegation also stepped forwards. 'We understood you were dead and Morthrir was to be crowned King. Then we find out you have returned and arrested him for attempting to usurp the Throne.'

'If you and your delegations come to the Amphitheatre for the celebrations tomorrow,' Kyros replied, 'I think all will become clear. Please accept my invitation to use the two Guest Boxes on either side of the dais.'

When the delegates had withdrawn, they turned back to the wedding party and Lenyé only just had time to react and catch the bouquet of flowers that Marie-anna tossed to her.

She went over, wrapped her arms around her friend's neck and kissed her. 'You didn't need to do that.'

'You're next. And our ceremony is but a foretaste of yours.'

'As ours will be of what is yet to come,' Lenyé replied.

'What do you mean?'

'Somehow there will be a joining of the True King with his People that will be like a marriage.'

'That is too lofty for me to understand. I'm more concerned with trying to be a good wife to my new husband.'

'As I will with Kyros after tomorrow. But I feel this deep in my heart. Every marriage is significant for those being joined together, no matter how simple or elaborate the celebration. For they all point towards that greater marriage to come. Please stay somewhere local tonight so you can be with us tomorrow.'

'You don't think I'd miss your Wedding Day do you? Of course I'll be there.'

'And when the two of you do go away on your own,' Lenyé continued, 'Ramâno is welcome to stay at the palace with the others until you get back. I'm sure he'll understand you and Harbona will want to be alone together for a few days.'

'Thank you.'

As she turned away, Lenyé glimpsed Olathe and Nasima through the crowd in their bridesmaids' dresses and suddenly thought of Beth. Marie-anna caught hold of her by the wrist.

'Despite your present happiness, Lenyé, I sense a deep sorrow in you. That can't be right on the eve of your Wedding Day. What's the matter? Please tell me.'

She tried to pull free, but Marie-anna wouldn't let go. Lenyé swung round and there were her friend's dark eyes gazing into her own, and such an expression of concern on her face.

'You know when we were on the ship,' Lenyé faltered, '*Brave Heart*, and everyone was helping with the anchor and capstan.'

Marie-anna nodded. 'I remember. Go on.'

'Kyros and I talked about Beth and Quinn and our grief over their loss. We ended up weeping in each other's arms.'

'Oh, Lenyé. I'm so sorry for you. I wish there was something I could do.'

She felt Marie-anna's arms slip around her, and sobbed into her friend's shoulder. 'I don't think either of us are over it yet. I wanted Beth to be my bridesmaid more than anything.'

Chapter Ninety

I, Kyros, eldest son of King Dareth and thereby Crown Prince of the Krêonor, was pacing up and down late that night in the private council chamber next to the Throne Room on the eve of the Great Day, contemplating the forthcoming Judgement I must pronounce on Uncle Morthrir, and anticipating my Coronation and Marriage to Lenyé. I was thinking of Lenyé's reminder concerning my Birthday. She was right, I had come of age. Suddenly I was caught up to a place I knew instinctively to be the Realm of the Blessèd Throne.

For I appeared to be in a vast building with an overarching ceiling of solid stone judging by the many voices echoing the surpassing greatness of the True King, and the paean of praise as more voices were lifted up in exquisite song that pierced my heart with a thousand blades of sweetness. The floor beneath my feet trembled and shook as though the stones would be loosened in their sockets and fall away, such was the potency of the words and song. But as I glanced down and then up above my head in wonder, no sign of any physical substance could I discern and I seemed to be standing in nothingness.

I heard behind me a loud voice saying: 'Write what you see and hear and make it available to those who dwell in the Waking World, that they may know the True King tests all those he loves, as human parents prepare their children for life. This is a day of reckoning to give an account of all that you have done with the freedom I gave you.'

I turned to see who was speaking to me and beheld him upon

whom I have set my heart's affection, seated on his Throne. He was clothed in a long white robe, and his feet were shod with sandals fashioned of gold. His eyes blazed like living fire and consumed me and his voice rolled over me like the power of the sea. Upon his head blazed a Crown of ruby-red, so like to the Krêon of Tulá-kâhju that I thought he must have reached down his hand and taken the one secured in the palace strong-room at Terrazarema. In his right hand he held the Sceptre of Authority and in his left, the golden Orb of Dominion. And I fell at his feet as one dead, unable to bear his searching gaze and my heart was in despair, for though I had completed the tests he set me, I only had one of the emblems that marked him out as King.

I felt him take hold of me by the shoulder. 'Do not be afraid.'

His voice was as the gentlest sea, lapping softly on white sands, and I dared to lift my head and saw his feet in the golden sandals. I was lying in a sea of molten glass that sparkled and reflected the Light of the True King. It glowed with a strong ruby-red as it mirrored the Krêon of Tulá-kâhju about his head, to act as a permanent reminder in the Realm of the Blessèd Throne of the cost that enables humankind to be in his presence. And I realised I had come to him through the shed blood of his sacrifice.

He raised me up and sat me on a chair in front of him as he resumed his Throne, and all about us fell quiet. In the silence he spoke one word: 'Well?'

I stumbled through the tests of obeying his voice when my own faculty of sight was blinded; of rescuing Harbona when he was still my enemy; of speaking his name against the Dé-monos; of destroying Malvi-Quîdda by the use of that name; of reversing my Uncle's words of power; of my heart-struggle over Lenyé and Yanantha; and finally of recovering the Crown of Life; but feeling all the time that I was missing some vital link.

I recalled Hoffengrégor's words to me: "*Any man can set his will to achieve an objective. It is not what you accomplish that is*

297

important so much as what you become. The True King is far more interested in you developing a relationship with him and the effect that will have on your character, rather than what you do".

I looked up and this time held his gaze without flinching. 'All these are but one test, my King. To know you and to love you and to walk in your ways. For you have revealed yourself to me not only as the True King, but also as Luchianó-bé, Lord of Light. Who am I that you should take hold of me like this and change me so much?'

'You may have recovered the Crown, Kyros, yet your heart remains broken over the Sundering of the Peoples long ago. Your Uncle gathered Tsé-shâmé and Harmoth delegates to force them to accept his Kingship. But that is not the way of healing. Only by a King who walks before me can the reconciliation of the Peoples be accomplished. As they witness your Wedding and Coronation, their hearts will be changed to accept you.'

To my wonderment, as if a veil had been drawn aside, I beheld a greater Throne to his left and slightly behind his and recognised the description of the Prophet. And I found myself thinking, why have I been shown this now, and who is the one greater yet to be revealed of whom the Prophet spoke?

I rose from my chair and knelt before him. 'My life is no longer my own. I offer myself unreservedly to you so that you may do in me and through me all that you seek to accomplish.'

He also rose from his Throne and raised me up and then knelt in front of me.

'What is the meaning of this, my King,' I objected.

He looked up at me and smiled. 'I offer you my life, unreservedly. Call on me, take of me and be one with me. For as I am in the Waking World, so you are in the Realm of the Blessèd Throne; and as I am in the Realm of the Blessèd Throne, so you are in the Waking World. Sit with me in my Throne and together we will rule and reign in the Waking World.'

I frowned, not fully grasping what he meant, and thinking

again of the missing Orb and Sceptre.

'Do not be dismayed, for all things shall come to fulfilment in their season. As in the Realm of the Blessèd Throne, so also in the Waking World. I send you back for the three things you face: Judgement, Kingship, and Marriage. By means of these offices all Peoples shall come to know me for themselves. But the last is the greatest, for through your fidelity to the one you love, my love is visible to all.'

The True King rose to his feet and we both stepped forwards to embrace each other at exactly the same moment. I felt again that intense feeling of peace, and the deep love that was kindled in my heart when Luchianó-bé rescued me from the River Lammista-ké. It arose afresh in me to become the overwhelming force of my life.

He smiled at me. 'Well done, my good and faithful friend. Enter into the joy of your Lord.'

'Please,' I faltered, not quite sure how to phrase the question, or whether it was even allowed of me to ask. But that unveiling of the Greater Throne must have been for a reason.

'Go ahead.'

'The Empty Throne. When will it be filled?'

'It is not for you to know the times and seasons of all things. Not yet.'

I spoke again with a sudden urgency that seized me. If I didn't know now, I never would. 'But who is the one, spoken of by the Prophet, who will fill the Throne?'

The whole scenario faded before my eyes. I glanced up and could still see the Throne Room above, then looked down to see the Throne Room at Terrazarema below and the private council chamber next to it for which I was heading. Just before my feet touched the floor, I heard his voice in my heart: *'You have asked the deepest question in the Known Universe. The answer is, my Father.'*

Chapter Ninety One

That night Beth drifted off to sleep straight into a vivid dream. She was standing on top of the processional archway at one end of the Amphitheatre in Terrazarema. Courtiers were preparing the vast elliptical arena for a state celebration.

A red carpet was unrolled from the foot of the arch below her along the centre of the arena to the raised dais at the far end. A shorter one was unrolled from the smaller archways at either side of the dais to cross the central one and form a gigantic red sword. Two Thrones were set in place on the dais looking down the length of the arena towards her. Folding chairs were arranged in rows on either side of the long carpet to face the dais, and reaching a third of the way down the arena. The tiered stone seats around the curved sides of the Amphitheatre had the dust brushed from them, and wooden chairs were set out in the boxes reserved for special visitors.

Then the scene changed. The Amphitheatre was packed with people in the tiered seats, the boxes were full of Tsé-shâmé and Harmoth delegates judging by their features and colouring, and the folding chairs on the floor of the arena seated many guests she recognised as family friends and higher ranking members of Krêonor society. The atmosphere was alive with chattering and shouting and the different coloured clothing.

A herald blew three notes on his long silver bugle and there was silence. Everyone stood up. A man in formal clothes, and sitting on the front row of the folding chairs facing the dais, was the last to stand. Beth recognised him, even with his back to her.

Kyros!

Next to Kyros was one of Uncle Morthrir's Captains, with a warrior-boy standing beside him. What was going on?

The band started playing a wedding march. Beth was distracted by a movement below her and leaned over the edge of the archway in time to see two page boys walking backwards and strewing blue cornflowers on the carpet: Lenyé's favourite flower. She recognised her brothers, Wilf and Festé. There was a blur of white as a woman emerged from under the archway. The white lace sleeves ended at the wrists in a slight bell-shape; the hands clasping a bouquet of white flowers shot through with yellows and blues and framed with green leaves. The bodice was overlaid with lace and gathered at the waist to emphasise the billowing white skirts that merged with the train. Her head and face were covered by a white veil. Beth wasn't sure who it was but as the two bridesmaids emerged holding the train, she recognised her cousins, Olathe and Nasima. So it must be Lenyé.

Behind them paced a lioness with a she-bear and a cobra on either side, and an eagle hovering overhead.

But no sign of Quinn or herself or their parents. Who was going to give the bride away if her Father wasn't there?

Had the wedding already taken place and she was excluded? Of all the occasions she wanted to attend, her sister's wedding would be the most special. And she'd missed it.

She watched the bridal party process along the carpet, towards the standing crowd of guests who were craning round to glimpse the bride.

Then everything went blurry and Lenyé was running in a swirl of white fabric and Beth was caught up in the shock of the moment and felt herself wrapped in the same fabric and falling, falling, falling... Harsh words filled her mind and she cried out for Ishi-mi-réjá to bring that old woman and let her tell her story, for suddenly it seemed so important. But they weren't there.

Chapter Ninety Two

Morthrir was locked in one of the palace bedrooms for the night in anticipation of his trial the following day. He paced up and down, smacking his hand on the furniture and fuming, 'What kind of court is this going to be?' He stopped in the middle of the room, adopted his flexed-knee stance and commanded Vashtani to appear and whisk him away, but nothing happened.

He crossed to the writing bureau, sat down, opened the lid and drummed his fingers on the leather writing section, preparing to write his last will and testament.

Morthrir was suddenly aware of a presence in the room, slipped off his chair and bowed down in awe as he recognised Abbérron and heard the deep voice as the great being spoke.

'Vashtani and the others are banished. It's just you and me.'

'My Lord, can you get me out of here?'

'I have a better idea. Where is the *Imbrésonite* you found?'

'In the Vault of Malrema where I left it.'

'It's not there now. Where would they have taken it?'

'I don't know.' Morthrir frowned, 'What will you use it for?'

'Never you mind,' and with that, the image was gone.

Morthrir sat at the bureau again and started writing, his mind suddenly clear: *I leave no possessions of this world, but only the conviction of my heart. Abbérron is greatest and to be revered above all others. By his power he will arise to rule in the Waking World.*

He dated the document and signed it, brief though it was, sealed it with wax, and placed it in his pocket.

Chapter Ninety Three

Quinn was eager to be off the following morning and woke the others early.

'Lenyé needs us urgently.' Beth talked about the dream of her sister's wedding as they ate breakfast 'It was more specific this time. We have to get to Terrazarema by noon today.'

'Noon?' Quinn spoke through his mouthful. 'You said three days. That takes us to this evening. We'll never make it through the Main Gates by noon.'

'We have to,' Beth was adamant, 'or we'll miss it!'

They rode further South before leaving the protection of the trees, so as to out-distance those warriors.

Quinn was ahead, but hoped the others had seen where he left the woods and started cantering across the rough ground to the Main Gates. He turned in the saddle to see Beth following him. The others, bunched in a group, were not far behind.

He led the way, but Beth was keeping up with him. He glanced back and saw his Father dismount and stroke one of the legs of Aunt Faria's horse. It obviously had a stone in its shoe by the way it was limping. Should he stop and wait, or carry on?

'Why are you slowing down?' Beth was level with him.

He nodded behind them, 'Aunt Faria's horse.'

Beth whipped round, 'We've got to keep going to be in the city by noon, or we'll be too late! They'll have to catch us up.'

Quinn nodded and kicked his horse up to the faster pace as his Mother and Beth's parents came clustering in behind. He twisted round and saw his Father dig something out of the horse's hoof. Then they mounted and Aunt Faria tried out the horse for a few paces before they galloped towards him.

He also saw the troop of warriors on the Eastern side of the city, and heard a shout. The warriors started chasing after them. Quinn pointed in alarm and saw the others whip round. His Father and Aunt Faria were still some way behind but catching up fast.

Quinn looked up at the sun as they clattered onto the cobbles under the archway of the Main Gates.

'It's gone noon,' he yelled at Beth.

'Faster,' she cried out in reply. 'We're going to miss it!'

They swept through the deserted streets and into the Central Square.

'Where is everyone?' he frowned at Beth.

'I don't know. Just keep going.'

He heard his Father calling, 'Head for the palace. We can find out what's going on there.'

'No,' Beth shouted in return. 'We must get to the Amphitheatre.'

As Quinn looked to the front again, Beth's horse was already some way ahead. He galloped after his cousin. As they neared the Amphitheatre he was vaguely aware of the main entrance being closed and saw Beth carry on round the Western side and aim for the rear entrance, but still he couldn't catch her.

By the time he reached the entrance, Beth was already off her horse and racing under the arch. He dismounted, threw the reins to a startled guard and chased after her.

Chapter Ninety Four

'Beth!' Lenyé's scream riveted all eyes in the Amphitheatre on her. Even Kyros whipped round, despite having steeled himself not to glance at his bride until she was standing beside him.

Kyros saw the rest of the bridal party falter with her half way along the red carpet as she stooped to struggle with her shoes. Then she flung them aside and raced, barefoot, down the aisle, her train wrenched from her bridesmaids' hands and billowing out behind her. The bridesmaids and page boys chased after her, trying to grab the swirling fabric. As she reached the front Lenyé veered left and away from him along the other carpet.

He looked up, saw Beth and realised why Lenyé was running.

'Quinn!' he yelled as another figure emerged from the left-hand archway. He chased after the bridal party and began overhauling them. But Lenyé arrived first, arms outstretched, and caught her sister in mid-flight as the younger girl hurled herself off the ground and they both went down in a flurry of arms and legs and entwining white silk.

Then he was up with them, grabbed Quinn tight to his chest and whirled him round. Dizzy with joy he staggered backwards, set his brother down and stooped slightly to embrace him again. But as he glanced over his brother's shoulder he felt frozen in time as five other figures stepped out of the shadow of the archway and began walking towards him.

Gently he pushed his brother aside, stood up fully and took a pace forwards, before going down on one knee. 'Father! Mother! Uncle Alkram! Aunt Niamh! Aunt Faria! We thought you were dead.'

Lenyé jerked her head up, scrambled to her hands and knees, and tried to yank the fabric of her train away from Beth and stand up. In her confusion all she could do was kneel there, opened mouthed, and too surprised to say anything.

In a daze Kyros watched his Father walk towards him, take him by the hand and raise him to his feet. Then he felt his Father's warm embrace. 'My son. In all the weeks of our captivity I have longed to look once again on your face. And now I am full of joy.'

Then Kyros was in his Mother's arms and there were tears on both sides as they were re-united.

And Lenyé was hugging and embracing her parents with tears aplenty, before both sets of parents were hugging and kissing the rest of the children.

'What is this?' Lenyé's Father stepped back and held her at arms length. 'All dressed up for a wedding? Beth was right after all. We arrived in the nick of time.'

'Forgive me, Uncle Alkram,' again Kyros went down on one knee. 'I tried to seek you out before you departed to Fantrios for the holidays, but missed you, and asked Lenyé for her hand in marriage without your permission. When we learned of your supposed deaths, I went ahead with the wedding arrangements. I beg your pardon.'

'My pardon? Don't be ridiculous. This match has been long in the making for all to see. Who am I to hinder it from happening? Since we are denied a private audience, I will ask you two questions in public. Do you love her?'

'Most certainly I do.'

'And will you lay down your life for her?'

'Most certainly I will.'

Uncle Alkram stretched out his hand, raised Kyros to his feet and embraced him. 'Then I gladly welcome you into our Family as a son. Let the ceremony proceed.'

'Father,' Beth interrupted. 'Now that we're here, I want to be at the wedding as well. But not in these clothes.'

'You're quite right, my child.' Alkram smiled at his youngest daughter. 'And neither can we.' He glanced at his wife, and across to his brother and sister-in-law.

'What about the Coronation,' Lenyé looked at her Father and then to her Uncle Dareth. 'Kyros was due to be crowned King straight after the wedding. We can't send all these people away disappointed.'

'And we need to decide what to do about Uncle Morthrir,' Kyros added.

Dareth spoke for them all. 'Let the heralds announce a delay in the proceedings for two hours due to the re-union of the Royal Families while we change our clothing, discuss what's necessary and re-assemble.'

'That sounds about right,' Alkram smiled. 'For my wife and I need time with Lenyé as well. And I need a few moments with her alone before I give my eldest daughter away in marriage.'

Chapter Ninety Five

Kyros completed his signature on the marriage certificate and handed the quill pen to Lenyé. He glanced at both sets of parents waiting their turn, and at Quinn and Beth where they sat with the rest of their families. This was such a time of joy, for they had returned, against all expectations, as if from the dead.

He stared over the head of the Royal Scrivener, who would complete the register and apply the official seal, and gazed at the wedding guests seated in front of him and the vast crowd that filled the rest of the arena. He thought of his words to Lenyé when they were reconciled at the Pool of Alesco, "*And you, My Lady...will be drawn to my side that we may walk together and our union will unlock the Restoration, and our wedding feast shall be a time of reconciliation for the Ancient Peoples*". There were so many Tsé-shâmé and Harmoth delegates in the guest boxes at either side of the dais, and many more from both races in the audience, that he knew it was happening today.

He smiled at Yanantha as he caught her eye. There was no one more fitting, not even Hoffengrégor, to join Lenyé and himself in marriage: to hear their vows and speak the words of blessing over them. For she had journeyed with them, especially Lenyé, in succour and comfort and wisdom and advice. And borne the conflict of emotions with him, and the pain of obedience to the True King. So their wedding was very much the fruit of Yanantha's long and patient faithfulness, watching over the Krêonor and anticipating the Restoration.

He heard the scratching of nib on parchment as the other signatures were completed. When the musicians began playing the recessional, he lifted Lenyé's hand to his lips, and led her to the head of the central aisle. He was aware of Beth amongst the bridesmaids, holding a bouquet of flowers as the other two gathered up Lenyé's train; and the page boys, led by Quinn, followed him. Ariella, Mamma Uza-Mâté, Chuah-te-mok and Ra-Na-Jiri closed in behind and the respective parents took up their positions. They walked forwards, through the guest seats, and passed into the Guard of Honour selected from Hanniel's men and Harbona's warriors. The air was a-flutter with white rose petals as friends and relatives flung handfuls over them.

When they reached the end of the Guard, the whole party stopped. Kyros bowed and Lenyé curtsied to the crowd in the rest of the Amphitheatre. Then they turned and the wedding procession parted to allow them through and followed while the Royal couple retraced their steps. As they approached the two Thrones in the middle of the dais, Kyros noticed two other Thrones had been placed to their right and slightly behind, and was reminded of the True King and the greater Throne.

Hoffengrégor mounted the steps of the dais and gestured for Kyros and Lenyé to sit on the central Thrones. Once Lenyé's train was arranged, the old Prophet indicated to Kyros' Father and Mother to take their places on the other Thrones. The rest of the wedding party was escorted to their seats facing the dais, and the four animal-friends found spaces at each end of the same row.

The Ancient Prophet raised his arms for silence.

'My friends,' he cried, turning to right and left to include everyone in the tiered seats around the curved sides of the arena and the seated assembly in front of the dais. 'This is indeed a special day. For not only are Kyros and Lenyé married, but will now fulfil words spoken long ago of a young Prince who accedes to the Throne and becomes King while his Father is still alive and King before him. There will be no lessening of King Dareth's authority, but rather his reign will be much enhanced. For the Father is always greater than the son, by virtue of being before him and giving him life; and the son will be the right hand of his strength. And so the Thrones are arranged today to reflect that.'

There was a murmur of approval from the vast crowd.

'Before we proceed to the Coronation, Kyros and Lenyé are to be presented with the Sword of Justice. It is theirs by right, to fulfil words sung over Lenyé and to honour the prowess of Kyros who was obedient to the True King in another Realm.'

A courtier ascended the steps and gave two swords to Hoffengrégor. The old Prophet raised his voice, 'One of these is the Sword of Justice, fashioned in the Realm of the Blessèd Throne, and presented to Zerigor by the True King himself. The other is a copy, forged in this world, to deceive others; and so the wrongful use of the real Sword by another is made more difficult. Kyros and Lenyé have decided to retain both swords, for the real blade can only be discerned by them and no one else.'

He knelt before Kyros and Lenyé and laid a sword across each of their knees. 'Receive what is rightfully yours, for before the Coronation can take place there is a certain judgement that has to be exercised over those who have tried to undermine the Throne of the Krêonor for their own purposes. Without the Sword of Justice in your hands, this cannot take place.'

Hoffengrégor gestured to one of the officers. 'Let the prisoners be escorted here. And bring the *Imbrésonite* as well.'

Five men, with their hands tied, emerged from the same archway where some of the Royal Family had appeared, and were led to the foot of the dais. They were followed by four soldiers carrying a heavy bundle. There was a craning of heads and whispers amongst the crowd: 'Is that Morthrir?' someone cried out. 'He looks so much older, I hardly recognise him.'

Hoffengrégor spoke again, 'Eawen, once known as the Henosite and formerly Chief Priest associated with these five men, has interceded for the other Priests and asked that they be questioned in private. Only Rafé remains unaccounted for and must answer to this court in person.'

The Ancient Prophet then addressed the five men. 'Morthrir, you are charged with High Treason for abducting your two brothers and their wives to have them disposed of so you could usurp the Throne; of waging war against Kyros and the rest of the Royal youngsters to remove any contenders; and seeking to have your own wife, Faria, murdered, so you could seize Lenyé and force her to become your bride, thus undermining the lawfully established line of succession for your own purposes. These offences all carry the death penalty. But in view of your own Royal birth and position, you may appeal to Prince Kyros for clemency if he will grant it. These other men, known as the Summoners, are indicted for seeking to place you on the Throne and seize power throughout the Waking World. This is a longstanding conspiracy, and now you, together with Morthrir, must face the consequences of your actions.'

Kyros glanced at the four Summoners and then sat watching his Uncle carefully.

'I do not accept judgement by my nephew,' Morthrir shouted. 'Nor do I acknowledge this gathering as an official court!'

'You are still obliged to answer to these charges that we may discern what has been going on.'

'Very well.' Kyros saw his Uncle take a deep breath before continuing. He then refuted everything Hoffengrégor challenged him on, saying he was trying to find the Royal Family and protect them from any more attempts on their lives.

Kyros sensed Lenyé's mounting anger: these were all the issues they agreed would be hard to prove. He raised a warning finger to his lips as Hoffengrégor continued.

'You convinced Lenyé that Faria died in a hunting accident.'

'That's what was reported to me after I came to Terrazarema. I was so distressed; but to learn she is alive gives me great joy.'

'We have Quinn and Beth's testimony that they saw you

participating in a convocation at Druis-cyf-rin, the Great Oak Tree, to locate Kyros and Lenyé. That implies you were seeking to use spiritual power to accomplish your purposes.'

'Everything else had failed and I was desperate to find them.'

'Your exact words were: *"Find him for me, and tell me how I am to triumph over him"*.'

'Triumph in the sense that he fled in confusion about my intentions towards him and evaded all my efforts to find him.'

'You then said: *"I need to know the whereabouts of my eldest niece, Lenyé"*.'

'I had to find her for her own safety!'

'Quinn and Beth also saw you at Mount Malkamet when you spoke a word of power from Abbérron to force a new Breaking-in and release the Dé-monos into the Waking World.'

'All resistance to the Priests and Summoners at the Grand Convocation was broken down before that happened. They must have been overcome and couldn't possibly have seen it.'

'So you do acknowledge you were there, and you knew they were deliberately opposing you to try and stop you.'

'I, er…' Kyros heard the hesitation in his Uncle's voice.

'We have Lenyé's testimony concerning a child sacrifice that you carried out in a bizarrely decorated cellar in the palace.'

'The boy is not dead. I've seen him in this gathering.'

'How do you know which boy we're talking about?'

'I, er…' again the hesitation.

So you confirm the ceremony took place and was only stopped by Lenyé's direct intervention.

'I…'

'Morthrir. What you have been doing is totally evil to bring about the destruction of all that is good in the Waking World and set up your own rule in its place. Regardless of the other charges, these last two are the worst: to use an evil spiritual power and invoke it by the attempted murder of an innocent victim.'

'That's a lie. And you cannot prove any of it!'

Chapter Ninety Six

Kyros was distracted as Beth jumped up from her seat and raced towards the entrance. He saw two old women emerge from the archway: one very sprightly, carrying something long and straight rolled up in a cloth; the other quite frail, and leaning on her companion until Beth could help.

When they reached the dais, he saw the old woman falter as she passed the four Summoners. Then she glanced beyond Kyros to his Father. She let go of her companions, climbed up the steps and flung herself in front of his Father's Throne.

'Please, Sire. Forgive me for the wrong I have done you and your brother in the past.' She turned and looked at Lord Alkram.

'Chenai?' Lord Alkram exclaimed. 'It is you, isn't it?'

'Our old nursemaid?' Kyros heard the tremor in his Father's voice. 'You left so suddenly after Morthrir's birth we were totally devastated. What happened?'

'I will only tell the story if you grant me Royal protection.' Kyros saw her eyes flick across to the four Summoners and back to his Father.

'Of course. Please continue.'

'The night your Mother gave birth,' Chenai sobbed, 'we were at the Royal Hunting Lodge. She called him Ibarno. It was a difficult birth and the Queen was exhausted. As I laid him to her breast, I found he had passed away. I panicked, grabbed him, flung a cloak about us and hurried out into the night, terrified that the shock of his death would be too much for the Queen in her weakened state. I fled into the shelter of the woods.'

She paused and gulped for breath. 'I was crying out for help, and well into the woods, stumbling over tree roots in the dark before bursting into a clearing. Someone grabbed me by the arm.'

'"*What are you carrying under that cloak?*" His voice was soft and menacing, and I was instantly terrified. How did he know?'

'He ripped the cloak open. "*A dead boy. If this was an ordinary baby it would have been buried without any problem. So I assume he is the son of King Lakané, Father of Prince Dareth and Prince Alkram.*"'

'"*No, no. You're mistaken. I wouldn't do a thing like that.*"'

'"*Like what?*" He dragged me close and whispered in my ear. "*So no one else knows that the child is dead. Am I right?*" And he twisted my arm so hard I thought it was broken.'

'I nodded.'

'"*Let us make an agreement,*" he sounded pleased. "*I am travelling with three companions and a girl with a baby boy we wish to be rid of. Give me your dead baby, and I will give you mine. Take him back to the Queen, and pretend nothing is wrong. Will you do that?*"'

'I nodded again. This was the answer to my cry for help.'

'"*Good. I will dispose of yours so that no one will ever know. If I find out you've told anyone, I will kill you. Do you understand?*"'

'I nodded a third time, too terrified to say anything and the exchange was done. He escorted me to the Lodge, but before I left the clearing, I heard the sound of spades and glimpsed three men at work. They were burying the dead baby, and I was so relieved my secret was safe.'

Lenyé pointed at Morthrir, 'So you're not my Uncle after all.'

'How can you believe that old woman? She's making it up!'

Beth stepped forwards. 'Ishi-mi-réjá took Quinn and me to a cottage in the forest to meet Chenai. Eventually she agreed to tell her story if she could appear before the King on his Throne.'

'That's right,' Ishi-mi-réjá spoke up. 'She took us to a clearing in the woods and we dug down to find two skeletons.'

'One was the skeleton of a baby,' Beth continued, 'which she now has wrapped in a shawl. The other was of a young woman with damage to the ribs over her heart.' Beth glanced at Morthrir and back to the dais. 'Lenyé, you have to believe us.'

Lenyé turned to Chenai, 'If only we can find the men involved to confirm your story.'

Chenai rose from where she'd been kneeling in front of Kyros' Father and pointed directly at Jumar-jé, the leader of the Summoners, standing next to Morthrir. Her hand was trembling.

'That's the man who spoke to me in the woods, and those other three were with him. I'd recognise them anywhere.'

Jumar-jé shook his head, 'You can't prove that.'

'Maybe she can't. But I can.'

Lenyé glanced up in surprise as Ishi-mi-réjá intervened.

'When I contested the Grand Convocation with Beth and Quinn on Mount Malkamet, you and the other Summoners tried to destroy me. But I saw into your minds about a journey heading North, thirty five years ago, with your newly married young wife who was eight and a half months pregnant. When you reached the Great Oak Tree, she gave birth, and you offered the baby to Abbérron and received the name Morthrir for him. You spoke death over the Queen and her baby, and willed the nursemaid to run into your arms so you could place Morthrir in the Royal Family. Then you took your wife and child and travelled all the next day, till you were in that clearing near Fantrios the following night.'

'That's nonsense,' Jumar-jé stared at Lenyé. 'You cannot accept this dream or vision or whatever it was as evidence!'

There was a disturbance from the audience and an old man emerged. 'Prince Kyros, I am Eawen, and you released me from imprisonment by your Uncle. May I proceed?'

Lenyé glanced at Kyros and saw him nod.

'As Chief Priest I arranged the Summoners' convocations and was often drawn to Druis-cyf-rin because of the power released there. On one occasion, I was startled by voices, and recognised Jumar-jé and the other Summoners, but remained hidden. I heard all that Ishi-mi-réjá has described. That is how I learned of the name "*Morthrir*" and was able to pass it in on to him.'

'But we weren't near Fantrios on the night the Queen died,' Jumar-jé objected. 'We journeyed to Druis-cyf-rin in early September for the Feast of Ingathering at the Autumn Equinox.'

'Her death was kept quiet for three months,' Chenai spoke up. 'Not until the Royal party returned to Terrazarema was the funeral announced. She went into labour in the early hours of June 21st, and gave birth late that night. She died about an hour after I returned with the living child. No one outside the immediate family knew the date of her death.'

'Eawen,' Lenyé looked at the old man. 'When were you at Druis-cyf-rin and witness to this event?'

'It was the night and dawn of the 20th to 21st of June.'

'The Summer Solstice?' Ishi-mi-réjá rounded on Jumar-jé. 'You invoked Abbérron's name on the most powerful date in the year and forced an early birth to accomplish your purposes. No wonder the Queen died going into labour like that for so long!'

'So you were there that night.' Lenyé held Jumar-jé's gaze and saw the shock in the man's eyes. 'Ishi-mi-réjá spoke the truth and Eawen confirms it. You are guilty of three things: firstly, murdering your own wife to keep her silent, hence the other skeleton; secondly, invoking the power of Abbérron to accomplish your purposes in bringing about the death of my Grandmother and her child; and thirdly, introducing a changeling into the Royal Family to give you power through the Throne when he came of age.'

Chapter Ninety Seven

Rafé covered the distance to Terrazarema in a few days of hard riding, still mulling over the golden globe and the power he felt. It couldn't be anything to do with the Nastrim because of that sword. It was exactly the same as Lenyé's. So the golden globe must have a greater significance than the Nastrim race. But somehow, it must be linked to them as it had lain hidden under Mount Nastâri for so long. Maybe Lenyé could shed some light on the matter, but how was he going to find her?

He entered the city by mid-afternoon and was astonished at the empty streets. Where was everyone? He rode towards the palace, not knowing if he would encounter Morthrir or not, but then heard shouts coming from the Amphitheatre.

Rafé headed for the Western side and the rear entrance, to avoid the main gates under the processional archway and be seen by the whole audience. He dismounted and approached one of the guards. 'What's going on?'

The man indicated with a jerk of the head, 'We've just had the Wedding of Princess Lenyé to Prince Kyros.'

'Did you say, "*Princess Lenyé's Wedding?*"' Rafé heaved a sigh of relief. He couldn't think of a better opportunity to give her the golden globe. 'I have a present for her.'

'I suppose you want me to let you in?'

'Yes please.'

'Wait here until they've finished debating about what to do with Morthrir.'

Chapter Ninety Eight

Kyros glanced at Lenyé and their eyes met in understanding. At her nod of consent, he turned to Morthrir. 'By taking the name Morthrir you indicate some knowledge of what we have discussed. Also, you abducted our parents and spoke a word of power, invoking Abbérron's name in order to destroy the rest of us and seize Lenyé for your bride...'

'That's nonsense. You can't prove it.'

'Yes I can. The great cellar in the palace was transformed into a *centre of evil* from which the activities of Abbérron were carried out, including an attempted child sacrifice. Next to the remains of an altar was this bundle of *Imbrésonite*,' he gestured towards it with his hand. 'It was the outer covering of Abbérron before he was cast down from the Realm of the Blessèd Throne. Why its scattered fragments were gathered together at the Beginning, no one knows. I assume it was for some purpose of Abbérron's...'

Kyros was interrupted by a court official walking up the aisle, mounting the steps, and presenting two scrolls.

'These were in the Royal safe, Sire. The Chief Scrivener had never seen them before, and asked me to bring them to you.' The man stood up and strode back down the aisle.

Kyros passed one to Lenyé and studied the other before swapping. He looked up at Morthrir. 'The keys to the Royal safe were missing, and the door has just been opened. These two parchments were found amongst your personal effects.'

He watched Morthrir intently and saw the colour drain from his face. 'One is a contract signed by you and Abbérron, who styled himself as, *"Prince over the Realm of the Waking World"* and referred to you as his, *"…Regent, to reach out your hand and take all that you desire"*. Do you deny ever signing such a document?'

Morthrir shook his head. 'You had no right to open the Royal safe without my permission.'

'The second document,' Kyros glanced at the parchment in his hand, 'records an encounter with Lammista-ké, King of Death, where he commands you to, *"Write what you see and hear, lest you forget what is revealed, and keep the document hidden for your own use. Do not let anyone else see it, or destruction will certainly come upon you"*.'

Kyros looked up and saw Morthrir trembling.

'You have engaged with two of the most powerful evil beings in the entire Known Universe. I now pronounce judgement over you and the Summoners. According to the anointing that rests upon me and the authority granted to me by the True King, I consign you to the Realm of Consumption, reserved for Abbérron and all those in league with him.'

A cry of dismay went up from Morthrir and the four Summoners. 'You cannot do that to humans!' Morthrir shouted.

'You are so closely allied to Abbérron,' Kyros replied, 'that it is impossible to separate you!' He lifted the sword from his knees, stood up, swept the blade from its scabbard and knew by the weight that it was the Sword of Justice. He bowed to Lenyé and handed it to her. 'Not only in battle but also in judgement is this Sword a powerful weapon in your hands to discern between good and evil. The honour therefore is yours to wield it now. Please join me in this pronouncement.'

Lenyé stood up and raised the Sword above her head.

Kyros turned back to Morthrir and cried out, 'Let the judgement befall you.' Lenyé brought the Sword down in a swift cutting motion. There was a crack of thunder, the ground split open in front of the five accused men, and they fell forwards into the chasm. A rush of flame and belch of heat stifled their agonised cries.

Kyros hadn't finished. 'I command Lammista-ké, King of Death, to appear before me.' Immediately a dark figure with a black scythe in his left hand took shape on the edge of the chasm where Morthrir and the Summoners had been standing.

'The power of Death in the Waking World was broken by the True King's sacrifice of old,' Kyros' words throbbed in the air. 'I call forth judgement upon you. In the Name of the True King, you are also cast down to the Realm of Consumption.' Again Lenyé swung the Sword. Lammista-ké sagged at the knees and collapsed into the chasm, still clutching his scythe.

As they sat down on their Thrones, Kyros saw a figure appear at the processional archway at the far end of the arena, and walk towards the dais along the carpeted aisle. The person was robed in simple attire and carried a water pot on its left shoulder. The hood of its cloak drooped forwards and hid the head and face.

Kyros whispered in his heart to the True King for wisdom. "*Do not be fooled*", the inner voice replied. "*Though he comes in peace, his heart is bent on destruction. Do not trust him*".

He felt Lenyé's hand on his arm. 'I do not know who this man is, but I sense from the True King that he is the embodiment of the words Yanantha spoke over me of "*...a greater power that sits behind Morthrir, that we have to bring down and vanquish*". You have returned with the power of the True King's words in your mouth, and I have the Sword of Justice in my hands. I give you my full agreement to deal with him accordingly.'

Kyros smiled at her and nodded. 'You confirm what the True King said to me, and I'm grateful we both hear his voice alike.'

He sat back and continued to watch the approaching figure.

When the individual reached the edge of the chasm it stopped, drew back its hood and was revealed as a young man with blue eyes and fair hair. 'You have consigned living beings to the hottest place in the Known Universe not caring what will happen to them. I have brought water from the Deep Well of the

Waking World.' The man lifted the water pot and poured the contents into the chasm. The flame and heat died down as he did so. 'That will ease their journey and forever link the Realm of Consumption to the Waking World. A time of drought and famine will plague this land, and you will beg me to break the link before you all die of hunger and thirst and go down to the Realm of Consumption yourselves.'

A gasp of shock went up from those within earshot.

Kyros heard the True King's voice in his heart, "*This is Abbérron, in person, brought to the Throne of Judgement because of your words spoken over him. Be careful, for he is at his wiliest. You must revoke what he has just said*".

Kyros stood up. Lenyé stood with him and raised the Sword again. 'You speak lies, Abbérron,' Kyros' voice carried great authority, 'as you have always done and so ensnared the unwary. I reverse your words.' He raised his right hand against his enemy, 'In the Name of the True King, before whom I stand, I cast you down from the Waking World to the deepest Pit. And so, may the source of evil be destroyed.'

As Lenyé swept the Sword down for the third time, the figure fell forwards into the chasm with a terrible cry, but twisted to seize the bundle of *Imbrésonite*. His voice drifted up for those in close proximity to hear, 'I will take what is rightfully mine!'

The jaws of the chasm closed after him with a loud crash.

Chapter Ninety Nine

A herald blew three notes on his bugle. The whole Amphitheatre settled into silence as Hoffengrégor stepped forwards.

'Now is the time for the Coronation of Kyros and Lenyé.'

But before he could continue, a lone figure appeared at the Western entrance and walked along the carpet towards the dais.

Lenyé nudged Kyros, 'That's Rafé. I'm sure of it.'

Kyros waited till the man knelt in front of them. 'Well, Rafé. What do you have to say for yourself?'

Ra-Na-Jiri slithered to the dais. 'Lenyé, if this is Rafé, then he was the one watching you through my eyes.'

'Really?' Lenyé frowned at Rafé. 'You have a lot to explain.'

'My Lady,' Rafé replied 'I hope to prove my innocence.' He talked about his concerns over the threat of Morthrir's warriors and suggested a coup to make their Uncle overreach himself.

'Why didn't you warn us?' Lenyé glared at him with a furious expression on her face. 'Kyros was very nearly killed!'

Rafé held up his hands in self-defence. 'If anyone else knew, it would leak out to Morthrir. I couldn't even tell your Fathers.'

'What about his involvement with the Hidden Power,' Kyros queried, 'and being in league with Abbérron?'

'I didn't know about that, but still tried to bring him down. That's why I sent the cobra to watch Lenyé and feed Morthrir with false information about her. By Eawen's counsel, I have severed any connection with the cobra, rejected my involvement with the Priesthood, renounced all ties to Abbérron and chosen to follow the True King.'

Kyros spoke up, 'Very well. I ratify your choice.'

Rafé turned to Lenyé. 'We discovered a source of power at Mount Nastâri, and I persuaded Morthrir to let me go and bring it back.' He pulled the golden globe from its covering, and pointed to the top. 'That looks like a replica of your Sword.'

'Let me see,' Hoffengrégor examined it. 'This is the Royal Orb of Dominion I hurled to the North to prevent Zerigor's enemies seizing it. Mount Nastâri must have grown up to hide it.'

'Lenyé,' Ra-Na-Jiri spoke up. 'That's the source of my peaceful feelings. Now I don't need to return to Mount Nastâri, but can stay here with you.'

'I'm very pleased to hear that,' Lenyé smiled. 'You have been a faithful friend to me, despite not being sent by Yanantha like the others. I would hate to lose you at this stage.'

'Wait,' Quinn stood up. 'We found something at Druis-cyf-rin that Kyros needs for the Coronation.' He took the rod-shaped bundle from Ishi-mi-réjá, removed the cloth and gestured to Beth to join him. 'Ishi-mi-réjá thinks it's the Sceptre of Authority.'

Hoffengrégor inspected the rod. 'She's right. I flung this to the East away from the battle on that fateful day when Zerigor was slain. The Great Oak Tree must have sprung up to protect it.'

'I am delighted we have the items I saw the True King had,' Kyros interrupted. 'Before we proceed there are a few positions Lenyé and I wish to clarify.' He glanced around. 'Firstly, Rafé. The exposure of your link to the cobra and its effect on Lenyé indicates that all secrets will be revealed before the Throne of Judgement. My Father confirms our parents owe their lives to you for delaying Morthrir's actions against them. And by bringing the Royal Orb of Dominion to Lenyé indicates you were acting in the best interests of the Royal Family all the time. I therefore confirm your position as trusted counsellor to the Throne. But you are not to take the initiative in any matter and play the lone wolf again without consulting us.'

'Yes, Sire.'

'Secondly,' Lenyé intervened. 'Doctor Nostrea.' She waited as the man mounted the steps and knelt in front of her. 'Prepare the skeleton of the baby Chenai has for burial in the Royal Cemetery. After all, he was our real Uncle. Then take Ishi-mi-réjá and exhume the remains of that dead woman in the woods and have her properly buried. Also, for your part in the misidentification of the corpse that was buried instead of Kyros, I release you from any fear of the Royal Throne that may have arisen when Morthrir was in control. Similarly, the two corpses that were buried instead of Quinn and Beth also need to be exhumed, identified, if possible, and the matter resolved. I therefore confirm you in the position of Royal Apothecary with no blame attaching to you as a result of these unfortunate incidents.'

'Thank you, Your Highness.' The Doctor returned to his seat.

'Thirdly,' Kyros spoke up. 'Aunt Faria.'

His Aunt came forwards and knelt before him.

'I have to authorise the tearing down and destruction of Morthrir's unlawful statue in the Central Square, and remove his name and entitlements from the records. But I am saddened for you at what has happened within your marriage, and the fate of your husband. I know of no complicity from you in these matters whatsoever. Do not be ashamed of taking time to mourn and grieve, for the evidence and judgement today must have come as a shock. I speak words of release that you may be free of any unwholesome hold Morthrir ever had over you. And be at peace, for Lenyé and I would love you to continue as part of the Royal Family should you wish to maintain the relationship.'

'Thank you, My Lord.'

'Fourthly, Yanantha,' Lenyé broke in with such eagerness, and rose to her feet as Yanantha climbed the steps. 'Dearest friend. Without you I wouldn't be here today, or accomplished the things I have achieved, or become the person I now am. I therefore appoint you as Prophetess to the Throne, to continue to watch faithfully over the Krêonor and guide me in wisdom and truth.' She flung her arms around Yanantha's neck and they embraced each other.

'Thank you, Your Highness.'

'Fifthly,' Kyros also stood up. 'The four animal-friends.' He waited as they made their way to the front. 'You three were sent by Yanantha to protect Lenyé, and Ra-Na-Jiri was sent to spy on her by Rafé, but has proved worthy of her trust. And you have all been of great help to me. Ra-Na-Jiri, I confirm your affinity with the Orb and appoint you with the three others to guard the emblems Lenyé and I now carry: Sword, Crown, Sceptre and Orb. And we also adopt your four images to be displayed on banners in the Throne Room to represent our Thrones in the Waking World: the Eagle for vision and discernment, the Lioness for courage and strength, the She-bear for power and mercy and the Cobra for wisdom and faithfulness.'

They nodded their acceptance and returned to their places.

'And finally,' Kyros continued, 'Eawen and Ramâno.'

The elderly man climbed the steps with the boy at his side.

'Eawen, I appoint you as my spiritual advisor, to spend your days listening to the voice of the True King and reporting to me what he says, that the laws of this Realm may be guided by a higher power than a mere physical King.'

'Thank you, Sire. I trust that I can rise to such a high office.'

'You were born for this role. But the deception of Abbérron hindered you for most of your life. Now the True King will make up for those lost years and enhance your ministry beyond what you could ever achieve in your own strength.'

The old man bowed his head and retreated down the steps.

'Now for you, Ramâno,' Kyros continued. 'Words cannot express what you have come to mean to me in the short time we have known each other. I take you into my service to hear the voice of the True King for yourself, and to grow into all that he would have you do. You wanted to be a healer. No one can take that role to himself, but I speak over you words to release you into your calling. You have seen many people healed, but that is nothing in comparison to what is yet to come. For we are about to be caught up in the healing of the nations.'

With tears of joy, Ramâno flung himself into Kyros' arms, accompanied by a great cheer from the whole assembly.

Hoffengrégor stepped forwards and held up his hands for silence. When the cheering died down he announced again: 'Let the Coronation begin.'

Kyros and Lenyé sat on their Thrones with a sword across their knees and Hoffengrégor stood before them.

'Receive the Sceptre of Authority,' Hoffengrégor spoke softly as he presented it to Kyros, 'and the Royal Orb of Dominion I give to Lenyé. I anoint you both with oil in the sign of the Sword of Justice, so that it might stand between you and all the judgements you have to make.'

The Prophet lifted both swords from their knees and placed the hilts in their right hands.

'Arise, Kyros. For now you are come into your Kingship. Arise, Lenyé, for you are worthy to be Queen. You are joined in marriage and have become as one. I also place you this day under a joint-anointing to be as one in rulership.'

They both stood and raised the swords.

'No one but you knows which is the Sword of Justice. Let it ever be so. Return to me the other two tokens.'

The Prophet raised the emblems to the People. 'These are for you. The Orb represents dominion over your own hearts and it is fitting that it should come to Lenyé because of her association with the Nastrim. They once struggled with their two conflicting inner natures. Recovering the Orb from Mount Nastâri frees you to rule your own hearts in love and humility before the True King. The Sceptre represents spiritual life and Kyros is the rightful keeper. At Druis-cyf-rin, some tried to gain unlawful access to that life. Retrieving the Sceptre from under the Great

Oak Tree releases you to approach the True King for yourselves and regain it. The good things of the True King were subverted for a while by those who practised evil and twisted them from their original intention. But today they are reinstated to release good, for Lenyé is appointed to watch over our hearts and Kyros will bring us into spiritual life. Do you accept these emblems and the rule of the True King through Kyros and Lenyé?'

'We do,' the vast crowd spoke as with one voice.

'Then, with these tokens, I seal the Sovereignty of Kyros and Lenyé. Let them be King and Queen amongst us.'

Hoffengrégor turned back to them. 'Kneel before me.'

Kyros and Lenyé did as they were asked.

'Receive back the Sceptre of Authority, so that your supremacy may go before you; and the Royal Orb of Dominion, so that rulership may be established through you.'

Kyros stole a sideways glance at Lenyé. He wasn't sure how to think of her any more: his best friend; his bride; or in a few minutes, his Queen. She had changed so much. For she had put off her cut-down blue dress and cloak and long boots, all that was to hand in the urgency of fleeing from Morthrir and striving against the evil he released, and was now clothed in white to reflect the culmination of all her endeavours. Even the swords strapped across her back and marking her out as a fearless leader were replaced by the softening of the veil tumbling over her shoulders in their place. She knelt there, eyes closed, Sword in one hand and Orb in the other, ready to receive the anointing as Queen that was about to come. But she also radiated the presence of the True King in the pure whiteness of her raiment, and her simple trust of the proceedings and the gentleness of her expression. Kyros stared at her in awe. Who was this woman he'd grown up with and known most of his life and come to love, that she should captivate him so much now? It wasn't just her beauty; there was a mystique about her he'd never discerned before, but entranced him all the more. She was the one he'd pledged to cherish for the rest of his life and grow to know fully.

He heard afresh the words of the True King in his heart: *"As in the Realm of the Blessèd Throne, so also in the Waking World"* and realised that in their oneness through marriage and as King and Queen, he and Lenyé fully represented the True King in the Waking World.

The Prophet received a newly-fashioned golden Crown from the hands of Yanantha. It consisted of two circlets, one above the other, the top studded with sapphires and the bottom with emeralds to reflect the blue and green colours of the Waking World. Hoffengrégor turned back to Lenyé. 'Repeat after me...'

Lenyé raised her voice and spoke clearly, 'I swear by the name of the True King, to maintain Justice within the Waking World, to allow everyone to live in peace and harmony and to watch over the hearts of the people.'

'I place this Crown upon your head,' the Prophet reached forwards, 'to confirm what you have spoken.'

Then he turned to Ramâno as the boy approached with the Krêon of Tulá-kâhju on a cushion. Hoffengrégor took the Crown and faced Kyros. 'Repeat after me...'

Kyros spoke boldly all the words of the Prophet, 'I swear by the name of the True King, to maintain Justice within the Waking World, to allow everyone to live in peace and harmony and to bring all those who are willing into spiritual life.'

'I place this Crown upon your head,' the Prophet continued, 'as the final act of the Restoration to release again the Kingship that Zerigor once bore.'

He glanced from one to the other. 'Arise now as King and Queen over us.'

As they stood to their feet, Hoffengrégor lifted his arms and held his hands above their heads. 'Together, may you prevail where Zerigor, carrying this rulership alone, stumbled and failed.'

Chapter One Hundred

'Behold our King and Queen,' Hoffengrégor exclaimed, and the cry was taken up by the whole assembly.

'Look,' Ramâno shouted. 'The Light about Kyros' head. I've always been able to see it. But now it shines through the Crown of Life. I saw it once on the ship when the Crown was placed on his head in mockery. Doesn't anyone else see it?'

'I do,' Eawen spoke up. 'I felt something around his head when I was blind. Now I see for myself. It dazzles blood red through the Crown, to remind us of the sacrifice of the True King at the Beginning, and that Rulership can only come through his blood, shed for us, that we may be delivered from our enemies.'

Kyros laid his sword on his Throne and addressed the crowd, 'My friends. You see me as I now am only through the trials and testings of the True King, and his strength to bring me to this point. And Lenyé, through courage, faithfulness and prowess in battle and judgement, stands with me. But a King and Queen without a People are of little value. You too can receive what has been given to me.' He addressed Hoffengrégor. 'We return these two tokens to you for safekeeping as Zerigor once did of old.'

Kyros embraced Lenyé and was astonished at the Light of Life blazing red, yellow and blue through the sapphires and emeralds of her Crown before settling into a dazzling white. He heard the True King's voice in his heart: *'This is my gift to your Queen, so that she may complement the red of your Crown with the colours of the Waking World to reflect the sacrifice and union in the coming together of your Realm and mine.'*

Kyros moved on and embraced his Father, then the Prophet and finally, Ramâno. 'You too, my friend,' he whispered as he wrapped his arms about the boy.

'Is it happening to me?' Ramâno cried in delight.

Kyros nodded. 'Even faster than the others. How quickly do little children enter in when others hold back!'

He released the lad and stood up. 'Come, my Father, and Lenyé, and Hoffengrégor and Ramâno. It is from the five of us that all others will receive this gift.'

King Dareth embraced his wife and led her down the steps to their children. Lenyé laid her sword on the arms of her Throne, then raced to Beth and her parents and her brothers. Kyros and Hoffengrégor descended the steps. The Prophet embraced Yanantha and Eawen before walking to the tiered seating on one side; Kyros hurried to the Tsé-shâmé and Harmoth delegates.

Ramâno was left on the dais. 'Who wants to receive the Light of Life from me?' he yelled, and bounded down the steps.

All the children broke out of the standing crowd or jumped up from their seats and came running towards him. 'Touch someone else,' he cried aloud to the first few he embraced. 'Don't keep it to yourselves. It's a free gift for everyone!'

Kyros smiled as Quinn and Beth ran after Ramâno with the other Royal youngsters, the Light of Life blazing about their heads. Chenai held Ishi-mi-réjá's hand and shared the gift they'd both received. Rafé embraced Dr Nostrea. Hanniel moved amongst the Royal Guard. Kyros flung his arms around Harbona and saw Lenyé do the same to Marie-anna. 'Move amongst your People and impart this gift,' he whispered to his friend. 'Take your wife with you, for they hold you in great esteem.' Then he embraced the Tsé-shâmé and Harmoth leaders, 'Spread the Light of Life so that our three races may be intermingled once more and the long Sundering of our Peoples fully healed.'

He looked up and saw the Light shining from so many heads already, and it was mainly due to the children racing back to their families and then moving on to others. The whole arena was ablaze as the Light of Life took hold and settled to an unwavering brilliance. But it was Lenyé who held his gaze. The Light through her Crown was so much whiter and more intense as it radiated with the beauty of the Waking World about her head and marked her out from everyone else. Kyros loved her more now than ever. He couldn't take his eyes off her.

A herald blew three blasts on his silver bugle and King Dareth stood at the top of the dais and cried in a loud voice, 'My friends. This is the most glorious day I have lived to see, and it will be more special yet. For I invite you all to the wedding feast of my son, Kyros, and his beautiful wife, Lenyé.'

Then the leader of the Tsé-shâmé cried out, 'My Lord, I beg you to allow those in my delegation to prepare food and drink, for that is our greatest gift to the new King and Queen.'

Similarly the leader of the Harmoth responded, 'My Lord, please allow those in my delegation to paint pictures to commemorate this day and play music so your guests may dance, for that is our greatest gift to the new King and Queen.'

As fire troughs were dragged into the arena and the aroma of cooking food arose and goblets of drink were passed round, the sound of music filled the air, and people began dancing.

Kyros and Lenyé mingled with the crowd talking and laughing and welcoming everyone.

When the food was ready, the herald sounded his bugle again for silence. Quinn climbed on to the dais to give thanks for the events of the day, and Beth accompanied him to give thanks for the food. Then the feasting and merrymaking continued in earnest and everyone toasted the Royal couple.

Finally, the fire troughs and tables were cleared away and the whole crowd formed a corridor around the red carpet down the length of the arena and arched over with their raised arms. Kyros and Lenyé walked along the tunnel sensing the love and well-wishing of all the people. The air was once more a-flutter with white rose petals, but this time interleaved with red: white for the joy of their Wedding, and red for the solemnity of their Coronation with its reminder of the True King's sacrifice; the whole atmosphere was tinged with the scent of roses.

When they reached the far end and were under the processional archway, Kyros lifted Lenyé in his arms and mounted the steps of an open carriage.

He turned to face the vast crowd with Lenyé still in his arms. 'My friends,' he cried, 'I charge you, when you return to your homes and your own countries, to spread the Light of Life about you to those who have not yet received this gift. For you are emissaries to take the good news of this day to all Peoples.'

He paused as Ariella, Mamma Uza-Mâté, Chuah-te-mok and Ra-Na-Jiri approached.

'What about us, Kyros?' Ariella growled.

'I confirm over the four of you Hoffengrégor's words: "*You will be amongst those who take the good news of peace to every creature in the Waking World*".'

'Thank you.'

'Also,' Kyros continued, 'I appoint you and your descendants to guard Lenyé and myself and our descendants in case the Light of Life ever flickers again and is lost to the Royal Throne.'

Kyros raised his voice so everyone could hear, 'Lenyé and I will return to you soon, but for now we need time to ourselves. When we do return we will make formal visits to your lands to embrace all people. For we are also servants of the True King.'

With that, he placed Lenyé on the rear seat and sat beside her and they both turned to wave. As the carriage passed under the great arch, even more red and white petals cascaded down and fluttered around them in the scented air.

'Farewell,' Lenyé waved her hand. 'Until we meet again.'

Kyros lifted her in his arms once more, stood up and turned to face the crowd. 'Until we meet again,' he echoed. 'May the presence of the True King be with you and his peace rest upon you now and for evermore. So let it be!'

THE RESTORATION OF THE CROWN OF LIFE

I, Hoffengrégor, called by the True King himself, who is Lord over all the Realms, and appointed by him to give an account of the Restoration; to all the sons and daughters who ever live to walk in the benefit they have received as they rejoice in the presence of the True King amongst us.

For something like a great weight has been lifted from us, and the Light of Life about everyone's head is rekindled and the Krêon of Tulá-kâhju, the Crown of Life, blazes around the head of Kyros for all to see. I perceive that Kyros and his delightful Queen, Lenyé have arisen amongst us to heal the rift between the Peoples that came about at the Beginning. For now each one regards another more highly than themselves, and treats others as they would have others treat them. And once more, ruling has sprung forth with love and mercy, and the pleasure of hard work for everyone's benefit rather than selfish ambition has taken root, where the joy of serving is reward in itself. And the dreams planted at birth in each heart by the True King are coming to fruition with a great release of giftings for the common good. And the Peoples have come together again with a harmonious disposition, and have embraced the True King's teachings to sustain the reality of their encounter with him. And life is unending, for the capping of the lifespan at one hundred and twenty years is no more, and the Realm of the Departed is now reserved only for those who lose their lives through unavoidable accident. Now I see afresh the perfection of the Peoples.

And emissaries have taken the good news of peace to every creature in the Waking World, for the gift of speaking and understanding the language of all creatures has been granted afresh. For now the lioness lies down with the gazelle, and the she-bear allows her cubs to frolic carefree amongst humans, and the eagle soars aloft with the dove, and a little child plays with the cobra while its parents watch with untroubled hearts. And the lush flora has again sprung up where it is needed for food that tastes so delicious, and the choking of thorns and briars is a thing of the past; and I deem the Waking World has passed from chaos to exceed its former glory; for the Peoples now fill the whole Waking World with the Light of Life, as was originally intended. And joy and laughter are ever present and the sound of singing has burst out in all lands and rises to blend with the song of the En-luchés, to reach the very Throne of the True King himself and bring him pleasure from all his long labours in preparing the Waking World for his dwelling place.

I would like to consider the Restoration to have been fully completed, and humankind to live in untroubled blessing forever. Yet I do not think this can be.

For certain misgivings disquieten my heart. Sadly my eye remains closed despite Kyros' words spoken over me, and the bed of the lake remains as it was, and the Eye of Hoffengrégor continues as an island. And I retain the office of Prophet, for I still see in part, like looking through a darkened glass, or discern things from afar, as though gazing through the wrong end of a telescope; and I prophesy in part, according to the wisdom and discernment granted to me. But that should not be in the Restoration. The role of the Prophet should have been wrapped up and put away: for greatly have I longed to see as I was always meant to see, and know as I am fully known.

Even though Lammista-ké was cast down, the Realm of the Departed has not yet given up its dead. And had I not seen

Abbérron seize the bundle of Imbrésonite even as he was cast down to destruction? What manner of mischief may he yet contrive in cheating the Realm of Consumption of its appointed task: to keep all those who go down to the Pit, bound in eternal flame? What if his entrapment is but for a season and Abbérron should arise again and bring the others with him? Not only would the Waking World be at risk, but also the rest of the Known Universe, for Abbérron's ultimate aim was to seize the Highest Throne for himself.

But then the prophecy Lenyé spoke over Kyros has yet to be fulfilled: "A day will come, My Lord, when you will ride forth with the Sword of Justice at your side and the very words of your mouth will be like a sharp, two-edged Sword. None shall withstand you and all the enemies of the True King will be brought low and vanquished before you!" For Kyros has put away evil from the Waking World as an uncrowned Prince, but has never gone to war bearing the Sword of Justice. There is yet to be a destroying of evil throughout the entire Known Universe. I tremble for that day when the wrath of the King is revealed.

I wrestle with these thoughts, not wanting to dismay others in the joy of what they have recently come into. Nevertheless, I am obliged to commit them to writing, lest the Peoples of the Waking World lapse into complacency and by lack of vigilance allow Abbérron to regain a foothold once more in their lives. These are my forebodings concerning an evil yet to come.

Signed and sealed this day by my hand, in the twenty-fifth year since Kyros was crowned King with the Krêon of Tulá-kâhju and married to our beautiful Queen, Lenyé,

Hoffengrégor,
Prophet to the True King.

335

and so we have

THE END

OF

BOOK III

concerning

THE
RESTORATION OF THE CROWN OF LIFE

and

AN
INKLING OF WHAT IS YET TO COME!

A COLLECTION OF WRITINGS

A COSMOGRAPHY OF THE KNOWN UNIVERSE

I, Hoffengrégor, called by the True King himself, do hereby set forth an account of all the Realms in the Known Universe.

Before the Great Inundation and the Scattering of the Peoples, I was standing, musing on the beauty of the Waking World, when I heard a loud voice in the skies above my head commanding me: 'Come up here!' I looked and beheld a door opened for me in the clouds and a figure in white, who blazed with light stronger than the sun, beckoned to me, and immediately I was lifted up and joined him on the threshold. He welcomed me and told me his name was Stellatus, sent to open my eyes to the ordering of the Known Universe that I might see and understand and convey my knowledge to others and so begin instructing the Peoples of the Waking World in wisdom.

As I entered in through the doorway I saw a ladder of many thousand steps, rising above the place where I stood, and also descending beyond the extent of my vision.

'There are seven Realms,' Stellatus informed me. 'Ordered as follows:

1. *The Realm of the Blessèd Throne,*
2. *The Realm of Eternal Flight,*
3. *The Realm of Dominion,*
4. *The Realm of the Waking World,*
5. *The Realm of the Departed,*
6. *The Realm of Travail, and*
7. *The Realm of Consumption.'*

Stellatus held out his hand to me and said, 'Come. For I will show you what is above.'

As he led me up the ladder, it seemed that new strength was given to me and an indescribable eagerness gripped me, for I easily climbed the many rungs until we came to the top and I was able to look ahead and behold what manner of place I had come to.

'This is the Realm of the Blessèd Throne, where the True King ever dwells wrapped in the Light of Life, and sends out his light to all other Realms that they may know him and walk with him.' Stellatus' whisper was soft in my ear as though he was too overawed to speak any louder.

And I beheld winged beings, filled with an intensity of light, ever circling the Throne and crying with a loud voice that shook the pillars of the Throne itself, and they were forever declaring the greatness of the True King.

And then I beheld Him: the True King, seated on his Throne in such splendour and majesty that words fail me to describe Him. And to his left, and slightly removed behind Him was another, even greater Throne, but it was as yet unoccupied and remained empty for all the time I was there.

'What is the meaning of the Empty Throne, My Lord,' I asked Stellatus.

'This is not the time or the place to explain, my friend,' he replied. 'For there is One greater yet to be revealed. Only when the Light of Life fills the entire Known Universe will He step forth and be seated. Then the True King will present Him with all his dominion and the two of them will be joined in great harmony and peace.'

Such utter perfection was contained within this Realm and emanated from Him who sat upon the Throne that I wished never to depart, and always wanted to remain there enveloped in the beauty of the True King's presence. For a great ecstasy swept over me and filled my heart so that I thought I would burst if it did not cease; but also, it was so wonderful, and I felt so alive and fresh and invigorated, that I never wanted it to end either.

But alas, it was not to be; for Stellatus took me by the hand and led me back down the ladder. Reluctant was my step, and a lethargy gripped me, as though my feet were unable to respond to my will. Even as I left that Place I knew for a surety that this Realm was not big enough to contain the perfection I saw, but it must enter into every other Realm and so bring the Light of Life to them.

We descended the ladder to the Realm of Eternal Flight, and I saw beings like Stellatus, filled with the same light, but of greater stature, and winged so that their movement was of swift flight, ever circling around the ladder and stooping down upon the Realms below to bring to pass the command of the True King and so intervene in the workings of those other Realms.

'These are the Great En-Luchés,' Stellatus whispered to me. 'The highest members of my order, and have direct access to the Blessèd Throne.'

And then my eyes were lifted up and I looked and beheld two others, like unto the Great En-luchés, but of a majesty and grandeur almost rivalling that of the True King himself.

'Who are these, My Lord?' I whispered to Stellatus.

'They are the two foremost amongst the Great En-luchés and ever stand in the presence of the True King and remain loyal to his cause and direct the activities of all the En-luchés in whatever Realm they are despatched to.'

And I delighted to be here, for I felt a power emanating from these great beings, flowing out from them to accomplish the will of the True King and I was reassured and happy, for surely the purposes of the True King would come to pass.

Also I saw other figures, more like men and women than En-luchés, for they were cloaked and hooded in brown raiment, and seated at desks with quills in their hands; and parchments were spread before them that they might write down all that passes in each of the Realms. And other figures, attired in grey robes and hoods, were sent forth to survey every Realm and required to report back.

I turned to Stellatus, 'Who are these, My Lord?' I enquired.

'They are the Recorders who will one day present their scrolls to the True King and have the seals broken open that he may read, and the Watchers who will give a verbal account, so that he may hear of all that has passed in every Realm.'

I glanced over the shoulder of one of the Recorders and saw my name at the top of his scroll. But immediately Stellatus covered my eyes with his hand and led me away.

'Come. It is not for you to know what is recorded; for your days are numbered according to the will of the True King, and it is your choice whether to walk in his ways and fulfil all that has been determined for you.'

We descended several hundred steps until he brought me to the Realm of Dominion and I saw many beings in the likeness of those I saw in the Realm of Eternal Flight, but the Light of Life was no longer in them, and a darkness, almost of intense hatred, emanated from them.

'Who are these, My Lord?'

'They were formerly numbered amongst the Great En-Luchés who once circled the Blessèd Throne and cried aloud as heralds of the True King for all to hear. For they were exalted to the same level as those whom you saw in the Realm of Eternal Flight. Alas, they were led astray, for they sought to supplant the True King and establish the Lord Abbérron on the Throne in his place and were cast down from their high office as a result. Now the Lord Abbérron rules from this Realm, for it was given to him before the rebellion and cannot easily be taken back.'

A great rage swept over me and I tried to rush forwards to destroy such rebellious creatures who had dared to defy the glory of the True King, for they occupied a Realm that lay between the other two and the Waking World, and so must *hinder all communication from the True King to the world where I dwelled and back again.*

But Stellatus restrained me with his hand. 'I understand your intentions, my friend, for they are good and right and honourable, and display your loyalty to the True King. But you have not the strength to contest such powerful creatures, even in their present state.'

'Then what is the answer to this problem, My Lord?'

'Know this,' Stellatus' voice rang with authority. 'Abbérron holds sway over every Realm beneath this, save one alone, which he fears above all else.'

'Which one is that, My Lord?'

'Have patience a while longer and I will show you.'

He brought me down the steps a little lower, and I found myself standing on a cloud and looking down upon the Waking World, and I marvelled afresh at its beauty: the indescribable aura of blue that shrouded the whole Waking World and the great swathes of green that covered the ground and swept down to the shores of the vast oceans. For a love of my own dwelling place flooded through me and a sense of unspeakable gratitude for the beauty of all I saw filled my heart.

'Even though the Lord Abbérron rules here,' the voice of Stellatus startled me as I gazed in wonder; 'the True King seeks to bring the Light of Life into this Realm through the race of men and women. Even now, Zerigor wears the Krêon of Tulá-kâhju, the Crown of Life, that demonstrates the presence of the True King with him and reveals the Light of Life blazing from him to enlighten all the Peoples. He must remain faithful to the True King, and all the Peoples with him, for the Light of Life to triumph in all other Realms.'

Again he brought me down more steps, and I was engulfed in a dim twilit world in which even the light of my companion was veiled and I could barely discern his outline.

'Where is this, My Lord?'

'The Realm of the Departed.'

Stellatus' voice sounded muffled and I turned to him in wonder for it seemed to me to be more than just the oppressive atmosphere of this place that affected his speech. 'What is this Realm for?' I enquired.

'If anyone from the Waking World should ever perish through physical accident that claims their life, their body returns to the dust of the ground, but that is not the end of them. They will live on. This Realm will forever remain empty if Zerigor prevails and all the Peoples walk in the Light of Life.'

'And if he fails...?' I let my voice tail away, for I was full of consternation at what his answer might bring.

'Then this Realm is set here by the wisdom of the True King to act as a place of succour until he comes to them and restores their physical presence.'

I felt a deep sadness in my heart that a place like this should exist, even if by the benevolent provision of the True King. I yearned eagerly that it would forever remain empty and so exonerate the trust which the True King had placed in Zerigor to lead the Peoples aright. For if he prevailed, that would safeguard their physical state and no such misfortune would ever befall them, and no one would have to descend to this terrible Place.

He took me down several hundred more steps and showed me the Realm of Travail, and I saw many beings like those in the Realm of Dominion, but without wings and of lesser stature; more like to Stellatus, but emanating darkness rather than light.

'These are the Dé-monos, who are like the En-luchés of my order.' Stellatus continued in my instruction. 'For at the rebellion, they were cast down here and are contained that they may not work any mischief in the Waking World.'

Again I felt an anger sweep over me, not as intense as in the

Realm of Dominion, for here, it seemed to me, that these beings were more easily overcome than their greater masters who still dwelled above. For my anger raged against their attempts to break into my world and so lead the Peoples astray from the call of the True King.

He took me down many thousands more steps until we arrived at the bottom of the ladder, and a great dread filled me and reluctant were my feet to approach, so that Stellatus had to take me by the hand and pull me down the last few steps. For it was utter darkness, yet by the light that emanated from Stellatus I was able to discern that our way was barred by a massive door reinforced with great straps of iron. But Stellatus led me by the hand and spoke a word of command and we walked through the very fabric of the door into a great chamber that was lit by a flickering flame. At the far end was the open mouth of a furnace and the heat in the place was unbearable.

'Behold the Realm of Consumption that lies at the core of the Known Universe,' Stellatus continued to instruct me. 'This is the place that Abbérron, and all who follow him, fears the most. For every being will stand before the True King and listen to the reading of the Scroll written by the Recorders and hear the verdict of the Watchers on their life and receive the decision of the True King concerning their destiny.'

'Then each in turn shall walk through the Fiery Furnace.'

'Those who served the True King and persevered in his ways will have all hindrances in their lives burned away, like grass withering in a forest fire. And he will perfect them like a silver smith skimming away the dross on the surface of the molten metal that he might see the reflection of his face mirrored in their lives. For he will walk with them and guard them in the furnace, so that not even the smell of burning shall stick to their hair or clothing. And they will emerge from the fire in readiness for what lies ahead.'

'But those who have turned away from the knowledge of the True King will face the Furnace by themselves. Some will pass through, but everything they treasured highly will be stripped from them by the rigour of the flames.'

'Those who knowingly rejected him will enter and be consumed.'

'That is why Abbérron fears it so. It is here that the fate of the Known Universe will be decided: those who remain or those who are consumed, either human or of a higher order.'

'And you must return to the Waking World, my friend, and charge the Peoples of what awaits them and how they should continue in the ways of The True King in preparation. For if you do not warn them, who will?'

Stellatus brought me back up the ladder, and bade me farewell when we reached the Waking World. As I stepped through a doorway onto firm ground and turned to look afresh at the ladder, it was gone, and only a sweet fragrance lingered where Stellatus had stood beside me.

As I pondered on what I had just beheld, it seemed to me that the best way to describe these Realms to any other person that they may fully understand, was to present them as hollow spheres within hollow spheres; for each one fully encompassed another, from the Realm of the Blessèd Throne right down to the Realm of Consumption. It was as though the Realm of the Blessèd Throne was so vast that it held all other Realms within itself.

Each Realm was an entirety in itself, for the sun and moon of the Waking World did not appear in other Realms as these were lit according to their nature by lights in their skies that I deemed to be suns and moons of a different order. For the sun in the Realm of Travail burned far brighter and hotter than the one in the Waking World I was most familiar with.

And each Realm was separate from another, even those which lay closest to each other within the structure of the spheres. For if you could take the wings of the wind in the Waking World and fly to the moon above, and beyond that to the furthest night-time stars, you would never enter either the Realm of Dominion above, or the Realm of Travail below, or even the Realm of the Departed. For only by the provision of the True King, or some great trauma yet to be devised, could you pass from one Realm to another, as I had done with my journey on the ladder.

According to my musing, the Realm of Consumption would appear as the smallest sphere, right at the heart of the Known Universe.

But it occurred to me that this could not be so, for surely the Realm of the Blessèd Throne must lie at the heart of the Known Universe and be contained by all other realms that the Light of Life might emanate from it and so fill all others? And surely the Realm of Consumption was at the utter periphery of the Known Universe and as far removed from all others as possible?

How to resolve this puzzle lay beyond the extent of my wit. All I could say was that the Realm of the Blessèd Throne lay both at the heart and periphery of the Known Universe to inspire and to contain; but so also did the Realm of Consumption, to warn and, finally, to consume.

When I began instructing those who sought my wisdom after the Inundation had swept survivors to my shore, one quiet young man observed: 'Surely it doesn't matter which way you cast the Known Universe from the greatest to the least? For whichever way you view the structure of the Known Universe, the Waking World is always the same expanse of distance from the Realm of the Blessèd Throne and the Realm of Consumption, being set at the fourth position, marking it out as the Central Realm for the focus of the entire Known Universe.'

I looked at him a long while considering all that he said. For often the seeds of wisdom are born in quietness and reflection. 'My friend,' I replied at last. 'The significance of what you have just said has yet to be borne out in the events ahead of us.'

For in that instant I perceived, as if by revelation, that the current state of the Known Universe was one of war: for those in the Realm of Dominion struggled against those in the Realm of Eternal Flight, trying to regain their former position. And those contained in the Realm of Travail struggled to burst their bonds and so come to the Waking World and influence the Peoples away from their knowledge of the True King. And the Realm of the Departed was ever hungry for those who would come down to that domain, which I deemed to be little more than a prison, and so destroy the lives of those who dwelled in the Waking World by seeking to hold them bound, even against the intervention of the True King.

And herein I saw the key to all things: that the Known Universe was in balance and contained and waiting. For the final struggle, if it should ever come, would be waged in the Waking World.

THE ENTERING IN OF EVIL

I, Hoffengrégor, called by the True King himself to guide and teach the Peoples of the Waking World, do hereby set forth an account of what has been revealed to me concerning this matter.

Not long after the Inundation, I was in great sorrow over the state of humankind, and set my face to seek the True King to give me understanding. I hardly ate any food, so desperate was I.

After three weeks, I was standing by the bank of the River Rubichinó, near the Krêonor encampment, and lifted up my eyes and beheld a figure, ablaze with light, and recognised Stellatus.

He said to me, 'From the first day you set your heart to seek the True King, you were heard; and I have been sent. But the Lord of the Realm of Dominion withstood me twenty-one days, for such is the significance of this; not until one of the Great En-luchés helped me, was I released to you. The knowledge you will gain is crucial for the final destruction of evil. Write what you see and hear, and seal it up for the appointed time.'

He lifted me up and I beheld a mountain. Near its peak was a trough full of burning stones, bubbling and oozing and heaving with an intense heat that I could feel from where I stood. Within the living flame was the most beautiful being I had ever seen: like a man in shape and feature, but of far greater stature. It seemed to be asleep with its hands folded on its chest. But I saw the eyelids flicker and the being stretched and thrust itself up till it stood in the bubbling trough, and walked back and forth in the midst of the fiery stones. It appeared to be fashioned of gold, but the light in it blazed a dazzling white, as though refracted through a coating of many colours. And I knew, intuitively, that this substance only came from the Realm of the Blessèd Throne, and converted intense heat to the opposite degree of cold, which was why the being could withstand such a high temperature.

'Where are we, My Lord?' I whispered to my companion. 'And who is this I behold?'

'You have come to the Mountain of the True King between the Realms of Eternal Flight and of the Blessèd Throne, and are witnessing the beginning of Rabborné, the Teacher of Light, one of the three pre-eminent amongst the Great En-luchés. Some say he is greater than the other two, for rulership of the Realm of Dominion has been granted to him. But others declare that the Three are equal in stature and wisdom and might.'

I watched Rabborné as he knelt amidst the fiery stones and smoothed a patch with his hand. Immediately I was at his shoulder, looking down into a golden mirror that reflected his face. And I thought: 'There is no one more beautiful to behold. Who can fail to be captivated and bow down before him?' I felt his mind probing who he was and the pride in self-knowledge that took root within him and the disdain he had for others. I saw his looks suddenly marred by the sneer of his upper lip, not from distaste of himself, but at what others might expect of him.

Then there occurred a great concourse of En-luchés as representatives from the Realms of Dominion and of Eternal Flight gathered before him. Rabborné stepped off the fiery stones and addressed them all. But as I listened, I realised he was sowing seeds of doubt in the minds of his hearers concerning their relationship with the True King. So skilled was he that I found myself struggling to remain faithful in my heart to the True King. I noticed others shake their heads as if to clear their minds, and counter what he had just said.

But before anyone could speak, Rabborné was lifted up and carried away, and all the En-luchés went with him; and my companion and I were permitted to follow. And I beheld afresh the True King, seated on his Throne, with the Empty Throne behind him and slightly to his left. He made as if to rise in greeting as Rabborné appeared. But Rabborné strode past the True King and sat down in the Empty Throne.

The ensuing scenario seemed very strange, as if the True King was frozen in time, making no sound of speech or sign of any further movement, and the winged beings surrounding his Throne were locked with him. I realised I was no longer in time as in the Waking World, governed by the rising and setting of the sun and bounded by the seasons. Instead, I was in an eternal realm where everything that is said or done continues forever.

Nothing was actually verbalised, but I caught Rabborné's words as they echoed within my mind. I knew then that the thoughts of an intelligent being resound more loudly in The Realm of the Blessèd Throne than any spoken words; and I could no longer remain unaffected. Only by meditating on the words of the True King did I have any chance of resisting them. My eyes were opened and I saw into every Realm, and focused on every being as far as the Realm of Dominion; for what we in the Realm of the Waking World call the Beginning, had not yet come to pass. And I knew of a certainty that whoever heard those words had to respond: either to obey them and follow Rabborné, or remain faithful to the True King. Again the words were soft and persuasive and crept into the inner heart like molten honey, and spoke of throwing off the yoke of servanthood and becoming your own master, and thereby being free.

Rabborné sat drumming the fingers of his right hand on the arm of the Throne, impatient for something to happen.

The True King started as though awakened from a trance and turned to him. 'When you are invited into my presence, choose the lowest seat that I might honour you by raising you to your rightful place, that others may acknowledge your real position.' But Rabborné leaped to his feet in fury and stormed past the True King towards Stellatus and myself. I heard him muttering, 'One day I will sit in that Throne and everyone in the Known Universe will bow down before me; including the True King!'

There arose a great tumult of voices and violent movements as the entire entourage of the True King either sided with Rabborné, or sought to oppose him. Great was the battle, almost destroying the Throne Room itself. At last the voice of the True

King cut through the turmoil: 'Rabborné, you have said in your heart, "I will ascend to the Highest Throne", and so your arrogance has betrayed you. For you were one of the anointed amongst the three foremost Great En-Luchés, to carry the Light of Life throughout the Known Universe, but especially to lead my work in the Waking World and meet with the Prophet I have set in place and teach him to instruct humankind how best to walk with me and know me. I established you in the fire of my Mountain and you were perfected in your ways from the day you were fully formed, until this iniquity of rebellion was found in you. Your knowledge can never now be tempered with wisdom. Therefore you will be brought down to the lowest Pit.'

I observed the letters of Rabborné's name forming above his head, as if the True King was writing with his finger in the air: that Rabborné had been weighed in the scales and found wanting; that his days were numbered; and his pre-eminence was to end before he was cast down. Those who sided with him were cast down also, as far as the Realm of Dominion. But I saw Rabborné fall much further, like lightning, and Stellatus and I followed his dreadful descent and watched him hurtle into an island surrounded by blue seas, and disappear in a great crater, such was his impact; and I realised I was looking down on the island of Bara-mâla in the Waking World. His beautiful outer covering was stripped from him as he plunged head foremost into the ground, and I knew the Light of Life in him was broken, and the different elements of his covering settled out into a golden substance impregnated with gems of blue and red and yellow and white, that seeped into the soil in various locations on the island where they had fallen, and disappeared with him. The designation of his covering grew in my mind: Imbrésonite.

And the letters of his name, falling more slowly than he did, came to rest on the ground, but they too were broken. A light breeze arose and blew them together for an instant, and I saw them re-gather to form the changed name of "Abbérron", before they also disappeared into the soil.

But I knew he would attempt to raise the same rebellion in the Realm of the Waking World that existed in the other two Realms. For this surely is the entering in of evil: the malicious will of Abbérron actively turning others from following the True King and depriving them of living in the good of his light and life and heart-peace; by enticing them to be their own master and only knowing the wretchedness of darkness and death and heart-tyranny that results from obeying Abbérron's voice.

Then I saw a hand reach down from the skies, holding a long stake with what appeared to be the upper jaws and teeth of some great sea creature attached to the end, and raked seven times across the length and breadth of the island, filling in the crater and flattening the debris of Abbérron's fall.

And I heard the True King speaking to me, 'The Waking World is now the arena for the entire Known Universe where the battle against evil will triumph. Humankind must suffer with me to bring him down to the lowest Pit, but will also be amongst the first to share with me in the joy that is yet to come. I choose the exact spot of Abbérron's demise to begin, where his Light source was broken beyond repair and his name became fallen and twisted and unmade from what I originally intended for him. Here the first community of humankind can establish in innocence through their walk with me what is good, not only in the Waking World, but also throughout the Known Universe.'

So mindful was I of Stellatus' instruction to seal up what I had witnessed that I have only let one man ever read this parchment: Zerigor, as he lay dying. He gave me a lockable cylinder in which to conceal it and told me of the key he had hidden on the island of Bara-mâla, and said, 'Though I cannot complete the True King's purposes, another will arise after me.' So I decided to carry the cylinder with me until I find the one for whom this knowledge is appointed amongst Zerigor's heirs.

THE LAY OF HOFFENGRÉGOR:
A SONG FROM THE BOOK OF BEGINNINGS

On the Isle of Bara-mâla
Lived the Bara-mâla-ké
Ancient People, ancient Nation
Blessèd Kingdom, blessèd Day

But the People were three races
Krêonor and Tsé-shâmé
One the ruling, one the serving
There must be a better way

In their midst sat idle Harmoth
Allied to the Krêonor
Always wanting, never giving
Stoked the flame of what's in store

For some Krêonor, the misfits
Tall and dark, defiant stood
Lured by secrets of the Shâmé
Turned their back on all that's good

These then sided with the Shâmé
Rebels through their lustful pride
Trained and raised a brand new army
Set themselves to be their guide

But the Harmoth, blind and wanting
Found that asking was their knack
Drove the Shâmé to distraction
Broke their spirit, broke their back

Ruling masters failed to notice
Seeds of mounting tensions, or
Face the Harmoth with their grasping;
Ignorant Lords, Krêonor

Came a mighty Tset-Tse-shâmé
Challenging the Krêonor
Marching out their powerful army
Led to shake up and to war

Many were the doughty fallen
Krêonor and Tsé-shâmé
Even hosts of idle Harmoth
Caught between, were swept away

But the waves of Asa-Dura
Round the fated Mâla-ké
Could not bear to see the life blood
Of the Peoples ebb away

So in anger, Asa-Dura
Raised a mighty Invadrook
Rushing inwards, cleansing ocean
Sank the island: all forsook

From the West'ring, riven Mâla
Came canoes of Krêonor
And the war boats of the Shâmé
Heading for a safer shore

To the flotsam and the jetsam
Bobbing on the fearsome wave
Clung the ever idle Harmoth
Nothing but their skins could save

All the wealth and garnered treasure
All the knowledge, tomèd: gone
Only in the hearts emerging;
Would this wisdom linger on?

Crawling up the proffered landfall
Fleeing from the wrecking tide
Parted now, the grieving Peoples
Sundered from each others' side

SOME NAUTICAL TERMS USED

Term	Description
belay	an order to stop
bilge	the lowest point of a ship's inner hull
bows	front of ship
broached	the ship has turned parallel to the waves
capstan	vertical cylinder for raising the anchor
close-hauled	sailing as close to the wind as possible
companionway	steps leading between decks
courses	lowest sails on fore and main masts
crosstrees	struts on a mast to spread the rigging
davits	spars to hoist items over the side
deckhead	underside of a deck
fo'c's'le	upper deck, forwards of the foremast
galley	kitchen
gunwale	upper edge of a ship's side
hawser	a thick rope for mooring a ship
heave to	stop the ship while underway
listed	leaned badly to one side
mizzen	mast to the rear of the mainmast
pintles	pins or bolts on which a rudder turns
pitch poled	a ship flipped end-over-end
poop deck	rear deck over cabins
quarter	side of a ship between the stern and midships (port & starboard)
quarter deck	a raised deck behind the main mast
ratlines	rope ladders for climbing aloft
reef/ed	part of a sail rolled and tied down
scuppers	a deck drain for water to flow overboard
sea anchor	a canvas cone towed behind the ship in rough weather
shrouds	ropes supporting a mast
spanker	lowest sail on the mizzen mast
spars	poles to support the rigging and sails

Term	Description
starboard	right, when facing forwards
stern	rear of ship
sticks	slang for masts
stunsails	sails extended outboard for extra speed
tack/ing	cutting across a headwind alternately to port and starboard
topgallant	highest sail on mast
watch/es	divisions of the day, with one bell ring for each half hour period
weigh anchor	haul up the anchor
yard/yard arm	a spar on a mast from which sails are set
yawed	behaved erratically when struck by a heavy sea

SHIPS

Name	Commissioned by:
Brave Heart	Kyros and Lenyé
Flying Cloud	Morthrir
Tempest	Morthrir
Monarch of the Seas	Morthrir (flagship)
Sea Sprite	Morthrir

LIST OF CHARACTERS

Name	Description
Abbérron	The Hidden Power
Acwellan	The Nastrim Lord High Executioner
Alkram	Lenyé's Father
Ariella	The lioness who rescues Lenyé
Asa-Dura	The Sea
Beth	Lenyé's younger sister
Chenai	Old woman from the woods
Chuah-te-mok	The eagle sent to Lenyé by Yanantha
Dareth	King of the Krêonor and Father of Kyros

Name	Description
Eawen	Former Chief Priest to Abbérron
Faria	Morthrir's wife
Festé	One of Lenyé's brothers
Hanniel	Former Captain in the Royal Garrison
Harbona	Former Captain in Morthrir's army
Hoffengrégor	The Ancient Prophet
Josiah	Captain of *Brave Heart*
Jumar-jé	Leader of the Summoners
Ishi-mi-réjá	Lady of miraculous powers
Kyros	A Prince of the Royal Krêonor Family
Lammista-ké	King of Death
Lenyé	A Princess of the Royal Krêonor Family
Luchianó-bé	The True King
Mamma Uza-Mâté	The She-bear who comforts Lenyé
Marie-anna	Ramâno's Mother
Morthrir	Uncle of Kyros and Lenyé
Nasima	One of Kyros' sisters
Nastâr	A fallen Great En-luchés
Nostrea	Apothecary
Ogandés	King of the Nastrim
Olathe	One of Kyros' sisters
Osâcah	Leader of the Sacred Pilgrims of Lohr
Paco	Warrior and friend of Beth's
Quinn	Younger brother of Kyros
Rabborné	Teacher of Light
Rafé	Royal counsellor
Ramâno	Warrior boy
Ranyak	Marie-anna's late husband
Ra-Na-Jiri	Cobra who comes to Lenyé's aid
Sorentina	Daughter of Zerigor
Stellatus	A Leader of the En-luchés
Tadeas	Ship's Crafter at Pordé-Sûnca
The Henosite	Original spiritual designation of Eawen

Name	Description
True King	Lord over all Realms
Vashtani	Dé-monos Leader and Acwellan's Father
Yanantha	Prophetess who sings over Lenyé
Youdlh	Commander of Morthrir's army
Wilf	One of Lenyé's brothers
Zerigor	First King of the Krêonor

PLACES

Bara-mâla	Island of the first civilisation
Dangst Rock	Place-of-Chaining
Druis-cyf-rin	The Great Oak Tree
Eye of Hoffengrégor	Islet on Lake Sanchéso
Lammista-ké	The River guarding the Realm of the Departed
Malkamet	Mountain used by Abbérron
Malvi-Quîdda	Fortress of the Dé-monos in the Realm of Travail
Nastâri	Mountain of the Nastrim
Onadestra	Morthrir's Castle & City
Pordé-Sûnca	Port on the Westernmost bulge of the coast
Rubichinó	River leading to Onadestra
Sanchéso	Lake, but formerly a Plain
Terrazarema	Capital of the Krêonor

THE THREE ANCIENT PEOPLES

Bara-mâla-ké	Collective name of the:
Krêonor,	
Tsé-shâmé, and	
Harmoth	

For Further Details of the Trilogy

visit

www.crownoflifelegend.com

If you enjoyed the book, please go to the "Books" page on the website, click the "Post a Review" button, and add a review on Amazon.